# THE ULTIMATE
# HALLOWEEN

# THE ULTIMATE HALLOWEEN

*edited by*

## MARVIN KAYE

*and written by:*
Esther Freisner • Terry Kaye • Darrell Schweitzer
Marc Bilgray • Al Sarrantonio • R.J. Lewis
Marilyn Mattie Brahen • Edward D. Hoch
John Gregory Betancourt • Edith Wharton
Carole Buggé • Ron Goulart • H.P. Lovecraft
William F. Nolan • Parke Godwin
Herminie T. Kavanagh

## ibooks
new york
www.ibooksinc.com

DISTRIBUTED BY SIMON & SCHUSTER, INC

# contents

# CONTENTS

# THE MANY MASKS
# OF HALLOWEEN

## AN INTRODUCTION BY MARVIN KAYE

Pumpkins, bats, pranksters, ghoulies and ghosties, and all those shivery things that lurk near the gates of graveyards—communion with the beloved spirits of our ancestors—harvest home and the death of the sun—Halloween means many things to different people, or it used to before Hallmark got hold of it. The notion of a holiday devoted to ghosts and evil creatures is an old one, but hitting up the neighbors for treats is a comparatively new add-on. The supernatural elements of All Hallows Eve are not the holiday's oldest aspect.

The ancient Wiccan observation of Samhain, or summer's end, set off the culmination of the harvest season and the storing of food for winter. The holiday, complete with the kind of Circle worship, dance and music that Parke Godwin eloquently described in the science-fiction novel, *Wintermind*, was observed on the evening of October 31st. A thousand years ago, the Celts of Scotland and Ireland chose November 1st as their New Year's Day, and when Christianity began to be accreted onto older spiritual tradition, the festival was retained, first as Allhallomas, then All Hallows E'en, and ultimately, Halloween, when all saints were revered. The turning of the year symbolically embodied future, present, and past, which is where the ghosts first came in. The Conrad Aiken poem, "Hallowe'en," accurately depicts the holiday as a time when the spirits of one's ancestors revisited their kinfolk "to rattle our latches and sit at the table." There is an analogous Asian festival called The Feast of the Hungry Ghosts, in which families offer meals for their kinfolk, and even the Jewish Passover dinner honors the spirit of the prophet Elijah by setting out a glass of wine for him.

It takes no great leap of the imagination to extend the holiday's commemorative nature to the darker sense that *every* spirit—good, bad, purposeful, vengeful, tormented— might walk the world that fateful October night. In this regard, Halloween echoes a later Germanic custom of Walpurgisnacht, when witches were alleged to hold their unholy sabbath on the last evening of April. And in middle Europe, at least according to Bram Stoker in *Dracula*, the night of May 4th, St. George's Day, is another occasion when evil spirits are permitted to walk the earth again.

Walpurgisnacht witches supposedly flew to Germany's Harz mountains on broomsticks, props which have become as identified with modern Halloween ambience as black cats, ducking for apples, and jack-o'-lanterns. The cats, of course, were the witches' familiar spirits; apple-ducking may be a throwback to the merciless Trial by Water, in which suspected witches were thrown into a body of water; if they floated, they were obviously pawns of the devil; if they drowned, they were innocent and on their way to heaven. The leering faces carved into pumpkins probably derive from the ancient custom of tribes ringing their circle of fire with the skulls of enemies: a warning to would-be aggressors similar to the practice of the Hungarian prince Vlad, the historic prototype of Dracula, who filled trenches at the edges of his land with corpses of foes impaled on great wooden stakes. As Halloween ritual became stylized, the skulls were replaced by turnips with faces carved into them, and in the New World, the more available pumpkin got the job.

In an old Irish custom associated with All Hallows Eve, peasants begged largesse from door to door; the polled givers were distinguished by their generosity or meanness in giving; a similar custom was practiced at New Year's in Germany, and these traditions eventually surfaced in America in the 1930s as "Trick or Treat," though the very real pranks that were played in the earlier decades of the twentieth century eventually disappeared. In his splendid book of essays, *Remember, Remember*, the late Charles Beaumont lamented how the commercial spirit vanquished the supernatural spirit, and Halloween lost its spirit and became a time to go to K-Mart for prepackaged costumes and plastic pumpkins for toddlers to collect candy and small coin on behalf of politically correct charities.

All of these aspects of Halloween are represented in *The Ultimate Halloween*, which gets off to a semi-traditional start by focusing on kids at Halloween. Esther Friesner has a refreshingly curmudgeonly "take" on the subject; Terry Kaye gives a witch's-eye view of the subject. Children are also important in the stories by Al Sarrantonio, who neatly balances compassion and terror in a tale that may call up echoes of the *Halloween* films; William F. Nolan, who introduces an equally scary bogeyman; John Gregory Betancourt, whose *conte cruelle* features a golem-child, and Carole Buggé, whose reminiscence of her late father's love for his children weds laughter with heartbreak.

# INTRODUCTION

In the spirit of diversity, the stories by Ron Goulart and Edward D. Hoch are Halloween mysteries; the theme of spirits who walk again highlight Marc Bilgray's and H. P. Lovecraft's tales; Marilyn Mattie Brahen gives trick or treating a unique twist, while Parke Godwin's and Terry McGarry's offbeat selections need their own category: *Strange Things Happen at Halloween!*

Halloween's Darker Powers manifest themselves in Edith Wharton's chilling puzzler, while Satan makes personal appearances in R. J. Lewis's and Darrell Schweitzer's tales. And for a spectacular conclusion, H. T. Kavanagh's wonderful Darby O'Gill novella boasts a full complement of supernatural beings, including one banshee, the Costa Bower, or Death Coach, an itinerant witch, a whole county of ghosts, and none other than King Brian Connors himself and his leprechauns.

Now turn down the lights, pass the cider, and try not to interrupt the spell too often by shouting *BOO!*

—MARVIN KAYE
New York City
July 2001

# THE ULTIMATE
# HALLOWEEN

# AUNTIE ELSPETH'S HALLOWEEN STORY
# OR
# THE GOURD, THE BAD, AND THE UGLY

## ESTHER M. FRIESNER

Hello, children, what brings you here to see your kindly old Auntie Elspeth? Parents fed up with you again? Well, never you mind. Auntie Elspeth knows what it's like to be unwanted, especially by the very same people who claim to love and cherish you, but who'll shove you into a so-called senior citizens' community—spelled "hellhole"—so fast that your wheelchair leaves skidmarks on the linoleum.

Now, now, don't whimper, and for heaven's sake don't look at me with those great big sad puppydog eyes. You don't want to know what I did to the last real puppydog who tried that crap on me. Face the facts, kiddies: Mommy and Daddy want you the hell out of their hair for awhile, probably because they want to play Hide the Hamster—no, you do not need to know what that means—but they also want an ooey-gooey feelgood excuse for doing it. That's why they parked you here with me. Probably said something like, "Oh my, won't dear old Auntie Elspeth love having some quality time with the children?"

No, Tommy, the word you are looking for to describe what Mommy and Daddy said is not "fibbing." The word you want is "bullshit." See if you can remember to say that when Mommy and Daddy come to pick you up, you and the rest of this clutch of young harpies-in-training. You see, dearie? Being with Auntie Elspeth is *educational*. That's another word Mommy and Daddy use a whole lot, I'll bet, especially when they want to justify plunking you brats down for a four-hour stint in front of the television.

As long as we're stuck with each other for—When did your parents say they were coming back? What? *That* long?! Why, those stinking, lousy, rotten sons-of-! Just because I'm old, do they think I've got nothing better to do with my time than hang out with the spawn of their loins? Bah.

Oh, to hell with it. Open the top drawer of that nightstand over there, kids; it's full of candy. Help yourself to as much as you want. Maybe if I send you back to them tanked up on sugar they'll think twice before farming you out to me again.

Hm? What's that, Cindy? You don't want any candy? What the hell's the matter with you?

Ohhhh. Not hungry, just bored. And bor-*ing* too, for the record. You want a story? Well, here's one: Once upon a time there was a nice old woman who was minding her own business when her nephew and his bimbo wife dumped their three kids on her doorstep and as soon as the old lady got the chance she sold the little buggers to a traveling circus where they had to spend the rest of their days biting the heads off chickens. The. End.

Happy?

Damn it, shut your yap and quit your bawling before one of the guards sticks his thick head in here. I'm not supposed to have all that candy, you know. Lousy screws will confiscate it if they find it. Look, I tell you what: How about if kindly old Auntie Elspeth tells you a *different* story? Once upon a time there were three little trichinosis-infected pigs who—

What?

You don't want that story either? Picky little snot, ain'tcha. Well then, what kind of story *does* Her Royal Heinieness desire?

A Halloween tale? Child there just might be some hope for you, after all. October is getting on. Halloween will be at our throats before you know it, and it just so happens to be your kindly old Auntie Elspeth's favorite holiday.

I heard that, Billy. If you're going to be malicious, at least have the stones to do it out loud so a person can hear you. Halloween is not my favorite holiday because I'm an old witch, I don't care what your Mommy said. Your Mommy also said she was a virgin when she married your Daddy, but between you and me and the Seventh Fleet—

Cindy, dear, it's not polite to interrupt. However, since you *did* ask, a virgin is a mythological creature, okay? Sort of like a dragon or a unicorn or a compassionate conservative or—

Look, grow up, learn to read, look up the words you don't know in the dictionary, and shut the hell up for two seconds. I don't have time to answer a lot of stupid questions.

Daddy told you there's no such thing as a stupid question? Daddy was wrong.

Do you want a Halloween story or not?

Now this is called "How the Vampire Prince Plunged His Fangs into the Heaving White Bosom of the Helpless Maiden and Devoured Her Still-Beating Heart." Once upon a time—

*Now* what?

Yes, Tommy, I know that Cindy is only four years old. Yes, I know that your Mommy and Daddy don't want any of you mini-weasels exposed to undue levels of violence. Speaking of which, where did a peewee pissant like you come up with such a mouthful of buzzwords?

Ah. Educational television. I should have known. All right, in that case I suppose I could tidy up the vampire story a bit and—

No vampires allowed? None at all? Not even a little one? He doesn't have to devour the maiden's still-beating heart, if you're going to be a big bunch of wussies about it. He can just devour it after he's sated his hellish thirst on the helpless maiden's blood and her heart *stops* beating, all right?

Okay, fine. Be that way. Sissies.

Ahem: The merciless sun of the Egyptian desert beat down upon the City of the Dead, but within the tomb of the Pharaoh's daughter it was cold; cold as the bellies of the deadly native vipers whose bite means a lingering, agonizing death; cold as the blade of a fanatical assassin as it slits the throat of the foreign devil rash enough to defy the ancient curses sealing the princess' final resting place; cold as the steely nerves of Sir Henry Battabout-Montescue as he strode into the burial chamber and laid impious hands upon the lid of the princess' sarcophagus. But before he could defile the royal virgin's eternal sleep, an unholy roar came from behind him. He turned in time to see the figure of a mummy—a hideous, deformed, desiccated corpse, rank with the putridity of centuries, trailing the dusty wrappings of its entombment—come lurching toward him. Hands like the talons of the sacred vulture closed around his windpipe and his last breath was overwhelmed by the fetor of the creature's—

Good Lord, *now* what's wrong, Cindy? Stop making noises like a dachshund with the hiccups and speak up! Billy, Tommy, try to make yourselves useful for a change and get that rabbity little sister of yours to stop crying.

What do you mean, I scared her? How could a simple little story about one insignificant, bloodthristy, vengeance-obsessed mummy bother anyone? It's even got a *moral*, for pity's sake: If you touch stuff you're told not to touch, you die a hideous, unnatural death. That's an *excellent* moral, in my humble opinion. Eminently practical. And the story's full of all kinds of fascinating facts about ancient Egypt. It's *educational!*

Gawd.

You know, in my day when we asked for a Halloween story we wanted to be scared spitless. And we all dressed up like ghosts and ghouls and goblins because we wanted to scare all the other kids so bad they'd walk home with their shoes squishing. At least tell me *that* hasn't changed.

Oh. So Cindy's going to be a fairy princess and Billy's going to be a teddy bear. Pass me that plastic basin from under the nightstand, Tommy; Auntie Elspeth's feeling a mite poorly and I don't want to pitch my porridge all over my clean shoes.

And what are you going to be this Halloween? A tofu burger?

Ahhhh, a *ghost*! Good boy. At least that's a step in the right—

7

The ghost of Anton van Loewen*who*?

Jesus, take me now. Do you little fluff-bunnies have blood in your veins or maple syrup?

Look, grab another fistful of taffy, stop your gobs, and Auntie Elspeth is going to tell you a Halloween story if it kills me. (Which it will, if there's a just and merciful God who doesn't want to see me suffer away the rest of this afternoon.) Don't worry, it won't be about vampires or mummies or zombies or anything nifty like that. It's going to be just the way your parents want *you* to be: Sweet and safe and sanitized for their protection. All that Auntie Elspeth's going to ask of you darling moppets is that you sit down, pay attention, and let your imaginations take you down the lovely garden path that leads to the Enchanted Pumpkin Patch, because *this*, children, is the story of Jo-Jo the Jolly Jack o' Lantern:

Once upon a time there was a little pumpkin named Jo-Jo. He grew up round and plump and happy with all of his little pumpkin friends in old Farmer Nosferatu's pumpkin patch. Oh, such jolly times they all had! The sun warmed them and the rain watered them and every time a traveling salesman came a-calling at the farmhouse, old Farmer Nosferatu would invite him inside, out of sight, and very soon afterwards he'd make a special trip down to the pumpkin patch to give the happy little pumpkins a great big dose of bonemeal fertilizer. *Dear* old Farmer Nosferatu!

It was a good life, but it wasn't enough for Jo-Jo. You see, Jo-Jo was a pumpkin with a dream. More than anything else, Jo-Jo wanted to grow up to be big enough and round enough and just the perfect shade of orange to be made into a jack o' lantern in time for Halloween.

Now Jo-Jo didn't really know all there was to know about being a jack o' lantern, because he had still been only a seed the last time October 31 rolled around. Everything he'd ever heard about Halloween came from wise old Mr. Hooty Owl who lived in the lightning-blasted tree over by the north fence near the graveyard. Night after night, wise old Mr. Hooty Owl would scare himself up a fine fuzzy field mouse dinner, then sit on the pumpkin patch fence while he gobbled down every juicy morsel. And in between munchy, crunchy bites he'd tell all of the little pumpkins stories about Halloween.

"It's just the most wonderful holiday that ever was," he'd say. "It's the time of year when magic happens—real, honest-to-goodness magic! But if it weren't for you pumpkins, Halloween wouldn't be half so grand nor magical, no indeedy. You see, when the air starts to snap like a bone-crushing bear trap and the leaves on the tree bleed red and purple and gold, and the night starts to come in darker and sooner, crowded with lorn, lost souls, why that's when Halloween comes dancing down the lane. And that's when folks start looking for pumpkins to make into jack o' lanterns to light up the nights and keep away whatever's wandering in the dark."

What's that, Billy? What *is* wandering in the dark that the jack o' lanterns have to keep away? Gracious, I can't tell you that. Your parents wouldn't approve. So I guess you'll just have to sit up at night all by yourself, staring out into the darkness, and imagine what *might* be waiting out there. Waiting and watching and biding its time until it knows you're sound asleep and can't see it coming. Mercy sakes, whatever might it be? Will it have fangs or scales or claws or all three or something even worse than that? Will it be hungry? Will it know how to climb up walls and through windows, even when they're locked down tight, or will it just ring the doorbell, hm? I won't tell—that would spoil the surprise—but you go right ahead and imagine it.

Won't that be fun?

You know, none of the little pumpkins who lived in Jo-Jo's patch ever interrupted wise old Mr. Hooty Owl when *he* was telling a story. They knew that if they did, wise old Mr. Hooty Owl would ring for the nurse and pretend he wanted to take a nap and all the blabby little pumpkins would have to sit in the sun room where the only channel you can get on the television is CNN. And because they were smart little pumpkins and really didn't enjoy the smell of bleach and wee-wee they didn't butt in on wise old Mr. Hooty Owl's story any more.

"Oh, it's marvelous to be a jack o' lantern," wise old Mr. Hooty Owl would say. "One minute you're a pumpkin like a hundred others, the next you're all aglow with light, just like a star. Then people put you in their windows or out on their front steps or balanced on the porch railing so that all the world can see just how bright and beautiful you are. They're pleased as punch to have you—almost think of you like a member of the family, they do—and when the little children see you, their eyes get *that* wide, and their mouths become just as round as can be, and they can't help but cry out over what a fine jack o' lantern you are. Yes, sir—" And he bit off the dead mouse's head and chewed it contentedly while he finished his speech. "—Halloween's a magical time to be a pumpkin."

Of course that was when a big chunk of mouse skull went down the wrong way and choked the life out of wise old Mr. Hooty Owl because wise old Mr. Hooty Owl wasn't quite wise enough and didn't know any better than to talk with his mouth full.

Jo-Jo couldn't wait for Halloween to come. All through the summer he did his best to soak up the sun and the rain until his round little body swelled up like a tick and he went from a teensy-weensy green thing the size of a tennis ball to a great big orange thing the size of a full-grown pumpkin.

Okay, so I never said my name was Auntie Metaphor. Sue me.

Pretty soon it got on for being close to Halloween and old Farmer Nosferatu came out to harvest his pumpkin patch. He was very pleased with what he saw, but not half so pleased as Jo-Jo. That clever little pumpkin knew from the way Farmer Nosferatu smiled down at him that he was a fine, ripe pumpkin and would be chosen to become a for-real-and-for-true jack o' lantern. Jo-Jo was so proud and so happy that he didn't even mind the searing pain he endured when Farmer Nosferatu took out his ever-so-sharp sickle and slashed through the stem holding Jo-Jo to the pumpkin vine.

Actually I'm lying. He *did* mind it. In fact, *minding* it doesn't even begin to cover little Jo-Jo's feelings. He hated it. It *hurt* to be cut off the vine. It hurt so bad that I can't tell you. You just imagine how *you'd* feel if you were holding hands with your Mommy and someone came along who wanted to snatch you away, only you were holding onto Mommy's hand so tight that they couldn't make you let go and so they had to take a great big ax and chopped right through your—

But I don't need to tell you everything, do I? You're such *bright* children. You can imagine that for yourselves.

Poor little Jo-Jo passed out entirely from the pain and when he woke up again, his stem throbbing, he discovered that he was sitting in a market. I'll spare you the tedious details and all the philosophical crap about what Jo-Jo learned from observing the interactions of human society. (See, Tommy? You're not the only show-off who watches educational television.) Jo-Jo wasn't paying a whole lot of attention to the people in the market anyhow. He was concentrating on his future, and what a merry future it would be once he became a jack o' lantern. It helped to take his mind off the pain.

How happy Jo-Jo was on the day that a dear little boy name Jeremy Jinx came into the market with his Mommy and picked three pumpkins! There was no doubt what Jeremy Jinx and his Mommy were going to do with those pumpkins, no sirree, because Jo-Jo heard Jeremy Jinx ask his Mommy right out loud, "Can we have this pumpkin to make into a jack o' lantern for Halloween? And this one? And this one? Oh, and this one, too? And that one over there? And the big one? Can we, can we, can we, huh, please, please, please?" And he heard Jeremy Jinx's Mommy reply, "We shall pick out one pumpkin for you, and one for me, and one for your darling Daddy. And then you can put a sock in it because I've got a three-martini headache so have some mercy and shut up."

Jeremy Jinx looked at all the pumpkins on display. Jo-Jo watched him. If he'd had a heart it would have been in his mouth, if he'd had a mouth. *Pick me!* he thought fiercely. *I want to be a jack o'lantern more than anything else in the whole, wide world. I want to be your jack o'lantern! Oh, please, please, please pick me!*

Lo and behold, Jo-Jo's fervent wish was granted, for little Jeremy Jinx looked straight at him, and put his dear, chubby little arms around him, and lifted him right off the display and said, "I want *this* one, Mommy. He's my very special friend, and he told me that more than anything else in the whole, wide world, he wants to be *my* jack o' lantern, and I love him."

"Great, now the kid's talking to vegetables," his Mommy muttered. She picked out two other pumpkins and dumped them in her shopping cart. "As soon as we get home, I'm calling your therapist."

Pretty soon Jo-Jo was safe and warm in his new home. He sat on the kitchen table with the other two pumpkins that Jeremy Jinx and his Mommy had chosen. He looked around, but he really wasn't paying attention to his surroundings. He was still thinking about becoming a jack o' lantern. In fact, Jo-Jo never thought about anything much except becoming a jack o' lantern. Come to think of it, Jo-Jo had a very unhealthy psychological obsession with becoming a jack o' lantern, so it's no wonder that when he finally learned the truth about jack o' lanterns—

But I'm getting ahead of myself.

On second thought, no, I'm not. Because you see, the very next morning, just as soon as Jeremy Jinx got on the school bus, when the air was fresh with frost and the sun was peeking in through the frilly white curtains at the kitchen window, Jeremy Jinx's Mommy spread a double layer of old newspaper over the kitchen table, set the first pumpkin right in the middle of it, took the biggest, sharpest knife in the whole kitchen, and plunged it straight through the soft and yielding skin right near the stem, ker-CHUNK!!!

Poor Jo-Jo! He was so shocked by this apparent act of wanton cruelty that he couldn't bring himself to look away. So he was still watching while Jeremy Jinx's mother sawed her knife all the way around the stem and pulled out the plug of dripping orange meat and then jabbed a big metal spoon deep into the helpless pumpkin's body. Jo-Jo saw how coolly the she-beast ladled out glob after sticky glob of seeds and dumped them into the garbage can, casually destroying generations of pumpkins yet unborn, but there was only so much a young vegetable could take. The horror was overwhelming and Jo-Jo fainted.

He awoke to a pain that made old Farmer Nosferatu's assault on his stem seem like a walk in the park. Mercifully, he passed out again before it completely registered on him that the source of his agony was because it was his turn under the knife and the spoon.

When Jo-Jo next became aware of the world around

him, he felt strangely light-headed, or perhaps I ought to say light-shelled. Kids, can you say "dramatic irony"?

Well, I'll bet you *could* say it if you'd stop goggling at me like a bunch of strangled frogs. Oh, never mind.

Anyhow, Jo-Jo felt different, very, very different from the innocent little pumpkin he used to be.

"What has happened to me?" he asked. Then he did a double-take. Had those words actually come out of his *mouth*?

But pumpkins don't have mouths.

Jack o' lanterns do.

Jo-Jo was still coming to grips with an altered reality when he glanced to his left. There was something shiny there, something that looked like a small silver box. Jo-Jo had no way of knowing that this was a toaster. All he knew was that when he turned, he could see himself in the brightly polished surface.

Oh, what a sight he was! For Jeremy Jinx's Mommy had taken all of the impotent rage she always kept bottled up inside her—a ferocious, long-smoldering rage which came from years of living under the regime of a repressive, patri-archal society—and had used it. And how had she used it? Why on carving the Halloween pumpkins, of course! She had given each of them the scowliest eyes and the pointiest noses and the biggest, widest, most sinister grins you can imagine.

And what is a big, wide, sinister grin unless it's full of big, sharp, nastily pointed teeth?

"Wow," said Jo-Jo, giving his reflection the once-over. "Cool."

"It won't be cool for long, squashboy," came an unfa-miliar voice. Jo-Jo turned—very slowly and in a wobbly manner—to confront the other two pumpkins that Jeremy Jinx's mother had also carved into jack o' lanterns. The one that had called out to Jo-Jo looked a lot like him, only not quite so scary, but the other one—

The other one was hollow and smashed and dead.

Jo-Jo gasped at the shattered, oozing shell. "What—what happened to *her*?" he demanded.

If a pumpkin could shrug, that's exactly what the other jack o' lantern would have done. "Mulch happens. The knife slipped. So the seed-scooping monster lost her temper and knocked the poor kid smack off the table by . . . 'accident.' "

"How awful!" Jo-Jo cried. Fat, slimy tears dripped from his freshly gouged-out eye-holes.

"Save your tears for yourself," the other pumpkin told him. "As soon as the seed-scooper comes back with the candles, it's all over for us."

Jo-Jo didn't understand.

"Geez, sprout, didn't anyone ever tell you?" the other pumpkin said. "Don't you know what it means to be a jack o' lantern?"

So Jo-Jo told the other pumpkin all about the pumpkin patch back home, and old Farmer Nosferatu, and wise old Mister Hooty Owl's stories. And when he was done, the other pumpkin was laughing fit to burst himself into a pile of puréed pie filling.

"Funny, you don't *look* green," he said when he finally got control of himself. "And you *believed* those stories? Sprout, those are the sort of thing 'most everyone tells you when you're young because being young means being dumb as a rock and it's fun to see just how many lies you'll swallow before you wise up!"

"Then it wasn't true?" Jo-Jo said, and he sounded so sorrowful and pathetic it would've made a high school guidance counselor cry real tears. "Not a single word?"

"Bless your blossoms, there's *some* truth to what you were told," the other pumpkin said. "All the best lies come wrapped up in half-truths so they're easier to believe. Halloween *is* a magical time of year for us poor pumpkins. How else do you think you got the power to move yourself around like that, even a little, and to talk like we're doing right now? But the magic doesn't last and neither do we. Oh, they'll use us to light up their Halloween night, all right! But how do you think they make us glow? Not by magic, nuh-uh. By fire."

Jo-Jo gasped. Fire was something he understood. It was something all vegetables understood without ever needing to be taught, a primal fear bred so deeply into every leaf and stem, fruit and flower, that it came to them as natural as soaking up sunlight and rain. Fire cooked. Fire killed.

"That's right, sprout, I said fire," the other pumpkin went on. "Something called a candle. They lift off the top of your shell, stick that thing upright inside you, and then they set it aflame. And as soon as the first little spark of it catches hold and the fire blazes up in your shell, the magic's over. You're dead. Beautiful and bright, but dead."

"Nooooooo!" Jo-Jo wailed. And he rocked back and forth on the kitchen table, because the magic of Halloween had given him the power to move himself around like that, in a most un-vegetable-like manner. More tears streamed from his eye-holes and he wiped them away frantically.

Then he realized something. *What* was he using to wipe away his tears?

"Where in heck did *these* come from?" he asked, holding up a pair of prehensile leaves. They trembled before his eye-holes, having burgeoned from the ends of a pair of sturdy pumpkin vines that had somehow erupted from the sides of his shell.

The other pumpkin chuckled. "Beats me, sprout. More of that 'magic of Halloween' crap in action, I guess. They say that if you want something bad enough, tonight of all nights, you get it. Anything short of wanting to save your own life, that is. Candle or no candle, we've only got until dawn."

"But I never wished for *these*," Jo-Jo protested, waving his vines about wildly.

"Hey, some things you want without knowing you want them," the other pumpkin said. "Some things, the magic knows you want them before you know it yourself."

Jo-Jo grew thoughtful. He continued to study his miraculous leaves and vines, flexing them testing them, reaching out with them, using them to pluck at the corners of the sodden newspapers still covering the kitchen tabletop. The leaves were very dexterous, just like human hands, only somehow Jo-Jo knew that the vines he'd grown instead of arms were much stronger than human arms.

"I guess the magic *does* know best," he said at last. "There *is* one thing I want to do before I go, and I won't so much mind dying after I've done it." As the other pumpkin watched, Jo-Jo began to shake and shiver, then all of sudden he sprouted two more vines, right out from under himself. Using his leaves, he laid hold of the table and let himself drop over the side just as his rapidly growing leg-vines reached their full size.

"Hey, sprout, what do you think you're–?" the other pumpkin began to ask. Just then the kitchen door swung open and Jeremy Jinx's Mommy came in with a couple of fat, white candles in her hands.

The other pumpkin saw Jo-Jo's vines snake back up onto the table top, lay hold of the carving knife and the scooping spoon, and drop from sight again just before he heard Jeremy Jinx's Mommy begin to scream.

The end.

What's that, Tommy? What do you mean, it can't be the end? Sure it can! Who's telling this story, huh? I'm only doing what your Mommy and Daddy want, shielding you, sheltering you from all the icky-sticky details. Why should I have to tell you what happened next, what Jo-Jo did with that carving knife and that scooping spoon and those candles? Can't you guess what little Jeremy Jinx found sitting on the front porch steps, waiting for him when he came home from school that day? It was a surprise, I can at least tell you that. A gaping, grinning surprise with a candle burning oh, ever so brightly inside!

Surely you don't need *me* to tell you what it was, do you? I didn't think so. Or to tell you what it was that little Jeremy Jinx found smeared all over the sharp, pointed, nastily carved teeth of the jolly jack o' lantern that sat on the *other* side of the front porch steps? A child's imagination is *such* a precious gift, dearie me, yes. Use it, yard-apes.

But what's that tapping at the door? Could it possibly be Jo-Jo the Jolly Jack o' Lantern, come to call? No, it's just your Mommy and Daddy, here to take you home again, thank God. Give Auntie Elspeth a kiss and—Oh, fine, no kiss, just try to stop screaming, okay?

Bye-bye, darlings. Happy Halloween.

# THE WITCH WHO HATED HALLOWEEN

## TERRY KAYE

**M**elissa Cooper woke up early Halloween morning and groaned. Halloween was definitely *not* her favorite day of the year.

Pluto, her little Yorkshire terrier, was perched at the foot of her bed. At the sound of her voice, he bounded into the air and onto her face. Once he felt his owner was sufficiently greeted—and Melissa felt sufficiently wet—Pluto settled down onto her stomach and gazed into her bright blue eyes.

"Well, at least one of us is having a happy Halloween," said Melissa, stroking Pluto as she studied the ceiling above her bed.

On it was a huge painting of the entire galaxy. The sun and our solar system was directly over her head, and the rest of the Milky Way spread out above her to the four corners of her bedroom.

Lots of kids had astronomical posters and paintings in their rooms, but Melissa knew that hers was special for two reasons. The first was that she helped her mother paint it when she was six years old, so she felt proud every time she looked at it.

The second reason was that *her* painting really *was* the galaxy—well, in miniature, anyway. The stars twinkled, the planets and moons rotated on their axes, and every now and then a shooting star would dash across the sky. Whatever happened in the heavens, Melissa watched it all unfold above her as she lay in her sleigh-bed.

One may wonder: how was this possible? One may answer: by magic! Melissa was a witch. Her parents were witches, and theirs before them, and so forth as far back as anyone can remember. Maybe even farther.

Melissa and her family were not the kind of witches who wore black dresses and pointy hats, who ate small children for breakfast, or who fed people poisoned apples and generally made life miserable. In fact, Melissa had never met a witch like that. Those were strictly fairy-tale creations, made up to scare little children and to help adults explain what they did not understand.

Real witches and wizards were generally quite dignified, kind and intelligent. Most had wonderful senses of humor—Melissa loved nothing better than to listen to the clever conversation at the parties her mother often threw. Sure, she was supposed to be asleep—but who could sleep with the promise of stolen snippets of puns, witticisms, and anecdotes right outside her door? Mother was usually so busy playing hostess that Melissa and Pluto could sneak into the hallway and listen for an hour or two unnoticed. Once or twice they fell asleep, curled up right there outside the bedroom door. Her mother would find them there—she'd be angry, if they weren't so darned cute!—and carry them off to bed.

But tonight, there would be no such entertainment. "Not for me, anyway," Melissa said with a sigh as she thought about the day and night to come. "Mama and Papa will be at the Crystal Ball, the most elegant event of the whole *year*! And where will I be?" Pluto cocked his head in anticipation of the answer. "I will be at Rebecca Leindecker's stupid Halloween party, being tortured as usual . . ."

"Meliiiiisa, I hope you're up, darling!" Helaine Cooper's voice rang out, singsongy, through the house. "Time to get ready for school! And you know what day it is, don't you? I have a surpriiiiise for you!"

"Ugh." Melissa fell back onto her goose down pillow. Pluto crawled gingerly up her torso and started licking her neck. "Ohhh . . . thanks, sweetie," cooed Melissa. "But I'm afraid nothing is going to make me feel better about *this* particular 'surprise'."

"Meliiiisa! Did you hear me, sweetheart?"

"Coming, Mother!"

"Well, hurry up, baby doll, your surprise awaits!"

Melissa rolled her eyes, hugged the dog, and took one last look at the ceiling. Her gaze rested on the planet Pluto, and the planet's furry namesake looked up to see what had captured her attention.

Melissa always felt a special affinity for the smallest planet, so far away, the vastness of space making it seem even tinier. She was sure it must be lonely all the way out there. And lately some scientists were saying that maybe Pluto wasn't a planet at all, that it was just a meteor drawn into orbit with the "real" eight planets. Melissa thought that must hurt, being picked on just because it was different, small and independent. In fact, she was sure she knew just how Pluto felt.

Melissa got up and dressed a little slower than usual. When she finally ventured out into the kitchen, her mother was waiting for her, holding a large package.

"There she is, my little munchkin. Now, what would you

like for breakfast this morning, today you may have anything you like."

"I'm really not that hungry, Mama . . ."

"Nonsense! You have to eat. So, how about I'll make up
a nice batch of oatmeal, with berries and brown sugar? It's
your favorite, yes?"

With a smile, Mama whisked her hand toward the stove.
Instantly a large saucepot appeared on the front burner,
brim full with hot oatmeal. It had a sweet cinnamonny
smell. Melissa's appetite picked up a bit at the aroma.

"Thanks, Mama." Melissa sat down at the table as her
mother conjured up a pitcher of orange juice and a heaping
bowl of every kind of berry.

"No time for cooking by hand today," she said. Mrs.
Cooper often did household chores "by hand," or without
magic; she enjoyed the "novelty" of it. She read *Good
Housekeeping* religiously and loved to try the recipes and
craft-making tips. She said they kept her on her toes.

These experiments tended to keep the rest of the family
on their toes, too, since they usually ended with something
on fire or melted or otherwise destroyed. One time she
decided to make "the most darling sweater" for the dog.
Unfortunately, she knitted poor Pluto right into the pink
and white wool. It took Melissa two days to unravel the
whimpering creature.

"So," Mrs. Cooper continued, "are you ready for your
surprise?" She handed Melissa the big box, wrapped in gold
foil with a large gold bow on top. Melissa accepted the gift
like a soldier going off to battle: she knew what lay ahead,
and grimly awaited her fate.

"Um, thanks, Mama . . . it's great."

"You haven't even opened it yet! Come on, I'm dying to
see your face."

"Okay . . . here goes," Melissa tore open the paper and

opened the box. Inside was a long black dress and matching hat, pointy-toed shoes, a set of claw-like glue-on finger-nails, and a vat of green greasepaint.

A witch's Halloween costume.

Melissa forced a smile that was closer to a grimace, and said, "Thanks, Mama."

"Oh, you're welcome, darling. I can't wait to see you in it!"

Her mother beamed and, in her excitement, accidentally levitated herself two feet off the floor. "Oops! I got carried up, up and away!" Mrs. Cooper giggled and Melissa couldn't help smiling. Helaine Cooper was a petite 5'4", 125 pounds, auburn-haired and full of energy. Melissa was sure the term "spitfire" had been coined for her mother.

"Okay, now finish your breakfast and hurry off to school! The sooner you go, the sooner you come home and get dressed for tonight!"

"Yes, mama—I know."

Mama bustled off then, humming happily as she whisked colorful decorations into place all over the house. Black and orange were strictly for the non-magical; real witches decorated for Halloween in bright, cheery, happy colors. Melissa always thought it looked like a rainbow had exploded in their living room. That was the part of Halloween she liked.

Melissa went upstairs, got her backpack, and mentally braced herself for the part of Halloween she didn't like ... which was, pretty much, all of the rest of it.

There was a time when Melissa enjoyed Halloween as much as the next kid—maybe more. Back then, all the children dressed up as witches, ghosts, goblins and whatnot. But as they got older, the other kids outgrew the mystical, became bored and disillusioned with the magical world. Witches and the like were fine for babies, but at 12 years old—and starting middle school, no less—no one would be caught dead in witch's garb.

No one except Melissa.

Melissa knew there was no point in protesting. She feebly suggested, last year, that it might be time for something new. She described to her parents in detail all of the wonderful costumes her schoolmates were wearing from Robin Hood and Huck Finn to Madonna and Bart Simpson. And she hinted ever so subtly that it might be fun, one day, to dress up as Juliet . . . so beautiful, elegant and dainty.

Her father regarded her sternly and reprimanded her for showing disrespect to her parents, her ancestors, and all of witchdom. Her mother looked bewildered, as if her daughter were speaking in tongues, or perhaps had suddenly sprouted two or three extra heads.

Nothing further was ever said on the subject. Melissa knew that for her parents, Halloween was sacred, a day to honor their long and rich magical heritage. And apparently, parading their daughter around in black robes was a part of it. No matter that the black "witch" ensemble was merely a perversion of the deep purple ceremonial robes that witches wore thousands of years ago. No matter that a real witch would never wear such a thing. "This is the way non-witches picture us," Mama always said, "so this is the way we shall celebrate in their midst." Case closed.

Melissa's parents did not understand how cruel seventh graders could be. Pluto understood, but that did not help the current situation.

Melissa arrived at her homeroom class before the bell, but not before Rebecca Leindecker and her clutch of giggling girlfriends. They were clustered in the center of the room, effectively forming a roadblock for anyone trying to cross to the seats along the back wall. Melissa paused in the doorway before entering the classroom.

"And *I* am going to be Britney Spears!" Rebecca chirped, to a chorus of excited squeals. "My mom let me pick out everything myself, and it is *so cute*! There's this little halter top, with lots of gold sparkles, and the pants are so tight and so hot and they have—*oh* . . . Melissa. I didn't even *notice* you."

*So what else is new?* thought Melissa, as seven body-waved heads turned in her direction.

"So, Missy, we're talking costumage . . ." said Rebecca. Melissa cringed inside; she hated to be called Missy. "I'm Britney, Sara here is Xena, Jasmine is Marilyn Monroe. . . . oh, and best of all Joshua Stevens is going to be Ricky Martin! How hot is *that*?"

Joshua Stevens was undoubtedly the cutest boy in the seventh grade—in the whole school, probably. Of course, Melissa had a huge crush on him—who didn't?—and she felt a lump rise in her throat. In all the time she'd known him, since the first day of the second grade, Melissa estimated that about ten words had been exchanged between them.

Rebecca, of course, would be draped all over him this evening. The image of Britney and Ricky (only cuter) arm in arm, laughing—*Oh, my God, maybe even kissing!*—made the lump in Melissa's throat grow to the size of a watermelon.

"Oh, Missy, I'm being rude," Rebecca cooed, her voice oozing with saccharine. "I haven't even asked you what *you* will be wearing."

"I'm going to be a witch," Melissa mumbled.

"Now Missy dear, you'll have to learn to speak up . . . and *enunciate*, so we can understand you!"

Melissa took a deep breath, and repeated, "I'm going to be a witch."

"Ooh, how *original* . . . Missy, you are so clever! We're all jealous, aren't we girls?" This was met with loud giggles and snickers from the others.

"Of course you realize, Missy," Rebecca continued, that the whole idea of Halloween is to be something *different* from what you are every day!"

At this, Rebecca and her groupies dissolved into peals of laughter. Of course, they had no idea of the truth of Rebecca's comment, and Melissa toyed with the idea of giving them a demonstration right there and then. Turning them all into crickets and feeding them to the class' pet frog was a very appealing notion. Luckily, just then the bell rang, and Melissa was relieved to escape into the world of literature, earth science and geometry.

The rest of the day went much as any other day in the young girl's life. Melissa was a good student and a favorite of all of her teachers. Outside of the classroom, at lunch and in the courtyard, she spent most of her time alone—reading, doing homework, or daydreaming. She was a shy girl by nature and at some point early on had been branded a loner. The label stuck, and eventually evolved from "loner" to "weird" to "freak." As a rule, kids either teased her or ignored her. She was used to both, and fond of neither.

After school, most of the kids rushed home to start getting ready for Rebecca's party. Melissa took her time, ambling through the park, stopping for a while to play on the swing set she'd loved since she was four years old.

She finally went home, walked Pluto and fed him, did her homework and had a quick supper of baked chicken, brown rice and broccoli. Usually one of her favorite meals, but tonight it seemed to have no flavor at all. She ate what she could, and asked to be excused.

"Did you hear that, Frank, she wants to be excused!"

"I heard." Frank Cooper was a wizard of few words.

"She can't wait to get dressed and ready," Helaine said, stroking Melissa's long brown hair.

Frank gave his daughter an appraising glance. She forced a weak smile.

"Well, go then. Have a good time at your party. And Melissa . . ."

"Yes, Papa?"

"Make us proud."

Melissa got dressed and made up quickly. *Like pulling off a band-aid*, she thought. *Just get it over with.* On her way out the door, she caught a glimpse of herself in the mirror over her dresser.

"Ugh," she said, to no one in particular. The image looking back at her was black and green, drab and ugly, right down to the long pointy prosthetic nose she'd found at the bottom of the costume box. "No wonder people think I'm a freak. If I didn't know me, *I'd* think I was a freak."

She joined her parents in the living room, and for a brief moment forgot her troubles. Standing before her were two of the handsomest people she'd ever seen.

Her mother was radiant in a sapphire blue silk gown, off the shoulder and flowing down to the floor. She wore sparkling sapphire earrings and a matching necklace that fell just along the line of her collarbone. Her hair was piled high on her head and blue glitter shimmered on her face, neck and shoulders.

Her father looked splendid in black tie and tails, with sapphire cufflinks that flashed like fire when the light hit them. They would no doubt be the most glorious couple at the Crystal Ball. Melissa wished with all her heart she could go with them.

"And just *look* at our daughter, Frank! How lovely she looks! Do you see, Frank?"

"Of course I see, Helaine, she's standing right there."

"Doesn't she look lovely?"

Frank took a long moment before answering, taking in

the picture, gazing at his daughter as only a father can. "Oh, yes, she does. She'll be the belle of the ball."

"Yes, indeed," agreed Mrs. Cooper. Melissa thought for a second her mother might actually start to cry. But instead, she clapped her hands and said, "So, let's go then. We'll drop you off on our way to the Ball."

When Melissa arrived at Rebecca Leindecker's house, the party was already going at full throttle. N'Sync blasted from the stereo, and a group of 20 or so costumed kids gyrated wildly in the center of the floor. Others were clustered around the spacious room, talking and laughing riotously. A few were visiting one of the three refreshment tables in various corners of the room. Each table offered a variety of goodies, and each had a huge punch bowl. At one table there was lemonade, at another, red berry punch, and at the third, a mango-pineapple concoction that was the hit of the evening.

Melissa glanced around the room from the doorway, making a quick assessment of the situation. Most of her classmates were too busy having fun to notice one little witch, she thought, and if she scurried past Batman and Hannibal Lector, edged past Hillary Clinton and ducked around the cast of Survivor, she might make it to the mango juice without incident. The plan from there was to hang out in the corner as much as possible, OD on mango madness, and leave at the earliest opportunity.

Satisfied with this idea, Melissa started shuffling across the dance floor. She successfully passed Hillary, dodged an unexpected Tarzan, and was almost to the Survivor pack with the safety of the beverage table in sight when—

"Missy!! *There* you are . . . we've been waiting for you!"

*Busted*, Melissa thought, looking up at a scantily-clad, blond-wigged Rebecca Leindecker. Rebecca had a grin on her face the size of Montana. Melissa acknowledged her hostess with a quick wave, and tried to continue on her path to the corner.

"Why, what's the hurry, Missy? Don't you want to show everyone your marvelous costume? Everybody, check out Missy's *fabulous* duds!" It seemed to Melissa that Rebecca's voice was as loud as a foghorn. Someone turned down the music and all eyes turned toward Melissa. At that moment she was glad that her face was covered with green paint. Underneath, she was sure, it was turning three shades of purple.

Rebecca, savoring every second in the spotlight, continued, "I mean, really, I *love* your get-up! In fact, I think I had an outfit just like it when I was three!"

This was greeted with loud laughter from the crowd, and Rebecca smiled even more broadly.

"You know, I think it's great, you wearing that . . . it's such a bold statement. Not everyone is willing to look totally, heinously ugly!"

More giggles, whispers and a few pitying looks. Melissa felt tears welling up in her eyes, but she would sooner have eaten ten cockroaches than to let Rebecca see her cry. Instead she found a gap in the crowd and pushed through, making eye contact with no one on the way.

"Enjoy the party!" shouted Rebecca after her. Then she turned around and yelled, "Hey, let's dance!"

Someone turned the music back up—now it was Eden's Crush—and gradually people filtered back onto the dance floor. In a few minutes the party was back in gear, the recent spectacle forgotten as quickly as it started.

Melissa looked from her corner at the scene before her. Everyone was enjoying the evening, it seemed. Some kids were starting to filter out the glass doors to the poolside patio. Melissa could smell the aroma of burgers, hot dogs and vegetables cooking on a grill. The normally pleasant scent was making her feel a little nauseous.

"I think it's cool," said a small voice by her right ear.

Melissa turned to see Elizabeth Ingram standing next to her. Elizabeth was a sweet girl, petite with curly brown hair and azure eyes. She was always kind and Melissa was grateful for it. They rarely saw each other outside of school but Melissa thought, in another life, they might have been close friends.

"Hi, Lizzie," replied Melissa. "You think what's cool?"

"Your costume," said Lizzie.

"You *do*?"

"Sure . . . I always thought Halloween was about witches and ghosts and stuff, anyway. I think you look great."

"Well, I don't know, but thanks," said Melissa. She looked at Lizzie's dress: a lovely silvery gown with empire waist and about 100 buttons all the way up her back. She wore white silk gloves and dainty silver shoes with bows. She looked just like the illustrations in Melissa's volume of the complete works of Shakespeare.

"Really, thank you . . . and by the way, I love your dress. I've always wanted to be Juliet . . ."

"Thanks."

"Hey, Lizard, are you coming out here, or what?" a voice yelled from the patio.

"I'm coming!" she hollered back. "Melissa, are you coming out?"

"Maybe later. You go, though."

"Well, okay . . . see you later, then."

Elizabeth wandered off to join the others, leaving Melissa once again alone in the midst of all the frivolity.

"You know, sometimes it's almost like I'm invisible," she

said to herself as she poured a glass of the mango potion. She took a long sip—it was good—and then she froze in mid-gulp.

*Invisible*, she thought. *Now that might just make this evening a little more exciting.*

She drained her cup, set it down on the table, and stole around the corner into the foyer. It was empty and completely out of view of the main party area.

*Perfect*, she thought.

Melissa closed her eyes and placed her hands on her temples. She concentrated as hard as she could, until she felt a wave of energy fill her body, starting in the tips of her toes and flowing up to the top of her head. Finally she opened her eyes, and surveyed her image in the large oak-framed mirror hanging on the wall. Or more accurately, her *non-image*, since she had successfully become invisible.

"Excellent. Now, let's party!"

Melissa floated back into the party undetected and now she did venture out to the patio. First, she saw a large swimming pool, recently drained in anticipation of winter. She looked around at the landscaping, beautifully sculpted shrubbery and several tall trees, perfect for climbing. Some of their branches were so long that they almost touched, high above the empty pool.

A glance over at the grilling area confirmed that Rebecca was not outside. So Melissa headed back to the dance room, where a couple dozen kids were still bopping to the Backstreet Boys.

At first she didn't see her quarry. She was just about to check by the pool again when she spotted her target, not-so-subtly flirting with Joshua Stevens by the snack table with the red punch.

Melissa crept toward them until she was close enough to hear their conversation.

"I just *adore* your costume, Joshua . . . Ricky Martin is, like, the hottest dude *ever!*"

"Yeah, I guess . . ."

"No, I mean it . . . he is so hot. But you know what? You're even hotter."

"Um, okay, Beck, if you say so . . ."

"I *do* say so. *All* the girls are talking about you." She sidled in closer to him, brushing against his arm. Melissa wasn't sure, but she thought she saw Joshua inch away a little.

"But, lucky me, it seems I have you all to myself." Savage Garden came over the stereo as if on cue, singing *I Knew I Loved You Before I Met You.* "Ooh, a slow song. So, does Ricky wanna dance with Britney?"

This was about all Melissa could stand. So, before Joshua could answer, she took action.

First, she waved her hand at the large framed portrait above the snack table. One of the nails it hung on suddenly sprang out, hitting Rebecca squarely on the head before clattering to the floor. The picture flopped down and dangled, swaying back and forth on its one remaining nail.

"Ow! What the—" Rebecca started; then gasped as she saw the portrait, precariously perched directly above the bowl of bright red punch.

"Oh, no! No, no!! That's my grandmother! I mean, her portrait—my mom will kill me if it gets ruined!"

She reached across the table to grab the picture before it fell, but the folding table was a little too wide and her arms a little too short. The dancers looked on silently. The group on the patio heard Rebecca's shouts and they started drifting in to see what was going on.

*Oh, this is too good*, thought Melissa. It was all she could do not to giggle out loud. She watched with glee as

Rebecca followed her plan to a T. *You would think she had a script!*

"Joshua, give me a boost onto the table, would you?" Rebecca asked. He complied and shortly Rebecca was balanced on the tabletop, reaching for her grandmother's portrait.

"Okay . . . okay . . . almost got it . . . there! Hey—noooo!!"

Melissa had one invisible finger pointed at the framed canvas. Just as Rebecca was about to reach it, it slid right out of her grasp.

"That's not possible! Okay . . . come . . . here!" Rebecca swiped at the frame again, with the same result.

"Do you want some help with that?" asked Joshua.

"No, no, I've got it . . . just . . . like . . . this!" Rebecca had to stretch as far as she was able in order to reach the edge of the frame. This time Melissa let her have it.

And then, she let her *have* it.

Melissa focused her mind on the two legs at the near end of the table. She held up both hands, pointed at the corners of the table where it joined to the legs, and flicked her index fingers as if she were flicking ants off a picnic table. Immediately the legs collapsed inward, and with a loud THUNK, the table hit the floor. The framed portrait flew out of Rebecca's hand and landed on the floor yards away, undamaged. Rebecca was not damaged either, but her ego was. She hurtled to the floor, shrieking and flailing in a futile attempt to steady herself. She landed hard, with a thud and a squish—the plate of grapes and berries had beaten her to the ground. *Well, that'll make for an interesting tie-dye job*, Melissa thought, *considering which part of her landed on it.*

Next came the plates of chips, dip, and cookies, which

mostly ended up in Rebecca's lap. A large bowl of green Jell-o crashed to the floor by her feet, and some of the sticky substance oozed out onto her shoes. Finally, the *pièce de resistance* . . . the enormous bowl of beet red fruit punch. Melissa concentrated on the bowl, one finger pointing directly at it, slowly allowing it to slide down the now empty table. Rebecca gaped in bewilderment, unable to move, bracing herself for the inevitable. Suddenly the bowl flew up into the air, hovering directly above Rebecca's head. It held there for a moment, and a loud gasp came from the crowd. Melissa knew she was going too far now, but she couldn't resist. She held the punch bowl in place for a good five seconds. Then, all at once, she let her arm go limp.

The punch bowl went limp, too, depositing all of its contents over Rebecca's head before it deposited itself there like a ridiculous crown. There was an explosion of laughter and a few flashes of light from those who ran to get their cameras.

Rebecca just sat, defeated and dazed, not moving from the spot where she landed. She seemed not to notice the ruckus around her.

Melissa, still invisible, looked on and waited for her own laughter to come. But it did not. She wanted to revel in her triumph, but she felt hollow. And sad. And small.

"Revenge is never right," she heard her mother telling her. "You think it will heal your wounds, but it only opens them wider." *You were right, Mama*, she thought. *I'm sorry.*

By now, Rebecca was coming out of her stupor and beginning to take in the scene around her. The view was a colorful tableau, a hundred 12-year-olds frozen in place, a few still smothering laughs and whispers in the stillness.

"What are you all looking at? What do you—" She abruptly cut off as something caught her eye. Motion, something . . . just a hint . . . something black. She struggled to focus as the blurry object came into view. The others followed her gaze.

The object became more solid, took on a defined shape. It was Melissa. The remorse she felt over her behavior upset her so that she'd lost her concentration, and without realizing it, she also lost her invisibility spell. Rebecca and the others stared on wide-eyed as she materialized.

*"You!!"* Rebecca shrieked, getting to her feet, slipping a little in the multicolored slime. "You did this!! You had to—the picture! And the table!! And the *punch*!! And—and—you were invisible!!! I saw you—I mean, I *didn't* see you!!"

Melissa suddenly understood what was happening and stood frozen, horrified. This was the worst thing she could have done, misusing her power and letting a horde of non-witches see her do it. She didn't know what the punishment was for this, but it would be worse than anything she'd ever experienced.

"I . . . I'm sorry . . . I . . ."

"You're *sorry*?" Rebecca was over her shock now, and the look in her eyes told Melissa she meant business. "You *will* be sorry! Because now I know—we *all* know. You're not just a freak! You're a *WITCH*!"

Melissa looked around, helpless, hoping to find one pair of friendly eyes in the crowd. There were none. Those who caught her gaze at all had terror in their eyes. Most looked down at the floor. Even Lizzie Ingram did not raise her eyes.

"I . . . I should go . . ." murmured Melissa. It was all she could think of to say. She crept toward the front door, past the motionless throng. Only Rebecca shouted after her.

"That's right, slink off to your nasty witch parents and your nasty witch house! You have no friends here—WITCH!"

Just as Melissa reached the door, there was a loud CRACK and a scream. She whirled around to look—it sounded like it came from the patio.

"What have you done now, witch?" yelled Rebecca.

"Oh my God! *Kevin!*" someone screamed, and several more voices followed. "Kevin, NO!" "Help him!" "Oh, God, we forgot about Kevin!!"

There was a mad rush out to the patio. Melissa followed tentatively, wanting to help but not sure if her help was welcome. She saw Lizzie at the back of the pack and grabbed her arm.

"What happened?"

"Kevin Mullaney. They dared him . . ."

"Dared him to do what?"

"The trees—climb the trees!"

Melissa didn't understand. "What's the big deal with climbing a tree?"

Lizzie paused, caught her breath. "Not *a* tree . . . *the trees* . . . he had to climb one, go across the branches, and go down another!"

Melissa ran outside, Lizzie close on her heels, and looked up. There, dangling from a broken branch, was Kevin Mullaney. Kevin was a smart boy, a little overweight and a little on the short side. He was constantly trying to prove himself to the popular, athletic boys—who were more than willing to come up with new and improved ways for Kevin to amuse them.

No one was laughing now, because Kevin was holding on for dear life, about ten feet above their heads. What was worse, the branch supporting him was directly above the empty swimming pool.

"He must have jumped across to the second tree when we all went inside—and it broke!" wailed Lizzie.

Some kids were shouting a frantic chorus of "Hang on, Kevin—don't worry, we'll get you down, Kev!" Others were too horror stricken to speak. All were beginning to realize the truth . . . there was no branch near enough for anyone to reach him, and the one he clung to would not hold out long enough for help to arrive. The drop into the pool was 20-plus feet onto solid concrete. He'd probably break his neck if he fell.

Melissa reacted without thinking. When she ducked into the foyer to become invisible, she'd noticed a broom leaning up against the wall. She blocked out the cacophony of sound around her, focused on that broom, and in a flash it swept out the glass doors and into her hands. She climbed aboard and took off.

She raced up toward the spot where Kevin swayed in the breeze. She saw that his eyes were tightly shut and his skin was clammy and ashen. She reached him just as the branch snapped, catching him on the back of the broomstick while the branch fell to the bottom of the pool.

Kevin's eyes were still sealed shut when they landed gently on the grass. It took a moment for him to realize that he was no longer dangling, and that he was not dead. Then he opened his eyes and blinked in amazement at Melissa.

There was a moment of utter silence. Melissa looked around nervously at the sea of stunned faces. *This is it*, she thought. *They know what I am. There's no denying it now . . . my life is over.*

Then two things happened.

Kevin grabbed Melissa into the biggest bear hug she'd ever had. He squeezed her so tight she could hardly breathe.

And the silence was broken by an earth shattering cheer. Melissa had never heard anything like it—screams of joy, whistles, shouts of "Hurray! and "Yeah!" and "Woo-hoo!"—all directed at her!

When the excitement finally died down to a dull roar and Kevin pried himself off of his heroine, Melissa looked around and saw something she had never seen before: every student in the seventh grade, smiling—no, *beaming*—at her.

All but one.

Rebecca Leindecker pushed through the crowd toward Melissa, still covered in goop and seething with rage.

"What are you all cheering for? Have you lost your minds? She's a witch! She's *evil*!! She probably made the branch break in the first place!"

Silence and icy stares.

"Oh, come *on*, people! Are you crazy? Or just stupid? She's a *witch*!! She probably eats toads for breakfast! She probably tortures puppies and kittens for fun! She almost killed Kevin! And look at what she did to *me*!"

More silence.

"Okay, maybe you are all blind, but *I'm* not. I see what she is. And if you all are too dumb to do anything about it, I will! First thing tomorrow I'm going to the principal—no, the police—hell, maybe the freaking FBI!—and I'm telling them all there's a family of witches living right here in our town! *Poisoning* our town! And you all saw it—you are all witnesses!" She turned viciously on Melissa. "Then we'll see how much everybody loves you."

"I don't know what you're talking about," said a small but strong voice.

Everyone turned to see where the words came from. It was Lizzie Ingram.

"I mean, Becky," she continued, "I didn't see anything strange here at all tonight."

Rebecca stared at her in horror. "Of *course* you saw it. We *all* saw it! She had a *broomstick*, for crying out loud! She flew up there and—"

"Really, Beck," said Lizzie, "everyone knows there's no such thing as witches. You know, maybe you hit your head when you took that little spill earlier. You should get that checked out."

"I didn't take a spill—*she spilled me*! She did it on purpose! And she was invisible! You all saw her!!"

Now Kevin stepped forward. "Well, I don't know what you're talking about . . . since I was stuck in the tree and all . . . but it seems to me that if someone were invisible, then no one would have *seen* her . . ."

The group roared with laughter, and one by one the other kids came forward in Melissa's defense.

"Really! A witch! You've been reading too many scary stories, Becky."

"I didn't see anything . . . except Rebecca with a punch bowl on her head!"

"Rebecca, I've got to hand it to you . . . you have, like, the most vivid imagination *ever*."

The last came from Joshua Stevens. Utterly defeated and able to take no more, Rebecca let out a short *high*-pitched squeak and ran into the house. A moment later they all heard the SLAM! of her bedroom door.

Melissa looked around at her classmates—now perhaps her friends?—and murmured, "thank you . . ." It didn't seem enough but it was all that would come out.

"Hey, no problem." Melissa looked up to see Joshua standing right next to her. "I was thinking . . . maybe you could do something for us?" he asked tentatively.

"Anything!" exclaimed Melissa.

She spent the rest of the evening giving everybody rides on the broomstick, on the condition that no one would ever tell another soul about it. The kids agreed instantly, and they all had a marvelous time soaring and dipping around the courtyard.

Melissa had never been happier. She knew that Rebecca couldn't touch her now. If she tried, the others would deny seeing anything, and Becky would either be ignored or end up at the funny farm.

As for her new found popularity, Melissa knew it probably would not last. She would no longer be a "freak," and that was good. She might end up with a few close friends, and that was wonderful. Joshua Stevens might speak to her in the hallway, maybe even have a whole conversation, and *that* was incredible.

Most of her classmates, she knew, would eventually get over their fascination with her and go back to their routine. They wouldn't be close friends, but they also wouldn't be enemies. And that was just fine. Life wasn't going to change completely overnight. But it was a start.

She felt a light tap on her shoulder and looked to her left. It was Lizzie.

"Hey, Melissa, I was wondering ... you wanna come over tomorrow after school? We could study ... and we have a ping-pong table in the cellar. You could stay for dinner, if you want."

Melissa smiled. "I'd like that, Lizzie. I'd like that a lot."

"Cool." Lizzie paused a second before adding, "And Melissa, you know what? I was thinking, next Halloween?"

"Yeah?"

"I think I'm going to be a witch."

She gave Melissa a quick hug and joined the rest of the kids, who had moved back inside the house.

Melissa stood on the patio, alone now, and looked at the sky. There was a beautiful crescent moon, and the stars seemed especially bright. She gazed off in the direction where she knew Pluto would be, and smiled.

"Yes," she said, to no one in particular. "It's definitely a start."

# TOM O'BEDLAM'S NIGHT OUT

## DARRELL SCHWEITZER

S will! Filth! Horse piss!" yelled the ragged man as he threw his bowl onto the stone floor.

"Ah, Tom," said the gaoler. "Be grateful for what ye got."

"Put something in this slop! Meat! A man needs meat to be strong!"

"But meat's expensive, Tom. If ye had two pennies I'd give ye meat, but ye don't, so be quiet or else I'll call the doctor to purge your ill humours."

"I'll get two copper pennies then. I will!"

"Ha! A thief ye will be, too? For that they'll hang ye, Tom. Stay a loon and be safe."

And laughing, the gaoler left.

Sad Tom, mad Tom, tattered Tom, removed a bar from his window on this night of All Hallows, in the year of Our Lord 1537. He tied his blanket into a rope and climbed down to the muddy street below. He wandered through shadows and empty lanes beneath a round full moon, and the first person he met was met a half mile away, near the edge of King Harry's good town of London, and this person was a little boy.

"Are you the bogey-man?" he was asked, and if ever an answer was likely that was it.

But Tom made a face and waved his arms and stuck out his tongue and sputtered, "No! I'm the Devil! Gobblegobble-gobble!" and the child ran away in terror, screaming that he had seen the Devil.

Tom laughed. He went a little further and met a maid with a bucket in hand.

"Going a'milking?" said Tom. "Not a good night for that. The Devil's loose, I hear."

"I'm not milking, sir," replied she, drawing back.

"Then you should! You should!" He pinched her with both hands in two places where she would not be touched. The maid let out a shriek, Tom a yelp of delight, and the two of them were quickly parted. Tom continued on until the houses thinned out and the stink of the city was behind him. He came to a field, in the middle of which a rock moved.

It was a boulder larger than a man and much heavier too, and yet it moved up and down as if an unseen giant were hefting it. Then suddenly it flew up, up, up, and a star winked as it passed by.

"Won't be back till tomorrow," said a little piping voice. Tom looked down and saw a little man standing where the stone had been, a fellow not more than five inches tall and clad in an oak leaf.

"You are very strong," said Tom. "You must eat fine meat to get that way."

"Indeed," said the man. "The thighs of men roasted, the breasts of maids toasted, little babies whole and raw, your mother's rump, I eat them all—"

"I think I must be getting back. I can't be out this late." Tom began to run, but the little man's voice followed him.

"Wait! You I shall not eat, for the King of Elves holds court tonight and he has summoned you. There's a great reward waiting for you."

Tom stopped, turned around, and came back.

"A reward?"

"Yes. Follow me."

He followed, over fields and fences and walls, through hedges and trees, along roads and over them, into a swamp and out again, all the while falling behind as the other ignored the obstacles that so tormented Tom.

"Slow down," he called out at last, "or I'll lose you."

"You're not lost. You're found. You're here."

And Tom emerged from a final thicket of thorns onto a wide plain where there was a great bonfire tended by witches, and before long he came to the old log which was the throne of the King of Elves. He saw that the King was not tiny, but tall as a mortal man, with a robe of soft green and a flowing red beard. The Queen of Elves sat beside the King, also dressed in green, and there were strings of acorns in her hair. The King spoke.

"Thomas, you have been called here by me to be my champion. You must joust for me as one must every year for my honour with the enemy. If you are victorious a wish will be granted to you from the fullest resources of my magic."

"And if I lose?"

"Why then," laughed the King, "my tithe to Hell will be paid until next year."

Tom knew he was in dire peril then, but he knew also that there was no escape through the throngs around him, so he made the best of it and joined the feast that was being held for the occasion. He joked with the gnomes and dwarves, took fairies by the dozens into his lap, and he ate well of meats no one has tasted in a thousand years. He drank deep of the molten liquor they brewed, and would have forgotten his predicament entirely had not a bent old man with a white beard trailing along the ground, with lantern and thorn branch in hand and a mangy dog trailing behind, come into the midst of them wailing, "Hellgate is open. The time has come. The foe has arrived. The time has come."

"Who is that?" whispered Tom to one beside him.

"The Man In The Moon, although presently not in the Moon," was the reply.

"And the foe?"

"Look."

The crowd drew away from the fire as it flamed brighter than ever, and out of the middle of it came one who was unmistakably Satan himself, and after him a knight on a black horse wearing black armor, with the face of a skull revealed beneath his upraised visor. His lance was aflame and his eyes seemed to be. Smoke snorted from the nostrils of his mount.

Greetings were exchanged between the Devil and the King, and the Lord of Elves called on Tom.

"Rise and come forward, champion, and fight in my name."

"But—I have no horse—"

"Then take one, made of air." The King waved his hand and the dust beneath Tom's feet began to stir. He was caught in a whirlwind and raised up. He felt the muscles of a horse rippling beneath him. He felt a saddle, and his feet found stirrups, but to his eye there was nothing except a dim shape, like a cloud. His steed whinnied and stamped.

"I have no lance," said Tom.

"Then take one." A burning twig was brought from the edge of the fire.

"This is a lance?"

"Take it," commanded the King and Tom took it by the

end that wasn't afire. As soon as he touched it it lengthened and grew and became a fine, flaming lance indeed.

"Now the battle shall begin," said the King.

"But I lack a helmet," said Tom, desperate for excuses.

"Take one then." The same witch who had handed him the twig now offered a leaf, and he put it on his head where it became a silver helmet with two slits to see through. She gave him also a plate which expanded into a shield, and she said a word and his rags were armor. Now without any more ways to delay the inevitable, Tom gulped hard and muttered a prayer to the Saviour. As he did the whole company hissed like a thousand snakes, and the King said angrily, "Speak not such words!"

In silence Tom was led away from the fire on his horse of wind and dust, and the black knight followed to a place where there was plenty of room for combat. Only the King and the Devil stood near.

"Now fight," said the King, and Tom was terrified.

"But wait. I'm not ready. I don't know—"

"What don't you know?"

"Who am I fighting?"

"The same one who comes every year for this."

"You mean—nobody has ever beat him?"

"Tom, I have great hopes for you."

"Well, who is he?"

"The Knight of Ghosts and Shadows. His name is Kamathakalamailetheknafor."

"What?"

"Such is his name. It is said that no mortal can repeat it, and thus none can gain power over him."

"Then how shall I—?"

"Good luck, my champion."

A trumpet sounded. The Knight of Ghosts and Shadows lowered his visor, and his lance. With no further warning he spurred his horse and charged. Tom in his confusion fumbled for the invisible rein of his barely visible steed. At the same time he kicked it in the ribs and the creature bolted forward. His lance was up, then down, then swaying side to side. When the two met Tom's point missed his opponent entirely, while the other's crashed into his shield and broke it like the old plate it was. The force of the blow sent Tom tumbling to the ground.

He landed with a clang of metal and lay stunned. When next he was aware the Knight stood over him with a red hot sword upraised, and helpless Tom, who had raved wilder things before, cried out, "Oh spare me, Kamathakala-mailetheknafor, please!"

And the Knight of Ghosts and Shadows paused and began to sway, and then he fell over backwards. At the same time Tom's armor became his rags again, and with the weight off him he was able to sit up. He saw his smoldering spear on the ground a good way off, and at his feet was a skeleton in a rusty suit, which crumbled as he watched, became only a heap of bones, then dust, then nothing at all.

The King of Elves lifted him to his feet, and all shouted his praises except Satan, who scowled and stalked back into the fire, took the flames with him and shut the door to Hell. By the light of the stars and the moon another feast was held, and this time Tom was treated like a God.

"Now Champion," said the King after a while. "What reward will you take?"

"I—I—uh—hadn't thought—I don't know."

"Would you like to be King of India?"

"I don't know."

"Well then know." And the Elfking took a wand and touched Tom on the head with it. All the folk around him vanished, and the field did also. For a minute Tom was King of India, sitting on his throne while eunuchs fanned him with huge feathers, and a hundred African maidens danced before him."

"It's awfully hot there," he said when he came back, "and I don't know how to rule, anyway."

"Then do you desire riches?"

"Riches?"

"All the gold in the mountains of the Moon. Look up."

Tom looked up at the full moon which still had no man in it, and he felt himself floating. As if he were made of smoke he rose above the earth. Below him the field grew small and vanished, and he saw all of England, then all the sea, then all the world. The round face of the moon grew larger, until it filled the whole sky. Then he was falling down, not up, into the valleys and mountains of the moon. He came to a stop in the middle of a barren plain and saw huge ingots the size of elephants strewn about, and mountains of pure gold in the distance, and even a volcano which spewed forth a golden stream. Then he was back on earth again and he said, "I could never carry that."

"Will you make up your mind soon?" The King was growing impatient. "Dawn will be coming and you must choose before then."

And Tom, afraid of losing all the riches and power and privilege in the world, could say nothing at all.

"Well, think," said the King. "What did you most recently wish for? What did you want this morning?"

"Two copper pennies," blurted Tom, before he knew he'd said it.

"Done! Two copper pennies you shall have."

"Wait, I—"

"Two copper pennies." The King clapped his hands and did a little dance, and his shape began to change. He shifted into something not at all human, and he shrank and darkened, and sprouted feathers. His neck grew disproportionately long; his lips grew out from his face and became a bill; his arms flattened into wings. The King had turned himself into a black swan. Tom looked on in amazement, and he began to feel sick. He seemed to be falling. His limbs would not obey him, and he looked up to see how the Man Not In The Moon, the witches, and even the dwarves towered over him. In the place of his hands he discovered black feathers, and knew then that he had become a swan too.

"Follow," said the King in a voice that sounded odd coming from the bill of a swan.

The two of them took to the air. It was natural for Tom, like running or jumping. It seemed that he had always known how to fly. He soared with the King away from the field, away from the Isle of Britain entirely, over the channel, across France, and above another sea. The moon was a lantern to light their way, and when clouds closed beneath them there was yet another ocean, this one all of glowing mist. They overtook night owls in their flight, and bats, and even a witch on her broom. All were left behind as Tom followed the King until land was beneath them again. They dropped lower, passed two artificial mountains, and followed a river. They came at last to a hidden place, to the catacombs of Nephren-Ka in the forgotten valley of Hadoth by the banks of the Nile, to the tomb of a Pharaoh the histories never mention. At the door of the tomb they became men very briefly, then serpents, and on their bellies they wriggled between the stones, down into the deepest vault where the coffin of the Black Pharaoh lay. The snake who was the Elfking caused there to be a faint light, and Tom could see the grim, shrivelled face of the Pharaoh, and the two copper coins laid on his eyes.

"There are your pennies, Tom," said the King. "Take them in your mouth and come away. There isn't much time."

And so Tom wriggled over the corpse of the one who had rested there so many centuries and scooped up the two pennies off the eyes to reveal a hateful glare undiminished by time. He screamed at the sight and nearly swallowed the coins. The light went out, and in complete darkness the Elfking spoke.

"Come! Hurry!"

The two of them crawled back between the stones, and up out of the tomb. Tom followed the other only by the rustling of the King's dry body, and by smell, which was much more acute than it had been when he had a human nose. At last dim light appeared overhead, and they emerged onto the desert sand. To the east the sky was beginning to brighten.

"Be quick," said the King. "If daylight catches us we can never resume our true forms." He changed them both into swans once more, and off they flew, racing the dawn all the way back to England.

This time the clouds beneath them were not a sea but a land, a wondrous country brought alive by the sun, and hidden to those who dwell only on the ground. Tom thought he saw hills and valleys, bright castles with tall white towers overlooking glowing fields. Where the clouds broke there were vast cataracts dropping to the unimaginable world below.

They flew on until London was beneath them, and the swan that was the Elfking said to Tom, "Go now where you will, and touch ground only when you have arrived, for when you do you'll be a man again." Then he folded his wings and dropped away into the retreating darkness, and was seen no more.

Tom winged on, over the palace, over the bridge and the Thames, until he came to Bishopgate. He swooped very low and a night watchman saw him, and wondered what was the meaning of this strange thing, this swan with coins in its bill. The watchman came for a closer look as Tom dropped behind a fence. He found him there, looking dazed, but there was no swan. Tom had changed, spit out the coins, and pocketed them the instant before the guard arrived. He was recognized.

"You! What are you doing loose? You know where you belong."

"I know, and I've nowhere else to go."

"Then I'll take you back." The watchman took Tom by the scruff of the neck and dragged him through the still empty and dark streets as morning began to break over the city. He came to a familiar old building with a wooden sign swinging over the door which reads:

## BETHLEHEM HOSPITAL
## FOR THE DEMENTED
## God Help all ye
## who enter here.

"Is this one of yours?" demanded the guard of the gaoler.

"It is."

"Then see that he doesn't get out again."

When the watchman was gone, Tom said, "I've got the two pennies, like I said I would."

"Did ye now? Indeed."

"In fact and also in deed."

"Quick! Show me them before anyone else wakes up."

Tom gave him the two coins, and the gaoler puzzled over the unfamiliar designs on them.

"Will you put meat in my soup now?"

The gaoler dropped one penny in his pocket, and held

up the other. "The first is to make up for the trouble ye caused by running away, but the second will buy ye something for your dinner, as long as ye tell me where ye got them."

Tom told him the whole story, leaving out no details, and distorting it very little. When he was done he was not believed, as he had feared. The gaoler looked at him silently for a moment with a mixture of disgust and pity, then sighed, "Ah Tom, you're mad as ever and nothing will change that."

He put Tom back in his cell, and dropped the second coin in with the first, but the two did not rest there. The end was not yet, not quite anyway.

The gaoler sent a boy down into the cellar to kill a rat for the soup, then forgot about Tom altogether. He paced back and forth desperately, waiting for the long hours to pass until the shops would open, the coins like red-hot coals in his pocket, so eager was he to spend them. The gaoler was not a thrifty man.

At last a steeple clock struck nine, and the time was come. He ran out into the street, past windows filled with tempting things, and made his first stop an inn. Inside, he ordered a drink, had one of his new pennies changed, and it was only a moment before the innkeeper was turning the coin over and over in his hand and muttering, "This money isn't English. And it isn't French, or Spanish."

Just then the innkeeper's wife came by. She took one look and pronounced, "It's not money at all. It's fake!"

"Fake! Fraud! Counterfeit!" The cry was raised by all there, by all who stood in the street outside, and a mob formed. They chased the gaoler back the way he had come, yelling, and a sheriff joined them, and several guardsmen with pikes.

When they got to the hospital the crowd huddled outside while the sheriff and the guards went in one minute and came out the next with the offender in custody.

" 'Tis death to counterfeit," the sheriff intoned righteously.

"What?" came a voice. "Would you put to death a poor lunatic that doesn't know right from wrong?"

Everyone turned, and there was Tom standing in the street. He'd climbed out of the window again and come down to see what all the excitement was about. His eyes met the gaoler's and no words were spoken, but a message was passed:

Help me Tom. They'll kill me if ye don't. I'll do anything. Please.

"Who are you?" demanded the sheriff.

"I'm the keeper."

"What? He's the keeper!"

"Oh no, he's a lunatic. We let him play his game of being the keeper to keep him good. Otherwise he's violent. His wit's diseased."

And at that moment the gaoler was so astonished that he looked the part.

"You mean," said the sheriff, "that he's—mad?"

"Quite."

"Then he belongs in a cell, not out here loose!"

"He does."

The sheriff ordered the guards, "You there! Take him inside and lock him in a cell."

They did, and from their looks when they came out you'd think they had been handling a leper.

"Thank you," said Tom. "You've all been very helpful."

"See that he doesn't get out again," said the sheriff. "If he does, lunatic or not, I'll have his head."

"I'll keep him safe. Don't worry."

*  *  *

Some hours later Tom found the rat meat the boy had left, and he put it in the gaoler's soup.

"Here's meat for you," said Tom, "and I won't charge you for it. Not anything. Not a penny."

"Ah, Tom," the other sighed, "Ye're the soul of kindness."

# MIASMA

## TERRY MCGARRY

The generator blossomed into fragments. Its steel petals bloomed over the construction site, consuming unwary workers. The explosion thrust mangled trick-or-treaters and bloodied parents across Granger's path as harbingers of his own fate. He stood transfixed, watching the death wind billow toward him bearing its plague of shrapnel. He imagined, in the timeless moment, each jagged metal piece embedding in his skin, pulping his eyeballs, slicing the critical arteries in throat and thigh.

But the fragments did not reach him. The phantom bloom subsided back into a hulking, humming machine, a garish blur of children's costumes, a streak of passing car.

He was safe. He had kept his distance.

Were those parents insane, herding children through the streets in their flammable costumes and smothering masks? Suppose a toddler was snatched by some cruel madman? Or darted in front of a car? Or bit into a razored apple? Granger loved the trappings of Halloween, the objectifying of terror. But it was the most dangerous day of the year.

What kind of mother would take her child out on a day like this?

At least they hadn't waited till dark to go on their rounds. Shaking his head, he moved on—keeping well back from the curb in case someone lost control of a truck and ran up on the sidewalk, but also far enough away from the building behind him that nothing falling from it would hit him. Even a penny dropped from high enough could kill you.

He never took the subway, with its narrow platforms and lurking lunatics—watching for their chance to push you into the tracks, the way that flutist had been—and its escalators that might collapse from underneath you and grind your legs to bits in their machinery, like that woman in the department store. The autumn streets were the lesser evil. He took only jobs he could walk to.

During the week he worked as a typist for a big firm. He liked the way the words went into his eyes and came out of his fingers, leaving his conscious mind entirely free. He filled the empty weekend afternoons by sorting mail for a sweepstakes house. Because he had, in the blessed numbness induced by the tedious filling of cubbyholes with top sections, bottom sections, address changes, magazine orders, emptied more boxes than anyone else, he had been promoted to envelope-slitter.

But after an hour of watching the envelopes prepared like dead fish for evisceration, hearing the hum of the slicing and the whispers of the shreds piling into their coffin-like boxes, he began to feel dizzy, then faint.

What would it feel like, to be an envelope, to be cut open so that all your guts spilled out—and anything might come in?

Perhaps there were no guts inside him at all. Perhaps he was devoid of viscera—filled with air, or gas, some noxious vapor of cowardice. If the long-dreaded mugger were to slit him open, what would be released but a breath of stagnation, a final, mortal sigh of fear?

The machine caught a paper clip in its razor teeth and squealed. Startled, he jerked his hand back in the midst of grabbing the next bunch of envelopes, and cut his thumb on a staple. His blood made a small smear on the beige paper, like a squashed mosquito.

As he stood staring at the stain, his machine idling, a middle-aged woman stepped up from the row behind him, asked him if he was all right, and took his hand in both of hers, turning it over. Her hands were dark brown, and the nails were not painted, but in maneuvering his fingers to check the damage they looked exactly like his mother's— bony, competent, masculine hands that controlled but never broke whatever they touched. They became his mother's hands: the skin paled to pink, the nails lengthened, colored, then shortened again, bitten down, the skin wasting, turning gray, sallow, flaccid.

Granger gave a strangled cry, and fled.

They would fire him, of course. He hadn't even gone to the floor manager to plead sickness. It didn't matter; there were other mindless jobs.

In fact, it could be good timing. This might be the day when a fire broke out or some disgruntled former employee came in and let loose with an Uzi. Halloween made people crazy. And now he would get home before dark. The evening streets were unbearable, with their roving gangs and drug dealers, and tonight killers could wear masks with impunity. And suppose teenagers were throwing eggs? A shard could slice your eye . . .

There was a drugstore cattycorner to his apartment building. If he could make it across and back, without a bus's brakes giving out just as it approached his crosswalk, he would have a treat tonight.

It was Halloween. He deserved one.

As Granger approached the rack at the far end of the store, his hands grew clammy and his heart rate increased. It seemed he could not get enough air into his lungs. It seemed that the air itself had filled with grit, had thickened into some unbreathable substance—that it would suffocate him if he did not get what he needed quickly.

He scanned the shelf's contents, desperate now that he had made the decision to seek this pleasure. Disappointment threatened; his eyes stung. He had read almost everything here, and his category was sorely depleted by people buying books for Halloween. Then, with a yelp of triumph, he pounced: one unfamiliar book, shiny black, with a die-cut cover showing the malevolent faces of two children staring out a top-floor window. A glow surrounded them, like the light of a candle through the evil grin carved in a pumpkin. The embossed red letters of the title dripped down around the house.

It was perfect.

In the printed word, Granger found a depth of controlled terror that made him squirm. Disaster was inexorable, but left him whole and unscathed. Disaster was climax. "Don't go up the stairs!" he would cry to the characters, much as radio fans must have screamed to Fibber McGee, "Don't open the closet!" But Fibber McGee always opened the closet.

He made his purchase, and clutched the secure bulk of the book in his pocket as he left the store. This time the security alarm didn't even go off.

In his building, he collected his mail from the little steel box with his surname on it and began the six-flight climb to his apartment, which was low enough for egress in case of fire, but far enough above the boiler room that he would probably survive an explosion. He scanned the hallway for strangers before unlocking his door. Inside, he made his customary four-point check: smoke detectors working, fire extinguishers in place, gas off, electrical wires secure.

He had done this for his mother, in their house, every day of her life after Father died. She refused to follow his safety instructions; it had driven him nuts. Planes crash, she had said, but life has to go on, as she went gallivanting off to Turkey and Sri Lanka and Mozambique and every other disease- and terrorist-ridden place, later on with men she barely knew. The worst part had been taking care of himself: he was all she had left, no ill must befall him. With the crazy life she led—how could she go on after what it had done to Father, his body twisted in the Cessna wreckage, sliced by metal, seared by fire—it was crucial that Granger be the responsible one.

He had thought it would be easier when she was gone—from cancer, after all the risks she had taken. But her death only proved to him that you couldn't be too careful. It could come from anywhere, at any time, even from your own blood cells or your own marrow.

The light outside was fading by the time he had fixed a macrobiotic dinner, eaten it slowly to avoid taxing his digestive system, drunk two glasses of distilled water, and taken one aspirin from a new package that he inspected for signs of tampering. The doorbell had made him jump time after time—he never answered, not on Halloween, when anyone could be behind the mask seen through the peephole—but at last the assault of children ebbed and the bell went quiet. Granger sank gratefully into his plush recliner with the book in his lap and popped the footrest into place. This was his candy.

With a sense of formality and anticipation, he cracked the slick black binding; he liked to put his mark on a book, insinuate his strength and his finger oils into the pages, make it part of him. He read the teaser, the list of other books by the same author, the title, the copyright page, the half-title, the dedication; each part of the book brought him closer to the opening descriptions, the first niggling suspicions, the titillation of foreshadowing. He savored every step of fear as he went up the fictional stairs and approached that landing, at his own pace, knowing he could always stop, knowing he could always go back, and reveling in his courage when he didn't.

Ten o'clock passed, and eleven. As faraway parties drew to a close or moved to bars, as street noises grew fewer and televisions were turned off, the buzz of urban All Hallows' Eve faded from his carpeted cave. By twelve o'clock, the first murder had been committed by the evil children, and he jumped a little as his refrigerator abruptly stopped humming. By twelve-thirty, three baby-sitters lay mangled in the suburbs, and all he could hear was a faint, rhythmic clicking as the numbers on his old clock radio flipped over.

Even the room seemed darker. He looked up reluctantly. From wall to wall stretched a layer of heavy smoke, unmoving in the still air. He rubbed his eyes. It was still there.

Fire! For a moment he sat, paralyzed, unable to remember what to do in a real emergency. Then he wrenched himself from the chair and grabbed a fire extinguisher. Where were the flames? There were no flames. There was no smoke in the kitchen, or in the bedroom. None of the detectors had gone off. It didn't even smell like smoke.

He forced himself to walk through it to the front door. Both door and air felt cold, slimy; he unlocked the three locks, took off the chain, and turned the knob.

There was no smoke in the hall. Only in his living room.

He turned slowly, the door ajar, tempted to run into the hall, wanting to scream. But the hall was long, and dim, and silent, and the stairs at this hour were only marginally less terrifying than the elevator, and at the bottom there was no doorman, just the glaring, bare lobby and the gleaming ebony streets beyond. He came completely around and shut the door behind him.

The smoke had moved; it was almost vertical now, sucking itself into a thick pillar, sparkling like mica. It didn't even really look like smoke. It looked like—darkness. Tangible darkness, in the middle of a safe, well-lit room.

"Get away from me!" he cried. The smoky form seemed to waver a bit, lose substance; Granger thought he could see the wall through it now, and the television.

Television. Sound, light—weapons. He lunged for the remote on the side table, stabbing randomly at buttons so that Channel 4 blared at top volume from the box. It was a late-night comedy show, a lumbering parody of Franken-stein. Once he had the volume under control he began to feel better. The companionable presence of manufactured reality calmed him.

The smoke pulled back into the corners of the room, became indistinguishable from shadow. He would finish his book, and the hell with it. It was some trick of the new track lighting, that was all. Or a product of fatigue after his trau-matic day. Halloween put crazy images in your head. Or were his eyes going, was it some failure of his optic nerve, was he slowly blinding himself by reading so much?

. . . No. It could not be that. He groped for the book and pulled the narrative around him like a blanket.

The last baby-sitter was confronting the children now. It wasn't as scary as it had been, the flow of suspense inter-rupted, as if by a commercial—but before long he had recap-tured the delicious tingle.

He would not look up, he vowed; there would be no smoke. He continued to read until he had forgotten about the smoke, except that thinking about how he had forgotten about it brought it back to mind . . . but he was on the next-to-last page, he was so close to finishing . . . but he could no longer see the words clearly, the letters were lost in a dark haze, and he had to do it, he had to look up.

He was enveloped in it, the freezing, greasy smoke. He leaped out of the chair, ran to the door, opened it wide to find the hallway black with the stuff, impassable. Fumbling through the murk, he found the phone, dialed the number of the super on the first floor. There was no answer. Now the room was as dark as the night outside.

He punched 911 by feel and asked for the fire department, told them his address. Then, trembling and retching, he made his way to the window, throwing it open to release the smothering smoke. But it did not pour out; it stayed, coagulated, in the room, even when a crosswind whipped in. He whimpered in frustration and bafflement, blind. Outside, below, sirens wailed down the avenue.

He felt his way back to the door and waited; their knocks pounded so loudly that his body spasmed even though he'd heard them clomping along the hall. He fumbled the door open—they were here, he would be safe now—but he was not prepared for how large and fast-moving and brusque they were.

There was no fire, and they neither saw nor smelled smoke. Granger flinched from their anger, their threats of a citation for a false alarm; they left, disgusted, when he began to cry. "Freakin' Halloween," one grumbled. "Get some help, guy, okay?" said the last one out, the axe gleaming in his black-gloved hand. Granger nodded shakily and locked the door after him.

Yes, there it was again, as he turned; it was in the

corners, lurking, and Granger thought he heard laughter, but it must have been the firemen as they left the building. He went straight to the window and closed it against the chill air. The room felt like a meat locker.

The television was still on, muted. Its silent flickering reminded him of the fear that had made him turn it on. He stared at it and struggled to focus on the light, the little pretend lives inside the box, to screen out the menace—to deny the threatening darkness, the darkness that had oozed in past his defenses, moved through his walls and shields by osmosis, terror seeking its own level, the death and chaos of the world trying to balance the controlled thrill of the make-believe, all of it sucked toward him, the membrane that vibrated, with ecstasy or anguish, to the smallest hint of danger.

He had become a maelstrom of his own fears, and his fears, spinning into a vortex, were consuming him at last.

All Hallows' Eve. The night when the barrier between the worlds thinned, when spirits walked the earth, when graves opened and the dead roamed loose. But the walls of the netherworld were not the only walls breached on this unholy night. The walls of the mind were, too.

If he could hold on until dawn, until the saints came to claim their day, until morning light and ordinary fears drove back the demon . . .

It was too late. The thing was unleashed, was deepening to the hue of tar right before his swollen, aching eyes. He had not blinked, fixated on the screen he could no longer see, and tears were streaming down his cheeks. He was so tired, and so terrified, and he could not remember what feeling normal was like. He suspected he had never felt that way at all.

As the smoke enveloped him in the darkness that he realized had surrounded him all his life, as its gritty sparkling filled his ears, his mouth, his lungs, he thought, At least I won't have to worry about dying any more. There was pain in his chest now, a burning balloon inflating, and it was awful, yes, worse than he had ever imagined—

But it was wonderful, too. Now he knew; now he knew what agony was. Now he knew the exquisite torment of the legs chewed by the escalator's teeth, crushed by the derrick's weight; now he knew the sharp-numb agony of the fingers sliced off by the subway's wheels; now he knew the shocking pain of the entire body smashed flat by the elevator's fall, the shattering of bones, the pulping of organs.

He knew them all, in one endless, shrieking moment, and he loved them with a piercing sweetness, because now it was not they who owned him, but he who owned them, forever.

I die as I lived, he thought, hysterical laughter bubbling up on a clot of blood, and as he fell to the soaked, crimson carpeting—slowly, like the last dry leaf of a rotten tree, his unrecognizable body so ruined that it seemed immune to gravity, mangled into weightlessness—he had a vision of himself putting all his fears, books and tapes and shreds of dark imaginings made palpable, into a black plastic bag that rippled like a child's Dracula cape, stuffing the bag into the crusty garbage chute like a drunk pouring the last bottle of liquor down the drain, wiping the hands he no longer had, and turning away.

And he thought, No, they are mine, as the shattered Cessna wing sectioned his brain and the tumor swelled up to engulf him, leaving behind in his breached sanctum the one thing he had never offered the world until now, white as a plume and red as a jack-o'-lantern's eyes.

A smile of joy.

# EVENING SPIRIT

## MARC BILGREY

One day, my wife Michelle decided that she didn't love me anymore. We'd been married five years, and had moved from New York, to a small town just outside San Francisco. And then she left. I was devastated. At first, I blamed myself, but I saw that it was really both of us. There had been alot of tension over money and missed opportunities. I thought it could all be fixed, but she never wanted to talk about anything, and refused to see a marriage counselor. She went back to Connecticut, where she's from; I went back to New York.

It had been so long since I'd been home again, that most of my friends had left. They'd all gone to live in other parts of the country. Just about everyone I'd known was an artist, like me. Not that I'd sold much lately. That was one of the things my wife hated.

I was a starving artist, and she, a starving artist's wife. She had always wanted the finer things in life that money could buy. Only, I couldn't give them to her.

I'd been back in New York almost a month, but it had

felt like years. I no longer had any sense of time. I was still in love with my wife. I drifted through the days, in a perpetual state of shock. She'd meant the world to me. Without her, I was completely lost.

It was on a Halloween night, that I found myself wandering through the streets. I had no idea where I was going, just that I had to walk. It was a warm evening, the tail end of an Indian summer. It felt more like August than October. I'd started walking while it was still light, and now, the last bit of sunlight was fading from the sky. Kids in costumes ran by me. I saw a witch, a mummy and Superman. I'd began my marathon walk on the west side and had gradually made my way to the upper east side.

Someone threw an egg at me from a passing car and laughed like a lunatic. I managed to jump out of the egg's path and it exploded against the wall of a building on Lexington Avenue. Halloween, it's a lot of laughs.

A couple of blocks later, I figured out what I had to do. I decided that I needed to retreat from the world. I resolved to move to some remote tropical island and have nothing to do with anyone ever again. That way I could start over with no reminders of my previous existence.

I was really starting to like the idea, when I turned the corner and realized that I was standing in front of Denise's old apartment building. Denise had been my first love when I was twenty-one; twenty-four years earlier. We'd gone out for a year, then broke up. Ten years later I met my wife, Michelle.

For a split second, I thought about ringing Denise's bell, but then reality hit me. Denise had died three years earlier. I'd heard about it during a phone conversation with a friend. I hadn't even known that he knew her. And the truth was, he hardly did. He'd only met her a few times. She was involved with someone my friend knew. Oh, yeah, he'd said,

Don's girlfriend died. Her name was Denise. What was her last name, I'd asked. When he told me I nearly fainted.

But she was my age! I protested. Nevertheless, she was gone. A victim of cancer. I was numb. I read an obituary about her that someone had put on an art website. They also showed some of Denise's paintings. It took me months to come to terms with her death. The first woman I'd loved.

I started walking again, past Denise's building, when I heard a woman's voice say, "Hey, Mike, where are you going?"

I spun around and saw Denise standing in the doorway. It was impossible, I told myself, as I held my breath. I tentatively took a couple of steps toward her, as she said, "What's wrong? I won't bite."

I walked right up to her. She looked exactly as I'd remembered her. I hadn't seen her in at least ten years. There must have been a logical explanation, I thought. A twin sister? Someone who looked just like her? A clone?

"Yeah, it's me," she said, smiling. She was wearing a blue blouse and a pair of black jeans. Her long auburn hair glistened in the moonlight.

"But–" I said.

"All right," she said, "let's get it out of the way. Yes, I'm dead. Are you happy now?"

"No, I'm not happy. I'd like to know how–"

"I don't actually know how, myself. I just know that I'm here."

"Well," I said, "you're here, all right." Though I wasn't sure she really was. The thought occurred to me that I might be having a nervous breakdown.

"You're not going crazy," she said, as if reading my mind.

"You don't look like a ghost," I said.

"Yeah, I'm not transparent," she said, looking at her hands. "So, you want to take a walk?"

"Sure," I said, shrugging. I decided that I didn't care if she was real or not. I liked seeing her again.

"Which way do you want to go?" She asked.

"It doesn't matter." We started west, toward Park Avenue.

"What's new?" said Denise.

"I could ask you the same question."

"I asked you first," she said, smiling.

"I'm separated from my wife. We're going to get divorced."

"That's rough. See, if you'd married me you wouldn't be going through this."

"If I'd married you, I'd be a widower."

"Oh yeah," she said, wistfully.

Denise had proposed to me often. I was very young at the time, and hadn't wanted to get tied down. Also, we'd had our own set of problems.

"What's it like being dead?" I said, as we stopped for a red light.

"It's no fun," she replied.

"That's useful information," I said, smirking.

"I missed you, through the years. Of all the guys I'd met, you were the only one I really wanted."

"But we were always fighting," I said, as we crossed over to the west side of Park Avenue.

"No relationship is perfect," she said.

"I miss my wife."

"What's her name?"

"Michelle."

"Is she an artist?"

"No. When I met her she was working in a framing store."

"Close enough," said Denise, smiling.

We walked to Madison, then turned south. A group of

children in costumes walked by, followed by two women, who appeared to be guiding the flock.

"I feel like I'm in a Magritte painting," I said.

"Why," said Denise, "because you're with me?"

"That, and the fact that I've felt so out it since Michelle left."

"You're not going to do anything stupid, are you? Like slit your wrists?"

"I don't think so, but if I did, I'd be with you again."

"Nothing personal, but there's no rush."

I glanced at an abstract painting in the window of a gallery. It was a splotch of yellow and green. It looked like something I'd done as a child, with finger paints.

Denise noticed me looking at the painting and said, "I'm not missing much, am I?"

"Artwise, no," I said.

"That's a lot nicer," she said, pointing at another painting in a nearby window. It was a still life, a bowl of colorful flowers.

"I still don't understand why you came back," I said.

"Do I really need a reason? Suppose I just felt like it?"

"Okay," I said, deciding to drop the subject. I didn't want to risk saying the wrong thing and have her vanish in a puff of smoke.

We walked a couple of blocks without saying anything, then she gestured at an outdoor café, on a side street, and said, "Will you buy me a drink?"

"Sure," I said, and we walked to the cafe and found a table under an orange umbrella.

She ordered a white wine, just like she used to twenty-four years earlier. I had a Perrier. When the waiter brought her drink she took a sip and said, "This is nice. You, the drink, the restaurant."

"Yes, it is," I said.

"So, what are you going to do with your life, Mike?"

"I really don't know."

"When's the last time you painted something?"

"The day before Michelle left."

"That's a while ago."

"I've been too distraught to work."

"But, it's your life."

"I don't know what my life is anymore," I said, sipping my Perrier.

"You always said you wanted your work to hang in the Metropolitan."

"We were kids then. Barely twenty-one."

"Does that mean you don't have dreams any more?" she said.

"I've adjusted them."

"You mean, you've given up."

"Actually, I was thinking about dropping out. Leaving, and going someplace remote. Maybe I'll paint there."

"You're going to Tahiti to do the Gauguin bit?"

"What's wrong with that? I think he had the right idea."

"You can't escape from yourself."

I didn't respond. She really hadn't changed at all. Did she come back from the grave to have a fight with me? I wondered.

"I'm depressed," I said.

"Who isn't? You think it's a joy being dead?"

"I don't know."

"Well, it's not; and then you tell me you're thinking about chucking it all. And for what? Because some dame gives you your walking papers?"

"You sound like a 1940s movie."

"I've been renting a lot of videos lately."

"How's that possible?" I asked, but she ignored me and kept right on talking.

"I think your work is museum quality," she said.

"You haven't seen my work in years," I replied.

"You were good then, I'm sure you're even better now."

I watched her sip her white wine and looked across the street at Central Park, which was a dark clump of trees.

"Where would *you* go?" I asked. "Bora Bora is supposed to be beautiful. I've seen travel shows—"

"You're not really going to Bora Bora."

"Why not? Or maybe some other tiny island. There are thousands of little out of the way places. . . ."

"Paint here. This is where you grew up. New York is part of you."

"I don't even know if I'll ever paint again," I said.

I saw Denise frown. Then she stood up and said, "I've got to go."

I threw a few dollars on the table and followed her out of the cafe toward Fifth Avenue. "Wait," I said. "Where are you going?"

"I don't know," she said, her voice cold.

I caught up with her and said, "You came back to get me to continue working, didn't you?"

She shrugged and turned north on Fifth. We walked silently for a while.

"You're talented," she said, finally. "Don't throw it away."

"Why do you suddenly care?" I said.

She turned, looked at me and said, "I was cut down in the prime of my life. I never got the chance to see any of my dreams realized. I wanted to have my work in all the big galleries. The farthest I ever got was a group show in the East Village, and then it was too late for me. I don't want you to walk away from it all, just because your wife left you."

"She was my inspiration, the first one I'd show my

paintings to right after they were done. I painted hundreds of portraits of her. Now they're all in storage."

"Get another inspiration," said Denise, as we passed posh apartment buildings.

We walked a couple of blocks, and then the Metropolitan Museum appeared across the street.

"I want to see your work in there," said Denise, pointing at the museum.

"Easier said than done."

"So give up, see if I care."

She sped up, I kept pace with her. "Look," I said, "I don't know how you're doing it and I don't care. But stay here with me. We'll pick up right where we left off. We're both older, maybe we learned something over the years. We could try again, you and me. It could work."

"I only have tonight," she said softly.

"Why tonight?" I asked.

"Halloween. The border between the living and the dead becomes blurry. It's the only time that happens."

"Couldn't you sneak out once in a while?"

"I wish I could," she said, smiling sweetly.

We walked quietly for some blocks, then turned and began walking east.

"What happens now?" I asked.

"It's up to you," she said.

"I'm very sad about you leaving."

"You'll get over it. Remember, keep working."

"What about my wife?"

"Time will help that."

We stopped in front of Denise's apartment building, or what used to be her building. She looked at me and smiled.

"It was good seeing you again, Mike," she said.

"It was good seeing you, too," I replied.

She leaned over and kissed me. It was a warm kiss, just

like I'd remembered. Then she took a key out of her pocket and opened the lobby door. She looked back at me, waved, went inside and up the stairs.

I stood for a minute, and then began walking again. I thought about how wonderful it was to see her again, and how much I had missed her. After that, my thoughts drifted back to Michelle. The wound was still very fresh. I wondered if, despite Denise's advice, I should get into a cab, go straight to the airport and take the first plane that was leaving for anywhere. It would be easy to disappear forever.

As I walked back toward my apartment, I thought about Denise and how beautiful she'd looked sitting in that outdoor café. It would make a good painting, I decided.

# PUMPKIN HEAD

## AL SARRANTONIO

An orange and black afternoon.

Outside, under baring but still-robust trees, leaves tapped across sidewalks, a thousand fingernails drawn down a thousand dry blackboards.

Inside, a party beginning.

Ghouls loped up and down aisles between desks, shouting "Boo!" at one another. Crepe paper, crinkly and the colors of Halloween, crisscrossed over blackboards covered with mad and frightful doodlings in red and green chalk: snakes, rats, witches on broomsticks. Windowpanes were filled with cut-out black cats and ghosts with no eyes and giant O's for mouths.

A fat jack-o'-lantern, flickering orange behind its mouth and eyes and giving off spicy fumes, glared down from Ms. Grinby's desk.

Ms. Grinby, young, bright, and filled with enthusiasm, left the room to chase an errant goblin-child, and one blackboard witch was hastily labeled "Teacher." Ms. Grinby, bearing her captive, returned, saw her caricature, and smiled. "All right, who did this?" she asked, not expecting an answer and not getting one. She tried to look rueful. "Never mind; but I think you know I don't *really* look like that. Except maybe today." She produced a witch's peaked hat from her drawer and put it on with a flourish.

Laughter.

"Ah!" said Ms. Grinby, happy.

The party began.

Little bags were handed out, orange and white with freshly twisted tops and filled with orange and white candy corn.

Candy corn disappeared into pink little mouths.

There was much yelling, and the singing of Halloween songs with Ms. Grinby at the piano, and a game of pin the tail on the black cat. And then a ghost story, passed from child to child, one sentence each:

"It was a dark and rainy night—"

"—and . . . Peter had to come out of the storm—"

"—and he stopped at the only house on the road—"

"—and no one seemed to be home—"

"—because the house was empty and haunted—"

The story stopped dead at the last seat of the first row.

All eyes focused back on that corner.

The new child.

"Raylee," asked Ms. Grinby gently, "aren't you going to continue the story with us?"

Raylee, new in class that day; the quiet one, the shy one with black bangs and big eyes always looking down, sat with her small, grayish hands folded, her dark brown eyes straight ahead like a rabbit caught in a headlight beam.

"Raylee?"

Raylee's thin pale hands shook.

Ms. Grinby got up quickly and went down the aisle, setting her hand lightly on the girl's shoulder.

"Raylee is just shy," she said, smiling down at the unmoving top of the girl's head. She knelt down to face level, noticing two round fat beads of water at the corner of the girl's eyes. Her hands were clenched hard.

"Don't you want to join in with the rest of us?" Ms. Grinby whispered, a kindly look washing over her face. Empathy welled up in her. "Wouldn't you like to make friends with everyone here?"

Nothing. She stared straight ahead, the bag of candy, still neatly wrapped and twisted, resting on the varnished and dented desktop before her.

"She's a faggot!"

This from Judy Linthrop, one of the four Linthrop girls, aged six through eleven, and sometimes trouble.

"Now, Judy—" began Ms. Grinby.

"Faggot!" from Roger Mapleton.

"A *faggot!*"

Peter Pakinski, Randy Feffer, Jane Campbell.

All eyes on Raylee for reaction.

"A pale little faggot!"

"That's enough!" said Ms. Grinby, angry, and there was instant silence; the game had gone too far.

"Raylee," she said, softly. Her young heart went out to this girl; she longed to scream at her, "Don't be shy! There's no reason, the hurt isn't real, I know, I know!" Images of Ms. Grinby's own childhood, her awful loneliness, came back to her and with them a lump to her throat.

*I know, I know!*

"Raylee," she said, her voice a whisper in the party room, "don't you want to join in?"

Silence.

"Raylee—"

"I know a story of my own."

Ms. Grinby nearly gasped with the sound of the girl's

voice, it came so suddenly. Her upturned, sad little face abruptly came to life, took on color, became real. There was an earnestness in those eyes, which looked out from the girl's haunted, shy darkness to her and carried her voice with them.

"I'll tell a story of my own if you'll let me."

Ms. Grinby almost clapped her hands. "Of course!" she said. "Class," looking about her at the other child-faces: some interested, some smirking, some holding back with comments and jeers, seeking an opening, a place to be heard, "Raylee is going to tell us a story. A Halloween story?" she asked, bending back down toward the girl, and when Raylee nodded yes she straightened and smiled and preceded her to the front of the room.

Ms. Grinby sat down on her stool behind her desk.

Raylee stood silent for a moment, before all the eyes and the almost jeers and the smirks, under the crepe paper and cardboard monsters and goblins.

Her eyes were on the floor, and then she suddenly realized that she had taken her bag of candy with her, and stood alone clutching it before them all. Ms. Grinby saw it too, and, before Raylee began to shuffle her feet and stand with embarrassment or run from the room, the teacher stood and said, "Here, why don't you let me hold that for you until you're finished?"

She took it from the girl's sweaty hand and sat down again.

Raylee stood silent, eyes downcast.

Ms. Grinby prepared to get up, to save her again.

"This story," Raylee began suddenly, startling the teacher into settling back into her chair, "is a scary one. It's about a little boy named Pumpkin Head."

Ms. Grinby sucked in her breath; there were some whisperings from the class which she quieted with a stare.

"Pumpkin Head," Raylee went on, her voice small and low but clear and steady, "was very lonely. He had no friends. He was not a bad boy, and he liked to play, but no one would play with him because of the way he looked.

"He was called Pumpkin Head because his head was too big for his body. It had grown too fast for the rest of him, and was soft and large. He only had a little patch of hair, on the top of his head, and the skin on all of his head was soft and fat. You could almost pull it out into folds. His eyes, nose, and mouth were practically lost in all the fat on his face.

"Someone said Pumpkin Head looked that way because his father had worked at an atomic plant and had been in an accident before Pumpkin Head was born. But this wasn't his fault, and even his parents, though they loved him, were afraid of him because of the way he looked. When he stared into a mirror he was almost afraid of himself. At times he wanted to rip at his face with his fingers, or cut it with a knife, or hide it by wearing a bag over it with writing on it that said, 'I am me, I am normal just like you under here.' At times he felt so bad he wanted to bash his head against a wall, or go to the train tracks and let a train run over it."

Raylee paused, and Ms. Grinby almost stopped her, but noting the utter silence of the class, and Raylee's absorption with her story, she held her tongue.

"Finally, Pumpkin Head became so lonely that he decided to do anything he could to get a friend. He talked to everyone in his class, one by one, as nicely as he could, but no one would go near him. He tried again, but still no one would go near him. Then he finally stopped trying.

"One day he began to cry in class, right in the middle of a history lesson. No one, not even the teacher, could make him stop. The tears ran down Pumpkin Head's face, in furrows like on the hard furrows of a pumpkin. The teacher had to call his mother and father to come and get him, and even they had trouble taking him away because he sat in his chair with his hands tight around his seat and cried and cried. There didn't seem to be enough tears in Pumpkin Head's head for all his crying, and some of his classmates wondered if his pumpkin head was filled with water. But finally his parents brought him home and put him in his room, and there he stayed for three days, crying.

"After those three days passed, Pumpkin Head came out of his room. His tears had dried. He smiled through the ugly folds of skin on his face, and said that he wouldn't cry any more and that he would like to go back to school. His mother and father wondered if he was really all right, but secretly, Pumpkin Head knew, they sighed with relief because having him around all the time made them nervous. Some of their friends would not come to see them when Pumpkin Head was in the house.

"Pumpkin Head went back to school that morning, smiling. He swung his lunch pail in his hand, his head held high. His teacher and his classmates were very surprised to see him back, and everyone left him alone for a while.

"But then, in the middle of the second period, one of the boys in the class threw a piece of paper at Pumpkin Head, and then another. Someone hissed that his head was like a pumpkin, and that he had better plant it before Halloween. 'And on Halloween we'll break open his pumpkin head!" someone else yelled out.

"Pumpkin Head sat in his seat and carefully brought his lunch box up to his desk. He opened it quietly. Inside was his sandwich, made in a hurry by his mother, and an apple, and a bag of cookies. He took these out, and also the thermos filled with milk, and set them on the desk. He closed the lunch pail and snapped shut the lid.

"Pumpkin Head stood and walked to the front of the

room, carrying his lunch pail in his hand. He walked to the door and closed it, and then walked calmly to the teacher's desk, turning toward the class. He opened his lunch box.

" 'My lunch and dinner,' he said, 'my dinner and breakfast.'

"He took out a sharp kitchen knife from his lunch pail.

"Everyone in the classroom began to scream.

"They took Pumpkin Head away after that, and they put him in a place—"

Ms. Grinby abruptly stepped from behind her desk.

"That's all we have time for, Raylee," she interrupted gently, trying to smile. Inside she wanted to scream over the loneliness of this child. "That was a *very* scary story. Where did you get it from?"

There was silence in the classroom.

Raylee's eyes were back on the floor. "I made it up," she said in a whisper.

To make up something like that, Ms. Grinby thought. *I know, I know!*

She patted the little girl on her back. "Here's your candy; you can sit down now." The girl returned to her seat quickly, eyes averted.

All eyes were on her.

And then something that made Ms. Grinby's heart leap: "Neat story!" said Randy Feffer.

"Neat!"

"Wow!"

Roger Mapleton, Jane Campbell.

As she sat down Raylee was trembling but smiling shyly.

"Neat story!"

A bell rang somewhere.

"Can it be that time already?" Ms. Grinby looked at the full moon-faced wall clock. "Why it is! Time to go home. I

AL SARRANTONIO

hope everyone had a nice party—and remember! Don't eat too much candy!"

A small hand waved anxiously at her from the center of the room.

"Yes, Cleo!"

Cleo, red-freckled face and blue eyes, stood up. "Can I please tell the class, Ms. Grinby, that I'm having a party tonight, and that I can invite everyone in the class?"

Ms. Grinby smiled. "You may, Cleo, but there doesn't seem to be much left to tell, does there?"

"Well," said Cleo, smiling at Raylee, "only that everyone's invited."

Raylee smiled back and looked quickly away.

Books and candy bags were crumpled together, and all ran out under crepe paper, cats, and ghouls, under the watchful eyes of the jack-o'-lantern, into darkening afternoon.

A black and orange night.

Here came a black cat walking on two legs; there two percale sheet ghosts trailing paper bags with handles; here again a miniature man from outer space. The wind was up: leaves whipped along the serpentine sidewalk like racing cars. There was an apple-crisp smell in the air, an icicle down your spine, here-comes-winter chill. Pumpkins everywhere, and a half-harvest moon playing coyly with wisps of high shadowy clouds. A thousand dull yellow night-lights winked through breezy trees on a thousand festooned porches. A constant ringing of doorbells, the wash of goblin traffic: they traveled in twos, threes, or fours, these monsters, held together by Halloween gravity. Groups passed other groups, just coming up, or coming down, stairs, made faces, and said "Boo!" There were a million "Boo!" greetings this night.

80

On one particular porch in all that thousand, goblins went up the steps but did not come down again. The door opened a crack, then wider, and groups of ghosts, wizards, and spooks, instead of waiting patiently for a toss in a bag and then turning away, slipped through into the house and disappeared from the night. Disappeared into another night.

Through the hallway and kitchen and down another set of stairs to the cellar. A cellar transformed. A cellar of hell, this cellar—charcoal-pit black with eerie dim red lanterns glowing out of odd corners and cracks. An Edgar Allan Poe cellar—and there hung his portrait over the apple-bobbing tub, raven-bedecked and with a cracked grin under those dark-pool eyes and that ponderous brow. This was his cellar, to be sure, a Masque of the Red Death cellar.

And here were the Poe-people; miniature versions of his evil creatures: enough hideous beasts to fill page after page and all shrunk down to child size. Devils galore, with papier-mâché masks, and hooves and tails of red rope, each with a crimson fork on the end; a gaggle of poke-hole ghosts; a mechanical cardboard man; two wolfmen; four vampires with wax teeth; one mummy; one ten-tentacled sea beast; three Frankenstein monsters; one Bride of same; and one monster of indefinite shape and design, something like a jellyfish made of plastic bags.

And Raylee.

Raylee came last; was last to slip silently and trembling through the portal of the yellow front door, was last to slip even more silently down the creaking cellar steps to the Poe-cellar below. She came cat silent and cautious, holding her breath—was indeed dressed cat-like, in whiskered mask, black tights, and black rope tail, all black to mix silently with the black basement.

No one saw her come in; only the black-beetle eyes of Poe over the apple tub noted her arrival.

The apple tub was well in use by now, a host of devils, ghosts, and Frankensteins clamoring around it and eagerly awaiting a turn at its game under Poe's watchful eyes.

"I got one!" shouted one red devil, triumphantly pulling a glossy apple from his mouth; no devil mask here, but a red-painted face, red and dripping from the tub's water. It was Peter, one of the taunting boys in Raylee's class.

Raylee hung back in the shadows.

"I got one!" shouted a Frankenstein monster.

"And me!" from his Bride. Two crisp red apples were held aloft for Poe's inspection.

"And me!" "And me!" shouted Draculas, hunchbacks, little green men.

Spooks and wolfmen shouted, too.

One apple left.

"Who hasn't tried yet?" cried Cleo, resplendent in witch's garb. She was a miniature Ms. Grinby. She leaned her broom against the tub, called for attention.

"Who hasn't tried?"

Raylee tried to sink into the shadows' protection but could not. A deeper darkness was what she needed; she was spotted.

"Raylee! Raylee!" shouted Cleo. "Come get your apple!" It was a singsong, as Raylee held her hands out, apple-less, and stepped into the circle of ghouls.

She was terrified. She trembled so hard she could not hold her hands still on the side of the metal tub as she leaned over it. She wanted to bolt from the room, up the stairs and out through the yellow doorway into the dark night.

"Dunk! Dunk!" the ghoul circle began to chant, impatient.

Raylee stared down into the water, saw her dark-reflection and Poe's mingled by the ripples of the bobbing apple.

"Dunk! Dunk!" the circle chanted.

Raylee pushed herself from the reflection, stared at the faces surrounding her. "I don't want to!"

"Dunk! . . ." the chant faded.

Two dozen cool eyes surveyed her behind eye-holes, weighed her dispassionately in the sharp light of peer pressure. There were ghouls behind those ghoulish masks and eyes.

Someone hissed a laugh as the circle tightened around Raylee. Like a battered leaf with its stem caught under a rock in a high wind, she trembled.

Cleo, alone outside the circle, stepped quickly into it to protect her. She held out her hands. "Raylee—" she began soothingly.

The circle tightened still more, undaunted. Above them all, Poe's eyes in the low crimson light seemed to brighten with anticipation.

Desperate, Cleo suddenly said, "Raylee, tell us a story."

A moment of tension, and then a relaxed "Ah" from the circle.

Raylee shivered.

"Yes, tell us a story!"

This from someone in the suffocating circle, a wolfman, or perhaps a vampire.

"No, please," Raylee begged. Her cat whiskers and cat tail shivered. "I don't want to!"

"Story! Story!" the circle began to chant.

"No, please!"

"Tell us the rest of the other story!"

This from Peter in the back of the circle. A low voice, a command.

Another "Ah."

"Yes, tell us!"

Raylee held her hands to her ears. "No!"

"Tell us!"

*"No!"*

"Tell us now!"

"I thought you were my friends!" Raylee threw her cat-paw hands out at them, her eyes begging.

*"Tell us."*

A stifled cry escaped Raylee's throat.

Instinctively, the circle widened. They knew she would tell now. They had commanded her. To be one of them, she would do what they told her to do.

Cleo stepped helplessly back into the circle, leaving Raylee under Poe's twisted grin.

Raylee stood alone shivering for a moment. Then, her eyes on the floor, she ceased trembling, became very calm and still. There was a moment of silence. In the dark basement, all that could be heard was the snap of a candle in a far corner and the slapping of water against the lone apple in the tub behind her. When she looked up her eyes were dull, her voice quiet-calm.

She began to speak.

"They took Pumpkin Head away after that, and they put him in a place with crazy people in it. There was screaming all day and night. Someone was always screaming, or hitting his head against the wall, or crying all the time. Pumpkin Head was very lonely, and very scared.

"But Pumpkin Head's parents loved him more than he ever knew. They decided they couldn't let him stay in that place any longer. So they made a plan, a quiet plan.

"One day, when they went to visit him, they dressed him up in a disguise and carried him away. They carried him far away where no one would ever look for him, all the way across the country. They hid him, and kept him disguised while they tried to find some way to help him. And after a long search, they found a doctor.

"And the doctor did magical things. He worked for two years on Pumpkin Head, on his face and on his body. He cut into Pumpkin Head's face, and changed it. With plastic, he made it into a real face. He changed the rest of Pumpkin Head's head too, and gave him real hair. And he changed Pumpkin Head's body.

"Pumpkin Head's parents paid the doctor a lot of money, and the doctor did the work of a genius.

"He changed Pumpkin Head completely."

Raylee paused, and a light came into her dull eyes. The circle, and Poe above them, waited with indrawn breath.

Waited to say "Ah."

"He changed Pumpkin Head into a little girl."

Breath was pulled back deeper, or let out in little gasps.

The light grew in Raylee's eyes:

"There were things that Pumpkin Head, now not Pumpkin Head any more, had to do to be a girl. He had to be careful how he dressed, and how he acted. He had to be careful how he talked, and he always had to be calm. He was very frightened of what would happen if he didn't stay calm. For his face was really just a wonderful plastic one. The real Pumpkin Head was still inside, locked in, waiting to come out."

Raylee looked up at them, and her voice suddenly became something different. Hard and rasping.

Her eyes were stoked coals.

"All he ever wanted was friends."

Her cat mask fell away. Her little girl face became soft and bloated and began to grow as if someone were blowing up a balloon inside her. Her hair began to pull into the scalp, forming a circle knot at the top. Creases appeared up and down her face.

With a sickening, rubber-inflated sound, the sound of a melon breaking, Raylee's head burst open to its true shape.

Her eyes, ears, and nose became soft orange triangles, her mouth a lazy, grinning crescent. She began to breathe with harsh effort, and her voice became a sharp, wheezing lisp.

"He only wanted friends."

Slowly, with care, Raylee reached down into her costume for what lay hidden there.

She drew it out.

In the black cellar, under Poe's approving glare, there were screams.

"My lunch and dinner," she said, "my dinner and breakfast."

# TRICK OR TREAT
# WITH JESUS

MARILYN MATTIE BRAHEN

S ister Miriam hated Autumn. She knew the good Lord saw fit to color the trees in a blaze of red, yellow and orange, but so did He color the flames of Hell. It was appropriate, a warning to all good Christians. Halloween was coming, and she hated Halloween, the Devil's own holiday, and nothing holy about it.

Miriam trudged over to the bus stop, lugging her "Repent, Sinners, or Suffer Everlasting Torment" sandwich board. She had added biblical verses to the backside board, exhorting the lost souls to accept Jesus as their savior. When she got on the bus, dropped token and forty cents into the box, and was handed her transfer, she blessed the driver. This one didn't say thank you. He would roast, oh, sweet Jesus, he would roast. She could tell which ones would fail on Judgment Day.

The bus took her, as always, to the elevated train, the transfer bought her passage, and she rode above ground until the train descended into the tunnel beneath Center City Philadelphia and brought her to 15th Street. Her major audience awaited her there, those sinful commuters, leaving their jobs, going home for the day, thinking of mortal concerns and pleasures and nothing more. Well, when she finished with them, they might open up the bible instead of turning on the TV.

She got off the train and positioned the sandwich board around her body as people pushed by her, boarding the train. Miriam was feeling particularly fine about her calling. That morning, as she read her own bible, opening it randomly to see God's special message for her, the passage had blared: "Make a joyful noise unto the Lord."

Miriam needed no microphone or bullhorn. The noise she was capable of making was well-known in Center City. And they couldn't stop her. She was in the Lord's service.

She took a deep, lung-stretching breath, and her voice covered the enclosed station like a net seeking fish.

"YOU'RE ALL GOING TO HELL!"

When the fish—or commuters—dwindled to a trickle, Miriam crossed the overpass to the other side of the tracks. The train pulled in, half-empty at 7:00 p.m. Miriam stepped in, took off her sandwich board, and sat down. At 2nd Street, a young white man came on board and leaned near the door, ignoring the available seats. He spoke out in a moderate, calm voice. "Excuse me, people. What would you say if I told you I've brought a bomb on this train, right here in my knapsack?"

Miriam checked him out: olive green pants, white short-sleeved shirt, clean brown loafers. He carried a leather jacket in his hand. The knapsack, same color as the pants, rested on his back. He had short blond hair, neatly combed, a thin face and skinny body. He wore silver-framed glasses. He didn't look like a terrorist.

The other people on the train ignored him, but Miriam caught a few worried looks among their faces.

"If you were going to die," the boy said, "right now, would you be ready to face God? Have you lived a life in the service of your Maker if a bomb went off on this train? Could you face Jesus and be welcomed by Him into Heaven?"

A woman two seats down turned to a girl next to her and said, loud enough for others to hear: "Just what we need after a hard day's work. Someone trying to push their religion on us with scare tactics."

The boy took this as a call to arms—rightly, Miriam thought, although she hoped he was joshing about a bomb. Never could tell with folks today.

The boy looked at his challenger. "The Lord says I am the light and the way. Follow me or burn in the fires of the Beast." The woman stared back at him, defying him and denying him, another sinner, as sure as Jesus died for our sins. Miriam watched her pull a book out of her tote bag and open it to some page tagged by a bookmarker. It sure as hell wasn't the Good Book. Then the woman spoke, louder than before, but she wasn't shouting. An actress's voice, that's what she had, and it carried: "We are *all* God's children. The only sin here is the sin of pride, pretending you know which of those children God loves." Then she went back to reading her book.

It was more than Miriam could bear. She rose up, dragging her sandwich board over to the woman. "The Good Book tells us which ones Jesus loves," she bellowed. "Good deeds will avail you nothing. Good intentions will fling you into the pit. Only accepting Jesus Christ as your savior will bring you to the promised land." The woman cast her eyes at her, one brow arcing, then continued to read. Miriam felt a shaking rage build in her heart. She wanted to smite this unbeliever, but she knew the law. She could only wish she'd see this woman writhe in Lucifer's lava pits, boil in the volcano that awaited her.

Miriam walked over to the young man. "Jesus will reward you for speaking the truth." She lowered her voice now, speaking only to him. "Let the Devil take them if they won't believe."

The youth smiled at her. "God will reward me indeed very shortly." He looked at his watch and spoke softly now. "It's due to go off in about seven minutes."

Miriam stared into those cool grey eyes. "You don't have to play around with me, son. I'm a believer." The kid just stared back at her, calm and certain of grace. Miriam repeated, "I'm a believer. But it's up to God to punish the sinners, boy, not us."

The young man slowly shook his head. "It's war. The only way to teach those who defy Jesus." He turned slightly away from her, his face determined.

Miriam stared at his knapsack. "You gotta teach them the right way. Like every Halloween, those kids come, and I give out Chick pamphlets, to get them on a path to Jesus."

The youth checked his watch again. "Five minutes."

Five minutes. It would take her at least eight to her stop. "I hope you're not crazy, boy."

He turned back to her. "Aren't you ready to meet Jesus?" His tone taunted her. She stared at him and dragged her board over to a seat and sat down.

Three more stops to go. She glanced at the kid, but he was staring out the window, his back with the bulky knapsack turned to her. There was maybe two minutes left if he was serious. Not enough to make it home. What was in his sack? Did he really have a bomb?

The train pulled into Allegheny station, slowing down.

Miriam picked up her sandwich board and got off the train.

The woman who had sassed her, the girl beside her, and the kid with the knapsack all looked at her on the platform as the train doors shut and it pulled away.

Miriam watched it disappear down the track and stood there waiting, waiting for the explosion, but none came. She cursed the grey-eyed kid then, a tool of the Devil, trying to tempt her through mortal fear. What good was she to Jesus dead? The dead can't preach to the sinners.

The little pamphlets were stacked on a card table, set up near the front door. They told the story of Jesus, and the stories of those who had rejected the Lord and the punishment they suffered for their willful ignorance. They told how to get salvation, and how not to fall into the clutches of the false religions.

The doorbell rang, and Miriam answered it.

A boy dressed as a Ninja and a girl done up as a flapper from the Roaring Twenties greeted her. "Trick or Treat!"

Miriam took two pamphlets from the table. "Ain't no devil to do tricks here, and the only treat is saving your soul for Jesus." She dropped one pamphlet each into their bags. "God curses Halloween. You kids go home and find Jesus."

The children stared at her, then down at the pamphlets in their bags. They turned, disappointed, and left her house. Going to some other house, looking for devil's food to rot their teeth and souls.

She dropped more pamphlets into more outstretched Halloween bags, exhorting the children to abandon the witches' sabbath and seek the Lord. A few kids bad-mouthed her, but she stood there like a rock, unmoved, unwavering. One little girl insisted that Jesus already loved the little children. Miriam told her sternly, "Not when they kiss Lucifer's backside on Halloween. He's looking to snare you, girl, to take you to Hell and away from Jesus!" The child started crying, and Miriam thought perhaps the girl saw the error of her ways, but her friends drew her close and whispered to her, and the girl spat "You're crazy!" at her. Another lost one.

Around 10:00 p.m., the doorbell stopped ringing. Miriam began to put the rest of the pamphlets away. She locked her door and sat down in her easy chair, lifting the bible off the end table beside it. She opened it randomly to the 24th Psalm. "To you I lift up my soul, Oh, Lord, Oh, God. In you I trust; let me not be put to shame, let not my enemies exult over me. No one who waits for you shall be put to shame; those shall be put to shame who heedlessly break faith." She stopped reading it aloud; the last line was troubling. The doorbell rang.

She put the bible down, grabbed another Chick pamphlet and unlocked the door to stare at the man outside.

He was dressed in a creamy white robe belted with a rope; his brown hair and beard cascaded down upon it. His brown eyes stared sadly into her own. He held an opened green knapsack in in his hands, which he thrust forward at her. "Trick or treat."

"Trick," Miriam muttered. "You're a trick. Be gone from me, Lucifer."

The man didn't leave. "David also wrote: 'The sins of my youth and my frailties remember not, in your kindness remember me, because of your goodness, O Lord,' and 'For your name's sake, Lord, you will pardon my guilt, great as it is.' How could the Lord be as unmerciful as you paint him, Miriam?"

"You . . . you're the Lord? Did I die? Did I stay on that train and get blown up?"

"You got off the train, Miriam. You had to wait for another one to complete your journey. Nothing exploded."

"You're not real. You're the Devil tricking me." She tried to close the door in his face, but he held out his hand. He didn't touch the door, but it moved back, out of her hand, opening fully up.

She peered at him, and that's when she saw the others, the creatures behind him. One looked like a human bat, another, a green ghoul; another was a shapeless mass with three eyes midway, watching her mournfully.

"You're the Devil!"

He reached out to the three-eyed thing and gently stroked its quivering flesh. "Do you think I or my father would turn away from those who seek us from a different pathway than your own? Or hate them because they do not bow before us?" He moved into her living room with the monsters, pushing her backwards as he moved forward. And from behind them, children in Halloween costumes entered, crowding the small room, holding out their bags to her. Their eyes cut into her soul, demanding, angry.

Miriam backed against the wall. "Lord, save me!"

"I cannot save you, Miriam. Save yourself. Empty your heart of pride and prejudice and arrogance toward the children of the Creator. You are not their judge."

One by one, the children began emptying their bags. Candy bars, boxes of candy, lollipops, gum in balls, sticks and chicklets, jawbreakers, popcorn balls, apples, candy corns, marshmallow pumpkins, gummies shaped like worms and other wriggly things both sweet and sour, pretzels, potato chips and pennies began to pile up around Miriam.

Jesus spoke again as the wall of Halloween treats rose around her. "Even in the depths of Hell, where souls have lost their way, does the true Creator of all life reside and send spiritual succor to its inhabitants, so they might follow a thin thread of hope. How can a father abandon children, no matter how errant? How can a father deny creations who seek a different mode of praising him from other creations who have decided what that mode shall be? And who are you to decide another creation's path to his, her or its creator?"

The Halloween treats pillared up around her eyes. The children floated to the top, building her a prison of sugar and starch. And now they drew Chick pamphlets from their bags, raining them down on Miriam. The small space between her, the wall and the mounds of treats began filling up with the booklets. "Please, dear Lord! Forgive me, forgive me, forgive me!!!"

Silence. The cheap paper tracts stopped fluttering down on her. "Jesus? Jesus? You still there?"

No answer.

Miriam pushed at the mountain of goodies surrounding her. She tried to climb up it, but the treats she stepped into avalanched, tumbling down into the cushion of Chick pamphlets, knee deep around her. A second attempt buried her to her waist.

"Jesus! Jesus? God! Is anybody there?!"

She gave in to a couple of good crying jags over the next hour. Her body ached with weariness from standing up, stuck waist deep in the Halloween treats, but she feared sleep, feared falling into them, being suffocated.

She finally reached out and picked up a chocolate bar, slowly unwrapping it. She ate it slowly, then carefully lifted an apple from her Halloween prison cell.

Eventually she fell asleep, wondering if asphyxiation by treats would be painfully slow or painlessly fast.

Outside of Miriam's world, the trick-or-treaters were now asleep, some with the lingering taste of sweets on their breath. Their parents had checked their booty and put the good stuff away to be doled out over a reasonable period of time, saving their children from extra cavities and extra pounds. And inevitably, those parents snitched a candy or two, knowing their kids wouldn't mind, would let them taste a treat of Halloween and so remember their own pleasure in this night when they were young. On this night when the gates between the dimensions are opened and all manner of spirits can visit our world as if they'd never left it.

# INTO THE ABYSS

R.J.  LEWIS

The creature walked to the door and brought his huge green hands to the locks. The flat black fingernails reflected darkly as the hands inserted and turned the keys. The elongated forehead pulsed with the concentration of the task as finally the door came open.

The tall, green figure made a noise somewhere between a snarl and a sigh, filled with the exhaustion of its quest. It walked into the room, the shabby clothes clinging to the tall shoulders and the unsteady gait of a reanimated corpse.

It knew something was wrong. It walked to the dining room table, finding the note. The clumsy fingers opened the envelope and pulled the piece of paper free, leaving dark green fingerprints, as if its very flesh was sloughing off, the result of decomposition.

It held the note, close to its face.

*"DEAR STAN;*

*I'VE HAD IT! THIS IS NOT WHAT I BARGAINED FOR WHEN WE MOVED IN TOGETHER. I THOUGHT WE WERE 'ACTORS', BUT YOU'VE SOLD OUT. I CAN'T TAKE WHAT*

*YOU'VE BECOME—OR THE MESS. I'M MOVING IN WITH
A GIRL FRIEND AT WORK.*

 *DON'T TRY TO FIND ME.*

 *JULIE"*

The creature's mouth opened.

"Damn", Stanley Nathan said aloud.

He put the note down and walked to the bathroom. She
was right, it was a mess. Half open bottles of spirit gum,
ripped toilet paper, and coagulated droplets of liquid latex
decorated the sink, commode, and tub.

He took off the padded coat, with the huge shoulder pads
sewn into the decaying yoke, and bent to loosen the shoes
with the elevator heels. He pulled off the rope belt, the shabby
pants, and the turtleneck shirt, turning on the shower.

The startling contrast of the pale pink skin of his chest
and arms to the green on his hands was reflected in the mirror on the door. He stepped under the hot spray and picked
up a bottle of baby oil, rubbing the liquid on his face and
hands, causing the "crypt green" greasepaint to come loose
and run like blood down the drain.

He carefully and systematically pulled the rubber forehead free as the oil relaxed the adhesive, and he pulled the
headpiece—complete with hair—off his own head, uncover-
ing his thinning hair with the strong widow's peak.

He soaped himself, and used several different makeup
removers to turn himself from a movie perfect reproduction
of the Frankenstein monster back into plain old Stanley
Nathan.

*She really did it*, he thought, *I can't believe it!*

When he and Julie moved to New York from Ohio with
the intention to be actors, they arrived with very little
except a love for each other. Now they didn't even have
that. A year in the big, bad city, and she did three showcases
and held a job as a waitress.

But Stanley used a talent with makeup to perform at parties. Not small parties, but the fanciest ones the wealthy threw gobs of money at. He could become anyone, from movie stars to an accurate recreation of the Grinch. He cast his own rubber pieces, called prosthetics, and was in demand by more and more of the best party planners in Manhattan.

And this was his season, October–Halloween. Here on October 30th, he was returning from a party aboard the *Intrepid*, with people dining on caviar and vodka. Stanley met the guests at the door, as unmoving as a mannequin.

"Doesn't that look real!" one of the women in diamonds would say.

"Thank you," Stanley would reply, in his best Boris Karloff, causing the woman to shriek, at first with terror, and then laughter.

He was at that party for two hours, and would get a check that could easily cover the monthly rent of the small, one bedroom apartment in the part of town called "Alphabet City". The one he shared with Julie until this evening.

He got out of the shower and dried himself.

"She's just jealous," he said aloud, meeting his eyes in the mirror, "that I got so good with the makeup."

Eyes ringed with green stared back, coupled with a look of doubt that surprised him.

He pulled out a pad of eye makeup remover and wiped the last of the green from his pores. The expression of doubt remained.

He went to bed, every muscle aching from the stiff pose he'd assumed, and from all the nights previous. He was tired, but his mind wouldn't shut down.

He'd spent the month working almost every day: Frankenstein at one party; Dracula at another; even a stunning Hunchback, his face distorted grotesquely with a glass eye sticking out from a fake rubber brow.

Stanley wasn't completely surprised at Julie's departure. Arguments started once the party planners began calling regularly, and each job this month made the tension grow.

"You're too good for this!" she told him, her pretty face still clear in his mind. "You could be doing real acting, not just this dressing up shit. You're selling out!"

The image of her face stayed with him until he fell asleep.

The phone woke him the next morning.

"Julie—can you get that?" Stanley said, seeing her side of the bed empty. Then he remembered and stumbled out to the other room to grab the phone, cursing as he stubbed his toe.

"That's a nice way to talk to someone giving you work!" the woman with the graveled voice of too many cigarettes said. It was Annette Freling, one of his first party planners, who only booked high class events.

"What? Oh Annette! I'm sorry, I hit my foot," Stan muttered, still not awake. "What time is it?"

"Eight thirty, bubby!" Annette said, with as much of an apology in her voice as she was capable of. "I know it's early to call you, but I had to see if you were booked."

Stan opened the pages of his datebook, rubbing his eyes with his free hand, trying to bring them into focus.

"Sure, what date?"

"Tonight!" Annette bellowed.

"Tonight?"

"As in tonight, Halloween! I got a call from someone with a lot of money—now I told them you were probably booked—"

"No, I'm clear," Stanley said, gazing with surprise at his book. It was odd that he didn't have anything tonight of all nights. The days leading up to the big night he'd had events, but All Hallows Eve was available.

"You're kidding!" Annette shrieked. "Oh my God, this guy really is the luckiest son-of-a-bitch on the planet."

"Who?" Stanley asked, beginning to wake up.

"Michael Baal, the guy who's rebuilding half of Manhattan, and owns the other half, that's who! I got a call from his office, God forbid he should pick up a phone—"

"Isn't that the guy who is richer than Donald Trump, but no one ever sees him?"

"People see him, just not lowly rabble like us. This guy— Mr. Austere, if you can believe it—called from his office, and I think I can book you!"

"Tell me about it. What do they want? Frankenstein? Maybe the Wolfman?"

"No bubby, Mr. Austere said they wanted someone who was an expert. They want something special, a custom makeup."

"Christ, Annette. It takes days to do a custom job."

"Listen to me, Stanley," Annette croaked, "this is a special situation. Baal has this nightclub—it's only open one night a year—tonight."

"Then why did he wait until the last minute?" Stan said, disgusted.

"The point is, he wants what he wants, and usually gets it—money is no object."

"What does that mean?"

"It means, I'll double your last custom job."

Stanley held still for a moment. His last specialty design netted him enough to keep him going for months. And with Julie gone, he now would pay *all* the bills.

"I can't give you an answer until I see what they want," Stanley said, covering his options.

"It was just e-mailed to me. Can I send it along to you?"

"Okay. I'll call you back as soon as I figure out if I can even do it."

"You can do it, you're the best! I'll send it right away." Her excitement stimulated a coughing fit, and Stanley held the phone away from his ear until it passed.

"I'll speak to you soon," Stanley said, hanging up. He walked into the kitchen and started the coffee, then booted up his laptop—the one he'd paid for with events—and that night he'd gotten the $600.00 tip.

*Julie was jealous*, he thought, *she never made that kind of money as a waitress. I have a talent, I use it, and I take pride in what I can do. There's nothing wrong with that!*

But he knew that he was justifying his position. Had he sold out, like she said?

He opened the e-mail program, and in a few minutes downloaded and opened the message marked AAA MOST IMPORTANT, containing an attachment which the computer turned into a picture.

It was a very odd illustration. It looked like art work that might have graced the cover of a magazine like *Heavy Metal*. A demon—but not just a demon—it was an amazingly well crafted fallen angel with a bald head, small bumps suggesting horns, an exaggerated chin, and brilliant yellow eyes.

Stanley whistled, and leaned back in his chair. The overall effect was stunning. He expected the demon to be half naked with rippling muscles, but instead he was in a very fine tuxedo, looking very fashionable and attractive in a worldly way.

Stanley looked away from the image, the eyes were so intense they seemed to burn into his soul. He hit PRINT, and as his ink jet printer buzzed and whirred, he looked again at the likeness on the screen, trying to remain the observer.

He studied the facial structure to see if it would fit his face. The long chin—he'd need a new nose—the horns looked easy enough, more like knobs than what an animal might have.

He opened another program as the printer worked. It contained a drawn image of his face that he could alter with different additions. It was based on software that police sketch artists use, though not as sophisticated. It could only add things to the central figure—his own. He couldn't reduce his chin size or the placement of his eyes. Stanley found it a very useful tool to plan out a makeup before he started casting appliances.

He added a fake chin, stretching it to a new length, and then adjusted the brow of the head, and the nose.

He grabbed the finished rendition from the printer and placed it next to the computer screen. He made a few more changes. After a half-hour he called Annette.

"So, bubby, what's the story?" she said hoarsely.

"I can, but it's a lot of work. You need to triple that last job—"

"Triple? Are you out of your mind?"

"Annette, you said money was no object. If I'd gotten this a week ago, double would have done it, but I have to do it in one day. Just making the molds would normally take two days. As it is, I have to do the molds and cast the pieces today!"

"I know, but—"

"Quite frankly, there isn't a make-up artist outside of Hollywood that can do this, so that's the deal. If it's me, it's triple."

"Give me ten minutes," she muttered, and the line went dead.

Stanley hung up the phone and looked at his printed version of the demon. He could do the yellow eyes, he already had a pair of contact lenses that were darn close. The bald head could be done with a 'Woochie' brand head-piece. He owned several already cut to fit, and the red makeup would easily cover the hair underneath better than a flesh tone. He had red greasepaint, though he couldn't be sure of a perfect match.

He made a list of what he already owned, what he had to cast, and printed up the computer sketch of his face with the necessary additions.

He was excited, and wanted to do this job, even though it was a Hell of a lot of effort. It would be his best work to date.

The phone rang, it was Annette.

"You got it, bubby—Jeez, I can't believe it. I'll have you know I'm making nothing on this."

"I appreciate it, Annette," Stanley said. Annette said this every time she booked him, but he knew for a fact that she made a fine commission off everyone she got jobs for.

She gave him the address of the club, a converted downtown warehouse on Tenth Avenue.

"What time do I start?"

"Ten PM—and you go to Midnight. That's all," she said, and then added with a chuckle, "Damn fine money for two hours work! And you didn't even have to sell your soul!"

Stanley raised his head, again looking into the eyes of the demon on the paper before him.

"What makes you say that?" Stanley said, finding himself inexplicably troubled.

"It's just an expression, bubby," Annette croaked.

"Of course," Stanley said, trying to understand why it bothered him. "What's the place called?"

"Here's the best part—get this, it's called 'The Abyss'."

The rest of the day was a blur of activity. He called upon all the expertise he developed since his arrival in New York. He used clay and sculpting tools to mold the chin, nose, and forehead on the plaster cast of his face. It took over two hours, but the results matched the distinct look of the illustration.

He then mixed plaster of paris, adding the dry powder to water by handfuls, stirring to avoid lumps. He added until the mixture grew thick and began to warm. He waited until the last moment as it started to solidify, and carefully molded the head in three separate sections, using dams to separate each part of the demonic re-creation.

It was necessary to wait at least an hour to make sure the plaster cured completely, and he spent the time finding his yellow contact lenses, the bald cap, and the cold foam mix.

The latex based chemicals were easy to use. Earlier types of latex foam had to be heated and were difficult to work with. Cold foam required mixing just two ingredients, generating a chemical reaction thickening the foam into a spongy material with an outer layer that was so similar to skin that it could be blended perfectly.

The trouble was, those chemicals had to cure completely. It was now after noon, and full curing would take several hours.

"Damn lucky I don't start until ten," Stan said, as he carefully took the solid plaster molds off of the face. He then took his smaller sculpting pick and began to remove the clay that remained inside the mold.

It took another hour to remove all the bits of clay stuck to the inside, but soon Stan had three sets of clean molds. He put a releasing agent into each one, then placed the molds into several pots and pans from the kitchen filled with gravel to hold the castings in the correct position.

He mixed the two equal measures of latex goo and reagent. This had to be done with haste, and he observed the mixture for signs of the reaction. As bubbles began to form, he poured the latex mix into the molds, picking up each one and gently rolling it, so that all the surfaces of the casting were covered by the rubber.

He placed the molds into their specific pots, and walked out of the kitchen away from the ammonia smell of curing rubber.

"Now, it's just a matter of time. It either worked or it didn't," he said aloud to the room. His last custom job required him to cast each facial piece two or three times before he was satisfied. But there wasn't enough time. If the mold wasn't right, he wouldn't be able to cast another.

He sat down and turned on the television.

*My best work to date*, Stanley thought, *if it all comes out.*

At eight o'clock, Stanley stood in his bathroom in his underwear and T shirt. The first thing he did was slip in the yellow contact lenses while he had clean hands. He looked over the facial pieces, and put the final coating of castor oil and greasepaint on each section. They turned out perfectly, and Stanley knew it the minute he gently separated each piece from its mold with held breath and clenched teeth.

This was the moment that excited him most, applying the lifeless rubber to his face and making it look like living tissue. It gave him a thrill he imagined was akin to what Doctor Frankenstein felt when the lifeless corpse began to move.

He started with the bald cap, applying the spirit gum to the skin around his hair line, using the blow dryer to speed up the process. He slipped on the cap, unfolding it from the center of his head, and made minor adjustments as he flattened it to his flesh, avoiding any small wrinkles or puckering.

He then picked up the brow, its small, stubby horns protruding. He looked in the mirror to see where it would fit his face, and put spirit gum every place it would touch. Then, he carefully attached it.

It was a perfect fit, since it had been cast from a copy of his own head. He took a small brush and covered the places where it met his skin with liquid latex, making any of the joints disappear. He daubed the wet, white rubber with a stipple sponge, flattening it and adding texture.

He proceeded down the face, putting on the nose, being especially careful with the chin. He would be talking and laughing with the patrons at the nightclub, and if it was too close to his mouth it could work loose.

Soon his face was a mixture of the red prosthetics and white latex with his natural skin color on his cheeks and neck. He finished blow-drying the wet latex and examined his reflection again.

"Magic time," he said, grabbing the greasepaint. He touched the rubber with quick little pats, and softly rubbed the makeup on all the exposed places, and on the back of his neck.

He looked up at the face in the mirror. Gone were the streaks of different colored skin and rubber, the face was a uniform red. The face staring back at him with yellow eyes was so startling, his breath caught.

"Jesus!" he said, as the demon in the mirror moved its lips with him. "I got it! I got it dead on!"

He went to the door of the bathroom and called out, "Julie, Julie you have to see this—"

He stopped at the threshold, remembering that she was gone. Just like his own face vanished into this new creation.

"Stupid!" he spat, "she'd rather work as a waitress—be a real actress. Look what I can do!"

He returned to the image in the mirror, now even more

animated, and for a moment Stanley couldn't figure out why. He slowly realized his anger made the face even more alive.

Alive—and evil.

After powdering the makeup and brushing off any excess, he dressed in his good white shirt and tuxedo. He knew the red greasepaint might never come out of the collar, but after tonight he could buy new shirts—Hell, dozens.

As a final touch, Stanley washed his hands, and picked up a red "Disguise-Stix" which he applied to his wrists. He knew from the drawing that he would wear gray gloves, but he wanted to make sure that any exposed skin matched his face.

A last minute inspiration struck him, and he pulled out a short black cape with a red lining he used for Dracula a week or two earlier.

He went outside and walked down to Fourteenth Street to catch the crosstown bus. It was a little after nine and there were people out in the cool Autumn night. They looked at him, but they didn't point and laugh, like when he was Frankenstein or even the Hunchback. People stared, but their faces were grim—even frightened.

He got aboard the bus and swiped his Metrocard. The bus driver, a black man, looked up, his eyes wide.

"Good evening!" Stanley said. He decided this character would have an English accent.

"Uh, evening. Man, you look—" the driver said stopping in mid-sentence, trying to smile but unable to.

Stanley sat, the other patrons giving him a wide berth.

*There is a sense of power*, Stanley thought, *unlike anything I've ever experienced.*

It felt thrilling.

Stanley arrived at the club at nine forty, and as he approached, he saw a long line of partygoers in costumes.

They were beautifully and expensively garbed, some wore make-up, but nothing at the level of his skill.

And Stanley knew it.

His eyes were drawn to the door by the size of the two men standing there. They were huge, bigger than any bouncers he'd ever seen. And each wore a large demon head with impressive horns.

*Must be a Celastic molded head resting on the guy's shoulders*, Stanley thought. He decided that they were very good molds, as the eyes seemed to follow his every movement.

He moved past the roped area and right toward the door. He expected to be stopped by the two goons, but as he approached they bowed and stood aside from the door.

*Of course, they're expecting me.*

As he walked into a lobby, he saw a man standing in the corner who stared up at him. He was wearing glasses and a suit, and he looked like he'd dressed up as a nerd accountant for Halloween.

He approached, sweat beading his brow, his mouth moving, but no words coming out until he was right next to Stanley.

"S-sir, I—I—" he sputtered, his face blanching.

"Good evening," Stanley said in his clipped accent. "I'm Stanley Nathan. Who do I see to find out where I'm performing?"

The man's thin face turned a bright shade of scarlet, almost matching Stanley's temporary skin hue.

"O-of course!" he blurted out. "I'm Austere—Mister Austere, I'm the one who hired you. It's just that—well—the re-creation of what we sent—I mean—I was told you were good—"

"Thank you," Stanley said, proud of his work. Tonight

was a crowning achievement, even if Julie did run out on him. If she could see him now!

Mr. Austere called over another man with a mustache and van dyke beard, and murmured into his ear. The man nodded and approached Stanley smiling.

"Sir, would you like to look around?"

Stanley nodded, "Please! By the way, what is this character called?"

"Called?" the man said, stopping short.

"Does he have a name—I mean the drawing was so specific—"

"I don't know," the man said, becoming uncomfortable as he looked into Stanley's yellow eyes. "Satanic Majesty? Prince of Darkness? Anything you like."

"Prince," Stanley said, "I like that, call me 'The Prince'!"

"As you wish. Please follow me."

They stepped to the door that separated the lobby from the large nightclub beyond. Stanley heard the rhythmic pulse of a heavy bass beat. He didn't really hear it, so much as feel the pulse in the walls around him.

The man with the beard opened the door, and the music increased to the point of being painful, a combination of metal rock and garbled lyrics that sounded like screams. Stanley realized the one thing he'd forgotten tonight was his ear plugs.

As he entered, he completely forgot about his ears or the music. The main room was the most amazing display he'd ever seen. It was as if someone took an illustration of Dante's Inferno and brought it to horrific life in this one cavernous room.

There were several different levels and dance floors, and in the center was a huge pit which belched forth smoke containing a hint of sulfur.

*Nice touch!* Stanley thought.

Women wearing bat wings and very little else, ran and jumped from level to level acrobatically. Their lithe forms moved with such wanton abandon, that Stanley decided they must be nymphomaniacs as well as gymnasts.

There were chained figures, with stripes from whippings on their bare midriffs. The make-up was so stunning real, Stanley thought he could sense the tinny taste of the blood.

His entrance caused a commotion among the winged women. They stopped and stared, then leapt and cavorted in his direction. The man with the beard stepped out in front of Stanley as the writhing swarm of women landed near him and fell into a huddled mass.

"Go on—all of you—this fellow is here as part of the show!" he bellowed, and Stanley could barely hear him above the music. One of the women, who seemed terribly young, yet at the same time ancient and far too experienced, glanced at Stanley's crotch, and licked her lips so lasciviously, that he found it hard to breath. Her eyes promised such possibilities, with a desire to be debased as well as taken.

The women twittered and giggled as the bearded man fretted, finally moving away and returning to their perches throughout the room.

Stanley, freed from the temptress's glance, tried to concentrate on the room. Every corner he looked at contained more than he expected. Realistic fires burned and bodies shook in artificial torment on racks, or hung from manacles. Of any display of macabre decor Stanley had ever seen, this was the ultimate.

Then his eyes fell on the chair at one of the highest points in the room. No, it couldn't be called a mere chair. A throne, a station of royalty and power! This would be a place for him to sit that night! A Prince surveying the kingdom of the damned.

Stanley pointed at the chair. The bearded man grew pale and escorted him out to the lobby.

"That would be perfect–" Stanley was saying as they passed through the doors and the Hellish din was left behind.

"I'm sorry, but that's the one place you cannot go," the man said, firmly but with an apologetic tone. "Not before Midnight."

Stanley nodded, deciding that such a marvelous prop already had a purpose in the evening's festivities.

He glanced back at the room beyond the doors. "Quite a layout! And those women–"

"For your own safety, don't get too close. They'll eat you alive."

"What a way to go," Stanley sighed.

Mr. Austere appeared at Stanley's arm so suddenly Stanley jumped.

"It's time to open the doors!" Austere said, checking his watch.

"I'll greet people here to start off," Stanley said, in his character voice.

"That would be fine," Austere said, not meeting Stanley's eyes.

The doors opened and the revelers came in slowly. Stanley thought it odd that no one was collecting a cover charge or checking ID. They didn't even have invitations, but the bouncers wearing the big heads seemed to know who belonged and who didn't.

"Welcome to the Abyss! I am the Prince, your host," Stanley said, taking the job of the doorman. The reactions were much more varied than what Stanley was used to.

Some of the people were impressed by the makeup—that always happened—but most of them were disquieted by his presence, only smiling when they saw the inside of the club.

After a half-hour at the door, Stanley began to wander through the club. The music was still deafening and even more like screaming. He found that the guests were all very polite, offering him drinks and cigars, but still stand-offish.

Still Stanley plugged on, shaking hands, acknowledging the guests. He approached one of the winged woman and began to dance with her, much to the girl's delight. He wanted to get close enough to see what she was really wearing. Could it be a body stocking with anatomical features air-brushed on?

Five minutes into the dance, and though he held her with gloved hands, he was sure she was wearing no body stocking. Every bit of anatomy was gloriously her own. Except for a belt and leather contraption around her nether region, with leather straps that went up and over her shoulders, barely covering her nipples, she wore nothing at all.

Even more confusing, he couldn't see how the wings were attached. At first glance, he'd assumed they were held on by the leather straps going over her shoulders, but instead they seemed to be part of her flesh, attaching directly to her back.

Thinking about this, Stanley pulled her close, to look past her shoulder and see what held them on. Without a word or gesture, the nymph fell to her knees, grabbed him by the waist, and nibbled at his crotch.

Stanley reeled back, and the creature leapt up, laughed, and ran off. Stanley looked around, thankful that the make-up covered any flush of his skin.

However, his dance partner was not the only one who decided to indulge. There were couples—well—coupling—all over the room. On the dance floors, or any free space they could find. Groups of two or three, men on men, women on top of each other. It was as if a bell had gone off and everyone was copulating with the nearest recipient with no concern for anything, least of all gender.

*This is one of those nutty sex clubs!* Stanley thought, finding himself riveted by the sight. A part of him was enticed by the lust of the scene. He wanted to find his teasing dance partner and hurl her to the floor, tear away her harness and have his way with her.

He pulled himself out to the lobby to get some fresh air. It might be a sex club, but he was the hired help and had to control himself.

A tall, thin, bony man Stanley hadn't seen before ran up to him.

"Sir! Sir! It's almost Midnight, you have to get to the—"

The man stopped talking as Austere came into sight and raised a hand.

"Relax, this is Mr. Nathan. He is an expert on makeup."

The thin man's face drooped, his mouth fell open.

"Oh, sorry," he said, caught off guard and cowed by the presence of Austere. "I'll make sure everything is ready,"

The thin man ran off, Austere approached Stanley.

"Everything all right, Mr. Nathan?"

"Yeah, it's just a little crazy in there," Stanley said, trying to catch his breath.

"Oh, it will be much crazier after Midnight," Austere said, eyeing Stanley through his glasses. "Until dawn, I should think. Just be careful of the winged girls, they bite."

"So I've heard," Stanley said.

"That's why they wear the harnesses," he whispered hoarsely, "because they bite *down* there."

Stanley realized that the straps and leather on the girls resembled of all things—a dog's muzzle.

Austere glanced at his watch, and brought Stanley towards the door of the main room.

"Almost Midnight. You'll want to see this!" Austere said.

They walked into the club, just as a sound like thunder shook the air. People stood, breaking apart from their partners, and looked up at the throne. The rumble came again, and flashes of light exploded about the room with showers of sparks flying high into the air.

The people knelt, as a figure rose from behind the chair.

*This is going to be good!* Stanley thought.

The figure came forward, and the hairs on the back of Stanley's neck began to quiver, even glued down with rubber and spirit gum.

The figure looked just like Stanley in his makeup. But he projected such a presence, that it filled Stanley with awe.

The demonic figure stretched out his hand and the people bowed, even Mr. Austere. Stanley felt compelled to bow as well.

"Do what thou wilt," the voice said booming, "shall be the whole of the law!"

The kneeling figures let out a cheer, their voices raised in triumph. The demon sat on the throne—and with a flash of lightning—disappeared.

"Holy shit!" Stanley said, as the guests cheered even louder. The music began to play again, and Stanley saw food being served, and couples continuing where they left off. He also saw a woman put a man in shackles and pick up a whip.

Austere pulled Stanley out toward the lobby, not speaking until they went through the door.

"If you don't mind, Mr. Baal would like to speak to you," he said, leading Stanley toward an elevator he hadn't noticed before.

"Sure," Stanley said, his head spinning. "I have to ask

you, if you had one guy in the makeup, what did you need me for?"

The elevator door opened and Austere looked quizzically at Stanley, as if trying to absorb what he'd just said.

"Oh, you mean at Midnight!" Austere said as the elevator started to rise. "That's a very good question. This was, what do you call it? An audition of sorts. We have a great need for someone of your remarkable skills."

"Whatever for?"

"Mr. Baal would be the best person to answer that."

The elevator stopped with a soft "whoosh" and the door opened.

"Go in, Mr. Nathan. Mr. Baal is waiting for you."

"But I—"

"Just go, Mr. Nathan. I'll be there when you need me. I'm always nearby."

Stanley stepped out of the elevator and onto a carpet of such deep soft pile, he felt as if he was floating. He was in a penthouse, with the lights turned out, but ambient light entered through the many windows.

Stanley carefully walked forward, his eyes adjusting to the dim light of the room.

"M-Mr. Baal?" he said, just above a whisper.

A light came on, shining right into his eyes, blinding him. He lifted his hand to shield his eyes.

"No!" a booming voice called out. "Lower your hand, I want to get a good look at you. Come closer."

Stanley lowered his hand, and moved forward, unable to resist the sound of that voice. The light moved up and down Stanley's face for a good minute.

"Very nice!" the voice said. "Turn your head."

Stanley turned his head one way, then the other.

"Excellent!" the voice said. "Beyond my expectations. You, young man, are an artist!"

"Thank you, sir," Stanley said, "after I saw the other fellow in makeup, I thought—"

"Other fellow?" the voice asked.

"Yes, on the throne. I thought he did a better job than I did—"

The voice broke into hissing laughter that chilled Stanley.

"I imagine he did look better—perhaps more realistic?"

"Yes sir. I'm glad you still liked my work."

"Very much so!" the voice said. Stanley could now see a shadowy figure behind the light. "In fact, I want to hire you."

"Hire me?"

"To do this work you do for me—full time."

"You have more characters you want me to create?"

"No, just one character," the shadowy figure said. "In fact, it will be your finest work."

"Sir?"

The figure rose. "I've always loved this time of year. It's the one day I can walk freely among my fellow creatures." He bent and touched a button on the table.

Lights flashed on.

Stanley faced the figure, but it was as if he were staring into his mirror back in his bathroom at home.

It was the other man in makeup—only now Stanley was close enough to see that it wasn't greasepaint or rubber.

It was his face.

Stanley collapsed heavily into a nearby chair. The smiling demon went to a small bar and poured two brandies. He walked over to Stanley and gave him a snifter.

"Drink it, it will help you," he returned to the desk and sat. "You see, *I* am Michael Baal—or that's my name for public consumption. I've built an empire. Unfortunately, I now find that the public expects a face to go with my monuments of brick and mortar."

"No one has ever seen you–" Stanley said, sipping at the brandy, the heat of the liquid warming the cold chill seeping into his bones.

"A few loyal lieutenants, like Mr. Austere," he said and gestured to Austere, who appeared out of nowhere.

"With your help, Mr. Nathan, the world can see me," Baal said, very pleased with himself. "Consider it your most difficult assignment. If you can make yourself look like me– you can make me look–how shall I put it–a little less conspicuous?"

"And if I refuse?" Stanley said, trying to sound courageous.

"But you won't, Mr. Nathan," Baal said with a smile. "Think of the challenge. I've wanted someone with your skills for years, but I needed someone–who takes pride in his work."

The demon rose, sitting on the edge of the desk. "You will travel with me, I'll pay you very well, and you've seen some of the fringe benefits at the party."

Stanley shuddered, the memory of the nymph's teeth on his crotch and the masses of writhing bodies jumped into his mind. He looked at Baal sitting before him, poised and confident.

*"You've sold out,"* said Julie's voice in his head.

*"You didn't even have to sell your soul!"* croaked Annette.

*Is that what I'm doing?* Stanley thought. *Selling out? Selling my soul?*

But he remembered the feeling of power that he'd experienced tonight. It was even stronger in the presence of this creature.

He looked again at Baal, his mind racing. It was an interesting face. If he used a wig to cover the horns and a flesh tone grease with a good cover– perhaps jowls to lessen the effect of the chin . . .

Before he knew it, Stanley was on his feet approaching Baal, pulling the gloves from his hands, and gently touching one of the fleshy knobs protruding from his forehead. The demon didn't shy from his touch.

"Make you look like any face in the crowd."

"It would be your masterpiece," Baal said, his eyes burning into him.

Stanley cringed back from those eyes, finding his mind was overflowing with what Baal could give him, and do for him. If he wanted to be an actor, Baal could arrange it. Money? Baal would supply it. Women? Ready and willing like the ones downstairs.

All Baal wanted was one simple thing, which Stanley and only Stanley could give him. It would be his finest work—his masterpiece. And no one would ever know.

"Yeesss!" Stanley said with a sigh as he fell back into the chair, overwhelmed by possibilities.

Baal and Austere exchanged a smile.

# THE THEFT OF THE HALLOWEEN PUMPKIN

### EDWARD D. HOCH

Nick Velvet first saw the big multicolored hot-air balloons at an autumn rally on a farm in upstate New York one pleasant weekend when he and Gloria were driving aimlessly through the countryside.

"Oh, *look*, Nicky! Let's stop!" she cried—and since he was at least as interested as she was he pulled off the road into a field where other cars were parked.

There were about a dozen of the big balloons in all, crowded onto a farmer's field and looking a bit like some weird October crop come suddenly to maturity. Nick and Gloria walked among them, watching preparations for what was to be a cross-country balloon race. "Could *you* go up in one of those things?" Gloria asked.

"If I had to," Nick decided, viewing the gradually inflating balloons a bit uncertainly.

"They're perfectly safe," a freckle-faced young man assured them, overhearing their conversation. "Man has been flying in hot-air balloons for two hundred years."

"Is this one yours?" Nick asked.

"I don't own it but I fly it." He held out his hand. "My name's Roger Enfield." His red hair and a thin red mustache went well with the freckles. Nick guessed he was still in his early twenties.

He introduced himself and Gloria and Nick shook the young man's hand. "Where are you racing to today?"

"Where the wind takes us," Enfield answered with a laugh. "But we hope to head southeast across the Hudson and come down in Dutchess County."

"Can't you steer these things?"

"Oh, a little. You can go up and down by turning the burner on and off, regulating the amount of heated air in the balloon. Sometimes you can catch a stream of faster air aloft that's going in your direction. And we can always drop ballast if we have to. But a lot depends on the wind."

"Ready to go, Roger?" a tall man asked, striding through the crowd like an officer inspecting his troops. He wore riding boots and a tan-leather jacket reminiscent of the sort pilots wore during the barnstorming Twenties.

"Yes, Mr. Melrose," Enfield replied, and both of them climbed into the little gondola beneath the candy-striped balloon.

"That's Horace Melrose, the publisher," Gloria whispered. "I read somewhere that he's a nut about ballooning."

Melrose was snapping out commands as the ground crew released the ropes holding the balloon in place. Gradually it began to rise, clearing the trees and hovering for a moment as if seeking its way. Then a draft of air took it and it began drifting southeast toward the river.

"It looks like he's right on course," Gloria remarked as they strolled back to the car.

That was the first weekend in October, and Nick thought no more about Melrose, Enfield, and the balloon rally until three weeks later when he was far away, sunning himself on the beach of an expensive Acapulco resort. It was a nice place to visit in late October when the weather around New York began to turn damp and rainy, but Nick wouldn't have chosen it on his own without the urging of his latest client, who gave her name on the telephone as Rita Spangles.

"I can't come up there," she'd informed him. "And I can't do business over the telephone. Fly down here for a couple of days and I'll pay your expenses, in addition to your regular fee."

"All right," he'd agreed. "I'll phone you when I get in."

"No. Be on the beach the day after tomorrow. Have you got a bathing suit?"

"Yes."

"What color?"

"You get your choice of black or red trunks. Like a roulette wheel."

She laughed. "Wear the red. I always win on red."

"What will you be wearing?"

"A white maillot. I'll look for you around one o'clock."

So there he was, a half hour early, basking in the sun with a copy of yesterday's *New York Times*, looking, he hoped, like a typical businessman on vacation. Then he saw her, a few minutes before the appointed hour, strolling across the sand in her white one-piece bathing suit, carrying a striped beach jacket over one shoulder.

He tried not to look up too obviously as she passed, and she paused at his feet to ask, "Velvet?"

"Hello there," he said, glancing up with a smile. "Join me on my blanket?"

She sank down beside him. "From what people told me about you, I expected a younger man."

"Don't let the grey hairs fool you. I'm in disguise."

"I see." She picked up a handful of sand. "You steal things, right?"

"Right. Nothing of value. No money, art works, or securities. Worthless stuff only. My fee's twenty-five thousand."

"I know all that. Would you steal a pumpkin?"

"What kind of a pumpkin?"

"A Halloween pumpkin. A jack-o-lantern. Next Sunday's Halloween."

"So it is. Where will the pumpkin be? In a store? In a farmer's field?"

"On the front porch of a friend of mine."

Nick rolled over on his stomach. "Miss Spangles, pardon me for mentioning it, but you could hire a couple of neighborhood kids to steal a pumpkin off somebody's front porch. They'd probably do it for a couple of candy bars."

"Not from this porch, they wouldn't. It's on an estate that's surrounded by a wall and has guards and dogs patrolling the grounds."

"Then why do they bother with a pumpkin if they don't encourage visitors?"

"A family custom. I think it's his wife's idea."

"Where is this place?"

She'd uncapped a plastic bottle and was spreading suntan lotion carefully along her firm thighs. Her hair was blonde and her complexion fair. She probably burned easily. "Dutchess County, north of New York. Do you know the area?"

"Sure."

"He's a publisher, name of Horace Melrose. He owns a chain of newspapers in cities around the country."

"I've met him briefly," Nick said.

"Can you do it? Steal the pumpkin from his porch on Halloween night?"

"It sounds easy enough. What's your connection with Melrose?"

"We were friends—" she began, and then corrected herself. "Hell, I was his mistress for eight years. Now I'm in exile down here. He pays the bills as long as I stay away."

"And the pumpkin?"

"That's a personal matter. You don't need to know any more."

"You want me to steal it as a sign? To remind him you're still around?"

"Something like that." She looked away, out to sea. "Just bring me the pumpkin."

"Is it a real one, or—"

"I know they use the same decorations every year, and then store them away. It's probably plastic or something." She reached into the drawstring bag she carried with her. "Here's a check for your travel expenses. You'll get your fee when you deliver."

Nick Velvet nodded. She was the sort of woman he liked to deal with, and not just because of the way she looked in a bathing suit. "You'll have it the day after Halloween," he assured her.

Roger Enfield was having a beer in a Poughkeepsie bar when Nick found him. It took a moment for recognition to dawn. "Sure, I remember you. At the balloon race. You had a nice-looking woman."

"Gloria will be happy to hear that," Nick murmured, signaling the bartender. "Who won the race?"

"Fella from New Mexico. Hot-air balloons are a big thing down there. They have races all the time."

"You work for Horace Melrose?"

"Hell, no! He acts like I do sometimes, though. For the

races he hires the balloon *and* me from the promotion company I work for."

"Then your balloon's for hire?" Nick said with interest, ordering a beer for himself.

"Sure. What'd you have in mind?"

"A sort of promotion. On Halloween night."

"I don't take it up after dark. It's too easy to get tangled in power lines."

"Late afternoon, then. Just before dark." Nick hoped the pumpkin would be out on the porch then. It was a chance he'd have to take. "I'd want to go up, touch down at a certain spot, and then go up again. Could you do that?"

"Sure, if the weather cooperates. I don't go up if it's rainy or windy."

"The pay would be good," Nick assured him. "I'd want you to land on the Melrose property."

"What—on Halloween?" Enfield's voice rose in alarm. "Not a chance, mister! Not after what happened there last year!"

"Oh? I wasn't aware anything happened there last year. Why don't we move over to a booth and you can tell me about it."

Enfield wiped the foam from his red mustache and picked up his half finished beer. "Sure, I'll tell you. It's no secret. It was in all the papers." They settled down in one of the wooden booths where there was more privacy and Nick ordered another round of beers.

The story Enfield told him was simple enough. On Halloween of the previous year, a man had been shot on Melrose property near the front porch of the house. A security guard had mistaken him for a prowler, and when the man started running the guard had fired. The man's name was Tom Reynolds and he was a sportswriter for a Philadelphia newspaper. He'd died at the hospital a few hours later. No one ever established what he was doing on the Melrose property.

"So you see what I mean about Halloween," Roger Enfield said. "If I landed that balloon there Sunday night, the guards would probably pump it full of holes."

"What's Melrose got to hide?" Nick wondered.

"Nothing. He just likes his privacy. He told me once he's around so many people every day he likes to get away from them on weekends."

Nick was struck by a thought. "He's a newspaper publisher. Did this man Reynolds work for him?"

"No. Melrose doesn't own any big-city papers. They didn't even know each other. That's why no one could figure out what Reynolds was doing there."

"Did the police bring charges against anyone?"

Enfield shook his head. "The Melroses are pretty important people up here. And Reynolds was trespassing, after all."

Rita Spangles had mentioned a wife. "What about Mrs. Melrose?"

"Jenny? She's a fine woman—very involved with social issues. She serves on a lot of committees."

Nick finished his beer. "Are you sure you won't change your mind about the balloon?"

"On Halloween? Not a chance! Take my advice. If you don't want to get shot, stay away from the Melrose place. If anything, those guards are more trigger-happy now than they were a year ago."

Until then, it had seemed like a simple and uncomplicated assignment. In fact, it had seemed so simple that Nick had dreamed up the balloon landing to spice it up a bit. The idea of using a hot-air balloon to steal a pumpkin and then escaping the same way appealed to his sense of the dramatic. If it couldn't be done, there were plenty of other ways to accomplish the theft. But the news about the man named Tom Reynolds being shot and killed there the previous Halloween bothered him. What if Rita Spangles had hired Reynolds to steal the plastic pumpkin, too? What if the whole thing was some sort of bizarre ritual to lure someone to his death each Halloween?

Later when he told Gloria of this idea, she scoffed. "Honestly, Nicky, you get the craziest ideas sometimes! You should be writing these horror movies the kids like so much. You could call this one *Halloween 4½* or something."

"I suppose I did let my imagination go too far," he admitted. "But Tom Reynolds is dead, there's no denying that. And he was trespassing on their property, the same as I'll be doing."

"Can't you find out if there was any connection between Reynolds and this woman who hired you?"

It was a good suggestion and he wondered why he hadn't thought of it. "I've only got a few days but maybe I can find out something," he decided.

The following morning Nick was in Philadelphia, calling on Tom Reynolds' former editor at the newspaper office on Market Street. The editor's name was Paul Karoski, and his thin hair and pale skin indicated that his was a sporting life spent mainly indoors.

"Reynolds was one of the best young sportswriters I had," he told Nick. "It was a shame what happened to him."

"Exactly what did happen?"

"He was onto a story of some sort. He never did tell me what it was. It brought him to the Melrose estate for some reason and he got himself shot. That's about all I know."

"The story must have been involved with sports somehow," Nick reasoned.

"Sure. Football, I think, because for a couple of days before he died he kept replaying a videotape from the Eagles-Rams game of a few weeks earlier. I even looked at it myself after the shooting, but I couldn't see anything unusual on it."

"Do you still have that tape?" Nick asked.

Karoski thought about it. Then he got up and shuffled through a stack of videotapes on top of a filing cabinet. "Maybe I erased—no, here it is. Eagles-Rams, from last October."

"Could I borrow it?"

The sports editor frowned at Nick. "What's your connection with all this? Are you a detective or something?"

"An investigator. I'm working on another matter and someone suggested I look into Tom Reynolds' death."

"All right," Karoski decided. "Take the tape, but bring it back. Give me a receipt for it."

"Gladly." Nick slipped the video cassette into the briefcase he'd brought along and reached for a pen. "One other thing. Did you or Reynolds know a woman named Rita Spangles?"

Karoski thought about it. "I don't, but I had no way of knowing all Tom's friends. He was a good-looking fellow, unmarried—Hold on. Wait a minute. Rita Spangles—I think that was the name of the woman at the hospital."

"What woman?"

"After he was shot, Reynolds lived about five hours. The hospital phoned me because they found his press card on him. I drove right up there, but he was dead by the time I reached the hospital. It was about a three-hour drive. They told me the only person he'd seen was this woman, and I think her name was Rita Spangles. I saw her only briefly, as she was leaving the hospital. I figured it was one of his girl friends."

"Did she seem upset by his death?"

"Yes. But she didn't talk to me."

"I'll get this tape back to you," Nick promised, giving Karoski his asked-for receipt as he left.

That evening he played it on their machine at home. Gloria looked in from the kitchen and sighed. "Don't we get enough football on Sundays and Monday nights?"

"This is work. It's a tape Reynolds was studying before he was killed."

"It looks like any other football game to me," Gloria said after watching it a while.

"That's the trouble," Nick agreed. He sat through the entire game—nearly three hours of it—without seeing anything unusual. It was just like any other football game.

On Friday night he looked for and found Roger Enfield in the same bar. "Are you back with your balloon plan?" the young man asked.

"A new one this time. You don't have to take me up, and you don't have to land the balloon. But could you fly over the Melrose place Sunday evening, just before dark?"

Enfield thought about it. "Daylight Savings Time ends Saturday. It'll be dark a little after five o'clock on Sunday."

"All right—around that time, then."

"Where'll you be?"

Nick took some money from his wallet and slid it across the table. "I'll be around. You just come in low and attract lots of attention."

The following morning Nick drove up to the Melrose place, stopping along the way to phone Jenny Melrose for an appointment. He represented himself as a free-lance writer wanting to interview her for an article he was preparing on gracious living in the Hudson Valley. He suspected that would perk her interest and it did.

She was a pleasant woman in her late thirties, a bit younger than her husband but with the same commanding personality. The sunny living room in which she greeted him had been decorated in expensive good taste—a bit old-fashioned by Nick's standards but still attractive. "Where will your article appear, Mr. Nicholas?" she asked, arranging herself on the sofa opposite him.

"I'm hoping for *The New York Times Magazine*, or perhaps *Country Gentleman*."

"I see."

"Could you tell me a bit about your style of living here?" Nick asked. "How you celebrate holidays, Halloween, for instance, since it's coming up tomorrow. Do you get any trick-or-treaters here?"

"Heavens, no. The gate is closed and there are guards. My husband is very security-conscious."

"How about decorations? Do you do anything special?"

"For Halloween?" She smiled at his question, perhaps at the absurdity of it. "No, no special decorations."

Nick pursued doggedly, "Not even a pumpkin?"

"Oh, we put a couple out on the porch with candles in them. They can be seen from the road. But that's as far as we go."

"I'd like to get a picture of those if I could."

She spread her hands helplessly. "I don't even know where they're stored. I must remember to have one of the servants get them out tomorrow."

"Perhaps I could come back then. The front of your house is so lovely it would make a very effective picture in my story."

"I'm afraid tomorrow wouldn't be convenient."

"I wouldn't have to disturb you. You could just leave word at the gate that I'm expected. One of your security men can stay with me while I snap a photograph of the house on Halloween evening."

"Very well," she agreed. "I suppose there's no harm in that."

Nick forced himself to remain for another forty-five minutes, pursuing his line of questioning about holiday celebrations. Then he departed, confident that he had prepared the way. She had surprised him when she mentioned two pumpkins, but that wouldn't stop him. He'd steal them both.

Halloween proved to be a crisp autumn day in Dutchess County, with the last of the leaves drifting down through sunlit skies. Wearing a black turtleneck sweater and slacks, Nick arrived back at the Melrose estate a little after four o'clock, let himself in the chained entranceway, and drove up the curving driveway. He was just taking a camera from his car when Horace Melrose, coming around from the side of the house, accosted him.

"What are you doing here?" the publisher asked.

"Nicholas is the name," Nick said, extending his hand. "I had a most informative interview with Mrs. Melrose yesterday and she gave me permission to return today for some pictures of the outside of the house."

Melrose ignored Nick's hand. "There's supposed to be a security guard with you. We've had trouble before with reporters."

"I'm not a reporter, Mr. Melrose. I'm a free-lance writer doing a magazine article."

"Nevertheless, no one's allowed on these grounds unaccompanied." He walked quickly down the drive to speak some brief harsh words to the security guard on duty. The man came hurrying up to Nick.

"Get your pictures and be on your way, mister," he growled.

"The lighting has got to be right," Nick answered, looking at the sky. Enfield's balloon was due any minute.

As Nick fussed with the camera, Jenny Melrose appeared in the doorway with two large glowing plastic pumpkins. "Here they are," she announced. "I'm sorry to have kept you waiting." She placed one on either side of the wide steps and inspected the scene with a critical eye. "Can you get them both in the photo?"

"I think so," Nick said, looking through the viewfinder and taking a step backward, thinking ironically that the pumpkins were reasonable copies of the real thing and would actually photograph very well. "Let me just move them slightly," he said, noticing that Horace Melrose was no longer on the scene and the guard was taking only a casual interest in the proceedings. He lifted the nearer pumpkin, careful not to disturb the flickering candle inside. There seemed nothing unusual about it to make it valuable to Rita Spangles or anyone else. A grease-penciled number on the bottom—274—seemed to indicate what its price had been.

"What's that?" the guard said, pointing at the sky.

"It looks like Roger Enfield's balloon," Jenny Melrose said. She and the guard moved out beyond Nick's car for a better view. "I wonder what he's doing up so late in the afternoon."

Nick had a look at the second pumpkin by then, but there was no price marked on it. While Mrs. Melrose and the guard watched the descending balloon, he blew out both candles and tossed the pumpkins through the open window of his car.

"I think he's trying to land," the guard said, unsnapping the holster at his side.

The big striped balloon, settling toward the front lawn

of the Melrose estate, did indeed look as if it might land. Nick climbed quickly into his car. "Thanks a lot," he called out to Jenny Melrose, "I've got my pictures!"

"What?" She turned, startled. "Already?"

Nick was already wheeling the car around the circular driveway. He heard her say something about the pumpkins, and then the guard shouted at him, but he kept going.

His car hit the slender chain across the gate and snapped it like a string. He saw a little puff of white in the rearview mirror and thought he heard the bark of the guard's gun fired after him. Overhead, Roger Enfield's balloon lifted high into the twilight sky, out of harm's way.

"What did *you* do for Halloween?" Nick asked Rita Spangles the following day, gazing out of her hotel-room window at the golden sand of the Acapulco beach.

"Trick or treat, like everyone else," she answered. "The treat was a bottle of French champagne in a nice man's room." She lit a cigarette and studied the two plastic pumpkins on the table in front of her. "Don't think I'm paying you *fifty* thousand just because you stole *two* of them."

"The second one's on me," Nick said generously. "I didn't know which one you needed."

She continued staring at them. "To tell you the truth, I don't either. How come the heat from the candle doesn't melt the plastic?"

"They make it with a high melting point for uses like this."

"You think there's something inside the candles?"

Nick shook his head. "I checked on that. They're solid. Look, maybe I can help with your problem if you tell me about it."

"Is that included in your fee?"

"Sometimes."

"All right," she agreed with a sigh, sitting on the edge of the bed. "As you know, I was Horace's mistress. I still am, I suppose, though I haven't seen him in a long time. Just over a year ago, this reporter named Tom Reynolds, a sports-writer and photo editor for a Philadelphia paper, started nosing around. That's when Horace sent me out of town. Reynolds tracked me to Florida and started asking questions."

"What sort of questions?"

"Horace's firm wanted to buy a paper in the Midwest and someone out there tried to block the sale by claiming he had links to organized crime. They said he was a business associate of Norman Elba, who's involved in illegal sports gambling."

"The sports connection—that's what interested Reynolds!" Nick remembered the videotape of the football game. Luckily he'd brought it in his suitcase on the off-chance Rita knew something about it.

"I suppose so," she agreed. "Anyway, Reynolds asked me about Horace, about what we did on certain dates he named. At first I clammed up, but later, when I knew Horace was about to ditch me, I started talking. I didn't have any solid information about Norman Elba, though."

"What was Reynolds doing at the Melrose home last Halloween?"

"He'd learned something and he went to confront Horace with it. Horace thought it was a routine interview and agreed to see him. I told Reynolds he should have settled for a statement over the phone, but he wanted to see Horace's face. He saw it, all right, and got a bullet for his trouble."

"You were at the hospital when he died," Nick said.

She looked surprised. "How did you know that?"

"His editor told me."

"Yeah, well, I went up there with him. You know. He was a handsome guy, young."

"Then you saw the shooting?"

"Not really. I was waiting in the car out on the main road, so Horace wouldn't see me. I followed the ambulance to the hospital and told them I was his fiancée."

"Did he talk to you?"

"Just a few words before he died. He said to get the pumpkin. 'It's on the pumpkin.' Those were his exact words."

"*On* the pumpkin, not *in* it?"

"*On.* I'm sure of that. But the next day when I returned to Horace's place, the pumpkins were gone—stored away for another year. Horace didn't want me snooping around with his wife there—he sent me away and warned me not to come back. He promised to send me money, and he has, but I keep remembering Tom Reynolds, a nice guy who didn't deserve what he got. And I keep remembering the dirty deal Horace handed me. When another Halloween rolled around I decided I should try to even the score, for Reynolds and me both."

Nick turned over the orange plastic globes, searching again for markings. "There's only the price on this one. Unless—"

"What is it?"

"This 274 scrawled on here with a black grease pencil. You said Reynolds was a photo editor besides being a sportswriter. He might have carried a grease pencil to mark photos, and when he saw the Melrose security guards drawing their guns he managed to mark this number on the pumpkin."

"I thought it was the price," Rita said.

"So did I. But $2.74 isn't a likely price for it. And there's no decimal point. It's not a price at all, but a number."

"A date?"

"February 1974? I doubt it. He'd have had time to put a line or dash separating the numbers if he meant them to be separated."

"Then what could it be?"

"Something important to him. The key to whatever he'd uncovered about Melrose and Norman Elba. I wonder—"

Nick was interrupted by a knock at the door. "Room service!"

Rita Spangles looked blank. "I didn't order anything."

"Open the door slowly," Nick whispered, slipping behind it.

But as soon as her hand turned the knob the door sprang open, propelled by a brawny man who barreled forward to grab Rita and cover her mouth before she could scream. Nick shoved back on the door, knocking a second man off balance, then dove for the one holding Rita. As they toppled, wrestling, to the floor, the second man recovered enough to shout, "Get the pumpkins!"

Rita snatched up a lamp and brought it down on the head of Nick's adversary, stunning him. Then she turned toward the man who had spoken. "I know you," she said, "you're Norman Elba!"

The gambler smiled and reached inside his jacket. Nick moved fast, almost by reflex, hurling the broken lamp at Elba's head just as a snub-nosed revolver appeared in his hand.

It was a brief battle. When it was over, Nick and Rita had Norman Elba and his henchman tied hand and foot with a haphazard collection of pantyhose, neckties, and a torn-up pillowcase.

"Melrose knew where to find you," Nick explained to Rita. "He guessed you hired me to steal the pumpkins and sent Elba after you." He turned to the gambler. "Isn't that right?"

"Go to hell!"

Nick held up the pumpkin. "What does 274 mean?"

"You tell me. You wanted it bad enough to steal it."

"It was Tom Reynolds' dying message, hidden for a year after his murder, and somehow it ties you and Melrose together."

Elba merely smiled. Rita appealed to Nick. "We can't hold him here forever."

"No," he agreed. There was a sound from the room next door. It sounded like a football game on television, and he remembered that the games from the States were shown here on cable. It would be Monday evening back East. Then he thought again of the videotape Paul Karoski had loaned him. "Of course—that's it!"

"What is?"

"Does the hotel have a video recorder somewhere?"

"There's one in the lounge downstairs. They play tapes of horse races in the afternoon and the guests make small wagers."

"Come on," Nick said. "I've got a tape in my room I want to play."

The lounge was unoccupied when they reached it and he slipped the tape into the machine. Then he turned on the set and pushed the FAST FORWARD button on the video recorder.

"What are you doing?" Rita asked.

"These machines all have digital counters to indicate the relative position of programs or scenes on a tape. See it there? It's almost to one hundred already. When it nears 274 we'll stop it and play the tape at its regular speed. I think we'll see something interesting—something Reynolds' editor missed because he didn't know where to look."

He waited another moment and stopped the tape at 270. Then he pushed the PLAY button. "But they're not even showing the game," Rita complained "The camera's panning over the crowd in the stands."

"And there it is!" Nick quickly pressed the PAUSE button and the image froze on the screen. It was a picture of Horace Melrose and Norman Elba with their heads together in deep conversation. "There's the proof Tom Reynolds spotted! When he confronted Melrose with what he had, Melrose ordered his security guards to shoot him. But Reynolds managed to scrawl that number on the pumpkin, and to tell you about it before he died."

"But why didn't Horace try to recover this tape?"

"Reynolds may not have been that specific about the nature of his evidence. Or Melrose might have figured it was better not to call attention to the tape at all. If he led Karoski to believe it was valuable, he could have gotten another copy easily enough and looked at it a bit more carefully."

"What should we do now?" she asked.

Nick thought about it as he rewound the video tape. "Phone Paul Karoski in Philadelphia and tell him what we've got. Then we'll turn Elba and his friend over to the local police and I'll be heading home—as soon as you pay me my fee."

# THE DEVIL'S OWN

JOHN GREGORY BETANCOURT

In the moment of my creation, I felt electricity.

That line conjures visions of Frankenstein's monster chained in the laboratory, of sparking electrodes and thunder storms and pyrotechnics. Nothing could be farther from the truth. Electricity—the ebb and flow of current, the gentle aliveness that filled me when my mistress first sanded down the roughness of my baked clay features with her power tools—was my initial sensation. Later, as she air-brushed the details of my perfect enamel face and delicate enamel hands, when she neatly etched my secret name to the back of my head, I tingled with awareness. It filled me with a buoyant energy that made me want to leap and shout. Electricity is one of the primal elements, and Elena Berman chained it to her will when she brought me forth from shapelessness.

Let me describe Elena. She was young as humans go, no more than twenty or twenty-one, with golden blond hair, blue eyes, and a honeyed complexion. You would not know her for a witch when you looked at her, but she was one.

She had a dark magic in her hands and heart and voice, and it showed as a single blemish on her throat—the devil's kiss, some call it, as if a demon had pressed his lips to that very spot.

Amidst the process of my creation, she would sometimes put me down and leave me alone on her workroom table for a day or more. Gradually my awareness would fade until I was little more than the sum of my parts: clay and straw, cloth and one small locket of her hair.

On the night of my completion, she dressed me as a doll in a frilly white dress, with shiny white shoes, tiny stockings, and a sun bonnet of pink and white. My white porcelain face shone; my wide blue eyes regarded her unblinkingly. Then she took me to the window and held me up to the moon, whispered thrice the secret name she had carved in the back of my head, and invoked the powers of darkness.

"Come forth, little girl, come forth!" she cried.

She cast me down toward the floor. For an instant I thought I would shatter on the tiles, ruined and dead forever, but instead I landed on my feet and felt my knees give almost gently. When I touched my face with warm, trembling fingers, I felt the flesh of my nose, my lips, my eyes, and my ears. I was real. She had made me live. I hardly dared breathe. When I did, it felt wonderful.

"Korina," she said, and she knelt and hugged me to her. "My darling Korina."

"What do you want of me?" I asked softly. "How may I serve you, mistress?"

She held me at arm's length and looked deeply into my eyes. "You are not here to serve anyone," she said. "I wanted a daughter, and you will be she. I will teach you all I know. We will be a family."

"I already know all that you know," I said. "I am part of you." I touched my hair, as golden as her own because it was her own. "Remember the lock you gave me?"

"Korina," she said, "I want to show you all that I have seen, to make you laugh with joy at the sunrise, to build you a doll house and watch you run and play and skip and dance in the sunlight."

"Why would I do those things?" I asked, a little scornfully. "I am not a child, mistress. Command and I will serve you."

"Then I command you to be a child!"

"I cannot change my nature, mistress. You might as well command me to be the wind or the rain or the darkness outside."

"Please . . ." she whispered. I could see tears welling up in her eyes, and I could not help but be moved by them. "I have done so much, given so much, for you already."

I bowed my head. "I will try . . . Mother."

Over the next few months I strived to forget all that I knew and become the perfect child. I dutifully went through the motions of playing with the dolls and stuffed animals she bought, holding pretend tea parties on the lawn or in the sitting room. I met other girls—insipid creatures, truly—and ran and jumped and skipped and hop-scotched with them, skinning my knees and elbows, getting dirty from mud pies, and doing all the things that six-year-olds do. One night we even had a pajama party, and Elena baked cookies and brownies all day in preparation. Seeing the joy on her face made it worth the boredom and suffering. These were the things she remembered from her own childhood, I realized, and reliving them from the role of parent made her feel young again inside, where the devil's blackness coiled around her heart.

With some surprise I realized she had become a witch to create me. Physically she could never have children of her own, I knew; she had been in an accident when she was sixteen, and the doctors had removed her womb. When she had promised her firstborn for a witch's power, she knew she had nothing to fear.

One fall evening, when the weather had grown chill, she took me aside and said we would be going to a special place.

"I know, Mother," I said. "It is All Hallow's Eve. Tonight is the Witch's Sabbath."

She dressed us both in black, and we drove downtown in her large blood-colored Cadillac. Elena's coven always rented out a large meeting hall for their meetings, and tonight was no different. As we walked to it from the parking lot, I saw half a dozen other witches strolling ahead of us, one with a huge slit-eyed Siamese cat perched on her shoulders. When the cat's yellow eyes met mine, there was a shock of mutual recognition. We were both made creatures, akin to one another.

Like a dutiful child, I took Elena's hand as we neared the meeting hall. I knew she liked little gestures like that. We went in and found seats in the large circle of folding chairs surrounding a small black altar.

The head of the coven was an old man named Patrick Smith. He wore black robes with an inverted gold crucifix around his neck, and when he saw us he came right over.

"My dear Elena," he said, "I see you've brought a guest tonight."

"This is my daughter, Korina," she said. "Korina, this is Mr. Smith."

"How do you do," I said, standing and curtsying.

"What's a charming child," he said with a smile that I

found rather too toothy and rather too quick. "May I borrow her some night?"

Before Elena could reply, I said, "That would be nice, sir, but I must warn you that I cannot be handled too roughly. I am only clay and straw and a little bit of magic."

"Ah," he said, and he seemed to lose interest. He forced another toothy smile. "We may have an important guest tonight," he said. "Do not be surprised if things run a little longer than usual."

"Of course," Elena said. "We have no other plans."

"Good, good." He moved on to greet another witch, an elderly man with only one arm.

Elena looked at me. "Thank you," she whispered.

"I only said what you would have, Mother," I replied.

Then the lights dimmed. The ceremony was about to begin. I sat in my seat, folded my hands in my lap, and gazed at the altar along with everyone else.

Beginning the black mass, Patrick Smith knelt and offered himself to the powers of darkness, and all the witches joined in chanting the final words. I had memories of countless similar ceremonies, all seen through Elena's eyes before my creation, and found nothing unusual in his actions. But when a strange sulfuric smell filled the air and a darkness gathered over our heads, I knew tonight was going to be extraordinary.

The lights suddenly went out. A red glow suffused the room. Patrick Smith had moved aside, I now saw, and in his place stood a huge hairy naked creature with the body of a man and the legs of a goat.

Slowly the creature paced around the circle of chanters, and as he drew near I found myself staring at his crotch and the wickedly barbed member that swayed between his legs at my eye level.

"Your firstborn," I heard him grunt to Elena, "by right will be mine."

"She is a golum," Elena said.

He shook his head, and every other part of him shook as well, left to right and back. I swallowed and felt Elena tense beside me. He reached out his hand and, trembling, she took it. I knew, as did she, that there could be no escape from this creature, not here, not tonight of all nights when his powers were strongest—when she had promised herself to him.

He led her to the altar, stripped off her clothes, and began pawing at her body. Elena sobbed briefly, then slumped forward and grew silent. The creature began to grunt, clawing at her back, thrusting itself forward again and again.

I felt a wave of cold rage go through me. The witches' chanting grew louder and more intense. That monstrous creature screamed in raw animal pleasure. Elena sobbed. I couldn't just watch, I thought. How could I? Elena was my mother. I felt it in my heart.

Leaping to my feet, I launched myself forward. The creature arched its neck and hissed at me, showing its wickedly forked tongue. I began pummeling it with my fists, kicking it with my feet, screaming, "Get off her! Get off her!"

Backhanded, it slapped me across the face. I flew across the room, hit the wall hard, and heard the sound of my clay head breaking.

I slumped to the floor. Through unblinking painted eyes I could only watch as the creature threw back its head and laughed.

The red glow vanished. When the lights flickered back to life, Patrick Smith moved forward to take his place before the altar. He covered my mother's body with a blanket, then picked her up. Others—I couldn't see who because I could no longer turn my head—picked up the pieces of my broken body and laid me all upon my mother's chest.

Smith carried us out to my mother's car and drove us home. I heard my mother moan once as she lay in the back seat, but she otherwise made no move. She might have been in shock. Broken, I could only slump in the front seat and stare into the dashboard.

Smith let himself into our house with my mother's key, carried us both upstairs to her bedroom and stretched us out on the bed. He made no effort to clean my mother up, though he arranged my pieces in their proper order next to her. Shaking his head, he left her covered with his blanket. I heard the front door slam and we were alone.

I tried to turn, to tell my mother how I felt, to comfort her as best I could, but of course I could do nothing. I was clay and cloth and straw once more. Even the lock of her hair had fallen out.

Sometime later, toward dawn, she stirred and opened her eyes. She seemed to be in a daze as she sat up. She pulled the blanket more closely around her shoulders and looked around in confusion.

"Korina—" she called.

Then she saw me, and I could tell she remembered. She picked me up and cradled me in her arms. The broken pieces of my head grated together.

"My poor, poor daughter," she murmured over and over, rocking me gently. "My poor, poor daughter."

Sometime later she rose, cleaned herself up, dressed in a robe, and carried me out to her workshop. There she put me back together as best she could with glue and string and wire, but I could tell I would never be the same again. That afternoon she sat me in the chair in the corner of her bedroom like a doll.

She left me there.

* * *

Without her touch, without her magic, I can feel the force of my life beginning to ebb like an outgoing tide. Each day I see and hear and understand a little less. Perhaps I have lasted so long because she made and loved me so well, or because I loved her so much.

It has been eight months now since the coven met on Halloween. My mother no longer practices magic, but the mark on her throat refuses to fade, and each morning the huge swell of her belly grows a little greater.

Her firstborn will truly be the devil's own, born of magic and evil and darkness.

I will not last long enough to see him. He is an intruder, a usurper, stealing my mother even as my life was stolen from me. Perhaps it is one last petty childishness, yet I cannot help but feel that she will never love him as she did me. And in that one small fact I find a little comfort.

# ALL SOULS'

## EDITH WHARTON

Queer and inexplicable as the business was, on the surface it appeared fairly simple—at the time, at least; but with the passing of years, and owing to there not having been a single witness of what happened except Sara Clayburn herself, the stories about it have become so exaggerated, and often so ridiculously inaccurate, that it seems necessary that some one connected with the affair, though not actually present—I repeat that when it happened my cousin was (or thought she was) quite alone in her house—should record the few facts actually known.

In those days I was often at Whitegates (as the place had always been called)—I was there, in fact, not long before, and almost immediately after, the strange happenings of those thirty-six hours. Jim Clayburn and his widow were both my cousins, and because of that, and of my intimacy with them, both families think I am more likely than anybody else to be able to get at the facts, as far as they can be called facts, and as anybody can get at them. So I have written down, as clearly as I could, the gist of the various talks I had with cousin Sara, when she could be got to talk—it wasn't often—about what occurred during that mysterious weekend.

I read the other day in a book by a fashionable essayist that ghosts went out when electric light came in. What nonsense! The writer, though he is fond of dabbling, in a literary way, in the supernatural, hasn't even reached the threshold of his subject. As between turreted castles patrolled by headless victims with clanking chains, and the comfortable suburban house with a refrigerator and central heating where you feel, as soon as you're in it, *that there's something wrong*, give me the latter for sending a chill down the spine! And, by the way, haven't you noticed that it's generally not the high-strung and imaginative who see ghosts, but the calm matter-of-fact people who don't believe in them, and are sure they wouldn't mind if they did see one? Well, that was the case with Sara Clayburn and her house. The house, in spite of its age—it was built, I believe about 1780—was open, airy, high-ceilinged, with electricity, central heating and all the modern appliances; and its mistress was—well, very much like her house. And, anyhow, this isn't exactly a ghost-story, and I've dragged in the analogy only as a way of showing you what kind of woman my cousin was, and how unlikely it would have seemed that what happened at Whitegates should have happened just there—or to her.

When Jim Clayburn died the family all thought that, as the couple had no children, his widow would give up Whitegates and move either to New York or Boston—for being of good Colonial stock, with many relatives and friends, she would have found a place ready for her in either. But Sally Clayburn seldom did what other people expected, and in this case she did exactly the contrary: she stayed at White-gates.

"What, turn my back on the old house—tear up all the family roots, and go and hang myself up in a bird-cage flat in one of those new sky-scrapers in Lexington Avenue, with a bunch of chick-weed and a cuttle-fish to replace my good Connecticut mutton? No, thank you. Here I belong, and here I stay till my executors hand the place over to Jim's next of kin—that stupid fat Presley boy. . . . Well, don't let's talk about him. But I tell you what—I'll keep him out of here as long as I can." And she did—for being still in the early fifties when her husband died, and a muscular, resolute figure of a woman, she was more than a match for the fat Presley boy, and attended his funeral a few years ago, in correct mourning, with a faint smile under her veil.

Whitegates was a pleasant hospitable-looking house, on a height overlooking the stately windings of the Connecti-cut river; but it was five or six miles from Norrington, the nearest town, and its situation would certainly have seemed remote and lonely to modern servants. Luckily, however, Sara Clayburn had inherited from her mother-in-law two or three old stand-bys who seemed as much a part of the fam-ily tradition as the roof they lived under; and I never heard of her having any trouble in her domestic arrangements.

The house, in Colonial days, had been four-square, with four spacious rooms on the ground-floor, an oak-floored hall dividing them, the usual kitchen-extension at the back, and a good attic under the roof. But Jim's grand-parents, when interest in the "Colonial" began to revive, in the early 'eighties, had added two wings, at right angles to the south front, so that the old "circle" before the front door became a grassy court, enclosed on three sides, with a big elm in the middle. Thus the house was turned into a roomy dwelling, in which the last three generations of Clayburns had exercised a large hospitality; but the architect had respected the character of the old house, and the enlargement made it more comfortable without lessening its simplicity. There was a lot of land about it, and Jim Clayburn, like his fathers before him, farmed it, not without profit, and played a considerable and respected part in state politics. The Clayburns were always spoken of as a "good influence" in the county, and the townspeople were glad when they learned that Sara did not mean to desert the place—"though it must be lonesome, winters, living all alone up there atop of that hill," they remarked as the days shortened, and the first snow began to pile up under the quadruple row of elms along the common.

Well, if I've given you a sufficiently clear idea of Whitegates and the Clayburns—who shared with their old house a sort of reassuring orderliness and dignity—I'll efface myself, and tell the tale, not in my cousin's words, for they were too confused and fragmentary, but as I built it up gradually out of her half-avowals and nervous reticences. If the thing happened at all—and I must leave you to judge of that—I think it must have happened in this way. . . .

# I

The morning had been bitter, with a driving sleet—though it was only the last day of October—but after lunch a watery sun showed for a while through banked-up woolly clouds, and tempted Sara Clayburn out. She was an energetic walker, and given, at that season, to tramping three or four miles along the valley road, and coming back by way of Shaker's wood. She had made her usual round, and was following the main drive to the house when she overtook a plainly dressed woman walking in the same direction. If the scene had not been so lonely—the way to Whitegates at the end of an autumn day was not a frequented one—Mrs. Clayburn might not have paid any attention to the woman, for she was in no way noticeable; but when she caught up with the intruder my cousin was surprised to find that she was a stranger—for the mistress of Whitegates prided herself on knowing, at least by sight, most of her country neighbours. It was almost dark, and the woman's face was hardly visible; but Mrs. Clayburn told me she recalled her as middle-aged, plain and rather pale.

Mrs. Clayburn greeted her, and then added: "You're going to the house?"

"Yes, ma'am," the woman answered, in a voice that the Connecticut valley in old days would have called "foreign," but that would have been unnoticed by ears used to the modern multiplicity of tongues. "No, I couldn't say where she came from," Sara always said. "What struck me as queer was that I didn't know her."

She asked the woman, politely, what she wanted, and the woman answered: "Only to see one of the girls." The answer was natural enough, and Mrs. Clayburn nodded and turned off from the drive to the lower part of the gardens, so that she saw no more of the visitor then or afterward. And, in fact, a half hour later something happened which put the stranger entirely out of her mind. The brisk and light-footed Mrs. Clayburn, as she approached the house, slipped on a frozen puddle, turned her ankle and lay suddenly helpless.

Price, the butler, and Agnes, the dour old Scottish maid whom Sara had inherited from her mother-in-law, of course knew exactly what to do. In no time they had their mistress stretched out on a lounge, and Dr. Selgrove had been called up from Norrington. When he arrived, he ordered Mrs. Clayburn to bed, did the necessary examining and bandaging, and shook his head over her ankle, which he feared was fractured. He thought, however, that if she would swear not to get up, or even shift the position of her leg, he could spare her the discomfort of putting it in plaster. Mrs. Clayburn agreed, the more promptly as the doctor warned her that any rash movement would prolong her immobility. Her quick imperious nature made the prospect trying, and she was annoyed with herself for having been so clumsy. But the mischief was done, and she immediately thought what an opportunity she would have for going over her accounts and catching up with her correspondence. So she settled down resignedly in her bed.

"And you won't miss much, you know, if you have to stay there a few days. It's beginning to snow, and it looks as if we were in for a good spell of it," the doctor remarked, glancing through the window as he gathered up his implements. "Well, we don't often get snow here as early as this; but winter's got to begin sometime," he concluded philosophically. At the door he stopped to add: "You don't want me to send up a nurse from Norrington? Not to nurse you, you know; there's nothing much to do till I see you again. But this is a pretty lonely place when the snow begins, and I thought maybe—"

Sara Clayburn laughed. "Lonely? With my old servants? You forget how many winters I've spent here alone with them. Two of them were with me in my mother-in-law's time."

"That's so," Dr. Selgrove agreed. "You're a good deal luckier than most people, that way. Well, let me see; this is Saturday. We'll have to let the inflammation go down before we can X-ray you. Monday morning, first thing, I'll be here with the X-ray man. If you want me sooner, call me up." And he was gone.

## II

The foot, at first, had not been very painful, but toward the small hours Mrs. Clayburn began to suffer. She was a bad patient, like most healthy and active people. Not being used to pain she did not know how to bear it; and the hours of wakefulness and immobility seemed endless. Agnes, before leaving her, had made everything as comfortable as possible. She had put a jug of lemonade within reach, and had even (Mrs. Clayburn thought it odd afterward) insisted on bringing in a tray with sandwiches and a thermos of tea. "In case you're hungry in the night, madam."

"Thank you; but I'm never hungry in the night. And I certainly shan't be tonight—only thirsty. I think I'm feverish."

"Well, there's the lemonade, madam."

"That will do. Take the other things away, please." (Sara had always hated the sight of unwanted food "messing about" in her room.)

"Very well, madam. Only you might—"

"Please take it away," Mrs. Clayburn repeated irritably.

"Very good, madam." But as Agnes went out, her mistress heard her set the tray down softly on a table behind the screen which shut off the door.

"Obstinate old goose!" she thought, rather touched by the old woman's insistence.

Sleep, once it had gone, would not return, and the long black hours moved more and more slowly. How late the dawn came in November! "If only I could move my leg," she grumbled.

She lay still and strained her ears for the first steps of the servants. Whitegates was an early house, its mistress setting the example; it would surely not be long now before one of the women came. She was tempted to ring for Agnes, but refrained. The woman had been up late, and this was Sunday morning, when the household was always allowed a little extra time. Mrs. Clayburn reflected restlessly: "I was a fool not to let her leave the tea beside the bed, as she wanted to. I wonder if I could get up and get it?" But she remembered the doctor's warning, and dared not move. Anything rather than risk prolonging her imprisonment. . . .

Ah, there was the stable-clock striking. How loud it sounded in the snowy stillness! One—two—three—four—five. . . .

What? Only five? Three hours and a quarter more before she could hope to hear the door-handle turned. . . . After a while she dozed off again, uncomfortably.

Another sound aroused her. Again the stable-clock. She listened. But the room was still in deep darkness, and only six strokes fell. . . . She thought of reciting something to put her to sleep; but she seldom read poetry, and being naturally a good sleeper, she could not remember any of the usual devices against insomnia. The whole of her leg felt like lead now. The bandages had grown terribly tight—her ankle must have swollen. . . . She lay staring at the dark windows, watching for the first glimmer of dawn. At last she saw a pale filter of daylight through the shutters. One by one the objects between the bed and the window recovered first their outline, then their bulk, and seemed to be stealthily re-grouping themselves, after goodness knows what secret displacements during the night. Who that has lived in an old house could possibly believe that the furniture in it stays still all night? Mrs. Clayburn almost fancied she saw one little slender-legged table slipping hastily back into its place.

"It knows Agnes is coming, and it's afraid," she thought whimsically. Her bad night must have made her imaginative, for such nonsense as that about the furniture had never occurred to her before. . . .

At length, after hours more, as it seemed, the stable-clock struck eight. Only another quarter of an hour. She watched the hand moving slowly across the face of the little clock beside her bed. . . . Ten minutes . . . five . . . only five! Agnes was as punctual as destiny . . . in two minutes now she would come. The two minutes passed, and she did not come. Poor Agnes—she had looked pale and tired the night before. She had overslept herself, no doubt—or perhaps she felt ill, and would send the house-maid to replace her. Mrs. Clayburn waited.

She waited half an hour; then she reached up to the bell at the head of the bed. Poor old Agnes—her mistress felt guilty about waking her. But Agnes did not appear—and after a considerable interval Mrs. Clayburn, now with a certain impatience, rang again. She rang once; twice; three times—but still no one came.

Once more she waited; then she said to herself: "There must be something wrong with the electricity." Well—she could find out by switching on the bed-lamp at her elbow (how admirably the room was equipped with each practical appliance!). She switched it on—but no light came. Electric current cut off; and it was Sunday, and nothing could be done about it till the next morning. Unless it turned out to be just a burnt-out fuse, which Price could remedy. Well, in a moment now some one would surely come to her door.

It was nine o'clock before she admitted to herself that something uncommonly strange must have happened in the house. She began to feel a nervous apprehension; but she was not the woman to encourage it. If only she had had the telephone put in her room, instead of out on the landing! She measured mentally the distance to be travelled, remembered Dr. Selgrove's admonition, and wondered if her broken ankle would carry her there. She dreaded the prospect of being put in plaster, but she had to get to the telephone, whatever happened.

She wrapped herself in her dressing-gown, found a walking stick, and resting heavily on it, dragged herself to the door. In her bedroom the careful Agnes had closed and fastened the shutters, so that it was not much lighter there than at dawn; but outside in the corridor the cold whiteness of the snowy morning seemed almost reassuring. Mysterious things—dreadful things—were associated with darkness; and here was the wholesome prosaic daylight come again to banish them. Mrs. Clayburn looked about her and listened. Silence. A deep nocturnal silence in that day-lit house, in which five people were presumably coming and going about their work. It was certainly strange. . . . She looked out of the window, hoping to see some one crossing the court or coming along the drive. But no one was in sight, and the snow seemed to have the place to itself: a quiet steady snow. It was still falling, with a business-like regularity, muffling the outer world in layers on layers of thick white velvet, and intensifying the silence within. A noiseless world—were people so sure that absence of noise was what they wanted? Let them first try a lonely country-house in a November snow-storm!

She dragged herself along the passage to the telephone. When she unhooked the receiver she noticed that her hand trembled.

She rang up the pantry—no answer. She rang again. Silence—more silence! It seemed to be piling itself up like the snow on the roof and in the gutters. Silence. How many people that she knew had any idea what silence was—and how loud it sounded when you really listened to it?

Again she waited; then she rang up "Central." No answer. She tried three times. After that she tried the pantry again. . . . The telephone was cut off, then; like the electric current. Who was at work downstairs, isolating her thus from the world? Her heart began to hammer. Luckily there was a chair near the telephone, and she sat down to recover her strength—or was it her courage?

Agnes and the housemaid slept in the nearest wing. She would certainly get as far as that when she had pulled herself together. Had she the courage—? Yes; of course she had. She had always been regarded as a plucky woman; and had so regarded herself. But this silence—

It occurred to her that by looking from the window of a neighbouring bathroom she could see the kitchen chimney. There ought to be smoke coming from it at that hour; and if there were she thought she would be less afraid to go on. She got as far as the bathroom and looking through the window saw that no smoke came from the chimney. Her sense of loneliness grew more acute. Whatever had happened below stairs must have happened before the morning's work had begun. The cook had not had time to light the fire, the other servants had not yet begun their round. She sank down on the nearest chair, struggling against her fears. What next would she discover if she carried on her investigations?

The pain in her ankle made progress difficult; but she was aware of it now only as an obstacle to haste. No matter what it cost her in physical suffering, she must find out what was happening below stairs—or had happened. But first she would go to the maid's room. And if that were empty—well, somehow she would have to get herself downstairs.

She limped along the passage, and on the way steadied herself by resting her hand on a radiator. It was stone-cold. Yet in that well-ordered house in winter the central heating, though damped down at night, was never allowed to go out, and by eight in the morning a mellow warmth pervaded the rooms. The icy chill of the pipes startled her. It was the chauffeur who looked after the heating—so he too was involved in the mystery, whatever it was, as well as the house-servants. But this only deepened the problem.

## III

At Agnes' door Mrs. Clayburn paused and knocked. She expected no answer, and there was none. She opened the door and went in. The room was dark and very cold. She went to the window and flung back the shutters; then she looked slowly around, vaguely apprehensive of what she might see. The room was empty; but what frightened her was not so much its emptiness as its air of scrupulous and undisturbed order. There was no sign of any one having lately dressed in it—or undressed the night before. And the bed had not been slept in.

Mrs. Clayburn leaned against the wall for a moment; then she crossed the floor and opened the cupboard. That was where Agnes kept her dresses; and the dresses were there, neatly hanging in a row. On the shelf above were Agnes' few and unfashionable hats, re-arrangements of her mistress' old ones. Mrs. Clayburn, who knew them all, looked at the shelf, and saw that one was missing. And so was also the warm winter coat she had given to Agnes the previous winter.

The woman was out, then; had gone out, no doubt, the night before, since the bed was unslept in, the dressing and washing appliances untouched. Agnes, who never set foot out of the house after dark, who despised the movies as much as she did the wireless, and could never be persuaded that a little innocent amusement was a necessary element in life, had deserted the house on a snowy winter night, while her mistress lay upstairs, suffering and helpless! Why had she gone, and where had she gone? When she was undressing Mrs. Clayburn the night before, taking her orders, trying to make her more comfortable, was she already planning this mysterious nocturnal escape? Or had something—the mysterious and dreadful Something for the clue of which Mrs. Clayburn was still groping—occurred later in the evening, sending the maid downstairs and out of doors into the bitter night. Perhaps one of the men at the garage—where the chauffeur and gardener lived—had been suddenly taken ill, and some one had run up to the house for Agnes. Yes—that must be the explanation. . . . Yet how much it left unexplained.

Next to Agnes' room was the linen-room; beyond that was the housemaid's door. Mrs. Clayburn went to it and knocked. "Mary!" No one answered, and she went in. The room was in the same immaculate order as her maid's, and here too the bed was unslept in, and there were no signs of dressing or undressing. The two women had no doubt gone out together—gone where?

More and more the cold unanswering silence of the house weighed down on Mrs. Clayburn. She had never thought of it as a big house, but now, in this snowy winter light, it seemed immense, and full of ominous corners around which one dared not look.

Beyond the housemaid's room were the back-stairs. It was the nearest way down, and every step that Mrs. Clayburn took was increasingly painful; but she decided to walk slowly back, the whole length of the passage, and go down by the front-stairs. She did not know why she did this; but she felt that at the moment she was past reasoning, and had better obey her instinct.

More than once she had explored the ground-floor alone in the small hours, in search of unwonted midnight noises; but now it was not the idea of noises that frightened her, but that inexorable and hostile silence, the sense that the house had retained in full daylight its nocturnal mystery, and was watching her as she was watching it; that in entering those empty orderly rooms she might be disturbing some unseen confabulation on which beings of flesh-and-blood had better not intrude.

The broad oak stairs were beautifully polished, and so slippery that she had to cling to the rail and let herself down tread by tread. And as she descended, the silence descended with her—heavier, denser, more absolute. She seemed to feel its steps just behind her, softly keeping time with hers. It had a quality she had never been aware of in any other silence, as though it were not merely an absence of sound, a thin barrier between the ear and the surging murmur of life just beyond, but an impenetrable substance made out of the world-wide cessation of all life and all movement.

Yes, that was what laid a chill on her: the feeling that there was no limit to this silence, no outer margin, nothing beyond it. By this time she had reached the foot of the stairs and was limping across the hall to the drawing-room. Whatever she found there, she was sure, would be mute and lifeless; but what would it be? The bodies of her dead servants, mown down by some homicidal maniac? And what if it were her turn next—if he were waiting for her behind the heavy curtains of the room she was about to enter? Well, she must find out—she must face whatever lay in wait. Not impelled by bravery—the last drop of courage had oozed out of her—but because anything, anything was better than to remain shut up in that snow-bound house without knowing whether she was alone in it or not. "I must find that out, I must find that out," she repeated to herself in a sort of meaningless sing-song.

The cold outer light flooded the drawing-room. The

shutters had not been closed, nor the curtains drawn. She looked about her. The room was empty, and every chair in its usual place. Her armchair was pushed up by the chimney, and the cold hearth was piled with the ashes of the fire at which she had warmed herself before starting on her ill-fated walk. Even her empty coffee cup stood on a table near the armchair. It was evident that the servants had not been in the room since she had left it the day before after luncheon. And suddenly the conviction entered into her that, as she found the drawing-room, so she would find the rest of the house: cold, orderly—and empty. She would find nothing, she would find no one. She no longer felt any dread of ordinary human dangers lurking in those dumb spaces ahead of her. She knew she was utterly alone under her own roof. She sat down to rest her aching ankle, and looked slowly about her.

There were the other rooms to be visited, and she was determined to go through them all—but she knew in advance that they would give no answer to her question. She knew it, seemingly, from the quality of the silence which enveloped her. There was no break, no thinnest crack in it anywhere. It had the cold continuity of the snow which was still falling steadily outside.

She had no idea how long she waited before nerving herself to continue her inspection. She no longer felt the pain in her ankle, but was only conscious that she must not bear her weight on it, and therefore moved very slowly, supporting herself on each piece of furniture in her path. On the ground-floor no shutter had been closed, no curtain drawn, and she progressed without difficulty from room to room: the library, her morning-room, the dining-room. In each of them, every piece of furniture was in its usual place. In the dining-room, the table had been laid for her dinner of the previous evening, and the candelabra, with candles unlit, stood reflected in the dark mahogany. She was not the kind of woman to nibble a poached egg on a tray when she was alone, but always came down to the dining-room, and had what she called a civilized meal.

The back premises remained to be visited. From the dining-room she entered the pantry, and there too everything was in irreproachable order. She opened the door and looked down the back passage with its neat linoleum floor-covering. The deep silence accompanied her; she still felt it moving watchfully at her side, as though she were its prisoner and it might throw itself upon her if she attempted to escape. She limped on toward the kitchen. That of course would be empty too, and immaculate. But she must see it.

She leaned a minute in the embrasure of a window in the passage. "It's like the *Mary Celeste—a Mary Celeste on terra firma*," she thought, recalling the unsolved sea-mystery of her childhood. "No one ever knew what happened on board the *Mary Celeste*. And perhaps no one will ever know what has happened here. Even I shan't know."

At the thought her latent fear seemed to take on a new quality. It was like an icy liquid running through every vein, and lying in a pool about her heart. She understood now that she had never before known what fear was, and that most of the people she had met had probably never known either. For this sensation was something quite different. . . .

It absorbed her so completely that she was not aware how long she remained leaning there. But suddenly a new impulse pushed her forward, and she walked on toward the scullery. She went there first because there was a service-slide in the wall, through which she might peep into the kitchen without being seen; and some indefinable instinct told her that the kitchen held the clue to the mystery. She still felt strongly that whatever had happened in the house must have its source and centre in the kitchen.

In the scullery, as she had expected, everything was clean and tidy. Whatever had happened, no one in the house appeared to have been taken by surprise; there was nowhere any sign of confusion or disorder. "It looks as if they'd known beforehand, and put everything straight," she thought. She glanced at the wall facing the door, and saw that the slide was open. And then, as she was approaching it, the silence was broken. A voice was speaking in the kitchen—a man's voice, low but emphatic, and which she had never heard before.

She stood still, cold with fear. But this fear was again a different one. Her previous terrors had been speculative, conjectural, a ghostly emanation of the surrounding silence. This was a plain every-day dread of evil-doers. Oh, God, why had she not remembered her husband's revolver, which ever since his death had lain in a drawer in her room?

She turned to retreat across the smooth slippery floor but halfway her stick slipped from her, and crashed down on the tiles. The noise seemed to echo on and on through the emptiness, and she stood still, aghast. Now that she had betrayed her presence, flight was useless. Whoever was beyond the kitchen door would be upon her in a second. . . .

But to her astonishment the voice went on speaking. It was as though neither the speaker nor his listeners had heard her. The invisible stranger spoke so low that she could not make out what he was saying, but the tone was passionately earnest, almost threatening. The next moment she realized that he was speaking in a foreign language, a language unknown to her. Once more her terror was surmounted by the urgent desire to know what was going on, so close to her yet unseen. She crept to the slide, peered cautiously through into the kitchen, and saw that it was as orderly and empty as the other rooms. But in the middle of the carefully scoured table stood a portable wireless, and the voice she heard came out of it. . . .

She must have fainted then, she supposed; at any rate she felt so weak and dizzy that her memory of what next happened remained indistinct. But in the course of time she groped her way back to the pantry, and there found a bottle of spirits—brandy or whisky, she could not remember which. She found a glass, poured herself a stiff drink, and while it was flushing through her veins, managed, she never knew with how many shuddering delays, to drag herself through the deserted ground-floor, up the stairs, and down the corridor to her own room. There, apparently, she fell across the threshold, again unconscious. . . .

When she came to, she remembered, her first care had been to lock herself in; then to recover her husband's revolver. It was not loaded, but she found some cartridges, and succeeded in loading it. Then she remembered that Agnes, on leaving her the evening before, had refused to carry away the tray with the tea and sandwiches, and she fell on them with a sudden hunger. She recalled also noticing that a flask of brandy had been put beside the thermos, and being vaguely surprised. Agnes' departure, then, had been deliberately planned, and she had known that her mistress, who never touched spirits, might have need of a stimulant before she returned. Mrs. Clayburn poured some of the brandy into her tea, and swallowed it greedily.

After that (she told me later) she remembered that she had managed to start a fire in her grate, and after warming herself, had got back into her bed, piling on it all the coverings she could find. The afternoon passed in a haze of pain, out of which there emerged now and then a dim shape of fear—the fear that she might lie there alone and untended till she died of cold, and of the terror of her solitude. For she was sure by this time that the house was empty—completely empty, from garret to cellar. She knew it was so, she could not tell why; but again she felt that it must be because of this peculiar quality of the silence—the silence which had dogged her steps wherever she went, and was now folded down on her like a pall. She was sure that the nearness of any other human being, however dumb and secret, would have made a faint crack in the texture of that silence, flawed it as a sheet of glass is flawed by a pebble thrown against it. . . .

## IV

"Is that easier?" the doctor asked, lifting himself from bending over her ankle. He shook his head disapprovingly. "Looks to me as if you'd disobeyed orders—eh? Been moving about, haven't you? And I guess Dr. Selgrove told you to keep quiet till he saw you again, didn't he?"

The speaker was a stranger, whom Mrs. Clayburn knew only by name. Her own doctor had been called away that morning to the bedside of an old patient in Baltimore, and had asked this young man, who was beginning to be known at Norrington, to replace him. The newcomer was shy, and somewhat familiar, as the shy often are, and Mrs. Clayburn decided that she did not much like him. But before she could convey this by the tone of her reply (and she was past-mistress of the shade of disapproval) she heard Agnes speaking—yes, Agnes, the same, the usual Agnes, standing behind the doctor, neat and stern-looking as ever. "Mrs. Clayburn must have got up and walked about in the night instead of ringing for me, as she'd ought to," Agnes intervened severely.

This was too much! In spite of the pain, which was now exquisite, Mrs. Clayburn laughed. "Ringing for you? How could I, with the electricity cut off?"

"The electricity cut off?" Agnes' surprise was masterly. "Why, when was it cut off?" She pressed her finger on the bell beside the bed, and the call tinkled through the quiet room. "I tried that bell before I left you last night, madam, because if there'd been anything wrong with it I'd have come and slept in the dressing-room sooner than leave you here alone."

Mrs. Clayburn lay speechless, staring up at her. "Last night? But last night I was all alone in the house."

Agnes' firm features did not alter. She folded her hands resignedly across her trim apron. "Perhaps the pain's made you a little confused, madam." She looked at the doctor, who nodded.

"The pain in your foot must have been pretty bad," he said.

"It was," Mrs. Clayburn replied. "But it was nothing to the horror of being left alone in this empty house since the day before yesterday, with the heat and the electricity cut off, and the telephone not working."

The doctor was looking at her in evident wonder. Agnes' sallow face flushed slightly, but only as if in indignation at an unjust charge. "But, madam, I made up your fire with my own hands last night—and look, it's smouldering still. I was getting ready to start it again just now, when the doctor came."

"That's so. She was down on her knees before it," the doctor corroborated.

Again Mrs. Clayburn laughed. Ingeniously as the tissue of lies was being woven about her, she felt she could still break through it. "I made up the fire myself yesterday—there was no one else to do it," she said, addressing the doctor, but keeping her eyes on her maid. "I got up twice to put on more coal, because the house was like a sepulchre. The central heating must have been out since Saturday afternoon."

At this incredible statement Agnes' face expressed only a polite distress; but the new doctor was evidently embarrassed at being drawn into an unintelligible controversy with which he had no time to deal. He said he had brought the X-ray photographer with him, but that the ankle was too much swollen to be photographed at present. He asked Mrs. Clayburn to excuse his haste, as he had all Dr. Selgrove's patients to visit besides his own, and promised to come back that evening to decide whether she could be X-rayed then, and whether, as he evidently feared, the ankle would have to be put in plaster. Then, handing his prescriptions to Agnes, he departed.

Mrs. Clayburn spent a feverish and suffering day. She did not feel well enough to carry on the discussion with Agnes; she did not ask to see the other servants. She grew drowsy, and understood that her mind was confused with fever. Agnes and the housemaid waited on her as attentively as usual, and by the time the doctor returned in the evening her temperature had fallen; but she decided not to speak of what was on her mind until Dr. Selgrove reappeared. He was to be back the following evening, and the new doctor preferred to wait for him before deciding to put the ankle in plaster—though he feared this was now inevitable.

## V

That afternoon Mrs. Clayburn had me summoned by telephone, and I arrived at Whitegates the following day. My cousin, who looked pale and nervous, merely pointed to her foot, which had been put in plaster, and thanked me for coming to keep her company. She explained that Dr. Selgrove had been taken suddenly ill in Baltimore, and would not be back for several days, but that the young man who replaced him seemed fairly competent. She made no allusion to the strange incidents I have set down, but I felt at once that she had received a shock which her accident, however painful, could not explain.

Finally, one evening, she told me the story of her strange weekend, as it had presented itself to her unusually clear and accurate mind, and as I have recorded it above. She did not tell me this till several weeks after my arrival; but she was still upstairs at the time, and obliged to divide her days between her bed and a lounge. During those endless intervening weeks, she told me, she had thought the whole matter over: and though the events of the mysterious thirty-six hours were still vivid to her, they had already lost something of their haunting terror, and she had finally decided not to re-open the question with Agnes, or to touch on it in speaking to the other servants. Dr. Selgrove's illness had been not only serious but prolonged. He had not yet returned, and it was reported that as soon as he was well enough he would go on a West Indian cruise, and not resume his practice at Norrington till the spring. Dr. Selgrove, as my cousin was perfectly aware, was the only person who could prove that thirty-six hours had elapsed between his visit and that of his successor; and the latter, a shy young man, burdened by the heavy additional practice suddenly thrown on his shoulders, told me (when I risked a little private talk with him) that in the haste of Dr. Selgrove's departure the only instructions he had given about Mrs. Clayburn were summed up in the brief memorandum: "Broken ankle. Have X-rayed."

Knowing my cousin's authoritative character, I was surprised at her decision not to speak to the servants of what had happened; but on thinking it over I concluded she was right. They were all exactly as they had been before that unexplained episode: efficient, devoted, respectful and respectable. She was dependent on them and felt at home with them, and she evidently preferred to put the whole matter out of her mind, as far as she could. She was absolutely certain that something strange had happened in her house, and I was more than ever convinced that she had received a shock which the accident of a broken ankle was not sufficient to account for; but in the end I agreed that nothing was to be gained by cross-questioning the servants or the new doctor.

I was at Whitegates off and on that winter and during the following summer, and when I went home to New York for good early in October I left my cousin in her old health and spirits. Dr. Selgrove had been ordered to Switzerland for the summer, and this further postponement of his return to his practice seemed to have put the happenings of the strange week-end out of her mind. Her life was going on as peacefully and normally as usual, and I left her without anxiety, and indeed without a thought of the mystery, which was now nearly a year old.

I was living then in a small flat in New York by myself, and I had hardly settled into it when, very late one evening—on the last day of October—I heard my bell ring. As it was my maid's evening out, and I was alone, I went to the door myself, and on the threshold, to my amazement, I saw Sara Clayburn. She was wrapped in a fur cloak, with a hat drawn down over her forehead, and a face so pale and haggard that I saw something dreadful must have happened to her. "Sara," I gasped, not knowing what I was saying, "where in the world have you come from at this hour?"

"From Whitegates. I missed the last train and came by car." She came in and sat down on the bench near the door. I saw that she could hardly stand, and sat down beside her, putting my arm about her. "For heaven's sake, tell me what's happened."

She looked at me without seeming to see me. "I telephoned to Nixon's and hired a car. It took me five hours and a quarter to get here." She looked about her. "Can you take me in for the night? I've left my luggage downstairs."

"For as many nights as you like. But you look so ill——"

She shook her head. "No; I'm not ill. I'm only frightened—deathly frightened," she repeated in a whisper.

Her voice was so strange, and the hands I was pressing between mine were so cold, that I drew her to her feet and led her straight to my little guest-room. My flat was in an old-fashioned building, not many stories high, and I was on more human terms with the staff than is possible in one of the modern Babels. I telephoned down to have my cousin's bags brought up, and meanwhile I filled a hot water bottle, warmed the bed, and got her into it as quickly as I could. I had never seen her as unquestioning and submissive, and that alarmed me even more than her pallor. She was not the woman to let herself be undressed and put to bed like a baby; but she submitted without a word, as though aware that she had reached the end of her tether.

"It's good to be here," she said in a quieter tone, as I tucked her up and smoothed the pillows. "Don't leave me yet, will you—not just yet."

"I'm not going to leave you for more than a minute— just to get you a cup of tea," I reassured her; and she lay still. I left the door open, so that she could hear me stirring about in the little pantry across the passage, and when I brought her the tea she swallowed it gratefully, and a little colour came into her face. I sat with her in silence for some time, but at last she began: "You see it's exactly a year——"

I should have preferred to have her put off till the next morning whatever she had to tell me; but I saw from her burning eyes that she was determined to rid her mind of what was burdening it, and that until she had done so it would be useless to proffer the sleeping-draught I had ready.

"A year since what?" I asked stupidly, not yet associating her precipitate arrival with the mysterious occurrences of the previous year at Whitegates.

She looked at me in surprise. "A year since I met that woman. Don't you remember—the strange woman who was coming up the drive that afternoon when I broke my ankle? I didn't think of it at the time, but it was on All Souls' eve that I met her."

"Yes," I said, "I remembered that it was."

"Well—and this is All Souls' eve, isn't it? I'm not as good as you are on Church dates, but I thought it was."

"Yes. This is All Souls' eve."

"I thought so. . . . Well, this afternoon I went out for my usual walk. I'd been writing letters, and paying bills, and didn't start till late; not till it was nearly dusk. But it was a lovely clear evening. And as I got near the gate, there was the woman coming in—the same woman . . . going toward the house. . . ."

I pressed my cousin's hand, which was hot and feverish now. "If it was dusk, could you be perfectly sure it was the same woman?" I asked.

"Oh, perfectly sure; the evening was so clear. I knew her and she knew me; and I could see she was angry at meeting me. I stopped her and asked: 'Where are you going?' just as I had asked her last year. And she said, in the same queer half-foreign voice: 'Only to see one of the girls,' as she had before. Then I felt angry all of a sudden, and I said: 'You shan't set foot in my house again. Do you hear me? I order you to leave.' And she laughed; yes, she laughed—very low, but distinctly. By that time it had got quite dark, as if a sudden storm was sweeping up over the sky, so that though she was so near me I could hardly see her. We were standing by the clump of hemlocks at the turn of the drive, and as I went up to her, furious at her impertinence, she passed behind the hemlocks, and when I followed her she wasn't there. . . . No; I swear to you she wasn't there. . . . And in the darkness I hurried back to the house, afraid that she would slip by me and get there first. And the queer thing was that as I reached the door the black cloud vanished, and there was the transparent twilight again. In the house everything seemed as usual, and the servants were busy about their work; but I couldn't get it out of my head that the woman, under the shadow of that cloud, had somehow got there before me." She paused for breath, and began again: "In the hall I stopped at the telephone and rang up Nixon, and told him to send me a car at once to go to New York, with a man he knew to drive me. And Nixon came with the car himself. . . ."

Her head sank back on the pillow, and she looked at me like a frightened child. "It was good of Nixon," she said.

"Yes; it was very good of him. But when they saw you leaving—the servants I mean. . . ."

"Yes. Well, when I got upstairs to my room I rang for Agnes. She came, looking just as cool and quiet as usual. And when I told her I was starting for New York in half an hour—I said it was on account of a sudden business call—well, then her presence of mind failed her for the first time. She forgot to look surprised, she even forgot to make an objection—and you know what an objector Agnes is. And as I watched her I could see a little secret spark of relief in her eyes, though she was so on her guard. And she just said: 'Very well, madam,' and asked me what I wanted to take with me. Just as if I were in the habit of dashing off to New York after dark on an autumn night to meet a business engagement! No, she made a mistake not to show any surprise—and not even to ask me why I didn't take my own car.

And her losing her head in that way frightened me more than anything else. For I saw she was so thankful I was going that she hardly dared speak, for fear she should betray herself, or I should change my mind."

After that Mrs. Clayburn lay a long while silent, breathing less unrestfully; and at last she closed her eyes, as though she felt more at ease now that she had spoken, and wanted to sleep. As I got up quietly to leave her, she turned her head a little and murmured: "I shall never go back to Whitegates again." Then she shut her eyes, and I saw that she was falling asleep.

I have set down above, I hope without omitting anything essential, the record of my cousin's strange experience as she told it to me. Of what happened at Whitegates that is all I can personally vouch for. The rest—and of course there is a rest—is pure conjecture, and I give it only as such.

My cousin's maid, Agnes, was from the isle of Skye, and the Hebrides, as everyone knows, are full of the supernatural—whether in the shape of ghostly presences, or the almost ghostlier sense of unseen watchers peopling the long nights of those stormy solitudes. My cousin, at any rate, always regarded Agnes as the—perhaps unconscious, at any rate irresponsible—channel through which communications from the other side of the veil reached the submissive household at Whitegates. Though Agnes had been with Mrs. Clayburn for a long time without any peculiar incident revealing this affinity with the unknown forces, the power to communicate with them may all the while have been latent in the woman, only awaiting a kindred touch; and that touch may have been given by the unknown visitor whom my cousin, two years in succession, had met coming up the drive at Whitegates on the eve of All Souls'. Certainly the date bears out my hypothesis; for I suppose that, even in this unimaginative age, a few people still remember that All Souls' eve is the night when the dead can walk—and when, by the same token, other spirits, piteous or malevolent, are also freed from the restrictions which secure the earth to the living on the other days of the year.

If the recurrence of this date is more than a coincidence—and for my part I think it is—then I take it that the strange woman who twice came up the drive at Whitegates on All Souls' eve was either a "fetch," or else, more probably, and more alarmingly, a living woman inhabited by a witch. The history of witchcraft, as is well known, abounds in such cases, and such a messenger might well have been delegated by the powers who rule in these matters to summon Agnes and her fellow-servants to a midnight "Coven" in some neighbouring solitude. To learn what happens at Covens, and the reason of the irresistible fascination they exercise over the timorous and superstitious, one need only address oneself to the immense body of literature dealing with these mysterious rites. Anyone who has once felt the faintest curiosity to assist at a Coven apparently soon finds the curiosity increase to desire, the desire to an uncontrollable longing, which, when the opportunity presents itself, breaks down all inhibitions; for those who have once taken part in a Coven will move heaven and earth to take part again.

Such is my—conjectural—explanation of the strange happenings at Whitegates. My cousin always said she could not believe that incidents which might fit into the desolate landscape of the Hebrides could occur in the cheerful and populous Connecticut valley; but if she did not believe, she at least feared—such moral paradoxes are not uncommon— and though she insisted that there must be some natural explanation of the mystery, she never returned to investigate it.

"No, no," she said with a little shiver, whenever I touched on the subject of her going back to Whitegates, "I don't want ever to risk seeing that woman again. . . ." And she never went back.

# UNCLE EVIL EYE

## CAROLE BUGGÉ

My father died quickly and cleanly in the waning days of autumn, just two months before the arrival of the year 2000. A massive neural hemorrhage took him; his brain, drowned in blood, was gone within hours. It was ironic that his own blood finally accomplished what years of alcoholism had not: as heavy as his drinking was, he remained utterly lucid and sharp until the early morning hours of a late October Tuesday, when a tiny blood vessel in his head gave way, loosening the flood of fluid that killed him. Until then, his memory, both short and long-term, remained unimpaired. True, his body was falling apart; his liver and heart were bad, he suffered from diabetes, gout, macular degeneration—you name it, he had it—but his mind remained the proverbial steel trap, sharp as the day he graduated with a Ph.D. from Harvard.

The week he died he was planning on attending a bridge tournament, where he was accruing points as a Grand Master. Bridge—let alone tournament bridge, which can be as serious and cutthroat as tournament chess—is a game requiring enormous concentration as well as keen memory, and until the moment the aneurism took him, my father had both.

My father was a mysteriously bitter man. It was as if he imbibed bitterness in the morning with his tea; it clung to him day and night, a relentless parasite of the soul. He sat at his end of the dining room table every evening, presiding over our family dinners, tearing his paper napkin into small pieces. You could always spot my father's place at the table: shreds of napkin lay in a pile to the right of his plate, a little heap of thin white strips, discarded worries.

Except that my father never could seem to rid himself of the sorrows that haunted him; even his laugh, a manic sort of giggle, had an edge of pain to it, a catch in the throat that was more like a sob. What exactly his past injuries were, or why he chose to hold onto them, no one really knew. He talked a lot about his Depression era childhood, about how he had been forced to support his family after the sudden death of his father, and the memory always seemed to fill him with bile—but I always suspected there was more, some key to his unhappiness, hidden deep within his psyche.

My mother reacted to my father's moroseness by developing a brittle shell of cheerfulness that she allowed few things to penetrate. It was a logical enough act of self-defense, though it served to polarize the family emotional life even more: my father was the gloomy one, my mother the eternal optimist, and we three children fell somewhere in the middle.

My father's repertoire as a parent may have been somewhat limited compared to my mother, but as an entertainer he could really pull out the stops. His greatest role—in fact, as I later came to believe, his alter ego—was Uncle Evil Eye, a surly one-eyed ancestor (or so he claimed) that skulked through the bedtime stories he told us like a menacing shadow, a sinister doppelgänger representing all that is dastardly and frightening to a young child. It was said that one glance from his evil eye could curse a person for life. Uncle Evil Eye played a mysterious game called Mumblety-peg, and even its name sounded sinister: *Mumblety-peg.* We didn't know how it was played, but the sound of it was deliciously scary.

Sometimes Uncle Evil Eye himself would come to us in the dead of night, circling our beds like the restless spirit he was, muttering and cackling, until finally he swooped down upon us, venting his evil spleen in the horrible manner of unquiet and tortured souls: violent, unrestrained tickling. His costuming was minimal, and consisted usually of a white bed-sheet pulled over his head so that only one eye showed—the evil one, of course.

When he became Uncle Evil Eye, it was as though all the bitterness inside my father dried up, and was replaced by the sneering but humorous persona of his ancestor; as if, in playing the part of the villain, my father liberated some part of himself that enjoyed life. Uncle Evil Eye may have been a scoundrel, but he was anything but glum. There was a gleam in my father's blue eyes when he took on the role of his alter ego. In the fiendish cackling of Uncle Evil Eye my father had found something—an expression of joie de vivre so absent from his day to day life.

Such was Uncle Evil Eye, and such was our terror of him, that our eyes lit up at the mere mention of his name. On warm summer nights when our cousins the Millers were visiting, we would sleep out in our "clubhouse"—an old shed behind our house we had cleaned up, lining the floor with a discarded carpet. My sister Katie even made curtains for the windows, and we dragged an old porch swing into the tiny backroom to serve as a bed. The front room we used as our "meeting room," and at night we lined it with army cots;

when we stuffed them in side by side we could just fit five of them.

The year I turned ten, a spell of warm weather hit north-eastern Ohio in late October, an Indian summer that coincided with a visit from the Millers. Halloween was on a Saturday that year, and we all went trick or treating together—the three Miller boys and the three Bowers girls—and then came back to spend the night in our clubhouse. It was so warm out that we hardly needed the coarse green army blankets that we had tucked neatly into our cots, and as we sat on the living floor sorting our candy, I looked through the French windows at the moon which rose ripe and full as the honeydew melons my father loved to eat for breakfast. A certain tingling in my stomach told me that this was a night for a visit from Uncle Evil Eye.

Indeed, how could he resist—it was Halloween! The harvest moon hung low over the horizon, orange and juicy as a cantaloupe. The warm air was full of the promise of fall—a rich briskness in the snap of a twig underfoot, a certain ripeness in the crisp rustle of the dead leaves piling up under the majestic red maple tree in the front lawn. If this wasn't a night for a haunting, then what was?

Tonight, however, we were ready for Uncle Evil Eye. We had spent the better part of the day rigging a special treat for him. We intended to welcome his next visit to the clubhouse with the most advanced weapons technology known to us: a bucket of water over the head. The bucket was attached to a limb of the old cherry tree which hung over the clubhouse, and the rope was strung into the main room through a narrow chimney pipe to which had once been attached a wood-burning stove. A good tug of the rope tipped the bucket from the branch upon which it rested; a second rope kept the bucket firmly attached to the branch so that only the water inside fell upon the victim below.

The Pentagon had nothing on us: we were in full control of our awesome technology, subjecting it to an extensive and grueling battery of tests. This consisted mainly of trial runs on a test subject—my cousin Donny, the youngest and therefore the most expendable member of our gang. We had Donny stand on various spots underneath the branch of the cherry tree upon which the bucket teetered precariously, filled to the brim with water, to see where the BSOI (Best Spot of Impact) was. Finally, after thoroughly drenching Donny with water many times, we determined that the BSOI was in fact right in front of the clubhouse window—a spot easily visible from inside. Could we have developed our secret weapon without the use of Donny as a guinea pig? We could. Would it have been as satisfying? It would not. Fortunately, Donny was both good-natured and gullible, and he remained convinced of the importance of the part he had played in the development of our weapon. We told no one of our plan, not even my mother: it was our secret.

Sure enough, as we prepared to go out to the clubhouse, my father alluded darkly to the possibility of an appearance from his most sinister of ancestors. His cheeks ruddy from roast beef and gin, his blue eyes crinkling with amusement, my father let us know that we might expect a visitation that evening.

"Hmm," he said, peering out at the plump round moon as we gathered on the back porch, dressed in our pajamas, blankets and pillows in our arms, ready to cross the back lawn to our clubhouse, which waited silently for us underneath the gnarled branches of the old sour cherry tree. "I wonder if it's a night for Uncle Evil Eye," he mused, almost to himself. A collective shiver passed through each of our spines. He always posed this possibility in the form of a question: *I wonder if Uncle Evil Eye will come out tonight?*

We knew then and there that he would, of course. We

lay wide awake on our army surplus cots, staring at the moon as it rose higher over the sloped roof of the big house, our toes tingling with excitement. Of course we knew that Uncle Evil Eye was actually our father disguised only in a bed-sheet thrown over his head; we knew and yet we didn't know, in that way children have of living in imaginary reality when it suits them.

The six of us were crammed into the little shack that night: me and my two sisters and the Miller boys. The Millers were all blond and sweet-natured, midwestern hayseeds with central Ohio twangs and cowlicks. Besides Cousin David and myself—both of us would turn ten in December—there was Cousin Bobby, the oldest at twelve, my sister Katie, a year younger than Bobby, my little sister Susan, who was almost seven, and Cousin Donny, the youngest at six.

We lay on our cots whispering and shivering, not from cold but out of excitement. Katie reclined on the porch swing in the tiny back room, looking very comfortable, with a book propped up on her knees. Katie was always reading; she was the intellectual in the family. I was more kinetic, restless, a fidgeter who needed always to be in motion. Finally, the suspense became too much for me and my cousin David. We threw off our scratchy green army blankets, and launched ourselves out into the night, leaving the clubhouse on a "spying" mission, a "reconnaissance maneuver," as Cousin Bobby called it, to alert the others when Uncle Evil Eye was on his way.

We stepped out into the cool air, startled by the first touch of wet grass on our bare feet. The night hugged us close; a full moon was on the rise and the air held the promise of adventure. The dew had gathered thickly not only on the lawn but upon everything: in the bright cold glow of moonlight everything glistened—the stump of the old oak tree, the swing set; even the pebbles on the driveway looked damp. I tiptoed across the lawn next to my cousin, excitement and anticipation forming a tight knot in my stomach. I heard the soft chortle of an owl in a tree somewhere above us as we approached the big house, which loomed up ahead, its white clapboards shining silver in the moonlight.

The lights blazed brightly from the living room window, and we crept up to it on our hands and knees and raised our heads high enough to peer inside. The grownups sat around the bridge table, drinks at their sides, immersed in the game. My father's piano stood in its corner, its maple veneer glistening with oil, the ivory keys white as bone. My mother was playing the bridge hand, and she leaned forward over the table, her back straight as ever, her long face composed in concentration, intent upon her task. My father stood at her shoulder watching as she snapped the cards down briskly on the table.

I couldn't hear the actual snap of the cards, but I could tell by the quickness of her movements that she had the hand sewed up; with my mother, once she started snapping the cards, you might as well throw down your hand. As she collected the tricks rapidly, I had a sudden longing to be in that room, to be sitting quietly next to my mother watching her play the hand. It was such a cozy scene, my parents and my Aunt Erma and Uncle Bob with their kind faces and soft, corn-fed bodies, and all at once I felt left out, standing here on the damp grass, the bottoms of my pajamas soggy with dew.

My cousin David's voice brought me out of my reverie.

"Look!" he whispered, gripping my shoulder.

I looked. My father was no longer in the room, and the others were leaning back in their chairs, sipping their drinks.

"He must be on his way!" David hissed, his hand tight as a claw on my shoulder.

"Okay—let's go back and tell the others," I replied, trying to sound calm, but I could feel my throat constricting from fear and excitement.

We dashed back toward the clubhouse—past the swing set, underneath the laundry line, toward the old twisted cherry tree, its branches hanging low over the roof of our clubhouse. Even these familiar objects took on a ghostly appearance, their shadows bent and misshapen in the half-light. A single lamp burned in the window of the tiny back room of the clubhouse, where my sister Katie lay on her porch swing reading. We tore open the door and burst inside.

"He's coming!" David cried breathlessly. The others looked up at us with wide eyes.

Bobby sat up in his cot. At twelve, he was the oldest, and was buck-toothed with a soft, bulky body—he looked as if he would make a perfect Lutheran minister someday. But because he was the oldest we all looked up to him.

"How do you know?" he asked.

"He's not at the bridge table," I answered.

"Maybe he went to the bathroom," Katie suggested. She was the only one who appeared unconcerned; she lay on her porch swing, a blanket over her knees, her book resting on her chest. She was beginning to grow breasts, a fact she was very proud of, and endeavored to draw attention to her chest whenever possible. She had been bra shopping earlier in the week, and wore her new bra all the time; I could see the white strap poking out from under her green flannel pajamas. I still wore the ribbed white undershirts I had always worn, and the thought of budding breasts made me shudder: to me they represented the end of childhood, a state I was not anxious to leave.

"Did you see Uncle Evil Eye?" said Susan. She was only

six, and the bridge between reality and fantasy was especially thin for her.

Cousin Donny was just a few months younger than Susan, though with his thin frame and blond hair he looked even younger. He looked up at me, his big blue eyes wide.

"Is he going to come get us?" His voice trembled a little, and I saw that he had wrapped his blanket tightly around his legs.

"I don't know," I said. "But it's Halloween, so I think so."

"Well, let me know if you see him," Katie yawned, going back to her book. I thought her air of indifference had to be feigned; she must be trying to impress us with how grownup she was. Perhaps as the oldest in our family she felt the need to rush headlong into adulthood, whereas I intended to cling to childhood as long as possible; I knew a good thing when I saw it, and I figured I had the rest of my life to be an adult.

"I'm going to hide," said Susan, "so he can't find me." With that she crawled under her cot. It was a tight fit; we had managed to cram the five canvas cots into the clubhouse, but only just barely, with no room to spare.

"Me too!" Donny chirped. He usually did whatever Susan did.

Bobby shrugged. As the oldest, he was expected to set an example, and so he could hardly crawl under his cot. Besides, Katie still reclined comfortably on her porch swing, book in hand—and she was only a girl. Bobby was required to set a standard for the rest of us, and he drew himself up with dignity.

"Well, we'll just have to wait and see what happens." His voice was unsteady, though, and a thin cold needle of fear pierced my stomach.

"Okay," I said.

Bobby took a deep breath. "Bucket ready?"

"Yep," I replied, my hand on the rope that dangled from the stove chimney. I noticed my palms were suddenly sweaty. I had been selected as the rope puller, since the whole caper was my idea in the first place. David was the "look out"—it was his job to give me the signal when Uncle Evil Eye was at the exact spot where the water would hit.

As so often happens in war, however, our best laid plans were replaced by the terror and chaos of the moment.

What happened was something like this: my cousin David was looking out the window when his face suddenly hardened into a mask of terror. His arm shot up and he pointed toward the window.

"There he is!" he cried, his voice high and shrill, then he turned from the window and abruptly dove under his bed. Katie let out a screech and covered her eyes. I looked around wildly for Bobby, but he, too, had joined the others quivering under their cots.

I was the only one left standing. Averting my face from the window—I could not bear to look—I groped blindly for the rope. As soon as I felt my fingers close around it, I pulled as hard as I could. There was the sound of the bucket falling from the tree limb, then a whoosh of water. I did not see any of this, however, because by this time I was already under my own cot.

After the whooshing sound came another sound—a kind of strangled gurgling. Through sheer dumb luck, it seemed our missile had found its target, after all. Then it occurred to me for the first time: what if Uncle Evil Eye was furious at our attack? How would he wreak his revenge? We braced ourselves. The door to the clubhouse opened slowly and we shivered in our skins—he was *here!*

There was a sloshing sound as he made his way toward us, and then we heard something that sounded like giggling.

I strained my ears to hear—yes, there was no mistaking it: my father was laughing uncontrollably. He came at us, sputtering and cackling, and dragged us from our hiding places to give us the tickling of our lives. It was like being embraced by Niagara Falls—he was soaked, his bed sheet a soggy mess. Still, he tickled us, laughing all the while. We screamed and squealed, and fought to throw off his embrace, but he held us tightly to his drenched body.

Finally, when we were all breathing heavily and Donny was beginning to hiccough, Uncle Evil Eye turned and left us as abruptly as he had arrived. We could hear him as he made his way back to the house, his high-pitched giggle trailing after him like the tail of a comet.

We would tell the story over and over at the breakfast table, in school, each with our own version; we never tired of describing how we had outsmarted the nefarious Uncle Evil Eye. My father would sit back in his chair, a partially shredded napkin between his fingers, smiling a secret smile. No one—then or since—ever referred directly to the fact that my father and Uncle Evil Eye were the same person. If we had, some of the magic would have been lost from the transformation; it would have been worse than Lois Lane suddenly realizing Superman and Clark Kent were the same person. We needed our fantasy, just as Clark Kent needed those stupid thick glasses to protect his identity.

The big house is gone now, condemned by the ever-present mercantile instinct of the American psyche, replaced by a used car lot, concrete and glass covering the land where our French windows once looked out over the broad lawn that led down to the clubhouse.

The clubhouse itself is long gone, also; only the cherry tree remains, more gnarled than ever, guarding used chevies now instead of our family. Every fall the little sour cherries still drop from its twisted branches to bounce off the roofs of the cars sitting side by side in the lot. Whenever I drive by there, which is infrequent, I remember that long ago Halloween night, lost in the mists of childhood.

I often wonder whether, as that final brain bleed took him, my father experienced his life flashing before his eyes, as so many survivors of near death experiences have reported seeing. I wonder, before he sank into the blackness that takes us all, whether he saw, if only for an instant, the events of that warm night in October when he became Uncle Evil Eye, immortal and unquiet spirit, wrestling with his laughing children, laughing himself, drenched to the skin, but laughing still, enjoying the joke even though it was at his own expense. It was, I think, Uncle Evil Eye's finest hour.

# THE PHANTOM HIGHWAYMAN

## RON GOULART

The first time they attempted to assassinate him, he had no idea why.

That was in London a few days before Halloween in October of 1899 at what had begun as a very sedate literary tea in the heart of Bloomsbury. Certainly not a place where you'd expect to be set upon by a trio of large, hooded men in formal attire and armed with sabers.

Before the case was over Harry Challenge would also have to contend with the ghost of a notorious 18th Century highwayman, a ruthless gang of espionage agents, the second cleverest criminal mastermind in all of Europe and a female equestrian with advanced ideas.

Harry was a man of middle height, lean, clean-shaven and a shade weather-beaten. He had recently turned thirty two and had little use for teas, literary or otherwise. But two days after he'd arrived in London, having successfully concluded an investigation into an outbreak of lycanthropy in a suburb of Paris, he'd received a cablegram from New York at the overpriced hotel on the Strand where his father always insisted he should stay.

*Dear Son: Quit lolling around decadent London clubs with ninnies and swells and get back to work. Attend literary tea at Lady Hammersmith's in Bloomsbury, Sat. 28 Oct., 5 PM. Client's daughter Elizabeth Beecher will contact you there. He's filthy rich and has the halfwit notion his country estate is haunted. I smell more big money for us. Your devoted father, the Challenge International Detective Agency.*

So there was Harry holding the same cup of weak tea he'd been holding for nearly a half hour and declining to avail himself of a chocolate napoleon from a passing tray. His client's daughter had yet to make an appearance at the crowded gathering and he was standing in a shadowy corner of the cluttered parlour of Lady Hammersmith's large townhouse.

A small poet in a nubby Norfolk suit was saying, "This bloody war is exactly what we Britons need to strengthen us, old man. I'm so taken up with fervour that I've already completed three stanzas of a patriotic ode I call *Take Up The Sword, Gird Up Thy Loins!*"

"I wouldn't keep that sword too close to my loins," said Harry. "What war?"

"Haven't you heard that Britain's at war with those benighted Boers in South Africa? The blighters declared war on us nearly a fortnight ago."

"Not on me," corrected Harry. "I'm from America."

"Ah, yes, you chaps are having your own little war with those benighted Spaniards in Cuba."

"Actually I'm sitting that one out, too."

The poet, wiping scone crumbs from his ample beard, eyed Harry a bit suspiciously. "You're not one of those blooming pacifists?"

"On the contrary, I'm almost insanely aggressive. Only yesterday I socked a bellicose poet for practically no reason at all."

Backing away a few steps, the poet said, "Well, old man, I've enjoyed our little—"

"Would a Mr. Harry Challenge be among those present?" inquired the thin bearded man who'd appeared in the parlour doorway.

"I'm Harry Challenge." He set his full tea cup on a small claw-footed marble-topped table.

Smiling, the thin man thrust two fingers into his mouth to produce a shrill, piercing whistle. "Here he is, my lads," he shouted. "Dispatch the bloke."

Harry was already reaching for the .38 revolver in his concealed shoulder holster. He'd decided to do that when he noticed a large portion of the man's beard falling off as he whistled.

Now he dived, gun in hand, to the Persian carpet and rolled swiftly to his left, knocking over a heavyset woman who'd earlier been introduced to him as a duchess. She went toppling onto an ottoman as Harry came up seated on the floor with his back pressing against the ornately carved leg of a candy stripe love seat.

A broad-shouldered man wearing evening clothes and a scarlet hood was pushing his way through the startled guests, brandishing a polished saber above his head. "It's all up with you, Challenge me lad," announced the man, the silken mask muffling his throaty voice some.

Harry merely grinned and shot the man in the thigh.

"I say, fellow," observed a heavyset gentleman with a substantial set of whiskers, "that's hardly sporting. I mean to say, this chap is only armed with a blade."

"He's an American," mentioned the poet to explain Harry's obvious lack of sportsmanship.

While the first hooded would-be assassin howled with pain and executed a ragged rigadoon on the stately carpet, Harry was vaulting a flowered divan.

He dodged to his right as two more similarly attired swordsmen came pushing into the now chaotic gathering.

"Oh, I say, you chaps," said the gentleman with the whiskers. "Now, I must point out, it's your side that's being far from sporting, don't you know? I mean to say, two against one is hardly cricket."

The leading assassin took a choppy swing at Harry with his saber.

He avoided that, delivering a solid punch to the man's ribs in passing. He followed that with a well-placed kick to the man's groin.

"A deucedly obvious foul," pointed out the gentleman. "Really, young sir, you must make more of an effort to fight fairly."

While the second man with a saber hopped in pain, Harry took aim at the third.

"Not bloody worth it," this one decided, spinning on his heel and shoving through the guests and into the hallway.

"Excuse me," said Harry, easing around a substantially built lady author of three-decker novels. He elbowed in the wake of the third assassin. "I really am curious to find out exactly what I did to annoy these louts."

The heavy oaken door was yanked open by the fleeing man. He went galloping down the brick steps and into the afternoon fog.

Still clutching his revolver, Harry went sprinting after him.

He was loping by a parked and driverless Hansom cab when the voice of a young woman cried out from inside it. "Please, won't someone help me?"

The thick midday fog parted and swirled as the train sped along the tracks toward Barsetshire. Elizabeth Beecher said,

"I can assure you, Mr. Challenge, that my dear father will also be forever grateful to you for your actions of yesterday afternoon."

"So you mentioned." Harry was sitting across from her in the First Class compartment they were sharing. Taking a thin cigar from his case, he lit it.

"I know I tend to repeat myself," said Elizabeth. "But that is quite simply because I'm so very much aware that had you not come along when you did, those scoundrels would have carried me off."

"You have no idea why they'd tie you up and tossed you in that cab?"

She was a slender blonde young woman of twenty four, wearing a tweed traveling suit and matching hat. Shaking her head, Elizabeth answered, "Perhaps to prevent me from consulting with you, Mr. Challenge. Or perhaps, the thought did occur to me while I lay trussed up in that vile Hansom cab and struggled desperately to loose my gag, that they might have intended to hold me for ransom. My father, as you may know, is a very wealthy man."

"My father told me, yes." Harry blew out smoke. "I think it's more likely, Miss Beecher, that this all has to do with the case your father's hired us to look into." More smoke. "They wanted to make sure you didn't talk to me and they also wanted to make absolutely certain that I'd never reach the village of Slumberleigh in Barsetshire to nose around."

The pretty young woman sighed, gloved hand idly drumming on the wicker basket that shared her seat with her. "Why, though, would a gang of masked ruffians care a fig for our ghost?"

"That's what I'll have to find out." He puffed on his stogie. "How many times did you say you've seen this phantom highwayman?"

"Possibly once." The train lurched as it rounded a bend, their compartment swayed and a bunch of fat purple grapes at the top of the basket nearly jumped free. "I've never seen the pumpkin, nor has my dear father."

Harry sat up. "Which pumpkin would that be, Miss Beecher?"

"As I say, I have never seen it myself but some of the villagers swear they have."

"Your ghost carries a pumpkin on his nocturnal rides?"

"He wears it."

Harry nodded. "Why? Some sort of Halloween prank?"

Elizabeth detached a few purple grapes. "The local legend, which absolutely no one informed us about when my father first journeyed here from Chicago and was negotiating to purchase Thorncliffe Manor, has it that a fabled highway robber who called himself the Jack-O'-Lantern plied his trade on the highway which runs from Barset to Slumberleigh and through the forest at the rear of our hundred and twenty acre estate. For some reason, possibly to frighten his victims, he wore a mask fashioned from a hollowed out pumpkin. This dashing daredevil flourished from 1705 to 1733. Then he was captured and hanged from the gibbet that used to stand near Druid's Hill."

"Don't tell me why it's known as Druid's Hill."

"Very well, Mr. Challenge, although it's merely because there's a small scale version of Stonehenge standing there."

"We have, then, a spectral highwayman who, in his heyday, chose to wear a pumpkin as a disguise," Harry said, tapping ashes off his stogie. "On top of which there's an ancient cairn where they probably used to stage human sacrifices. For good measure we also have a spot where they used to hang folks." He shook his head, grinning. "Colourful."

"This is, after all, England."

"True," he admitted.

"At any rate, Mr. Challenge, all my father wishes you to accomplish is to rid him of this ghost."

"Why exactly? I'd bet a good reliable spectre—one who's been manifesting himself as frequently as this lad has of late, according to what you've told me—would be an appealing tourist attraction. Add to the value of your property."

She smiled at him. "I quite agree with you," Elizabeth said. "Yet my father is much more conservative and, keep in mind, we're transplanted Americans and one of his major desires is to fit into the community. He feels one doesn't do that by standing out in any way." She paused to eat a few fat grapes. "Of more immediate concern is the fact that we're having a gala Halloween masquerade ball this coming Tuesday. Father is fearful that some of our two hundred invited guests will be frightened off if they hear the area is haunted. We've also been having a devil of a time hiring extra servants for the evening. The locals are a superstitious lot."

"You want this ghost exorcised no later than Tuesday, huh?"

"That would be ideal, yes. Can you do it?"

He grinned. "How many witnesses have seen your galloping highwayman thus far?"

"He apparently didn't recur until something like three weeks ago," she answered. "In that time, as far as we know, a half dozen. Of course, the accounts of the sighting have spread throughout Slumberleigh."

"Give me some details."

"The Jack-O'-Lantern usually appears near midnight on the high road, riding like fury. His steed is a powerful black stallion. Its eyes glow red and give off sparks and it exhales great clouds of smoke. At least according to those who claim to have seen it."

"Yep, that's one impressive horse."

Slightly perplexed, she watched his face for a few silent seconds. "Am I correct in assuming that you are adopting a somewhat flippant attitude toward the situation?"

"At this point I don't even know if this horse and rider are supernatural or not," he told her. "Therefore, Miss Beecher, I'm going to have to find out what exactly folks are seeing. Then I'll adopt a fitting attitude and let you know what it is."

She made a sound that came close to being a sigh. "Your agency comes highly recommended."

"With good reason," he assured her. Lowering the window on the outside door a few inches, he flipped his cigar butt out into the thick grey fog. "Who lives near you?"

"No one really," she answered. "Except the tenants who inhabit cottages on our farming land. Beyond that there's a substantial forest and then the village of Slumberleigh."

"Who's been doing all the noticing of the Jack-O'-Lantern, then?"

"Our gardener, some of the tenants and a traveling parson who was on his way to visit his sister in Slumberleigh," Elizabeth said, plucking a few more grapes. "Except for Parson Estling, who's back home in Barset again, you'll be able to question all of the witnesses. I'm sure you'll have some pertinent queries for them."

Harry leaned back in his seat. "And you have no other neighbours?"

"Well, I suppose we could count Professor Garroway and his daughter. Emily Garroway, I must say, is a very strange girl and I suspect that she's what they call a New Woman."

"Meaning what?"

"She has very advanced ideas, so I hear, and was actually seen in the village once smoking a cigarette. I've never had a conversation with her, but the rumour is that she advocates suffrage for women." Emily shook her head. "An idea such as that borders on the radical, in my opinion."

"Where do this radical and her father live?"

"In a place known as the Spectral Horseman Inn just off the high road to the village. A ramshackle, sprawling place, it was converted to a private residence in '87, I believe," she said. "Professor Garroway is said to be working on perfecting a horseless carriage. He has a small crew of workmen and the stables and out buildings have been converted to workshops. His daughter, who is an artist of some sort, also aids him in his work."

"This professor wouldn't be *Albert* Garroway, would he?"

"Yes, I believe that is his first name. Are you acquainted with—"

"He's the man who invented the Garroway Machine Gun," said Harry. "It was used by the British in the Zulu Wars. I doubt he's working on something as harmless as an automobile."

"Then what do you suspect the professor and his daughter are actually up to, Mr. Challenge?"

Harry shrugged his left shoulder. "That's one more thing I'll have to find out."

The magician appeared while the train was still more than an hour away from the Slumberleigh station. He tapped on the corridor door and, not waiting for an invitation, stepped into their compartment. He was a portly fellow, wrapped in a dark cloak and sporting an impressive top hat. "Ah, Harry, I had a strong hunch I'd find you here," he said. "I've come to warn you that—"

"Why, it's Mr. Lorenzo," exclaimed Elizabeth. "I had no notion that you were traveling on this selfsame train."

"I'm known as the Great Lorenzo," he corrected, smiling as he plucked a bouquet of yellow roses out of the air and handed them to the young women. "Now then, Harry my lad, as I was about to say, I've come to warn you that—"

"We've hired the Great Lorenzo to stage his famous magic show at our masked ball on Tuesday," Elizabeth explained to Harry.

"*World famous* magic show," the Great Lorenzo corrected. "Harry, as you know, while I make no claim to possessing true magical powers, I have on past occasions, when our paths have crossed in many of the glittering capitals of Europe, had visions and premonitions that have helped you pull your chestnuts out of the fire on more than one occasion."

"That you have, Lorenzo." Harry half stood, shaking hands with the plump magician. "Sit down and tell me about your latest premonition. Judging from the pained expression, it must be a real doozie."

Bowing toward Elizabeth, the Great Lorenzo placed her basket on the compartment floor and sat opposite Harry. "These portents of the future, as you well know, Harry, do not always reach me in crystal clear form. This afternoon, whilst I was sharing a magnum of rather inferior Ruritanian champagne with a slightly overweight ballerina who's traveling to Barsetshire to—"

"The premonition, Lorenzo."

"To be sure, although I always think colourful details add to the impact of a narrative." The magician fluffed his substantial greying sideburns. "In the vision I was suddenly visited with, I saw two men clad in tailcoats and crimson hoods attacking you with—"

"Only two?"

"It seems to me, my boy, that even two huge masked

blackguards waving sabers constitute a sufficient threat." The Great Lorenzo sounded a bit miffed.

Grinning, Harry held up his left hand in a placating gesture. "Sounds to me like you're going to have to fine tune your premonitions," he said. "Those hooded louts attacked me yesterday afternoon in London. And there were three of them, not two. I appreciate your warning, Lorenzo, but it's about a day late."

"Those same men also attempted to abduct me," added the young woman. "Had not Mr. Challenge routed them and noticed me in the Hansom cab where they—"

"Hush, my child," advised the magician.

"I'm not accustomed to being hushed by a person whom we've hired to—"

"Someone's walking on the roof of this car," amplified Lorenzo, pointing a gloved thumb at the ceiling.

Harry heard the thumping now. He stood, reaching toward his shoulder holster.

Outside their compartment and from above, a large man in a tailcoat and scarlet hood came swinging. His booted feet hit the door, slamming it open. He came stumbling into the compartment. He clutched a saber in his right fist. "Death has caught up with you, Challenge," he cried, lunging.

Harry shot him in the thigh. "Not just yet."

The unsuccessful assassin staggered back, teetered on the threshold, then fell out through the open doorway. He yelled as he went sailing through the swirling afternoon mist and then slammed onto the slanting hillside beyond the tracks.

Still clutching his revolver, Harry eyed the flapping door. "Two, you said, Lorenzo?"

The magician held up two fingers. "A pair, yes."

There was a skittering from above, thunking and then a

second man appeared. This one was upside down, however, dangling from a thick strand of greasy rope that was tangled around his ankle. There was no sign of his saber.

"Where's your weapon?" inquired Harry, watching the big masked man swing to and fro.

"I'm terribly chagrined, governor," admitted the dangling man. "The blasted thing went flying when I took a header off the bloody roof. I've never been all that fond of rail travel."

"I could pull you inside," suggested Harry.

"I'd be much obliged."

"Thing is, I'd first have to know what all this foolishness is about," Harry explained. "Who hired you lads and why?"

"That's a bit rum of you, sir," said the swaying assassin. "Granted that mine isn't an especially noble profession, still it has a certain code attached. Even though I'm not a gentleman, still I have ethics and. . . . Yow!"

The rope that had held him suddenly uncoiled, releasing the man.

He plummeted down, fell away from the train and was lost in the surrounding fog.

"Damn it," said Harry. "That's five of these bastards I haven't been able to question."

"I feel partially responsible for your inability to question the initial three," apologized Elizabeth. "Had you not stopped to untie me and—"

"Do you sense any more of these guys?" he asked the Great Lorenzo.

Lorenzo stroked his plump chin. "No, Harry, that's the last of them," he said. "However, my boy, I have a feeling that worse things are coming."

As the brougham that met them at the station and traveled along a narrow back lane neared the high stone walls that surrounded Thorncliffe Manor, Elizabeth said, her voice taking on a slightly apologetic tone, "It would be most thoughtful if neither of you mentioned pigs in my father's presence during your stay."

"Pigs?" Harry was sitting next to her.

"Does the old boy have some porcine bugaboo?" inquired the Great Lorenzo from his side of the carriage.

"Father is trying very hard to fit into British society," she explained, "and has an unreasoning, in my view, dread that the way he amassed his vast wealth is not quite . . . well, gentlemanly."

Harry said, "Then your father is the Pork King? The man behind Beecher's Southern-Baked Ham, Beecher's Country Pork Sausage and Beecher's Bottled Pickled Pigs' Feet?"

A bit forlornly, she nodded. "I fear he is," she answered. "I, in all the American yellow journals, am known as the Pork Heiress. That has been, I assure you, a considerable burden."

"One can well imagine, my dear." Lorenzo plucked a single daffodil out of the air and passed it to the girl. "You have our solemn promise that such words as pig, pork, pork chop, ham, ham hock and related terms shall not pass our lips while we dwell under your roof or—"

"Actually, Mr. Lorenzo, you won't be dwelling under our roof," Elizabeth corrected. "Father is putting the entertainers up in the old carriage house."

"Other entertainers? I was given to believe that the Great Lorenzo's International Magical Show would be the only entertainment offered at your gala costume extravaganza this—"

"Father decided to add the Costermongers' Music Hall Brass Band and a fellow who juggles," she told him. "Then, of course, your assistants will also be sharing those quarters."

"I see."

The carriage turned in at the open gateway and the roan horse went trotting along a wide, white gravel drive that led to a vast Tudor style mansion a quarter of a mile away and blurred by mist. On each side of the drive rose rows of stately pines and to the rear of the house showed part of a terraced formal garden.

A middle-aged couple materialized out of the mist on the roadway ahead. They were dressed in servants' livery, each carrying a fat suitcase.

"Oh, dear, it's the Folletts," said Elizabeth. Leaning out the window, she called to the carriage driver. "Emerson, will you halt the brougham for a moment, please."

"Yes, miss." The horse was reigned up and the carriage rattled to a stop.

"I'll just step out, Mr. Challenge, and see if I can persuade them to stay on—at least until after the masquerade."

"What's the problem?" Harry asked, following her out into the misty twilight.

"I imagine they've got the wind up about the ghost rider." She gathered up her long skirt and ran toward the resigning couple. "Mr. and Mrs. Follett, I do hope you don't intend to desert us in our hour of need. We depend on you as head cook and first butler to—"

"It's no go, miss," said Follett, a lean pale man. "The missus has made up her mind."

"Begging your pardon, miss," said the plump Mrs. Follett, "but we can't stay on at Thorncliffe Manor."

"The rumours of a ghost in the vicinity are greatly—"

"That's just it," the cook said. "A haunted *house* we can abide and have on prior jobs, but the fact that this particular spectre is in the *vicinity* and nobody can tell where he's likely to pop up is simply too much to bear. He might attack Alf while he was strolling to the pub of an evening or assault me when I was sunning myself in the garden."

"I sympathize with you, Mrs. Follett, yet—"

"Come along, Edwin," said the plump cook, "we've got a train to—"

"I'll give you two pounds a month more," called a deep, chesty voice.

A wide, heavyset man had come running up from the direction of the mansion. He was in his fifties, dressed in a tweedy jacket and knickerbockers. His face was flushed, he was wheezing slightly.

"It's no use, sir," said Follett, touching the peak of his cap. "She's fair made up her mind."

"And so have you, Edwin." His wife took hold of his arm with her free hand and tugged him off along the drive.

"Damn it all," said Beecher, watching them disappear into the mist. "We've already got fifty guests staying with us, with more to come, and no darned cook."

The Great Lorenzo stepped out of the brougham. "Let me point out, sir, that besides being a magician and illusionist of world renown, I am also a cordon bleu chef."

Beecher smiled. "Would you be willing to help out in this crisis?"

"Most gladly," said the magician. "Although I'm afraid it will be difficult to do from the carriage house."

"We'll put you up in the main house," promised Beecher, eyeing him hopefully.

The great Lorenzo bowed toward him. "Then I accept the offer," he said. "You'll hardly notice the additional fee."

After dinner, forty of Wallace Beecher's earliest-arriving guests gathered in the conservatory to listen to Elizabeth play the spinet piano and sing.

While she was rendering a sad ballad about an orphan lost in the snow, the Great Lorenzo made his way over to where Harry was standing, arms folded, near a potted banana palm.

"Do you have a magical cure for heartburn?" Harry asked him.

"The meal was excellent and any internal problems you happen to be experiencing are due to your devil-may-care manner of living," the magician assured him in a lowered voice. "What I want to ask you, my boy, is if you're involved in more than simply ghost hunting on this particular assignment."

"I think I must be," he answered. "Especially since Albert Garroway seems to be connected somehow."

Nodding, Lorenzo said, "That accounts for the person who was introduced to us as Lady Beresford."

Harry grinned. "Yep, that's Rowland Fleetway of the British Secret Service," he confirmed. "The man fancies himself a master of disguise."

"Three of the other guests strike me as somewhat less than legitimate," continued Lorenzo. "Guy Chumley is one. I doubt that anyone can really be as much a silly ass as he pretends."

"Chumley can," said Harry. "I met him in Antwerp a couple years ago. He's the heir to the Chumley's Excellent Elixir fortune and an authentic ninny. You can write him off."

"What's your opinion of Gabriel Litwin, supposed poet?"

"I'm not sure, Lorenzo. He's the same poet I met at Lady Hammersmith's tea party."

"The one where you were set upon by saber wavers?"

"That very same tea party, yeah."

Lorenzo tugged at his left sideburn. "I also sense that there may be something amiss about Sebastian Tree, alleged painter and member of the Royal Academy."

"Sebastian Tree is a respected landscape painter with a

rising reputation," said Harry. "This fellow, however, isn't really Sebastian Tree."

When the ancient grandfather clock in the second floor corridor of the left wing of the mansion struck a quarter past eleven, Harry very carefully eased open the door of his bedroom. The guests had all long since turned in and the house was quiet. A single gas bracket lamp burned dimly, pushing back the night shadows a bit.

Harry was wearing dark trousers, a dark sweater and a dark knit cap. He carried a bull's eye lantern, unlit, and his revolver was tucked into his waistband.

Cautiously he moved along the thickly carpeted hall toward the back stairs.

Earlier he'd talked to the gardener and collected a somewhat vague account of his brief nocturnal account with the ghostly horseman. Harry also obtained a detailed hand-drawn map of the exact location where the gardener had sighted the spectre a few nights earlier.

The mist was gone and a quarter moon showed in the clear, black sky.

Harry made his way up through the hedges, flower beds and marble statues of the large formal garden, then entered the thick woodlands that climbed to the roadway where the highwayman had been appearing.

His pocket watch showed him it was fifteen minutes shy of midnight when he reached the edge of the woods and saw the wide dirt road beyond.

He took a deep breath, set the unlit lantern on the ground and leaned back against a tree trunk.

Night birds called in the branches above, small unseen animals skittered over dry leaves.

A faint thumping commenced to his right.

The sound grew gradually louder, became a pounding gallop sound.

There was also now chugging and chuffing.

Edging nearer to the road, crouching behind a spiky cluster of brush, he looked in the direction of the growing noise.

He saw red sparks first, then billows of white steam. Out of that came galloping a large black stallion. On its back sat a slim figure wearing a billowing cape and some sort of mask.

"That's made of cloth," Harry concluded, "and not a true and authentic pumpkin."

The great horse and the rider were now about a hundred yards from where he was crouching.

Suddenly came a rasping twang. The huge steam-spouting horse tripped. Clanking and sputtering, it fell toward the moonlit road. The rider, who wasn't using a saddle, was thrown free.

The horse slammed into the road, legs going out from under it, producing a loud metallic clang.

The cloaked rider, meantime, had fallen into the brush on the other side of the roadway and remained sprawled there, moaning, not moving.

Quickly lighting the lantern with a wax match, Harry grabbed it up and sprinted over to the fallen figure.

Steaming water and glowing machine oil was spilling out of the toppled mechanical horse. He saw now that what had felled animal was a wire stretched across the road.

Harry dodged around the equine automaton and reached the side of the fallen rider.

He knelt. "You conscious?" he inquired.

"Go away." It was a young woman's voice.

"Not just yet, Miss Garroway." Placing the lantern on the road, he lifted the jack-o'-lantern mask from her face.

She was slim and dark-haired, not more than twenty five. "How the devil do you know my name?"

"Here's a more important question. Are you hurt?"

"No, I'm perfectly fine." Ignoring his proffered hand, Emily Garroway sat up. "Now answer my question."

"Anyone testing a mechanical horse in the vicinity of the Garroway homestead," he told her, "I figure must be a Garroway."

"You know my father?" She rubbed at her right ankle, wincing.

"Only by reputation. By unsavoury reputation, that is."

"He's not responsible for what mean-minded people do with his inventions. Although I have succeeded in persuading him to work on no more inventions that can be converted to bellicose uses."

"And yonder horse isn't intended to end up serving in the Boer War."

"Of course not, that's ridiculous." She made an attempt to rise, winced again. "It goes against my principles, but I'm going to have to ask you to help me to stand."

"Ankle sprained?"

"Merely twisted, I believe."

Bending, he slipped an arm around her waist and aided her in rising. "Will somebody from home come looking for you eventually?"

"Yes." Hobbling slightly, she walked over to the defunct mechanical horse. "I hope Dobbin III is not seriously damaged. He's the most advanced model my father's come up with thus far." She shook her head. "I don't understand what caused him to malfunction and fall."

"There's a metal wire stretched across the road."

She inhaled sharply. "That must mean someone was lying in wait for us."

"It does, which is a good reason to get you away from here as soon as—"

"We'll see to that." A tall, dapper man emerged from the

woods nearby, holding a hunting rifle cradled in his arms.

It was the man who wasn't Sebastian Tree.

Beyond the clearing at Druids' Hill rose steeply slanting hills, thick with brush and trees. The clearing itself had once held a circle of huge standing stones, but long centuries ago several had fallen and the circle was broken. The tallest of the nine megaliths still standing rose a good fifteen feet above the scrubby ground.

As Harry and Emily were urged across the moonlit clearing, he noticed writing in what he assumed was runic script had been cut into the bases of several of the huge and heavy sandstone pillars.

The fellow who wasn't Sebastian Tree was behind them, rifle in hand. He had two burly men with him, both clad in peacoats and dungarees and armed with pistols.

Looking back over his shoulder, Harry asked, "You planning to sacrifice us to a few pagan gods?"

"Nothing so picturesque, old man," answered the man with the rifle. "Being a humane sort at heart, I intend merely to detain you until we haul the working model of the Garroway Steam Combat Horse away and sell it to a certain foreign power."

"Weren't those humane louts who made two tries to kill me in your employ?"

"When I learned that you were heading here I decided you must be prevented from getting in my way," he admitted. "So perhaps I'm not as humane as I was just pretending to be. Keep that in mind."

"My father intends his steam horse for peaceful, basically agricultural purposes," insisted the girl. "Warmongers such as you are always trying to convert technological innovations to bellicose ends."

"Not I, Miss Garroway, but rather my client," he replied. "They intend to use the Dobbinses, each mounted with a

Garroway Machine Gun, on the field of battle, that's true."

"But my father intended them for—"

"He intends the British to use them against the Boers, dear lady."

"That's complete and utter nonsense. He's come around to my way of thinking about—"

"The old boy has hoodwinked you." Their captor laughed. "I've seen copies of the original communications between him and the British government." He laughed his nasal laugh once again.

Harry halted, turned to face him. "That laugh," he said, frowning. "Yeah, I heard it a year ago in Vienna when I was investigating the theft of the Rasmussen Torpedo plans. You were disguised then, but I later learned I'd been up against none other than Dr. Grimshaw, the second cleverest criminal mastermind in Europe."

Grimshaw sighed and smiled ruefully. "If it weren't for that blasted Professor Moriarty, I'd be right at the top of the list," he said. "Move along now, Challenge, I intend to lock you and the naïve Miss Garroway in the cave that we've renovated yonder. My colleagues and I will then transport the—"

"Woe betide thee!" boomed a deep and unearthly voice all at once. "Who dares desecrate the sacred temple of the mystical Druidic order?"

A white robed, hooded figure, fully seven feet tall, had stepped forth from behind the tallest stone column. His gloved hands were raised high and he was muttering now in what sounded like an ancient tongue.

Sudden blue lightning began crackling around the ancient stones. Thunder boomed and pungent yellow smoke commenced spewing up from a dozen spots.

"What the devil is this?" said Dr. Grimshaw, turning to stare at the robed Druid.

Harry dropped toward the sward, turning in midair and booting Grimshaw.

He connected with the mastermind's knee. The doctor cried out, went staggering back into his two associates.

Harry hit the ground, bounced up and tackled Dr. Grimshaw. He levered the rifle out of his grasp, jumped upright and pointed the weapon at the fallen mastermind.

Emily meantime had slugged one of the armed men, wrested his gun away from him and had it aimed at the other man's midsection.

"The ancient gods find themselves satisfied," announced the robed figure, swaying and then tipping over. "Drat it, I have never quite mastered the fine art of stilt-walking."

From out of the tangle of white cloth, the Great Lorenzo emerged. After dusting himself off, he bowed in their direction.

Harry grinned at him. "Another vision?"

"Nothing so arcane, my boy. I simply followed you when you went skulking away from Thorncliffe Manor."

"What about the fire and brimstone?" asked Emily.

"It is actually, my child, a modification of my Famous Egyptian Mystery Illusion, which has delighted and entertained the crowned heads of Europe, and a great number of uncrowned groundlings. I thought it might be useful in causing a diversion."

Harry said, "Then you must have had at least a small premonition."

Lorenzo admitted, "I did see you and a fetching young lady being sacrificed at a location much like this one."

"You're a very clever gentleman," said Emily.

"I am indeed," he agreed. "You have no doubt heard of me. I am the Great Lorenzo."

She shook her head. "Never, no," she answered. "I have no interest in the world of entertainment."

Harry asked, "Did you bring any rope in your bag of tricks, Lorenzo?"

"I did, yes."

"We'll tie these fellows up, escort them back to the manor house and turn them over to Rowland Fleetway of Her Majesty's Secret Service."

The young woman asked, "Why is there a Secret Service agent at Thorncliffe?"

"Because, as Dr. Grimshaw suggested, your father's steam horse is actually considered a weapon of war and the British Empire is keeping an eye on him," answered Harry. "Although he didn't do a very good job, Fleetway was supposed to prevent the likes of Dr. Grimshaw from swiping the horse or the plans for it."

Grimshaw laughed yet again. "Eventually, Challenge, I'll succeed. I usually do."

"Not often enough to cinch the number one position, though."

Emily gave a sad shake of her pretty head. "I'm terribly disillusioned. It seems evident that once again my father has fallen back on his word to me."

While he and Lorenzo trussed up the doctor and his henchmen, Harry asked her, "Why exactly did you wear that pumpkin mask?"

"We wanted to test the Dobbins automatons on a stretch of open road, rather than just on our compound grounds," she replied. "It was my idea that if I appeared as the ghostly Jack-O'-Lantern of local legend, any of the country people who might chance to see us would take me for a spirit and not someone testing a secret invention."

"Such a simpleminded ruse would hardly fool me," said the now rope-wrapped Dr. Grimshaw.

Moving closer to Harry, the young woman said, "I believe I'll return to London tomorrow and resume my life there, leaving my duplicitous father to fend for himself. Perhaps we can travel together, Mr. Challenge."

"Oh, you know who I am."

"This scoundrel's been dropping your name. Besides, I've read several accounts of your detective activities in the press in recent years," she said. "You seem, for all your rough edges, a man of principle."

"I am, relatively speaking," he admitted. "I wasn't planning to take my leave until after the masquerade ball. Although I'm not especially fond of such festivities, I want to attend Lorenzo's magic show."

"A pity, since I was hoping you'd be on my train tomorrow," Emily told him. "I realize this is not a conventional thing to say, Mr. Challenge, but I find you a very interesting man."

Lorenzo said, "Harry my lad, your devotion to my humble efforts is laudable. Keep in mind, however, that you've seen all the illusions I have planned for the Halloween gala performance before. Twice in some instances."

"You wouldn't be eternally chagrined if I accompany Miss Garroway to London tomorrow?"

"Not at all," the magician assured him. "Magic is important, but no substitute for romance."

# THE UNNAMABLE

## H.P. LOVECRAFT

We were sitting on a dilapidated seventeenth-century tomb in the late afternoon of an autumn day at the old burying ground in Arkham, and speculating about the unnamable. Looking toward the giant willow in the cemetery, whose trunk had nearly engulfed an ancient, illegible slab, I had made a fantastic remark about the spectral and unmentionable nourishment which the colossal roots must be sucking from that hoary, charnel earth; when my friend chided me for such nonsense and told me that since no interments had occurred there for over a century, nothing could possibly exist to nourish the tree in other than an ordinary manner. Besides, he added, my constant talk about "unnamable" and "unmentionable" things was a very puerile device, quite in keeping with my lowly standing as an author. I was too fond of ending my stories with sights or sounds which paralyzed my heroes' faculties and left them without courage, words, or associations to tell what they had experienced. We know things, he said, only through our five senses or our religious intuitions; wherefore it is quite impossible to refer to any object or spectacle which cannot be clearly depicted by the solid definitions of fact or the correct doctrines of theology—preferably those of the Congregationalists, with whatever modifications tradition and Sir Arthur Conan Doyle may supply.

With this friend, Joel Manton, I had often languidly disputed. He was principal of the East High School, born and bred in Boston and sharing New England's self-satisfied deafness to the delicate overtones of life. It was his view that only our normal, objective experiences possess any esthetic significance, and that it is the province of the artist not so much to rouse strong emotion by action, ecstasy, and astonishment, as to maintain a placid interest and appreciation by accurate, detailed transcripts of everyday affairs. Especially did he object to my preoccupation with the mystical and the unexplained; for although believing in the supernatural much more fully than I, he would not admit that it is sufficiently commonplace for literary treatment. That a mind can find its greatest pleasure in escapes from the daily treadmill, and in original and dramatic re-combinations of images usually thrown by habit and fatigue into the hackneyed patterns of actual existence, was something virtually incredible to his clear, practical, and logical intellect. With him all things and feelings had fixed dimensions, properties, causes, and effects; and although he vaguely knew that the mind sometimes holds visions and sensations of far less geometrical, classifiable, and workable nature, he believed himself justified in drawing an arbitrary line and ruling out of court all that cannot be experienced and understood by the average citizen. Besides, he was almost sure that nothing can be really "unnamable." It didn't sound sensible to him.

Though I well realized the futility of imaginative and metaphysical arguments against the complacency of an orthodox sun-dweller, something in the scene of this afternoon colloquy moved me to more than usual contentiousness. The crumbling slate slabs, the patriarchal trees, and the centuried gambrel roofs of the witch-haunted old town that stretched around, all combined to rouse my spirit in defense of my work; and I was soon carrying my thrusts into the enemy's own country. It was not, indeed, difficult to begin a counter-attack, for I knew that Joel Manton actually half clung to many old-wives' superstitions which sophisticated people had long outgrown; beliefs in the appearance of dying persons at distant places, and in the impressions left by old faces on the windows through which they had gazed all their lives. To credit these whisperings of rural grandmothers, I now insisted, argued a faith in the existence of spectral substances on the earth apart from and subsequent to their material counterparts. It argued a capability of believing in phenomena beyond all normal notions; for if a dead man can transmit his visible or tangible image half across the world, or down the stretch of the centuries, how can it be absurd to suppose that deserted houses are full of queer sentient things, or that old graveyards teem with the terrible, unbodied intelligence of generations? And since spirit, in order to cause all the manifestations attributed to it, cannot be limited by any of the laws of matter, why is it extravagant to imagine psychically living dead things in shapes—or absences of shapes—which must for human spectators be utterly and appallingly "unnamable"? "Common sense" in reflecting on these subjects, I assured my friend with some warmth, is merely a stupid absence of imagination and mental flexibility.

Twilight had now approached, but neither of us felt any wish to cease speaking. Manton seemed unimpressed by my arguments, and eager to refute them, having that confidence in his own opinions which had doubtless caused his success as a teacher; whilst I was too sure of my ground to fear defeat. The dusk fell, and lights faintly gleamed in some of the distant windows, but we did not move. Our seat on the tomb was very comfortable, and I knew that my prosaic friend would not mind the cavernous rift in the ancient, root-disturbed brickwork close behind us, or the utter blackness of the spot brought by the intervention of a tottering, deserted seventeenth-century house between us and the nearest lighted road. There in the dark, upon that riven tomb by the deserted house, we talked on about the "unnamable," and after my friend had finished his scoffing I told him of the awful evidence behind the story at which he had scoffed the most.

My tale had been called *The Attic Window*, and appeared in the January, 1922, issue of *Whispers*. In a good many places, especially the South and the Pacific coast, they took the magazines off the stands at the complaints of silly milksops; but New England didn't get the thrill and merely shrugged its shoulders at my extravagance. The thing, it was averred, was biologically impossible to start with; merely another of those crazy country mutterings which Cotton Mather had been gullible enough to dump into his chaotic *Magnalia Christi Americana*, and so poorly authenticated that even he had not ventured to name the locality where the horror occurred. And as to the way I amplified the bare jotting of the old mystic—that was quite impossible, and characteristic of a flighty and notional scribbler! Mather had indeed told of the thing as being born, but nobody but a cheap sensationalist would think of having it grow up, look into people's windows at night, and be hidden in the attic of a house, in flesh and in spirit, till someone saw it at the window centuries later and couldn't describe what it was that turned his hair gray. All this was flagrant trashiness, and my friend Manton was not slow to insist on that fact. Then I told him what I had found in an old diary kept between 1706 and 1723, unearthed among family papers not a mile from where we were sitting; that, and the certain reality of the scars on my ancestor's chest and back which the diary described. I told him, too, of the fears of others in that region, and how they were whispered down for generations; and how no mythical madness came to the boy who in 1793 entered an abandoned house to examine certain traces suspected to be there.

It had been an eldritch thing—no wonder sensitive students shudder at the Puritan age in Massachusetts. So little is known of what went on beneath the surface—so little, yet such a ghastly festering as it bubbles up putrescently in occasional ghoulish glimpses. The witchcraft terror is a horrible ray of light on what was stewing in men's crushed brains, but even that is a trifle. There was no beauty: no freedom—we can see that from the architectural and household remains, and the poisonous sermons of the cramped divines. And inside that rusted iron straitjacket lurked gibbering hideousness, perversion, and diabolism. Here, truly, was the apotheosis of the unnamable.

Cotton Mather, in that demoniac sixth book which no one should read after dark, minced no words as he flung forth his anathema. Stern as a Jewish prophet, and laconically unamazed as none since his day could be, he told of the beast that had brought forth what was more than beast but less than man—the thing with the blemished eye—and of the screaming drunken wretch that they hanged for having such an eye. This much he baldly told, yet without a hint of what came after. Perhaps he did not know, or perhaps he knew and did not dare to tell. Others knew, but did not dare to tell—there is no public hint of why they whispered about the lock on the door to the attic stairs in the house of a childless, broken, embittered old man who had put up a blank slate slab by an avoided grave, although one may trace enough evasive legends to curdle the thinnest blood.

It is all in that ancestral diary I found; all the hushed innuendoes and furtive tales of things with a blemished eye seen at windows in the night or in deserted meadows near the woods. Something had caught my ancestor on a dark valley road, leaving him with marks of horns on his chest and of apelike claws on his back; and when they looked for prints in the trampled dust they found the mixed marks of split hooves and vaguely anthropoid paws. Once a post-rider said he saw an old man chasing and calling to a frightful loping, nameless thing on Meadow Hill in the thinly moonlit hours before dawn, and many believed him. Certainly, there was strange talk one night in 1710 when the childless, broken old man was buried in the crypt behind his own house in sight of the blank slate slab. They never unlocked that attic door, but left the whole house as it was, dreaded and deserted. When noises came from it, they whispered and shivered; and hoped that the lock on that attic door was strong. Then they stopped hoping when the horror occurred at the parsonage, leaving not a soul alive or in one piece. With the years the legends take on a spectral character—I suppose the thing, if it was a living thing, must have died. The memory had lingered hideously—all the more hideous because it was so secret.

During this narration my friend Manton had become very silent, and I saw that my words had impressed him. He did not laugh as I paused, but asked quite seriously about the boy who went mad in 1793, and who had presumably been the hero of my fiction. I told him why the boy had gone to that shunned, deserted house, and remarked that he ought to be interested, since he believed that windows retained latent images of those who had sat at them. The boy had gone to look at the windows of that horrible attic, because of tales of things seen behind them, and had come back screaming maniacally.

Manton remained thoughtful as I said this, but gradually reverted to his analytical mood. He granted for the sake of argument that some unnatural monster had really existed, but reminded me that even the most morbid perversion of nature need not be *unnamable* or scientifically indescribable. I admired his clearness and persistence, and added some further revelations I had collected among the old people. Those later spectral legends, I made plain, related to monstrous apparitions more frightful than anything organic could be; apparitions of gigantic bestial forms sometimes visible and sometimes only tangible, which floated about on moonless nights and haunted the old house, the crypt behind it, and the grave where a sapling had sprouted beside an illegible slab. Whether or not such apparitions had ever gored or smothered people to death, as told in uncorroborated traditions, they had produced a strong and consistent impression; and were yet darkly feared by very aged natives, though largely forgotten by the last two generations—perhaps dying for lack of being thought about. Moreover, so far as esthetic theory was involved, if the psychic emanations of human creatures be grotesque distortions, what coherent representation could express or portray so gibbous and infamous a nebulosity as the specter of a malign, chaotic perversion, itself a morbid blasphemy against nature? Molded by the dead brain of a hybrid nightmare, would not such a vaporous terror constitute in all loathsome truth the exquisitely, the shriekingly *unnamable?*

The hour must now have grown very late. A singularly noiseless bat brushed by me, and I believe it touched Manton also, for although I could not see him I felt him raise his arm. Presently he spoke.

"But is that house with the attic window still standing and deserted?"

"Yes," I answered. "I have seen it."

"And did you find anything there—in the attic or anywhere else?"

"There were some bones up under the eaves. They may have been what that boy saw—if he was sensitive he wouldn't have needed anything in the window-glass to unhinge him. If they all came from the same object it must have been an hysterical, delirious monstrosity. It would have been blasphemous to leave such bones in the world, so I went back with a sack and took them to the tomb behind the house. There was an opening where I could dump them in. Don't think I was a fool—you ought to have seen that skull. It had four-inch horns, but a face and jaw something like yours and mine."

At last I could feel a real shiver run through Manton, who had moved very near. But his curiosity was undeterred.

"And what about the window-panes?"

"They were all gone. One window had lost its entire frame, and in all the others there was not a trace of glass in the little diamond apertures. They were that kind—the old lattice windows that went out of use before 1700. I don't believe they've had any glass for a hundred years or more—maybe the boy broke 'em if he got that far; the legend doesn't say."

Manton was reflecting again.

"I'd like to see that house, Carter. Where is it? Glass or no glass, I must explore it a little. And the tomb where you put those bones, and the other grave without an inscription—the whole thing must be a bit terrible."

"You did see it—until it got dark."

My friend was more wrought upon than I had suspected, for at this touch of harmless theatricalism he started neurotically away from me and actually cried out with a sort of gulping gasp which released a strain of previous repression. It was an odd cry, and all the more terrible because it was answered. For as it was still echoing, I heard a creaking sound through the pitchy blackness, and knew that a lattice window was opening in that accursed old house beside us. And because all the other frames were long since fallen, I knew that it was the grisly glassless frame of that demoniac attic window.

Then came a noxious rush of noisome, frigid air from that same dreaded direction, followed by a piercing shriek just beside me on that shocking rifted tomb of man and monster. In another instant I was knocked from my grue-some bench by the devilish threshing of some unseen entity of titanic size but undetermined nature; knocked sprawling on the root-clutched mold of that abhorrent graveyard, while from the tomb came such a stifled uproar of gasping and whirring that my fancy peopled the rayless gloom with Miltonic legions of the misshapen damned. There was a vor-tex of withering, ice-cold wind, and then the rattle of loose bricks and plaster; but I had mercifully fainted before I could learn what it meant.

Manton, though smaller than I, is more resilient; for we opened our eyes at almost the same instant, despite his greater injuries. Our couches were side by side, and we knew in a few seconds that we were in St. Mary's Hospital. Atten-dants were grouped about in tense curiosity, eager to aid our memory by telling us how we came there, and we soon heard of the farmer who had found us at noon in a lonely field beyond Meadow Hill, a mile from the old burying ground, on a spot where an ancient slaughterhouse is reputed to have stood. Manton had two malignant wounds in the chest, and some less severe cuts or gougings in the back. I was not so seriously hurt, but was covered with welts and contusions of the most bewildering character, including the print of a split hoof. It was plain that Manton knew more than I, but he told nothing to the puzzled and interested physicians till he had learned what our injuries were. Then he said we were the victims of a vicious bull—though the animal was a difficult thing to place and account for.

After the doctors and nurses had left, I whispered an awestruck question:

"Good God, Manton, but *what was it? Those scars—was it like that?"*

And I was too dazed to exult when he whispered back a thing I had half expected—

"No—*it wasn't that way at all.* It was everywhere—a gelatin—a slime—yet it had shapes, a thousand shapes of horror beyond all memory. There were eyes—and a blemish. It was the pit—the maelstrom—the ultimate abomination. Carter, *it was the unnamable!"*

# THE HALLOWEEN MAN

## WILLIAM F. NOLAN

O h, Katie believed in him for sure, the Halloween Man. Him with his long skinny-spindley arms and sharp-toothed mouth and eyes sunk deep in skull sockets like softly glowing embers, charcoal red. Him with his long coat of tatters, smelling of tombstones and grave dirt. All spider-hairy he was, the Halloween Man.

"You made him up!" said Jan the first time Katie told her about him. Jan was nine, a year younger than Katie, but she could run faster and jump higher. "He isn't real."

"Is so," said Katie.

"Is not."

"Is."

"*Isn't!*"

Jan slapped Katie. Hard. Hard enough to make her eyes sting.

"You're just mean," Jan declared. "Going around telling lies and scaring people."

"It's true," said Katie, trying not to cry. "He's real and he could be coming here on Halloween night—right to this town. This could be the year he comes here."

The town was Center City, a small farming community in the Missouri heartland, brightened by fire-colored October trees, with a high courthouse clock (Little Ben) to chime the hour, with plowed fields to the east and a sweep of sun-glittered lake to the west.

A neat little jewel of a town by day. By night, when the big oaks and maples bulked dark and the oozy lakewater was tar-black and brooding, Center City could be spooky for a ten-year-old who believed in demons.

Especially on Halloween night.

All month at school, all through October, Katie had been thinking about the Halloween Man, about what Todd Pepper had told her about him. Todd was very mature and very wise. And a lot older, too. Todd was thirteen. He came from a really big city, Indianapolis, and knew a lot of things that only big-city kids know. He was visiting his grandparents for the summer (old Mr. and Mrs. Willard) and Katie met him in the town library late in August when he was looking through a book on demons.

They got to talking, and Katie asked him if he'd ever seen a demon. He had narrow features with squinty eyes and a crooked grin that tucked up the left side of his face.

"Sure, I seen one," said Todd Pepper. "The old Halloween Man, I seen him. Wears a big pissy-smelling hat and carries a bag over one shoulder, like Santa. But he's got no toys in it, no sir. Not in *that* bag!"

"What's he got in it?"

"Souls. That's what he collects. Human souls."

Katie swallowed. "Where . . . where does he get them from?"

"From kids. Little kids. On Halloween night."

They were sitting at one of the big wooden library tables, and now he leaned across it, getting his narrow face closer to hers. "That's the only time you'll see him. It's the only night he's got *power*." And he gave her his crooked grin. "He comes slidin' along, in his rotty tattered coat, like a big scarecrow come alive, with those glowy red eyes of his, and the bag all ready. Steppin' along the sidewalk in the dark easy as you please, the old Halloween Man."

"How does he do it?" Katie wanted to know. "How does he get a kid's soul?"

"Puts his big hairy hands on both sides of the kid's head and gives it a terrible shake. Out pops the soul, like a cork out of a bottle. Bingo! And into the sack it goes."

Katie felt hot and excited. And shaky-scared. But she couldn't stop asking questions. "What does he do with all the kids' souls after he's collected them?"

Another crooked grin. "*Eats* 'em," said Todd. "They're his food for the year. Then, come Halloween, he gets hungry again and slinks out to collect a new batch—like a squirrel collecting nuts for the winter."

"And you—you saw him? Really *saw* him?"

"Sure did. The old Halloween Man, he chased me once when I was your age. In Havershim, Texas. Little bitty town, like this one. He *likes* small towns."

"How come?"

"Nowhere for kids to hide in a small town. Everything out in the open. He stays clear of the big cities."

Katie shifted on her chair. She bit her lower lip. "Did he catch you—that time in Texas?"

"No sir, not me." Todd squinched his eyes. "If he had of, I'd be dead—with my soul in his bag."

"How'd you get away?"

"Outran him. He was pretty quick, ran like a big lizard

he did, but I was quicker. Once I got shut of him, I hid out. Till after midnight. That's when he loses his power. After midnight he's just *gone*—like a puff of smoke."

"Well, *I've* never seen him, I know," said Katie softly. "I'd remember if I'd seen him."

"You bet," said Todd Pepper, nodding vigorously. "But then, he isn't always so easy to spot."

"What'da mean?"

"Magical, that old Halloween Man is. Can take over people. Big people, I mean. Just climbs right inside 'em, like steppin' into another room. One step, and he's inside lookin' out."

"Then how can you tell if it's *him*?" Katie asked.

"Can't," said Todd Pepper. "Not till he jumps at you. But if you're lookin' sharp for him, and you *know* he's around, then you can kind of spot him by instinct."

"What's that?"

"It's like an animal's got in the jungle when a hunter is after him. The animal gets an instinct about the hunter and knows when to run. It's that way with the ole Halloween Man—you can sort of sniff him out when you're sharp enough. He can't fool you then. Not if you're really concentrating. Then your instinct takes over."

"Is there a picture of him in that book?"

Todd riffled the pages casually. "Nope. No kid's ever lived long enough to take a picture of the Halloween Man. But I've described him to you—and unless he climbs inside somebody you'll be able to spot him easy."

"Thanks," said Katie. "I appreciate that." She looked pensive. "But maybe he'll never come to Center City."

"Maybe not." Todd shut the book of demons with a snap. "Then again, you never know. Like I said, he favors small towns. If you want my opinion, I'd say he's overdue in this one."

\* \* \*

And that was the only talk she'd had with Todd Pepper. At summer's end he went back to Indianapolis, to school, and Katie was left in Center City with a head full of new thoughts. About the Halloween Man.

And then it was October, with the leaves blowing orange and yellow and red-gold over her shoes when she walked to school, and the lake getting colder and darker off beyond the trees, and the gusting wind tugging at her coat and fingering her hair. Sometimes it rained, a chill October drizzle that gave the streets a wet-cat shine and made the sodden leaves stick to her clothes like dead skin.

Katie had never liked October, but *this* year was the worst, knowing about the Halloween Man, knowing that he could come walking through her town come Halloween night, with his grimy soul-bag over one shoulder and his red-coal eyes penetrating the dark.

Through the whole past week at school that was all Katie could think about and Miss Prentiss, her teacher, finally sent Katie home. With a note to her father that read:

Katie is not her normal self. She is listless and inattentive in class. She does not respond to lessons, nor will she answer questions related to them. She has not been completing her homework. Since Katie is one of our brightest children, I suggest you have her examined for possible illness.

"Are you sick, sugar?" her father had asked her. Her mother was dead and had been for as long as Katie could remember.

"I don't think so," Katie had replied. "But I feel kind of funny. I'll be all right after Halloween. I want to stay home from school till after Halloween."

Her father had been puzzled by this attitude. She had

always loved Halloween. It had been her favorite holiday. Out Trick-or-Treating soon as it got dark with her best friend Jan. Now Jan never called the house any more. Katie's father wondered why.

"I don't like her," Katie declared firmly. "She slapped me."

"Hey, that's not nice," said Katie's father. "Why did she do that?"

"She said I lied to her."

"About what?"

"I can't tell you." Katie looked down at her hands.

"Why not, sugar?"

"Cuz."

"Cuz why?"

"Cuz it's something too scary to talk about."

"Are you sure you can't tell your ole Daddy?"

She looked up at him. "Maybe after Halloween. *Then* I'll tell you."

"Okay, it'a deal. Halloween's just a few days off. So I guess I won't have long to wait."

And he smiled, ruffling her hair.

And now it was Halloween day and when it got dark it would be Halloween night.

Katie had a sure feeling that *this* year he'd show up in Center City. Somehow, she knew this would be the year.

That afternoon Katie moved through the town square in a kind of dazed fever. Her father had sent her downtown for some groceries and she had taken a long time getting them. It was so hard to remember what he wanted her to bring home. She had to keep checking the list in her purse. She just couldn't keep her mind on shopping.

Jan was on the street outside when Katie left Mr. Hakin's grocery store. They glared at each other.

"Do you take back what you said?" asked Jan, sullen and pouting. "About that awful, smelly man."

"No, I don't," said Katie. Her lips were tight.

"You lied!"

"I told the *truth*," declared Katie. "But you're just scared to believe it. If you try to slap me again, I'll kick your shins!"

Jan stepped back. "You're just the *meanest* person I know!"

"Listen, you'd better stay home tonight," warned Katie. "I mean it. If you don't want the Halloween Man to pop your soul and eat it."

Jan blinked at this but said nothing.

"I figure he'll be out tonight," nodded Katie. "He's *due*."

"You're crazy! I'm going Trick-or-Treating, like always."

"Well, don't say I didn't warn you," Katie told her. "When he grabs you, just remember what I said."

"I *hate* you!" Jan cried, and turned away.

Katie started home.

It was later than she thought. Katie had spent so much time shopping she'd lost track of the day. It had just slipped past.

Now it was almost dark.

God!

*Almost dark.*

The brightness had drained from the sky, and the westering sun was buried in thick-massed clouds. A thin rain was beginning to dampen the streets.

Katie shifted the heavy bag of groceries and began to walk faster. Only two miles and she'd be home. Just twenty blocks.

A rising wind had joined the rain, driving wet leaves against her face, whipping her coat.

Not many kids will be going out tonight, Katie thought.

Not in this kind of weather. Which meant lean pickings for the Halloween Man. If he shows up there won't be many souls to bag. Meaning he'll grab any kid he finds on the street. No pick and choose for him.

I'm all right, Katie told herself. I've still got time to make it home before it gets really dark . . .

But the clouds were thickening rapidly, drawing a heavy grey blanket across the sky.

It *was* getting dark.

Katie hurried. An orange fell from the top of the rain-damp sack, plopped to the walk. Katie stopped to pick it up.

And saw him.

Coming along the walk under the blowing trees, tall and skeleton-gaunt, with his rotted coat flapping in tatters around his stick-thin legs, and with his sack slung over one bony shoulder. The red of his deep-sunk eyes burned under a big wide-brimmed slouch hat.

He saw Katie.

The Halloween Man smiled.

She whirled around with an insucked cry, the soggy paper sack ripping, slipping from her fingers, the groceries tumbling to the sidewalk, cans rolling, split milk cartons spitting white foam across the dark concrete.

Katie ran.

Not looking back, heart triphammering her chest, she flung her body forward in strangled panic.

Where? Where to go? He was between her and home; she'd have to go back into the heart of town, run across the square and try to reach her house by another route.

But could she run that far? Jan was the runner; *she* could do it, she was faster and stronger. Already Katie felt a rising weakness in her legs. Terror was constricting her muscles, numbing her reflexes.

He could run like a lizard. That's what Todd had said, and lizards are fast. She didn't want to look back, didn't want to turn to see him, but she had to know how much distance she'd put between them. *Where was he?*

With a low moan, Katie swung her head around. And suddenly stopped running.

He was gone.

The long wet street stretched empty behind her, char black at its far end—just the wind-lashed trees, the gusting leaves, the blowing curtain of rain silvering the dark pavement. There was no sign of the Halloween Man.

He'd outfoxed her. He'd guessed her intention about doubling back and had cut across the square ahead of her. And he'd done the final demon-clever thing to trap her. He'd climbed inside.

But inside *who?* And *where?*

Concentrate, she told herself. Remember what Todd Pepper said about trusting your instinct. Oh, I'll know him when I see him!

Now Katie was in the middle of the town square. No matter which route she took home she had to pass several stores and shops—and he could be waiting in any doorway, ready to pounce.

She drew a long, shuddering breath, steeling herself for survival. Her head ached; she felt dizzy, but she was prepared to run.

Then, suddenly, horribly, a hand tugged at her shoulder!

Katie flinched like a dog under the whip, looked up in dry-mouthed terror—into the calm, smiling face of Dr. Peter Osgood.

"Your father tells me you've been ill, young lady," he said in his smooth doctor's voice. "Just step into my office and we'll find out what's wrong."

*Step into my parlor said the spider to the fly.*

Katie backed away from him. "No . . . no. Nothing's wrong. I'm fine."

"Your face looks flushed. You may have a touch of fever, Katie. Now, I really think we should—"

"Get away from me!" she screamed. "I'm not going any-where with you. I know who you are—you're *him*!"

And she broke into a pounding run.

Past Mr. Thurtle's candy shop: *Him*, waving from the window at her, with his red eyes shining . . .

Past the drug store: *Him*, standing at the door inside Mr. Joergens, smiling with his sharp shark's teeth. "In a big rush today, Katie?"

Yes, away from *you*! A big rush.

Across the street on the red light. *Him*, in a dirty Ford pickup, jamming on the brakes, poking his head out the window: "Watch where you're running, you little bitch!"

Oh, she knew the Halloween Man.

When Katie reached her house, on Oakvale, she fell to her knees on the cold wooden porch, gasping, eyes full of tears, ears ringing. Her head felt like a balloon about to burst, and she was hot and woozy and sick to her stomach.

But she was safe. She'd made it; he hadn't caught her.

Katie stood up shakily, got the door open and crossed the living room to the big rose sofa, dropped into it with a heavy, exhausted sigh.

Outside, a car pulled to the curb. She could see it through the window. A dark blue Chevy! *Dr. Osgood's car!*

"No!" screamed Katie, running back to the front door and throwing the bolt.

Her father came downstairs, looking confused. "What's wrong, sugar?"

Katie faced him, panting, her back tight against the

bolted door. "We can't let him in. He's gonna steal my soul!"

"It's just Dr. Osgood, Kate. I asked him to drop by and see you."

"No, it *isn't*, Daddy. He's not Dr. Osgood. He's *him!*"

"Him?"

"The Halloween Man. He can get into big people's bodies. And he's inside Dr. Osgood right now."

Her father smiled gently, then moved to unlock the door. "I think you've been watching too many scary movies. You don't have to be afraid of—"

But Katie didn't wait for him to finish. She rushed up the stairs, ran to her room at the end of the hall, hurried inside, and slammed the door.

Panic. There was no lock on her door, no way to keep him out. She ran to the bed, jumping under the covers the way she used to do when she was little and things scared her in the dark.

Below, muted sounds of greeting. Male voices. Daddy talking to *him.*

Then footsteps.

Coming up the stairs.

Katie leaped from the bed in a sudden frenzy, toppled over the tall wooden bookcase near her closet, dragged it over against the door. *It probably won't hold him, but . . .*

A rapping at the door. Rap-rap-rap. Rap-rap-rap.

"Katie!"

"Go way!" she yelled.

"Katie, open the door." It was Daddy's voice.

"No. You've got him with you. I know he's right there with you."

"Go to the window," her father told her. "See for yourself."

She ran across the room, stumbling over spilled books, and looked out. Dr. Osgood was just driving away through the misting rain in his blue Chevy.

Which meant that her *father* could now be—

He pushed the door open.

Katie swung around to face him. "Oh, no!" She was trembling. "It's true! Now *you're* him!"

Katie's father reached out, put a big hand on each side on her face. "Happy Halloween, sugar!" he said.

And gave her head a terrible shake.

# A MATTER
# OF TASTE

## PARKE GODWIN

**M**ediocrity lives in a crowded house. Perfection dwells alone. For Addison Solebury, life was lonely at the top. Even in the upper reaches of gastronomy his tastes were so lofty that no restaurant in the world could hope for his continued custom. In the main, he prepared his own meals, a process of considerable labor and research that only added zest to anticipation, feasts so rarefied in their reflection of taste that few could share, let alone cater them.

His standards were arcane but not inflexible. On an off night he could squeak by with properly aged filet mignon and vin ordinaire, but for the most part, Solebury's antipathy to the ordinary was visceral and had been all his life. He turned even paler than normal at the sight of margarine, fled a block out of his way to avoid the effluvium of pizza, and often woke whimpering from nightmares of canned tomato soup.

Food—his ecstatic, almost sexual vision of it—was an art he could not see coarsened; therefore, integrity exacted its price. The absence of sharing, of a woman, was the minor mode of Solebury's male lament. After all, not even the nightingale sang for the hell of it, but Solebury, through overspecialization, labored and dined for the most part alone. Time and again, he girded himself and went woman hunting, but with his intolerance of the mundane, his quest was akin to a majestic elk bugling for a mate in the city pound.

For most city singles, Christmas is the loneliest time; for Addison, despair set in like indigestion in mid-October and peaked perversely on Halloween, which day fate had chosen to bring him into the coarse-feeding world. He had spent too many lonely birthdays.

Many were called, none were chosen. He despaired of finding a woman of similar refinement. Even those for whom Solebury had the highest hopes revealed a gullet of clay. His fragile expectations would inevitably dampen as she attacked her salad, flickered as she swallowed garlic escarole with vulgar relish, guttered with the entree, and died over brandy and cheese. Failure upon failure, until the coming of Pristine Solent.

From the fast tentative conversation in the library reference room where he worked, Solebury felt right about Pristine. When he peered over her shoulder, he found her scanning just those sources he ferreted out in his pursuit of perfection. An exploratory dinner was even more promising. Craftily, he suggested the Four Seasons and was heartened when Pristine answered her door in sensible clothes rather than the coronation gown an ordinary woman might have worn for the occasion. Clothes were not important. The key, the subtle clue to the unerring rightness of his choice was in the way Pristine addressed herself to food. Looks counted for something, to be sure. Pristine was short and robust, with a pale but infinitely well-nourished complexion, a square face with faintly critical brows, and a wide, ready smile that displayed 90 percent of her perfect teeth. For his own appearance, she seemed tacitly to approve of him; pallid as herself with a clear skin, perhaps a small roll of flesh around his fortyish middle that only attested to many years of choosy but ample diet.

But her address to the food—ah, that was exquisite. Her fork balanced in a firm hand, Pristine studied the entree, turned it this way and that in the manner of an inquisitive coroner, then, resigned that the chef could come no closer to her ideals, speared, chewed, and reluctantly swallowed. Solebury's lips parted in silent admiration. He dared to hope.

"The best is none too good, is it?" he winked at her, then applied the test. Would she join him soon in a dinner of his own preparation? "I'm something of an expert on dining. In a small way."

"Small way" was the code phrase that separated cognoscenti from the uninitiated. He was instantly gratified.

"Why don't we?" Pristine touched her white hand to his, strong fingers curving intimately to touch his callused palm. She wrinkled her upturned nose at him. "It sounds memorable."

Solebury leaned forward and their eyes met over the forgotten trout almandine. "I think it could be. You know what it means to meet someone you can truly share with?"

"Yes, yes. I know." Pristine stroked the back of his slightly trembling hand. "So seldom. So rare. And *just* the right time of year."

A bubble of happiness swelled in Solebury's chest. "You're very beautiful."

"I feel beautiful tonight," said Pristine Solent.

They got out of the taxi a few blocks before her apartment, not wanting the evening to end, holding hands, heads close together. Solebury kissed her with clumsy ardor at her outside door. Pristine swayed into him, then threw back her head to the night sky with a little mew of contentment.

"What an evening. Oh, Addison, I hope there'll be a moon next time. I'm so damned romantic about these things. And a moon is part of it."

"It is. So important." Solebury positively quivered with joy.

"And what is a romantic dinner without moonlight?" Pristine squeezed his hand. "G'night."

If there was a sidewalk under him, Solebury didn't feel it. He floated to the corner and let three cabs approach, slow tentatively, and pass on before remembering he wanted one.

Like Lancelot, Solebury's love quest lay through great deeds. Such a dinner could not be conjured for the next evening or even within a week. Pristine would consider that careless. This called for his full mastery. Since the bone of genius is discipline, Solebury went back to basics, to research.

His own office, the library reference room, was his usual start. All the dailies were searched, torrents of fine print skimmed for the form of his menu. All professionals had their secrets; Solebury's lay in his insistence on a slightly pungent spice overlooked by all but a few masters and not commonly used for centuries. Only one establishment, Whittaker's, still used it in their prepared seasonings. Just a tiny dollop, but to Solebury it was sine qua non, adding an overtaste delicate as it was incomparable.

At length his entree was found. In a rising fever of concentration, Solebury turned his attention to the treacherous but crucial matter of wine.

Only a tyro considered geriatric vintages automatically best. Like any living thing, the grape had its youth, prime and declining age. Of recent years he gave serious consideration to only one: '92 of course—but '92 what? Even within the confines dictated by a white-meat entree, there were nuances of choice. Some masters—and Pristine could well be one—preferred a demi-sec where he would choose a drier variety. A blunder here, one false step, could shadow Pristine's judgment. She'd be kind, but Solebury would feel a door closing behind her charity, and successive evenings would find her otherwise engaged.

He let instinct guide him, recalling a champagne he'd chosen not two months back, a superb Chardonnay brut. His usual shop produced one remaining bottle at a larcenous price, but Solebury's heart sang as he hurried home. He knew all this was preamble, part of the labor of love. A great deal of delving remained.

One more choice awaited him: the time, more of a gamble than all the rest. Pristine wanted a moon, but though Solebury scanned the paper and the skies, one promised nothing and the other remained perversely overcast. At last came an evening when the early autumn moon entered like a diva from a proscenium of fleecy cumulus clouds. Solebury turned from his window and reached for the phone, at once stabbed to the heart and uplifted by Pristine's throaty greeting.

"Hello, Addison. I was just thinking about you."

He choked on his ecstasy. "You were?"

"Must be ESP. I was looking at the moon and thinking tonight might be—"

"Yes. Perfect. That's why I called. You wanted a romantic moon. Shall we dine? Something very special?"

"In a small way. Love to," Pristine whispered over the wire. "I'm famished for something special. If not Christmas, at least it's Halloween."

A world of promise throbbed in her honeyed contralto.

Solebury always dined late. Pristine was not surprised by the hour or the address, neither that fashionable.

"It's a perfect time, Addison. I'm never hungry much earlier than that. I'll be there."

Solebury hung up in a soft rush of joy. Here was a mate for all reasons.

Humming with busy pleasure, Solebury twirled the '92 down into the waiting ice. Even now, before Pristine arrived, there was spadework. He miscalculated slightly and was only half ready with final preparations when she appeared. If her first dinner costume had been sensible, her clothing tonight was downright utilitarian—jeans and boots and a windbreaker against the cool. She gave Solebury a cheerful little peck and surveyed his labors.

"Can I help?" she asked politely.

"Oh no, really. There's just a little further—"

"No, let me. You've already worked so hard."

It flattered Solebury to see Pristine pitch in. She was very sturdy, but no dining of this caliber was ever accomplished without hard physical labor. At length Pristine paused, wiping her brow with the back of one white hand, and drew the champagne from its bucket to browse the label with admiration.

"Lovely year, Addison." She turned again briefly to the last shovel work, then stepped aside for her host. "You'll want to open up and carve."

"Of course. You are a dear, Pristine." Descending into the grave, Solebury wielded his implement with a practiced economy of movement. Three deft snaps with the crowbar broke the casket seals. With a gustatory flourish, he threw it open for her approval.

"Bon appetite, darling."

He hovered, waiting under the October moon for the sunbeam of her approval, but he saw only a frown of disappointment.

"Beautifully aged," he assayed against her silence. "Buried Thursday."

Pristine sat down on the freshly turned earth. "Oh, Addison. Oh, dear . . ."

"What—what's wrong?"

"Everything!" she wailed.

He felt a premonitory chill. "But he's perfect. Buried from Whittaker's last Thursday. I use them exclusively, the only undertakers who still use myrrh in their preparation. You must know that."

Pristine's disappointment turned brittle. "Of course I know that. There is Whittaker's and only Whittaker's. But as you see, the entree is hardly Caucasian."

True, the entree was decidedly dark. There was no mention of that in the obituary. He'd assumed white meat; a minor variant and trivial. Solebury vaulted out of the grave to sit facing Pristine like a teacher. "Pristine, it doesn't really matter. Expertise is one thing, ivory tower another."

"Doesn't matter?" Pristine corrected him like an errant child. "Surely you know non-Caucasian flesh doesn't take the myrrh flavor well at all. It cancels it out."

"I beg to disagree." Solebury's pride was at stake, and she was dead wrong. "A difference, yes. A subtle piquance, if you will, but hardly canceled."

"Even if that were true," Pristine countered in a voice cool as the churchyard dark, "it completely negates champagne."

Solebury began to feel a bit waspish despite himself. "Oh, really! The principle is the same as dark meat on fowl. I took days choosing that champagne. I am not an amateur."

But her pretty head wagged back and forth through his protestations. "Cold Duck, Mister Solebury. Nothing else."

He went falsetto at the sacrilege. "Cold Duck? It's so bloody common!"

"But," Pristine riposted with a raised forefinger, "the uncommon choice." Her assertiveness quavered and broke. "I'm sorry, Addison, but I—"

"Oh, please, Pristine. I worked so hard."

"I know, but it's all so wrong."

"Please stay. I adore you."

"Oh, go to hell. Go to McDonald's—no. No, please, dear Addison, I didn't mean that. That was filthy. Just—" Her voice caught and shattered on a sob. "Just that I was looking for someone to share with. It's so lonely being the best. And I thought you . . ."

"I am, Pristine, darling. We could share so much."

"No, not with differences as wide as these. Don't say anything, just goodbye. I'm leaving. I won't look back. Don't call me. Oh, my dear Addison. You were so close to perfection."

Solebury choked out something in farewell and admission of his sins, following Pristine with eyes of tragedy as she receded forlornly through the cemetery gate. He slumped down on the turned earth, working without relish at the champagne cork. The pop was hollow as his hopes.

"So close to perfection," she had said. All right. He raised the glass to his better, though it cost him a love to learn. Life was still lonely near the top. The moon went down and the wind before dawn was desolate.

He could barely pick at supper.

# THE
# BANSHEE'S COMB

HERMINIE TEMPLETON
KAVANAGH

The story is told in dialect because, according to the author, *"These adventures were first related to me by Mr. Jerry Murtaugh, a reliable car-driver, who goes between Kilcuny and Ballinderg. He is a first cousin of Darby O'Gill's own mother."*

# CHAPTER I

## THE DIPLOMACY OF BRIDGET

### I

Twas the mendin' of clothes that All Sowls' afthernoon in Elizabeth Ann Egan's kitchen that naturally brought up the subject of husbands an' the best ways to manage them. An' if there's one thing more than another that makes me take me hat off to the women, 'tis the owdacious way the most down-throdden of their sex will brag about her blaggard husband.

Not that ayther one or the other of the foive busy-tongued and busy-fingered neighbour women who bint above their sewing or knitting that afthernoon were down-throdden; be no manner of manes; far, far from it. They were so filled with matrimonial contintedness that they fairly thrampled down one another to be first in praising the wondherful men of their choice. Every woman proudly claimed to own an' conthrol the handsomest, loikeliest man that ever throd in brogues.

They talked so fast an' they talked so loud that 'twas a thryin' long while before meek-woiced little Margit Doyle could squeege her husband, Dan'l John, sideways into the argyment. An' even when she did get him to the fore, the other women had appropryated all the hayroic qualifications for their own men, so that there was nothing left for Dan'l but the common lavings; an' that dayprivation nettled Margit an' vexed her sore. But she took her chanst when it came, poor as it was, an' boulted in.

Jabbing the air as though her needle were a dagger, she broke into the discoorse.

"I wouldn't thrade my Dan for the King of Rooshia or the Imperor of Chiney," says she, peering dayfiant around the room. No one sided with that raymark, an' no one argyed agin it, an' this vexed her the more.

"The Kingdom of Chiney is where the most supharior tay comes from," says Caycelia Crow. She was a large, solemn woman, was Misthress Crow, an a gr-r-reat histhorian.

"No," says Margit, scorning the intherruption, "not if the two men were rowled into one," says she.

"Why," says Caycelia Crow, an' her deep woice tolled like a passing bell—"why," says she, "should any dacint woman be wantin' to marry one of thim haythen Imperors? Sure they're all ambiguious," she says, looking around proud of the grand worrud.

Elizabeth Ann sthopped the spinning-wheel the betther to listen, while the others turned bothered faces to the histhorian.

"Ambiguious," says Misthress Crow, raisin' her woice in the middle part of the worrud; "ambiguious," she says again, "manes that accordin' to the laygal laws of some furrin parts, a man may marry four or five wives if he has a mind to."

At this Margit bristled up like a bantam-hin.

"Do you mane to say, Caycelia Crow," says she, dhroppin' in her lap the weskit she was mendin', "do you intind to substantiate that I'm wishin' to marry the Imperor of Chiney, or," she says, her woice growin' high an' cutting as an east wind, "do you wish to inferentiate that if my Dan'l had the lave he'd be ambiguious? Will you plaze tell these friends an' neighbours," she says, wavin' a hand, "which of the two of us you was minded to insinuate against?"

The attackt was so sudden an' so unexpected that Misthress Crow was too bewildhered to dayfind herself. The poor woman only sat starin' stupid at Margit.

The others sunk back in their chairs spacheless with consternaytion till Mollie Scanlan, wishin' to pacificate the sitiwation, an' winkin' friendly at Caycelia, spoke up sootherin'.

"Thrue for ye, Margit Doyle," says she. "What kind of talk is that for ye to be talkin', Caycelia?" says she. "Sure if Dan'l John were to be med the Imperor of Chiney to-morrow he'd hesitate an' day-liberate a long time before bringin' in one of them ambiguious women to you an' the childher. I'd like to see him thry it. It'ud be a sore an' a sorrowful day for him, I'm thinkin'."

At thim worruds, Margit, in her mind's eye, saw Dan'l John standin' ferninst her with an ambiguious haythen woman on aich side of him, an' the picture riled the blood in her heart.

"Oh, ho!" says she, turning on poor, shrinkin' Mollie with a smile, an' that same smile had loaded guns an' pistols in it. "An' will you plaze be so kind an' condesinden', Misthress Scanlan," says she, "to explain what you ever saw or heerd tell of in my Dan'l John's actions, that'ud make you think he'd contimplate such schoundrel endayvours," says she, thrimblin'.

The only answer to the question was from the tay-kettle. It was singin' high an' impident on the hob.

Now, Bridget O'Gill, knowin' woman that she was, had wisely kept out of the discoorse. She sat apart, calmly knittin' one of Darby's winther stockings. As she listened, howsumever, she couldn't keep back a sly smile that lifted one corner of her mouth.

"Isn't it a poor an' a pittiful case," said Misthress Doyle, glaring savage from one to the other, "that a dacint man, the father of noine childher, eight of them livin', an' one gone for a sojer—isn't it a burnin' shame," she says, whumperin', "that such a daycint man must have his charack-ther thrajuiced before his own wife—Will you be so good as to tell me what you're laughing at, Bridget O'Gill, ma'am?" she blazed.

Bridget, flutthering guilty, thried to hide the misfortunate smile, but 'twas too late.

"Bekase, if it is my husband you're mocking at," says Margit, "let me tell you, fair an' plain, his ayquils don't live in the County of Tipperary, let alone this parish! 'Tis thrue," she says, tossin' her head, "he hasn't spint six months with the Good People—he knows nothin' of the fairies—but he has more sinse than those that have. At any rate, he isn't afeard of ghosts like a knowledgeable man that I could mintion."

That last thrust touched a sore spot in the heart of Bridget. Although Darby O'Gill would fight a dozen livin' men, if needful, 'twas well known he had an unraysonable fear of ghosts. So, Bridget said never a worrud, but her brown eyes began to sparkle, an' her red lips were dhrawn up to the size of a button.

Margit saw how hard she'd hit, an' she wint on thriumphant.

"My Dan'l John'ud sleep in a churchyard. He's done it," says she, crowin'.

Bridget could hould in no longer. "I'd be sore an' sorry," she says, "if a husband of mine were druv to do so such a thing as that for the sake of a little pace and quiet," says she, turnin' her chowlder.

Tare an' 'ounds, but that was the sthroke! "The Lord bless us!" mutthered Mollie Scanlan. Margit's mind wint up in the air an' staid there whirlin', whilst she herself sat gasping an' panting for a rayply. 'Twas a thrilling, suspenseful minute.

The chiney shepherd and shepherdess on the mantel sthopped ogling their eyes an' looked shocked at aich other; at the same time Bob, the linnet, in his wooden cage at the door, quit his singin' an' cocked his head the betther to listen; the surprised tay-kettle gave a gasp an' a gurgle, an' splutthered over the fire. In the turrible silence Elizabeth Egan got up to wet the tay. Settin' the taypot in the fender she spoke, an' she spoke raysentful.

"Any sinsible man is afeard of ghosts," says she.

"Oh, indade," says Margit, ketching her breath. "Is that so? Well, sinsible or onsinsible," says she, "this will be Halloween, an' there's not a man in the parish who would walk past the churchyard up to Cormac McCarthy's house, where the Banshee keened last night, except my Dan'l!" says she, thriumphant.

The hurt pride in Bridget rose at that an' forced from her angry lips a foolish promise.

"Huh! we hear ducks talkin'," she says, coolly rowling up Darby's stocking, an' sticking the needle in the ball of yarn. "This afthernoon I was at Cormac McCarthy's," she says, "an' there wasn't a bit of tay in the house for poor Eileen, so I promised Cormac I'd send him up a handful. Now, be the same token, I promise you my Darby will make no bones of going on that errant this night."

"Ho! ho! ho!" laughed Margit. "If he has the courage to

do it bid him sthop in to me on his way back, an' I'll send to you a fine settin' of eggs from my black Spanish hin."

What sharp worrud Misthress O'Gill would have flung back in answer no one knows, bekase whin once purvoked she has few ayquils for sarcastic langwidge, but just then Elizabeth Ann put in Bridget's hand a steaming cup of good, sthrong tay. Now, whusky, ale, an' porther are all good enough in their places, yer honour—I've nothing to intimidate aginst them—but for a comforting, soothering, edayfing buverage give me a cup of foine black tay. So this day the cups were filled only the second time, when the subject of husbands was complately dhropped, an' the conwersation wandhered to the misdaymeanours of Anthony Sullivan's goat.

All this time the women had been so busy with their talkin' an' argyfyin' that the creeping darkness of a coming storm had stolen unnoticed into the room, making the fire glow brighter and redder on the hearth. A faint flare of lightning, follyed by a low grumble of thunder, brought the women to their feet.

"Marcy on us!" says Caycelia Crow, glad of an excuse to be gone, "do you hear that? We'll all be dhrownded before we raich home," says she.

In a minute the wisitors, afther dhraining their cups, were out in the road, aich hurryin' on her separate way, an' tying her bonnet-sthrings as she wint.

'Twas a heavy an' a guilty heart that Bridget carried home with her through the gathering storm. Although Darby was a nuntimate friend of the fairies, yet, as Margit Doyle said, he had such a black dhread of all other kinds of ghosts that to get him out on this threatening Halloween night, to walk past the churchyard, as he must do on his way to Cormac McCarthy's cottage, was a job ayquil to liftin' the Shannon bridge. How she was to manage it she couldn't for the life of her tell; but if the errant was left undone she would be the laughin'-stock of every woman in the parish.

But worst of all, an' what cut her heart the sorest, was that she had turned an act of neighbourly kindness into a wainglorious boast; an' that, she doubted not, was a mortal sin.

She had promised Cormac in the afthernoon that as soon as she got home she would send Darby over with some tay for poor little Eileen, an' now a big storm was gathering, an' before she could have supper ready, thry as hard as she could, black night might be upon them.

"To bring aise to the dying is the comfortingist privilege a man or woman can have, an' I've thraded it for a miserable settin' of eggs," she says. "Amn't I the unfortunit crachure," she thought, "to have let me pride rune me this away. What'll I do at all at all?" she cried. "Bad luck to the thought that took me out of me way to Elizabeth Egan's house!"

Then she med a wish that she might be able to get home in time to send Darby on his errant before the night came on. "If they laugh at me, that'll be my punishment, an' maybe it'll clane my sin," says she.

But the wish was in wain. For just as she crossed the stile to her own field the sun dhropped behind the hills as though he had been shot, an' the east wind swept up, carrying with it a sky full of black clouds an' rain.

## II

That same All Sowls' night Darby O'Gill, the friend of the fairies, sat, as he had often sat before, amidst the dancin' shadows, ferninst his own crackling turf and wood fire, listening to the storm beat against his cottage windows. Little

Mickey, his six-year-ould, cuddled asleep on his daddy's lap, whilst Bridget sat beside thim, the other childher cruedled around her. My, oh my, how the rain powered and hammered an' swirled!

Out in the highway the big dhrops smashed agin wayfarers' faces like blows from a fist, and once in a while, over the flooded moors and the far row of lonesome hills, the sullen lightning spurted red and angry, like the wicious flare of a wolcano.

You may well say 'twas perfect weather for Halloween—to-night whin the spirits of the dayparted dead visit once again their homes, and sit unseen, listening an' yearnin' about the ould hearthstones.

More than once that avenin' Darby'd shivered and shuddered at the wild shrieks and wails that swept over the chimney-tops; he bein' sartin sure that it wasn't the wind at all, but despairing woices that cried out to him from the could lips of the dead.

At last, afther one purticular doleful cry that rose and fell and lingered around the roof, the knowledgeable man raised his head and fetched a deep breath, and said to his wife Bridget:

"Do you hear that cry, avourneen? The dear Lord be marciful to the souls of the dayparted!" sighed he.

Bridget turned a throubled face toward him. "Amen," she says, speakin' softly; "and may He presarve them who are dying this night. Poor Eileen McCarthy—an' she the purty, light-footed colleen only married the few months! Haven't we the raysons to be thankul and grateful. We can never pray enough, Darby," says she.

Now the family had just got off their knees from night prayers, that had lasted half an hour, so thim last worruds worried Darby greatly.

"That woman," he says to himself, mighty sour, "is this

minute contimplaytin' an' insinuatin' that we haven't said prayers enough for Eileen, when as it is, me two poor knees have blisters on thim as big as hin's eggs from kneelin'. An' if I don't look out," he says to himself again, "she'll put the childher to bed and then she's down on her knees for another hour, and me wid her; I'd never advise anyone to marry such a pious woman. I'm fairly kilt with rayligion, so I am. I must disthract her mind an' prevent her intintions," he says to himself.

"Maybe, Bridget," he says, out loud, as he was readying his pipe, "it ain't so bad afther all for Eileen. If we keep hoping for the best, we'll chate the worst out of a few good hours at any rate," says the knowledgeable man.

But Bridget only rowled the apron about her folded arms and shook her head sorrowful at the fire. Darby squinted carefully down the stem of his pipe, blew in it, took a sly glance at his wife, and wint on:

"Don't you raymember, Bridget," he says, "whin ould Mrs. Rafferty lay sick of a bad informaytion of the stomick; well, the banshee sat for a full hour keening an' cryin' before their house—just as it did last night outside Cormac McCarthy's. An' you know the banshee cried but once at Rafferty's, but never rayturned the second time. The informaytion left Julia, and all the wide worruld knows, even the King of Spain might know if he'd send to ax, that Julia Rafferty, as strong as a horse, was diggin' petaties in her own field as late as yesterday."

"The banshee comes three nights before anyone dies, doesn't it, daddy?" says little Mickey, waking up, all excited.

"It does that," says Darby, smilin' proud at the child's knowledgeableness; "and it's come but once to Eileen McCarthy."

"An' while the banshee cries, she sits combing her hair with a comb of goold, don't she, daddy?"

Bridget sat onaisy, bitin' her lips. Always an' ever she had sthrove to keep from the childher tidings of fairies and of banshees an' ghosts an' other onnatural people. Twice she trun a warning look at Darby, but he, not noticin', wint on, strokin' the little lad's hair, an' sayin' to him:

"It does, indade, avick; an' as she came but once to Mrs. Rafferty's, so we have rayson to hope she'll come no more to Cormac McCarthy's."

"Hush that nonsinse!" says Bridget, lookin' daggers; "sure Jack Doolan says that 'twas no banshee at all that come to Rafferty's, but only himself who had taken a drop too much at the fair, an' on his way home sat down to rest himself by Rafferty's door. He says that he stharted singin' pious hymns to kape off the evil spirits, and everyone knows that the same Jack Doolan has as turrible a woice for singin' as any banshee that ever twishted a lip," she says.

The woman's conthrayriness vexed Darby so he pounded his knee with his fist as he answered her: "You'll not deny, maybe," he says, "that the Costa Bower sthopped one night at the Hall, and—"

"Whist!" cried Bridget; "lave off," she says; "sure that's no kind of talk to be talkin' this night before the childher," says she.

"But mammy, I *know* what the Costa Bower is," cried little Mickey, sitting up straight in Darby's lap an' pinting his finger at his mother; " 'tis I that knows well. The Costa Bower is a gr-r-reat black coach that comes in the night to carry down to Croagmah the dead people the banshee keened for."

The other childher by now were sitting boult upright, stiff as ramrods, and staring wild-eyed at Mickey.

"The coachman's head is cut off an' he houlds the reins this away," says the child, lettin' his hands fall limp an' open at his side. "Sometimes it's all wisable, an' then agin it's unwisable, but always whin it comes one can hear the turrible rumble of its wheels." Mickey's woice fell and, spreading out his hands, he spoke slow an' solemn. "One Halloween night in the woods down at the black pond, Danny Hogan heard it coming an' he jumped behind a stone. The threes couldn't sthop it, they wint right through it, an' as it passed Danny Hogan says he saw one white, dead face laned back agin the dark cushions, an' this is the night—All Sowls' night—whin it's sure to be out; now don't I know?" he says, thriumphant.

At that Bridget started to her feet. For a minute she stood spacheless with vexation at the wild, frighting notions that had got into the heads of her childher; then"Glory be!" she says, looking hard at Darby. You could have heard a pin dhrop in the room. Ould Malachi, the big yellow cat, who until this time lay coiled asleep on a stool, was the best judge of Bridget's charack-ter in that house. So, no sooner did he hear the worruds an' see Bridget start up, than he was on his own four feet, his back arched, his tail straight up, an' his two goolden eyes searchin' her face. One look was enough for him. The next instant he lept to the ground an' started for the far room. As he scampered through the door, he trew a swift look back at his comerades, the childher, an' that look said plain as any worruds could say:

"Run for it while you've time! Folly me; some one of us vagebones has done something murtherin'!"

Malachi was right; there would have been sayrious throuble for all hands, only that a softening thought was on Bridget that night which sobered her temper. She stopped a bit, the frown on her face clearing as she looked at the childher, an' she only said: "Come out of this! To bed with yez! I'm raising a pack of owdacious young romancers, an' I didn't know it. Mickey sthop that whimpering an' make haste with your clothes. The Lord help us, he's broke off another button. Look at that, now!" she says.

There was no help for thim. So, with longin' looks trun back at their father, sittin' cosey before the fire, an' with consolin' winks an' nods from him, the childher followed their mother to the bedroom.

Thin, whilst Bridget was tucking the covers about them, an' hushing their complainings, Darby sat with his elbows on his knees, doing in his head a sum in figures; an' that sum was this:

"How much would it be worth this All Sowls' night for a man to go out that door and walk past the churchyard up to Cormac McCarthy, the stone-cutter's house?" One time he made the answer as low as tin pounds two shillings and thruppence, but as he did so a purticular loud blast went shrieking past outside, an' he raised the answer to one thousand five hundred an' tunty pounds sterling. "And cheap at that," he said aloud.

While he was studyin' thim saygacious questions, Bridget stole quietly behind and put a light hand on his chowlder. For a minute, thin, nayther of thim said a worrud.

Surprised at the silence, an' puzzled that little Mickey had escaped a larruping, Malachi crept from the far room an' stood still in the doorway judging his misthress. An' expression was on her face the cat couldn't quite make out. 'Twas an elevayted, pitying, good-hearted, daytermined look, such as a man wears when he goes into the sty to kill one of his own pigs for Christmas.

Malachi, being a wise an' expayieranced baste, daycided to take no chances, so he backed through the door again an' hid undher the dhresser to listen.

"I was just thinking, Darby avourneen," says the woman, half whuspering, "how we might this blessed night earn great credit for our two sowls."

"Wait!" says the sly man, straightening himself, an' raising a hand. "The very thing you're going to spake was in my own mind. I was just dayliberatin' that I hadn't done justice to-night to poor Eileen. I haven't said me prayers farvint enough. I niver can whin we're praying together, or whin I'm kneeling down. Thin, like every way else, there's something quare about me. The foinest prayers I ever say is whin I'm be myself alone in the fields," says the conniving villyan. "So, do you, Bridget, go in an' kneel down by the childher for a half hour or so, an' I'll sit here doing my best. If you should happen to look out at me ye might aisily think," he says, "that I was only sittin' here comfortably smoking my pipe, but at the same time prayers'll be whirlin' inside of me like a wind-mill," says he.

"Oh, thin, ain't I glad an' happy to hear you say thim worruds," says his wife, puttin' one foine arrum about his neck; "you've taken a load off my heart that's been weighing heavy on it all night, for I thought maybe you'd be afeard."

"Afeard of what?" axed Darby, liftin' his eyebrows. Malachi throtted bouldly in an' jumped up on the stool.

"You know Father Cassidy says," whuspered Bridget, "that a loving deed of the hands done for the disthressed is itself a prayer worth a week of common prayers."

"I have nothin' agin that sayin'," says Darby, his head cocked, an' he growin' suspicious.

Bridget wiped her forehead with her apron. "Well, this afthernoon I was at McCarthy's house," she wint on, soothering his hair with one hand, "an', oh, but the poor child was disthressed! Her cheeks were flaming with the faver. An', Darby, the thirst, the awful thirst! I looked about for a pinch of tay—there's nothing so coolin' for one in the faver as a cup of wake tay—an' the sorra scrap of it was in the house, so I tould Cormac that to-night, as soon as the childher were in bed, I'd send you over with a pinch."

Every one of Darby's four bones stiffened an' a mortial chill sthruck into his heart.

"Listen, darlint," she says, "the storm's dying down, so while you're putting on your greatcoat I'll wrap up the bit of tay." He shook her hand from his chowldhers.

"Woman," he says, with bitther politeness, "I think you said that *we* had a great chanst to get credit for our *two* sowls. That's what I think you raymarked and stibulated," says he.

"Arrah, shouldn't a woman have great praise an' credit who'll send her husband out on such a night as this," his wife says. "The worse the con-ditions, the more credit she'll get. If a ghost were to jump at ye as you go past the church-yard, oughtn't I be the happy woman entirely?" says Brid-get.

There was a kind of a tinkle in her woice, such as comes when Bridget is telling jokes, so Darby, with a sudden hope in his mind, turned quick to look at her. But there she stood grim, unfeeling, an' daytermined as a pinted gun.

"Oh, ho! is that the way it is?" he says. "Well, here's luck an' good fortune to the ghost or skellington that lays his hand on me this blessed night!" He stuck his two hands deep in his pockets and whirled one leg across the other—the most aggrawating thing a man can do. But Bridget was not the laste discouraged; she only made up her mind to come at him on his soft side, so she spoke up an' said:

"Suppose I was dying of the faver, Darby O'Gill, an' Cormac rayfused to bring over a pinch of tay to *me*. What, then, would ye think of the stone-cutter?"

Malachi, the cat, stopped licking his paws, an' trun a sharp, inquiring eye at his master.

"Bridget," says the knowledgeable man, giving his hand an argifying wave. "We have two separate ways of being good. Your way is to scurry round an' do good acts. My way is to keep from doing bad ones. An' who knows," he says, with a pious sigh, "which way is the betther one. It isn't for us to judge," says he, shakin' his head solemn at the fire.

Bridget walked out in front of him an' fowlded her arms tight.

"So you won't go," she says, sharp an' suddin'.

"The divil a foot!" says he, beginnin' to whustle.

You'd think, now, Bridget was bate, but she still hildt her trump card, an' until that was played an' lost the lad wasn't safe. "All right, me brave hayro," says she; "do you sit there be the fire; I'll go meself," she says. With that she bounced into the childher's room an' began to get ready her cloak an' hood.

For a minute Darby sat pokin' the fire, muttherin' to himself an' feeling very discommodious. Thin, just to show he wasn't the laste bit onaisy, the lad cleared his throat, and waggin' his head at the fire, began to sing:

"Yarra! as I walked out one mor-r-nin' all in the
    month of June
The primrosies and daisies an' cowslips were in
    bloom,
I spied a purty fair maid a-sthrollin' on the lea,
An' Rory Bory Alice, nor any other ould ancient
    haythan goddess was not half so fair as she.
Says I, 'Me purty fair maid, I'll take you for me
    bride,
An' if you'll pay no at-TIN-tion——' "

Glancing up sudden, he saw Malachi's eye on him, and if ever the faytures of a cat spoke silent but plain langwidge Malachi's face talked that minute to its master, and this is what it said:

"Well, of all the cowardly, creaking bostheens I ever see in all me born days you are the worst, Darby O'Gill. You've not only guve impidence to your wife—an' she's worth four of you—but you've gone back on the friends you purtended to—"

Malachi's faytures got no further in their insultin' ray-marks, for at that Darby swooped up a big sod of turf an' let it fly at the owdacious baste.

Now it is well known that by a spontaneous trow like that no one ever yet hit a sinsible cat, but always an' ever in that unlucky endayvour he strikes a damaginger blow where it's not intinded. So it was this time.

Bridget, wearing her red cloak an' hood, was just com-ing through the door, an' that misfortunate sod of turf caught her fair an' square, right below the chist, an' she staggered back agin the wall.

Darby's consthernaytion an' complycation an' turpitay-tion were beyant imaginaytion.

Bridget laned there gasping. If she felt as bad as she looked, four Dublint surgunts with their saws an' knives couldn't have done her a ha-porth of good. Howsumever, for all that, the sly woman had seen Malachi dodge an' go gal-lopin' away, but she purtendid to think 'twas at herself the turf was trun. Not that she scolded, or anything so common as that, but she went on like an early Christian marthyer who was just goin' to be inthrojuiced to the roaring loins.

Well, as you may aisy see, the poor man, her husband, hadn't a chanst in the worruld afther that. Of course, to rightify himself, he'd face all the ghosts in Croaghmah. So, in a minute, he was standing in his greatcoat with his hand on the latch. There was a packet of tay in his pocket, an' he was a subdued an' conquered man.

He looked so woful that Bridget raypented an' almost raylinted.

"Raymember," he says, mournful, "if I'm caught this night by the Costa Bower, or by the banshee, take good care of the childher, an' raymember what I say—I didn't mane, Bridget, to hit ye with that sod of turf."

"Oh, ain't ye the foolish darlin' to be afeared," smiled Bridget back at him, but she was sayrious, too. "Don't you know that when one goes on an errant of marcy a score of God's white angels with swoords in their hands march before an' beside an' afther him, keeping his path free from danger?" With that she pulled his face down to hers, an' kissed him as she used in the ould courtin' days.

There's nothing puts so much high courage an' clear, steadfast purpose in a man's heart, if it be properly given, as a kiss from the woman he loves. So, with the warmth of that kiss to cheer him, Darby set his face agin the storm.

# CHAPTER II

## THE BANSHEE'S HALLOWEEN

### I

Halloween night, to all unhappy ghosts, is about the same as St. Patrick's Day is to you or to me—'tis a great holiday in every churchyard. An' no one knew this betther or felt it keener than did Darby O'Gill, that same Halloween night, as he stood on his own doorstep with the paper of black tay for Eileen McCarthy safely stowed away in the crown of his top-hat.

No one in that barony was quicker than he at an act of neighbourly kindness, but now, as he huddled himself together in the shelter of his own eaves, and thought of the dangers before, an' of the cheerful fire an' comfortable bed he was leaving behint, black raybellion rushed shouting across his heart.

"Oh, my, oh, my, what a perishin' night to turn a man out into!" he says. "It'd be half a comfort to know I was goin' to be kilt before I got back, just as a warnin' to Bridget," says he.

The misthrayted lad turned a sour eye on the chumul-tuous weather, an' groaned deep as he pulled closer about his chowldhers the cape of his greatcoat an' plunged into the daysarted an' flooded roadway.

Howsumever, 'twas not the pelting rain, nor the lashing wind, nor yet the pitchy darkness that bothered the heart out of him as he wint splashin' an' stumbling along the road. A thought of something more raylentless than the storm, more mystarious than the night's blackness put pounds of lead into the lad's unwilling brogues; for some-where in the shrouding darkness that covered McCarthy's house the banshee was waiting this minute, purhaps, ready to jump out at him as soon as he came near her.

And, oh, if the banshee nabbed him there, what in the worruld would the poor lad do to save himself?

At the raylisation of this sitiwation, the goose-flesh crept up his back an' settled on his neck an' chowldhers. He began to cast about in his mind for a bit of cheer or a scrap of com-fort, as a man in such sarcumstances will do. So, grumblin' an' sore-hearted, he turned over Bridget's parting words. "If one goes on an errant of marcy," Bridget had said, "a score of God's white angels with swoords in their hands march before an' beside an' afther him, keeping his path free from danger."

He felt anxious in his hat for the bit of charitable tay he was bringin', and was glad to find it there safe an' dhry enough, though the rest of him was drenched through an' through.

"Isn't this an act of charity I'm doin', to be bringin' a cooling drink to a dyin' woman?" he axed himself aloud. "To be sure it is. Well, then, what rayson have I to be afeared?" says he, pokin' his two hands into his pockets. Arrah, it's aisy enough to bolsther up one's heart with wise sayin' an' hayroic praycepts when sitting comodious by

one's own fire; but talkin' wise words to one's self is mighty
poor comfort when you're on the lonely high-road of a Halloween night, with a churchyard waitin' for ye on the top of
the hill not two hundred yards away. If there was only one
star to break through the thick sky an' shine for him, if there
was but one friendly cow to low or a distant cock to break
the teeming silence, 'twould put some heart into the man.
But not a sound was there only the swish and wailing of the
wind through the inwisible hedges.

"What's the matther with the whole worruld? Where is
it wanished to?" says Darby. "If a ghost were to jump at me
from the churchyard wall, where would I look for help? To
run is no use," he says, "an' to face it is—"

Just then the current of his misdoubtings ran whack
up against a sayin' of ould Peggy O'Callaghan. Mrs. O'Callaghan's repitation for truth and voracity, whin it come to
fairy tales or ghost stories, be it known, was ayquil if not
shuparior to the best in Tipperary. Now, Peggy had towld
Ned Mullin, an' Ned Mullin had towld Bill Donahue, the tinker, an' the tinker had adwised Darby that no one need ever
be afeared of ghosts if he only had the courage to face them.

Peggy said, "The poor crachures ain't roamin' about
shakin' chains an' moanin' an' groanin', just for the sport of
scarin' people, nor yet out of maneness. 'Tis always a throuble that's on their minds—a message they want sint, a saycret they're endayvouring to unload. So instead of flyin'
from the onhappy things, as most people generally do," she
said, "one should walk up bowld to the apparraytion, be it
gentle or common, male or faymale, an' say, 'What throubles ye, sir?' or 'What's amiss with ye, ma'am?' An' take my
worrud for it," says she, "ye'll find yourself a boneyfactor to
them when you laste expect it," she says.

'Twas a quare idea, but not so onraysonable afther all

whin one comes to think of it; an' the knowledgeable man fell to dayliberatin' whether he'd have the hardness to folly it out if the chanst came. Sometimes he thought he would, then agin he was sure he wouldn't. For Darby O'Gill was one who bint quick undher trouble like a young three before a hurrycane, but he only bint—the throuble never broke him. So, at times his courage wint down to a spark like the light of a candle in a gust of wind, but before you could turn on your heel 'twas blazing up sthrong and fiercer than before.

Whilst thus contimplatin' an' meditaytin', his foot sthruck the bridge in the hollow just below the berrin'-ground, an' there as the boy paused a minute, churning up bravery enough to carry him up the hill an' past the mystarious gravestones, there came a short quiver of lightning, an' in its sudden flare he was sure he saw not tin yards away, an' comin' down the hill toward him, a dim shape that took the breath out of his body.

"Oh, be the powers!" he gasped, his courage emptying out like wather from a spilt pail.

It moved, a slow, grey, formless thing without a head, an' so far as he was able to judge it might be about the size of an ulephant. The parsecuted lad swung himself sideways in the road, one arrum over his eyes an' the other stretched out at full length, as if to ward off the turrible wisitor.

The first thing that began to take any shape in his bewildhered brain was Peggy O'Callaghan's adwice. He thried to folly it out, but a chatterin' of teeth was the only sound he made. An' all this time a thraymendous splashin', like the floppin' of whales, was coming nearer an' nearer.

The splashin' stopped not three feet away, an' the ha'nted man felt in the spine of his back an' in the calves of his legs that a powerful, unhowly monsther towered over him.

Why he didn't swoonge in his tracks is the wondher. He

says he would have dhropped at last if it weren't for the distant bark of his own good dog. Sayser, that put a throb of courage intil his bones. At that friendly sound he opened his two dhry lips an' stutthered this sayin':

"Whoever you are, an' whatever shape ye come in, take heed that I'm not afeared," he says. "I command ye to tell me your throubles an' I'll be your boneyfactor. Then go back dacint an' rayspectable where you're buried. Spake an' I'll listen," says he.

He waited for a reply, an' getting none, a hot splinther of shame at bein' so badly frightened turned his sowl into wexation. "Spake up," he says, "but come no furder, for if you do, be the hokey I'll take one thry at ye, ghost or no ghost!" he says. Once more he waited, an' as he was lowering the arrum from his eyes for a peek, the ghost spoke up, an' its answer came in two pitiful, disthressed roars. A damp breath puffed acrost his face, an' openin' his eyes, what should the lad see but the two dhroopin' ears of Solomon, Mrs. Kilcannon's grey donkey. Foive different kinds of disgust biled up into Darby's throat an' almost sthrangled him. "Ye murdherin', big-headed imposture!" he gasped.

Half a minute afther a brown hoot-owl, which was shelthered in a near-by black-thorn three, called out to his brother's fambly which inhabited the belfry of the chapel above on the hill that some black-minded spalpeen had hoult of Solomon Kilcannon be the two ears an' was kickin' the ribs out of him, an' that the langwidge the man was usin' to the poor baste was worse than scan'lous.

Although Darby couldn't undherstand what the owl was sayin', he was startled be the blood-curdlin' hoot, an' that same hoot saved Solomon from any further exthrayornery throuncin', bekase as the angry man sthopped to hearken there flashed on him the rayilisation that he was bating an' crool maulthraytin' a blessing in dishguise. For this same

Solomon had the repitation of being the knowingest, sensiblist thing which walked on four legs in that parish. He was a fayvourite with young an' old, especially with childher, an' Mrs. Kilcannon said she could talk to him as if he were a human, an' she was sure he undershtood. In the face of thim facts the knowledgeable man changed his chune, an' puttin' his arrum friendly around the disthressed animal's neck, he said:

"Aren't ye ashamed of yerself, Solomon, to be payradin' an' mayandherin' around the churchyard Halloween night, dishguisin' yerself this away as an outlandish ghost, an' you havin' the foine repitation for daciency an' good manners?" he says, excusin' himself. "I'm ashamed of you, so I am, Solomon," says he, hauling the baste about in the road, an' turning him till his head faced once more the hillside. "Come back with me now to Cormac McCarthy's, avourneen. We've aich been in worse company, I'm thinkin'; at laste you have, Solomon," says he.

At that, kind an' friendly enough, the forgivin' baste turned with him, an' the two keeping aich other slitherin' company, went stumblin' an' scramblin' up the hill toward the chapel. On the way Darby kept up a one-sided conwersation about all manner of things, just so that the ring of a human woice, even if 'twas only his own, would take a bit of the crool lonesomeness out of the dark hedges.

"Did you notice McDonald's sthrame as you came along the night, Solomon? It must be a roarin' torrent be this, with the pourin' rains, an' we'll have to cross it," says he. "We could go over McDonald's stone bridge that stands ferninst McCarthy's house, with only Nolan's meadow betwixt the two, but," says Darby, laying a hand, confaydential on the ass's wet back, " 'tis only a fortnit since long Faylix, the blind beggarman, fell from the same bridge and broke his neck, an' what more natural," he axed, "than that the ghost of Faylix would be celebraytin' its first Halloween, *as a ghost*, at the spot where he was kilt?"

You may believe me or believe me not, but at thim worruds Solomon sthopped dead still in his thracks an' rayfused to go another step till Darby coaxed him on by sayin':

"Oh, thin, we won't cross it if you're afeared, little man," says he, "but we'll take the path through the fields on this side of it, and we'll cross the sthrame by McCarthy's own wooden foot-bridge. 'Tis within tunty feet of the house. Oh, ye needn't be afeared," he says agin; "I've seen the cows cross it, so it'll surely hould the both of us."

A sudden raymembrance whipped into his mind of how tall the stile was, ladin' into Nolan's meadow, an' the boy was puzzling deep in his mind to know how was Solomon to climb acrost that stile, whin all at once the gloomy western gate of the graveyard rose quick by their side.

The two shied to the opposite hedge, an' no wondher they did.

Fufty ghosts, all in their shrouds, sat cheek by jowl along the churchyard wall, never caring a ha'-porth for the wind or the rain.

There was little Ted Rogers, the humpback, who was dhrownded in Mullin's well four years come Michaelmas; there was black Mulligan, the gamekeeper, who shot Ryan, the poacher, sittin' with a gun on his lap, an' he glowerin'; beside the gamekeeper sat the poacher, with a jagged black hole in his forehead; there was Thady Finnegan, the scholar, who was disappointed in love an' died of a daycline; furder on sat Mrs. Houlihan, who dayparted this life from ating of pizen musherooms; next to *her* sat—oh, a hundhred others!

Not that Darby *saw* thim, do ye mind. He had too good sinse to look that way at all. He walked with his head turned out to the open fields, an' his eyes squeeged shut. But something in his mind toult him they were there, an' he felt in the marrow of his bones that if he gave them the encouragement of one glance two or three'd slip off the wall an' come moanin' over to tell him their throubles.

What Solomon saw an' what Solomon heard, as the two wint shrinkin' along'll never be known to living man, but once he gave a jump, an' twice Darby felt him thrimblin', an' whin they raiched at last the chapel wall the baste broke into a swift throt. Purty soon he galloped, an' Darby wint gallopin' with him, till two yellow blurs of light across in a field to the left marked the windys of the stone-cutter's cottage.

'Twas a few steps only, thin, to the stile over into Nolan's meadow, an' there the two stopped, lookin' helpless at aich other. Solomon had to be lifted, and there was the throuble. Three times Darby thried by main strength to hist his compagnen up the steps, but in vain, an' Solomon was clane dishgusted.

Only for the tendher corn on our hayro's left little toe, I think maybe that at length an' at last the pair would have got safe over. The kind-hearted lad had the donkey's two little hoofs planted on the top step, an' whilst he himself was liftin' the rest of the baste in his arrums, Solomon got onaisy that he was goin' to be trun, an' so began to twisht an' squirm; of course, as he did, Darby slipped an' wint thump on his back agin the stile, with Solomon sittin' comfortable on top of the lad's chist. But that wasn't the worst of it, for as the baste scrambled up he planted one hard little hoof on Darby's left foot, an' the knowledgeable man let a yowl out of him that must have frightened all the ghosts within miles.

Seein' he'd done wrong, Solomon boulted for the middle of the road an' stood there wiry an' attentive, listening to the names flung at him from where his late comerade sat on the lowest step of the stile nursin' the hurted foot.

'Twas an excited owl in the belfry that this time spoke up an' shouted to his brother down in the black-thorn:

"Come up, come up quick!" it says. "Darby O'Gill is just afther calling Solomon Kilcannon a malayfactor."

Darby rose at last, an' as he climbed over the stile he turned to shake his fist toward the middle of the road.

"Bad luck to ye for a thick-headed, on-grateful informer!" he says; "you go your way an' I'll go mine—we're sundhers," says he. So sayin', the crippled man wint limpin' an' grumplin' down the boreen, through the meadow, whilst his desarted friend sint rayproachful brays afther him that would go to your heart.

The throbbin' of our hayro's toe banished all pity for the baste, an' even all thoughts of the banshee, till a long, gurgling, swooping sound in front toult him that his fears about the rise in McDonald's sthrame were undher rather than over the actwil conditions.

Fearin' that the wooden foot-bridge might be swept away, as it had been the year purvious, he hurried on.

Most times this sthrame was only a quiet little brook that ran betwixt purty green banks, with hardly enough wather in it to turn the broken wheel in Chartres' runed mill; but to-night it swept along an angry, snarlin', growlin' river that overlept its banks an' dhragged wildly at the swaying willows.

By a narrow throw of light from McCarthy's side windy our thraveller could see the maddened wather sthrivin' an' tearing to pull with it the props of the little foot-bridge; an' the boards shook an' the centre swayed undher his feet as he passed over. "Bedad, I'll not cross this way goin' home, at any rate," he says, looking back at it.

The worruds were no sooner out of his mouth than there was a crack, an' the middle of the foot-bridge lifted in the air, twishted round for a second, an then hurled itself into the sthrame, laving the two inds still standing in their place on the banks.

"Tunder an' turf!" he cried, "I mustn't forget to tell the people within of this, for if ever there was a thrap set by evil spirits to drownd a poor, unwary mortial, there it stands. Oh, ain't the ghosts turrible wicious on Halloween!"

He stood dhrippin' a minute on the threshold, listening; thin, without knockin', lifted the latch an' stepped softly into the house.

## II

Two candles burned above the blue and white chiney dishes on the table, a bright fire blazed on the hearth, an' over in the corner where the low bed was set the stone-cutter was on his knees beside it.

Eileen lay on her side, her shining hair sthrealed out on the pillow. Her purty, flushed face was turned to Cormac, who knelt with his forehead hid on the bedcovers. The colleen's two little hands were clasped about the great fist of her husband, an' she was talking low, but so airnest that her whole life was in every worrud.

"God save all here!" said Darby, takin' off his hat, but there was no answer. So deep were Cormac an' Eileen in some conwersation they were having together that they didn't hear his coming. The knowledgeable man didn't know what to do. He raylised that a husband and wife about to part forever were lookin' into aich other's hearts, for maybe the last time. So he just sthood shifting from one foot to the other, watching thim, unable to daypart, an' not wishin' to obtrude.

"Oh, it isn't death at all that I fear," Eileen was saying. "No, no, Cormac asthore, 'tis not that I'm misdoubtful of; but, ochone mavrone, 'tis you I fear!"

The kneelin' man gave one swift upward glance, and dhrew his face nearer to the sick wife. She wint on, thin, spakin' tindher an' half smiling an' sthrokin' his hand:

"I know, darlint, I know well, so you needn't tell me, that if I were to live with you a thousand years you'd never sthray in mind or thought to any other woman, but it's when I'm gone—when the lonesome avenings folly aich other through days an' months, an' maybe years, an' you sitting here at this fireside without one to speak to, an' you so handsome an' gran', an' with the penny or two we've put away—"

"Oh, asthore machree, why can't ye banish thim black thoughts!" says the stone-cutter. "Maybe," he says, "the banshee will not come again. Ain't all the counthry-side prayin' for ye this night, an' didn't Father Cassidy himself bid you to hope? The saints in Heaven couldn't be so crool!" says he.

But the colleen wint on as though she hadn't heard him, or as if he hadn't intherrupted her:

"An' listen," says she; "they'll come urging ye, the neighbours, an' raysonin' with you. You're own flesh an' blood'll come, an', no doubt, me own with them, an' they all sthriving to push me out of your heart, an' to put another woman there in my place. I'll know it all, but I won't be able to call to you, Cormac machree, for I'll be lying silent undher the grass, or undher the snow up behind the church."

While she was sayin' thim last worruds, although Darby's heart was meltin' for Eileen, his mind began running over the colleens of that townland to pick out the one who'd be most likely to marry Cormac in the ind. You know how far-seeing an' quickminded was the knowledgeable man. He settled sudden on the Hanlon girl, an' daycided at once that she'd have Cormac before the year was out. The ondaycency of such a thing made him furious at her.

He says to himself, half crying, "Why, then, bad cess to you for a shameless, red-haired, forward baggage, Bridget Hanlon, to be runnin' afther the man, an' throwing yourself in his way, an' Eileen not yet cowld in her grave!" he says.

While he was saying them things to himself, McCarthy had been whuspering fierce to his wife, but what it was the stone-cutter said the friend of the fairies couldn't hear. Eileen herself spoke clean enough in answer, for the faver gave her onnatural strength.

"Don't think," she says, "that it's the first time this thought has come to me. Two months ago, whin I was sthrong an' well an' sittin' happy as a meadow-lark at your side, the same black shadow dhrifted over me heart. The worst of it an' the hardest to bear of all is that they'll be in the right, for what good can I do for you when I'm undher the clay," says she.

"It's different with a woman. If you were taken an' I left I'd wear your face in my heart through all me life, an' ax for no sweeter company."

"Eileen," says Cormac, liftin' his hand, an' his woice was hoarse as the roar of the say, "I swear to you on me bendid knees——"

With her hand on his lips, she sthopped him. "There'll come on ye by daygrees a great cravin' for sympathy, a hunger an' a longing for affection, an' you'll have only the shadow of my poor, wanished face to comfort you, an' a recollection of a woice that is gone for ever. A new, warm face'll keep pushin' itself betwixt us——"

"Bad luck to that red-headed hussy!" mutthered Darby, looking around disthressed. "I'll warn Father Cassidy of her an' of her intintions the day afther the funeral."

There was silence for a minute; Cormac, the poor lad, was sobbing like a child. By-and-by Eileen wint on again, but her woice was failing an' Darby could see that her cheeks were wet.

"The day'll come when you'll give over," she says. "Ah, I see how it'll all ind. Afther that you'll visit the churchyard by stealth, so as not to make the other woman sore-hearted."

"My, oh, my, isn't she the far-seein' woman?" thought Darby.

"Little childher'll come," she says, "an' their soft, warm arrums will hould you away. By-and-by you'll not go where I'm laid at all, an' all thoughts of these few happy months we've spent together—Oh! Mother in Heaven, how happy they were—"

The girl started to her elbow, for, sharp an' sudden, a wild, wailing cry just outside the windy startled the shuddering darkness. 'Twas a long cry of terror and of grief, not shrill, but piercing as a knife-thrust. Every hair on Darby's head stood up an' pricked him like a needle. 'Twas the banshee!

"Whist, listen!" says Eileen. "Oh, Cormac asthore, it's come for me again!" With that, stiff with terror, she buried herself undher the pillows.

A second cry follyed the first, only this time it was longer, and rose an' swelled into a kind of a song that broke at last into the heart-breakingest moan that ever fell on mortial ears. "Ochone!" it sobbed.

The knowledgeable man, his blood turned to ice, his legs thremblin' like a hare's, stood looking in spite of himself at the black windy-panes, expecting some frightful wision.

Afther that second cry the woice balanced itself up an' down into the awful death keen. One word made the whole song, and that was the turruble worrud, "Forever!"

"Forever an' forever, oh, forever!" swung the wild keen, until all the deep meaning of the worrud burned itself into Darby's sowl, thin the heart-breakin' sob, "Ochone!" inded always the varse.

Darby was just wondherin' whether he himself wouldn't go mad with fright, whin he gave a sudden jump at a hard, sthrained woice which spoke up at his very elbow.

"Darby O'Gill," it said, and it was the stone-cutter who spoke, "do you hear the death keen? It came last night; it'll come to-morrow night at this same hour, and thin—oh, my God!"

Darby tried to answer, but he could only stare at the white, set face an' the sunken eyes of the man before him.

There was, too, a kind of fierce quiet in the way McCarthy spoke that made Darby shiver.

The stone-cutter wint on talkin' the same as though he was goin' to dhrive a bargain. "They say you're a knowledgeable man, Darby O'Gill," he says, "an' that on a time you spint six months with the fairies. Now I make you this fair, square offer," he says, laying a forefinger in the palm of the other hand. "I have fifty-three pounds that Father Cassidy's keeping for me. Fifty-three pounds," he says agin. "An' I have this good bit of a farm that me father was born on, an' his father was born on, too, and the grandfather of him. An' I have the grass of seven cows. You know that. Well, I'll give it all to you, all, every stiver of it, if you'll only go outside an' dhrive away that cursed singer." He trew his head to one side an' looked anxious up at Darby.

The knowledgeable man racked his brains for something to speak, but all he could say was, "I've brought you a bit of tay from the wife, Cormac."

McCarthy took the tay with unfeeling hands, an' wint on talking in the same dull way. Only this time there came a hard lump in his throat now and then that he stopped to swally.

"The three cows I have go, of course, with the farm," says he. "So does the pony an' the five pigs. I have a good plough an' a foine harrow; but you must lave my stone-cutting tools, so little Eileen an' I can earn our way wherever we go, an' it's little the crachure ates the best of times."

The man's eyes were dhry an' blazin'; no doubt his mind was cracked with grief. There was a lump in Darby's throat, too, but for all that he spoke up scolding-like.

"Arrah, talk rayson, man," he says, putting two hands on Cormac's chowlders; "if I had the wit or the art to banish the banshee, wouldn't I be happy to do it an' not a fardin' to pay?"

"Well, then," says Cormac, scowling, an' pushin' Darby to one side, "I'll face her myself—I'll face her an' choke that song in her throat if Sattin himself stood at her side."

With those words, an' before Darby could sthop him, the stone-cutter flung open the door an' plunged out into the night. As he did so the song outside sthopped. Suddenly a quick splashing of feet, hoarse cries, and shouts gave tidings of a chase. The half-crazed gossoon had stharted the banshee—of that there could be no manner of doubt. A raymembrance of the awful things that she might do to his friend paythrefied the heart of Darby.

Even afther these cries died away he stood listening a full minute, the sowls of his two brogues glued to the floor. The only sounds he heard now were the deep ticking of a clock and a cricket that chirped slow an' solemn on the hearth, an' from somewhere outside came the sorrowful cry of a whipperwill. All at once a thought of the broken bridge an' of the black, treacherous waters caught him like the blow of a whip, an' for a second drove from his mind even the fear of the banshee.

In that one second, an' before he rayalised it, the lad was out undher the dhripping trees, and running for his life toward the broken foot-bridge. The night was whirling an' beating above him like the flapping of thraymendous wings, but as he ran Darby thought he heard above the rush of the water and through the swish of the wind Cormac's voice calling him.

The friend of the fairies stopped at the edge of the foot-bridge to listen. Although the storm had almost passed, a spiteful flare of lightning lept up now an' agin out of the western hills, an' afther it came the dull rumble of distant thunder; the water splashed spiteful against the bank, and Darby saw that seven good feet of the bridge had been torn out of its centre, laving uncovered that much of the black, deep flood.

He stood sthraining his eyes an' ears in wondheration, for now the woice of Cormac sounded from the other side of the sthrame, and seemed to be floating toward him through the field over the path Darby himself had just thravelled. At first he was mightily bewildhered at what might bring Cormac on the other side of the brook, till all at once the mur-dhering scheme of the banshee burst in his mind like a gunpowdher explosion.

Her plan was as plain as day—she meant to dhrown the stone-cutter. She had led the poor, days-thracted man straight from his own door down to and over the new stone bridge, an' was now dayludherin' him on the other side of the sthrame, back agin up the path that led to the broken foot-bridge.

In the glare of a sudden blinding flash from the middle of the sky Darby saw a sight he'll never forget till the day he dies. Cormac, the stone-cutter, was running toward the death-trap, his bare head trun back, an' his two arrums stretched out in front of him. A little above an' just out of raich of them, plain an' clear as Darby ever saw his wife Bridget, was the misty white figure of a woman. Her long, waving hair sthrealed back from her face, an' her face was the face of the dead.

At the sight of her Darby thried to call out a warning, but the words fell back into his throat. Thin again came the stifling darkness. He thried to run away, but his knees failed him, so he turned around to face the danger.

As he did so he could hear the splash of the man's feet in the soft mud. In less than a minute Cormac would be sthruggling in the wather. At the thought Darby, bracing himself body and sowl, let a warning howl out of him.

"Hould where you are!" he shouted; "she wants to drownd ye—the bridge is broke in the middle!" but he could tell, from the rushing footsteps an' from the hoarse swelling curses which came nearer an' nearer every second, that the dayludhered man, crazed with grief, was deaf an' blind to everything but the figure that floated before his eyes.

At that hopeless instant Bridget's parting words popped into Darby's head.

"When one goes on an errant of marcy a score of God's white angels, with swoords in their hands, march before an' beside an' afther him, keeping his path free from danger."

How it all come to pass he could never rightly tell, for he was like a man in a dhrame, but he recollects well standing on the broken ind of the bridge, Bridget's words ringing in his ears, the glistening black gulf benathe his feet, an' he swinging his arrums for a jump. Just one thought of herself and the childher, as he gathered himself for a spring, an' then he cleared the gap like a bird.

As his two feet touched the other side of the gap a turrific screech—not a screech, ayther, but an angry, frightened shriek—almost split his ears. He felt a rush of cowld, dead air agin his face, and caught a whiff of newly turned clay in his nosthrils; something white stopped quick before him, an' then, with a second shriek, it shot high in the darkness an' disappeared. Darby had frightened the wits out of the banshee.

The instant afther the two men were clinched an' rowling over an' over aich other down the muddy bank, their legs splashing as far as the knees in the dangerous wather, an' McCarthy raining wake blows on the knowledgeable man's head an' breast.

Darby felt himself goin' into the river. Bits of the bank caved undher him, splashing into the current, an' the lad's heart began clunking up an' down like a churn-dash.

"Lave off, lave off!" he cried, as soon as he could ketch his breath. "Do you take me for the banshee?" says he, giving a dusperate lurch an' rowling himself on top of the other.

"Who are you, then? If you're not a ghost you're the divil, at any rate," gasped the stone-cutter.

"Bad luck to ye!" cried Darby, clasping both arrums of the haunted man. "I'm no ghost, let lone the divil—I'm only your friend, Darby O'Gill."

Lying there, breathing hard, they stared into the faces of aich other a little space till the poor stone-cutter began to cry.

"Oh, is that you, Darby O'Gill? Where is the banshee? Oh, haven't I the bad fortune," he says, sthriving to raise himself.

"Rise up," says Darby, lifting the man to his feet an' steadying him there. The stone-cutter stared about like one stunned by a blow.

"I don't know where the banshee flew, but do you go back to Eileen as soon as you can," says the friend of the fairies. "Not that way, man alive," he says, as Cormac started to climb the foot-bridge, "it's broke in the middle; go down an' cross the stone bridge. I'll be afther you in a minute," he says.

Without a word, meek now and biddable as a child, Cormac turned, an' Darby saw him hurry away into the blackness.

The raysons Darby raymained behind were two: first an' foremost, he was a bit vexed at the way his clothes were muddied an' dhraggled, an' himself had been poundcd an' hammered; an' second, he wanted to think. He had a quare cowld feeling in his mind that something was wrong—a kind of a foreboding, as one might say.

As he stood thinking a rayalisation of the caylamity sthruck him all at once like a rap on the jaw—he had lost his fine brier pipe. The lad groaned as he began the anxious sarch. He slapped furiously at his chist an' side pockets, he dived into his throwsers and greatcoat, and at last, sprawlin' on his hands an' feet like a monkey, he groped savagely through the wet, sticky clay.

"This comes," says the poor lad, grumblin' an' gropin', "of pokin' your nose into other people's business. Hallo, what's this?" says he, straightening himself. " 'Tis a comb. By the powers of pewther, 'tis the banshee's comb."

An' so indade it was. He had picked up a goold comb the length of your hand an' almost the width of your two fingers. About an inch of one ind was broken off, an' dhropped into Darby's palm. Without thinkin', he put the broken bit into his weskit pocket, an' raised the biggest half close to his eyes, the betther to view it.

"May I never see sorrow," he says, "if the banshee mustn't have dhropped her comb. Look at that, now. Folks do be sayin' that 'tis this gives her the foine singing voice, bekase the comb is enchanted," he says. "If that sayin' be thrue, it's the faymous lad I am from this night. I'll thravel from fair to fair, an' maybe at the ind they'll send me to parliament."

With these worruds he lifted his caubeen an' stuck the comb in the top tuft of his hair.

Begor, he'd no sooner guv it a pull than a sour, singing feelin' begun at the bottom of his stomick, an' it rose higher an' higher. When it raiched his chist he was just going to let a bawl out of himself only that he caught sight of a thing ferninst him that froze the marrow in his bones.

He gasped short an' jerked the comb out of his hair, for there, not tin feet away, stood a dark, shadowy woman, tall, thin, an' motionless, laning on a crutch.

During a breath or two the parsecuted hayro lost his head completely, for he never doubted that the banshee had changed her shuit of clothes to chase hack afther him.

The first clear aymotion that rayturned to him was to fling the comb on the ground an' make a boult of it. On second thought he knew that 'twould be aisier to bate the wind in a race than to run away from the banshee.

"Well, there's a good Tipperary man done for this time," groaned the knowledgeable man, "unless in some way I can beguile her." He was fishing in his mind for its civilist worrud when the woman spoke up, an' Darby's heart jumped with gladness as he raycognised the cracked voice of Shee-lah Maguire, the spy for the fairies.

"The top of the avenin' to you, Darby O'Gill," says Shee-lah, peering at him from undher her hood, the two eyes of her glowing like tallow candles, "amn't I kilt with a-stonishment to see you here alone this time of the night," says the ould witch.

Now, the clever man knew as well as though he had been tould, when Sheelah said thim worruds, that the ban-shee had sent her to look for the comb, an' his heart grew bould; but he answered her polite enough, "Why, thin, luck to ye, Misthress Maguire, ma'am," he says, bowing grand, "sure, if you're kilt with a-stonishment, amn't I sphlit with inkerdoolity to find yourself mayandherin' in this lonesome place on Halloween night."

Sheelah hobbled a step or two nearer, an' whuspered confaydential.

"I was wandherin' hereabouts only this morning," she says, "an' I lost from me hair a goold comb one that I've had this forty years. Did ye see such a thing as that, agra?" An' her two eyes blazed.

"Faix, I dunno," says Darby, putting his two arrums behind him. "Was it about the length of ye're hand an' the width of ye're two fingers?" he axed.

"It was," says she, thrusting out a withered paw.

"Thin I didn't find it," says the tantalising man. "But maybe I did find something summillar, only 'twasn't yours at all, but the banshee's," he says, chuckling.

Whether the hag was intentioned to welt Darby with her staff, or whether she was only liftin' it for to make a sign of enchantment in the air, will never be known, but whatsomever she meant the hayro doubled his fists an' squared off; at that she lowered the stick, an' broke into a shrill, cackling laugh.

"Ho, ho!" she laughed, houldin' her sides, "but aren't ye the bould, distinguishable man. Becourse 'tis the banshee's comb; how well ye knew it! By the same token I'm sint to bring it away; so make haste to give it up, for she's hiding an' waiting for me down at Chartres' mill. Aren't you the courageous blaggard, to grabble at her, an' thry to ketch her. Sure, such a thing never happened before, since the worruld began," says Sheelah.

The idee that the banshee was hiding an' afeared to face him was great news to the hayro. But he only tossed his head an' smiled shuparior as he made answer.

" 'Tis yourself that knows well, Sheelah Maguire,

ma'am," answers back the proud man, slow an' day-liberate, "that whin one does a favour for an unearthly spirit he may daymand for pay the favours of three such wishes as the spirit has power to give. The worruld knows that. Now I'll take three good wishes, such as the banshee can bestow, or else I'll carry the goolden comb straight to Father Cassidy. The banshee hasn't goold nor wor'ly goods, as the sayin' is, but she has what suits me betther."

This cleverness angered the fairy-woman so she set in to abuse and to frighten Darby. She ballyragged, she browbate, she trajooced, she threatened, but 'twas no use. The bould man hildt firm, till at last she promised him the favours of the three wishes.

"First an' foremost," says he, "I'll want her never to put her spell on me or any of my kith an' kin."

"That wish she gives you, that wish she grants you, though it'll go sore agin the grain," snarled Sheelah.

"Then," says Darby, "my second wish is that the black spell be taken from Eileen McCarthy."

Sheelah flusthered about like an angry hin. "Wouldn't something else do as well?" she says.

"I'm not here to argify," says Darby, swingin' back an' forrud on his toes.

"Bad scran to you," says Sheelah. "I'll have to go an' ask the banshee herself about that. Don't stir from that spot till I come back."

You may believe it or not, but with that sayin' she bent the head of her crutch well forward, an' before Darby's very face she trew—savin' your presence—one leg over the stick as though it had been a horse, an' while one might say Jack Robinson the crutch riz into the air an' lifted her, an' she went sailing out of sight.

Darby was still gaping an' gawpin' at the darkness

where she disappeared whin—whisk! she was back agin an' dismountin' at his side.

"The luck is with you," says she, spiteful. "That wish I give, that wish I grant you. You'll find seven crossed rushes undher McCarthy's door-step; uncross them, put them in fire or in wather, an' the spell is lifted. Be quick with the third wish—out with it!"

"I'm in a more particular hurry about that than you are," says Darby. "You must find me my brier pipe," says he.

"You omadhaun," sneered the fairy-woman, " 'tis sthuck in the band of your hat, where you put it when you left your own house the night. No, no, not in front," she says, as Darby put up his hand to feel. "It's stuck in the back. Your caubeen's twishted," she says.

Whilst Darby was standing with the comb in one hand an' the pipe in the other, smiling daylighted, the comb was snatched from his fingers and he got a welt in the side of the head from the crutch. Looking up, he saw Sheelah tunty feet in the air, headed for Chartres' mill, an' she cacklin' an' screechin' with laughter. Rubbing his sore head an' mutthering unpious words to himself, Darby started for the new bridge.

In less than no time afther, he had found the seven crossed rushes undher McCarthy's door-step, an' had flung them into the stream. Thin, without knocking, he pushed open McCarthy's door an' tiptoed quietly in.

Cormac was kneelin' beside the bed with his face buried in the pillows, as he was when Darby first saw him that night. But Eileen was sleeping as sound as a child, with a sweet smile on her lips. Heavy pursperation beaded her forehead, showing that the faver was broke.

Without disturbing aither of them our hayro picked up the package of tay from the floor, put it on the dhresser, an' with a glad heart sthole out of the house an' closed the door softly behind him.

Turning toward Chartres' mill he lifted his hat an' bowed low. "Thank you kindly, Misthress Banshee," he says. " 'Tis well for us all I found your comb this night. Public or private, I'll always say this for you—you're a woman of your worrud," he says.

# CHAPTER III

## THE GHOSTS AT CHARTRES'
## MILL

For a little while afther Darby O'Gill sint the banshee back her comb, there was the duckens to pay in that townland. Aich night came stormier than the other. An' the rain—never, since Noey the Phœnaycian histed sail for Arrayat was there promised such a daynudherin' flood. (In one way or another we're all, even the Germin min an' the Fardowns, dayscendints of the Phœnaycians.)

Even at that the foul weather was the laste of the throuble—the counthry-side was ha'nted. Every ghost must have left Croaghmah as soon as twilight to wander abroad in the lonesome places. The farmyards and even the village itself was not safe.

One morning, just before cock-crow, big Joey Hooligan, the smith, woke up sudden, with a turrible feeling that some gashly person was lookin' in at him through the windy. Startin' up flurried in bed, what did he see but two eyes that were like burnin' coals of fire, an' they peerin' study into the room. One glance was enough. Givin' a thraymendous gasp, Joey dhropped back quakin' into the bed, an' covered his head with the bed-clothes. How long afther that the two heegous eyes kept starin' at the bed Joey can't rightly tell, for he never uncovered his head nor stirred hand nor foot agin till his wife Nancy had lighted the fire an' biled the stirabout.

Indade, it was a good month afther that before Joey found courage enough to get up first in the morning so as to light the fire. An' on that same mimorable mornin' he an' Nancy lay in bed argyfin' about it till nearly noon—the poor man was that frightened.

The avenin' afther Hooligan was wisited Mrs. Norah Clancy was in the stable milking her cow—Cornaylia by name—whin sudden she spied a tall, sthrange man in a top-coat standin' near the stable door an' he with his back turned toward her. At first she thought it a shadow, but it appeared a thrifle thicker than a shadow, so, a little afeared, she called out: "God save you kindly, sir!"

At that the shadow turned a dim, grey face toward her, so full of rayproachful woe that Mrs. Clancy let a screech out of her an' tumbled over with the pail of milk betwixt her knees. She lay on her back in the spilt milk unconscionable for full fufteen minutes.

The next night a very rayliable tinker, named Bothered Bill Donahue, while wandherin' near Chartres' ruined mill, came quite accidental upon tunty skillingtons, an' they colloguing an' confabbing together on the flat roof of the mill-shed.

But worst of all, an' something that sthruck deeper terror into every heart, was the news that six different persons at six different places had met with the turrible phantom coach, the Costa Bower.

Peggy Collins, a wandherin' beggar woman from the

west counthry, had a wild chase for it; an' if she'd been a second later raichin' the chapel steps an' laying her hand on the church-door it would have had her sure.

Things got on so that afther dark people only wentured out in couples or in crowds, an' in pint of piety that parish was growin' into an example an' patthron for the naytion.

But of all the persons whom thim con-ditions com-plicayted you may be sure that the worst harried an' implicayted was the knowledgeable man, Darby O'Gill.

There was a weight on his mind, but he couldn't tell why, an' a dhread in his heart that had no raysonable foun-daytion. He moped an' he moothered. Some of the time he felt like singin' doleful ballads an' death keens, an' the rest of the time he could hardly keep from cryin'. His appetite left him, but what confuged him worse than all the rest was the fondness that had come over him for hard worruk—cuttin' turf an' diggin' petaties, an' things like that.

To make matters more onsociable, his friend, Brian Con-nors, the King of the Fairies, hadn't showed a nose inside Darby's door for more than a fortnit; so the knowledgeable man had no one to adwise with.

In thim dismal sarcumstances Darby, growin' dusperate, harnessed the pony Clayopathra one morning and dhrove up to Clonmel to see the Masther Doctor—the raynowned McNamara. By this you may know how bad he felt, for no one, till he was almost at the pint of dissolation, ever wint to that crass, brow-batin' ould codger.

So, loath enough was our own hayro to face him, an' hard-hearted enough was the welcome the crabbed little docthor hilt out to Darby whin they met.

"What did you ate for breakwus?" the physician says, peerin' savage from undher his great eyebrows at Darby's tongue.

"Only a bowl of stirabout, an' a couple of petaties, an' a

bit of bacon, an' a few eggs." He was countin' on his fingers, "an'—an' somethin' or other I forgot. Do you think I'll go into a daycline, Doctor, agra?"

"Hump! ugh! ugh!" was all the comfort the sick man got from the blinkin' ould blaggard. But turnin' imaget to his medicine-table the surgent began studyin' the medicines. There was so much of it ferninst him he might have give a gallon an' never missed it. There was one foine big red bottle in particular Darby had his eye on, an' thought his dose 'ud surely come out of that. But NcNamara turns to a box the size of your hat, an' it filled to the top with little white, flat pills. Well, the stingy ould rascal counts out three and, handing them to Darby, says: "Take one before breakwus, another before dinner, an' the last one before suppher, an' give me four silver shillings, an' that'll cure ye," he says.

You may be sure that Darby biled up inside with madness at the onraysonableness of the price of the pills, but, houlding himself in, he says, very cool an' quite: "Will you write me out a rayceipt for the money, Doctor McNamara, if you plaze?" he says. An', whilst the ould chayter was turned to the writing, by the hokey if our hayro didn't half fill his pockets with pills from the box. By manes of them, as he dhrove along home, he was able to do a power of good to the neighbour people he met with on the road.

Whin you once get in the habit of it there's no pleasure in life which ayquils givin' other people medicine.

Darby ginerously med ould Peggy O'Callaghan take six of the little round things. He gave a swally to half-witted Red Durgan, an' a good mouthful to poor sick Eileen McCarthy (only she had to gulp them whole, poor thing, an' couldn't ate them as the others did—but maybe 'twas just as good). An' he gave a fistful aich to Judy Rafferty an' Dennis Hogan; an' he stood handsome thrate to a sthranger, who, the minute he got the taste well intil his mouth, wanted to fight Darby. Howsumever, the two only called aich other hard names for a while, then Darby joggled along, doin' good an' growin' lighter-hearted an' merrier-minded at every sthop he med. 'Twas this way with him till, just in front of Mrs. Kilcannon's, who should he see, scratching himself agin the wall, but Solomon, an' the baste lookin' bitther daynunciation out of the corner of his eye. Darby turned his head, ashamed to look the misthrayted donkey in the face. An' worse still nor that, just beyant Solomon, laning agin the same wall, was Bothered Bill Donahue, the deef tinker. That last sight dashed Darby entirely, for he knew as well as if he had been tould that the tinker was layin' in wait to ride home with him for a night's lodging.

It wasn't that Darby objected on his own account to takin' him home, for a tinker or a beggar-man, mind you, has a right, the worruld over, to claim a night's lodgin' an' a bit to ate wherever he goes; an' well, these honest people pay for it in the gossip an' news they furnish at the fireside an' in the good rayport of your family they'll spread through the counthry afthrwards.

Darby liked well to have them come, but through some unknown wakeness in her char-ack-ther Bridget hated the sight of them. Worst of all, she hated Bothered Bill. She even went so far as to say that Bill was not half so bothered as he purtendid—that he could hear well enough what was a-greeable for him to hear, an' that he was deef only to what he didn't like to listen to.

Well, anyhow there was the tinker in the road waitin' for the cart to come up, an' for a while what to do Darby didn't well know.

He couldn't rayfuse one who axed food to ate or shelther for a wandherer's four bones during the night (that would be a sin, besides it would bring bad luck upon the house), an' still he had a mortial dislike to go agin Bridget in this purtick'ler—she'd surely blame him for bringin' Bothered Bill home.

But at length an' at last he daycided, with a sigh, to put the whole case before Bill an' then let him come or stay.

Whilst he was meditaytin' on some way of conveyin' the news that'd be complaymintary to the tinker, an' that'd elevayte instid of smashing that thraveller's sinsitiveness, Bill came up to the cart.

"The top iv the day to you, dacint man," he says. " 'Tis gettin' toward dark an' I'll go home with ye for the night, I'm thinkin'," says he. The tinker, like most people who are hard of hearin', roared as though the listener was bothered.

Darby laid down the lines an' hilt out a handful of the little medicines.

"There's nothin' the matther with me, so why should I ate thim?" cried Bill.

"They're the best thing in the worruld for that," says Darby, forcing them into Bill's mouth. "You don't know whin you'll nade thim," he says, shoutin'. "It's betther meet sickness half-way," says he, "than to wait till it finds you."

And thin, whilst Bill, with an open hand aginst his car, was chawin' the pills an' lookin' up plaintiff into Darby's face, the knowledgeable man wint on in a blandishin' way to pint out the sitiwation.

"You see, 'tis this away, Wullum," he says. "It's only too daylighted I'd be to take you home with me. Indade, Bridget herself has wondherful admiraytion for you in an ord'nary way," says he. "She believes you're a raymarkable man intirely," he says, dayplomatic, "only she thinks you're not clane," says he.

The tinker must have misundherstood altogether, for he bawled, in rayply, "Wisha good luck to her," he says, "an' ain't I glad to have so foine opinion from so foine a woman," says he. "But sure, all the women notice how tidy I am, an' that's why they like to have me in the house. But we best be movin'," says he, coolly dhropping his bags of tools intil the cart, "for the night's at hand, an' a black an' stormy one it'll be," says Bill.

He put a foot onto the wheel of the cart. As he did so Darby, growin' very red in the face, pressed a shilling into the tinker's hand. "Go into Mrs. Kilcannon's for the night, Wullum," he says, "an' come to us for your breakwus, an' your dinner an' maybe your supper, me good fellow," says he.

But the deef man only pocketed the shillin' an' clambered up onto the sate beside Darby. "Faith, the shillin's welcome," he says; "but I'd go to such a commodious house as yours any time, Darby O'Gill, without a fardin's pay," says he, pattin' Darby kindly on the back. But Darby's jaw was hangin' for the loss of the shillin' right on top of the unwelcome wisitor.

"We'd betther hurry on," says the tinker, lighting his pipe; "for afther sundown who knows what'll catch up with us on the road," says he.

Sure, there was nothing for it but to make the best of a bad bargain, an' the two went on together, Darby gloomy an' vexed an' the deef man solomn but comfortable till they were almost at McHale's bridge. Then the tinker spoke up.

"Did ye hear the black threats Sheelah Maguire is makin' agin you?" he says.

"No," says Darby; "what in the worruld ails her?" says he.

"Bless the one of me knows," says the tinker, "nor anybody else for that matther. Only that last Halloween night Sheelah Maguire was bate black an' blue from head to foot, an' she lays the raysponsibility on you, Darby," he says.

The knowledgeable man had his mouth open for a question whin who should go runnin' acrost the road in front of them but Neddy McHale himself, an' his arrum full of sticks. "Go back! go back!" cries Neddy, wavin' an arrum wild. "The bridge's butther-worruks are washed out by the flood an' McDonald's bridge is down, too, so yez must go around by the mill," says Neddy.

Now here was bitther news for ye! 'Twas two miles out of the way to go by Chartres' mill, an' do the best possible they'd be passing that ha'nted place in the pitch dark.

"Faith, an' I've had worse luck than in pickin' you up this night, Bothered Bill Donahue," says Darby, "for it's loath I'd be to go alone—"

He turned to speak just in time, for the tinker had gathered up his bag an' had put his right foot on the cart-wheel, purparin' for a jump. Darby clutched the lad by the back of his neck an' joulted him back hard into the sate.

"Sit still, Wullum, till we raich me own house, avourneen," he says, sarcastic, "for if ye thry that move agin I'll not lave a whole bone in your body. I'll never let it be said," he says, lofty, "that I turned one who axed me for a night's lodgin' from me door," he says. An' as he spoke he wheeled the cart quick around in the road.

"Lave me down, Misther O'Gill! I think I'll stop the night with Neddy McHale," says Wullum, shiverin'. "Bridget don't think I'm clane," says he, as the pony started off.

"Who tould ye that, I'd like to know?" shouted Darby, growin' fierce; "who dared say that of ye? You're bothered, Wullum, you know, an' so you misthrupit langwidge," he says.

But Bill only cowered down sulky, an' the pony galloped down the side lane intil the woods, strivin' to bate the rain an' the darkness. But the elements were too swift-footed, an' the rain came down an' all the shadows met together, an' the dusk whirled quick intil blackness before they raiched the gloomy hill.

Ever and always Chartres' mill was a misfortunit place. It broke the heart of an' runed and kilt the man who built it; an' itself was a rune these last tunty years.

Many was the wild tale known throughout the counthry-side of the things that had been seen an' heard at that same mill, but the tale that kept Darby an' the tinker unwelcome company as the pony throtted along was what had happened there a couple of years before. One night, as Paddy Carroll was dhrivin' past the gloomy ould place, his best ear cocked an' his weather eye open for ghosts, there came sudden from the mill three agonised shrieks for help.

Thinkin' 'twas the spirits that were in it Paddy whipped up his pony an' hurried on his way. But the next morning, misdoubtin' whether 'twasn't a human woice, afther all, he had heard, Paddy gathered up a dozen of the neighbours an' went back to inwestigate. What did they find in one of the upper rooms but a peddler, lying flat on the floor, his pack ramsacked an' he dead as a door-nail. 'Twas *his* cries Paddy had heard as the poor thraveller was bein' murdhered.

Since that time a dozen people passing the mill at night had heard the cries of the same peddler, an' had seen the place blazin' with lights. So, that now no one who could help it ever alone passed the mill afther dark.

At the hill this side of that place the pony slowed down to a walk; nayther coaxin' nor batin' 'd injooce the baste to mend his steps. The horse'd stop a little an' wait, an' thin it'd go on thrimblin'.

They could all see the dim outlines of the empty mill glowerin' up at them, an' the nearer they came the more it glowered, an' the faster their two hearts bate. Half-way down the hill an ould sign-post pinted the way with its broken arm; just beyant that the bridge, an' afther that the long, level road an'—salwaytion.

But at the sign-post Clayopathra sthopped dead still,

starin' into some bushes just beyant. She was shakin' an' snortin' and her limbs thrimblin'.

At the same time, to tell the truth, she was no worse off than the two Christians sittin' in the cart behint her, only they were not so daymonsthray-ta-tive about it. Small blame to the lads at that, for they were both sure an' sartin that lurking in the black shadows was a thing waiting to freeze their hearts with terror, an' maybe to put a mark on thim that they'd carry to their graves.

Afther coaxing Clayopathra an' raysonin' with her in wain, Darby, his knees knocking, turned to the tinker, an' in the excitement of the events forgettin' that Bill was deef, whuspered, as cool an' as aisy-like as he could:

"Would ye mind doin' me the favour of steppin' out, avick, an' seein' what's in that road ahead of us, Wullum?"

But Bothered Bill answered back at once, just as cool an' aisy:

"I would mind, Darby," he says; "an' I wouldn't get down, asthore, to save you an' your family an' all their laneyal daysindents from the gallus-rope," says he.

"I thought you was deef," says Darby, growin' disrayspectful.

"This is no time for explaynations," says Wullum. "An' I thought meself," he wint on, turning his chowlder on Darby, "that I was in company with a brave man; but I'm sorry to find that I'm riding with no betther than an' outrageous coward," says he, bitther.

Whilst Wullum was sayin' them wexatious worruds Darby stood laning out of the cart with a hand on Clayopathra's back an' a foot on the shaft, goggling his eyes an' sthrivin' to pierce the darkness at the pony's head. Without turnin' round he med answer:

"Is that the way it is with you, Wullum?" he says, still sarcastic. "Faix, thin ye'll have that complaint no longer, for if yez don't climb down this minute I'll trow you bag an' baggage in the ditch," he says; "so *get* out immaget, darlint, or I'll *trow* you out," says he.

The worruds weren't well out of his mouth whin the owdacious tinker whipped out his scissors an' sint the sharp pint half an inch into Clayopathra's flank. Clayopathra jumped, an' Darby, legs an' arrums flying, took a back sommerset that he never ayquiled in his supplest days, for it landed him flat agin the hedge; an' the leap Clayopathra gave, if she could only keep it up'd fit her for the Curragh races. An' keep it up for a surprisin' while she did, at any rate, for as the knowledgeable man scrambled to his feet he could hear her furious gallop a hundhred yards down the road.

"Stop her, Wullum avourneen, I was only joking! Come back, ye shameless rogue of the univarse, or I'll have ye thransported!" he shouted, rushing a few steps afther them. But the lash of the whip on Clayopathra's sides was the only answer Wullum sint back to him.

To purshue was useless, so the daysarted man slacked down to a throt. I'd hate bad to have befall me any one of the hundhred things Darby wished aloud then an' there for Wullum.

Well, at all events, there was Darby, his head bint, plodding along through the storm, an' a fiercer storm than the wind or rain ever med kept ragin' in his heart.

Only that through the storm in his mind there flared now an' thin quivers of fear an' turpitation that sometimes hastened his steps an' thin again falthered thim. Howsumever, taking it all in all, he was making good pro-gress, an' had got to the bunch of willows at the near side of the mill whin one particular raymembrance of Sheelah Maguire and of the banshee's comb halted the lad in the middle of the road an' sint him fumblin' with narvous hands in his weskit pocket. There, sure enough, was the piece of the banshee's comb. The broken bit had lain forgotten in the lad's pocket since Halloween; an' now, as he felt it there next his thumping heart an' buried undher pipefuls of tobaccy, the rayalisation almost floored him with consthernaytion. All rushed over his sowl like a flood.

Who else could it be but the banshee that guv Sheelah Maguire that turrible batin' mintioned by the tinker? An' what was that bating for, unless the banshee a-ccused Sheelah of stealing the ind of the comb? An', mother of Moses! 'Twas sarchin' or that same bit of comb it was that brought the ghosts up from Croaghmah an' med the whole townland ha'nted.

Was ever such a dangerous purdicament! Here he was, with ghosts in the threes above him an' in the hedges, an' maybe lookin' over his chowlder, an' all of them sarchin' for the bit of enchanted comb that was in his own pocket. If they should find out where it lay what awful things they would do to him. Sure, they might call up the Costa Bower an' fling him into it, an' that 'ud be the last ever heard of Darby O'Gill in the land of the livin'.

With thim wild thoughts jumpin' up an' down in his mind he stood in the dark an' in the rain, gawmin' vacant over toward the shadowy ruin. An' he bein' much agitayted, the lad, without thinkin', did the foolishest thing a man in his sitiwaytion could well a-complish—he took out of his pocket the enchanted sliver of goold an' hildt it to his two eyes for a look.

The consequences came suddin', for as he stuck it back into the tobaccy there burst from the darkness of the willows the hallowest, most blood-curdlin' laugh that ever fell on mortial ears. "Ho! ho! ho!" it laughed.

The knowledgeable man's hair lifted the hat from his head.

An' as if the laugh wasn't enough to scatther the wits of anyone, at the same instant it sounded, an' quick as a flash, every windy in the ould mill blazed with a fierce blue light. Every batthered crack an' crevice seemed bursting with the glare for maybe the space of ten seconds, an' then, oh, Millia Murther! there broke from the upper floor three of the bitterest shrieks of pain an' terror ever heard in this worruld; an', with the last cry, the mill quinched itself into darkness agin an' stood lonely an' gloomy an' silent as before. The rain patthered down on the road an' the wind swished mournful in the threes, but there was no other sound.

The knowledgeable man turned to creep away very soft an' quiet; but as he did a monsthrous black thing that looked like a dog without a head crawled slowly out from the willows where the turrible laugh had come from, an' it crept into the gloom of the opposite hedge an' there it stood, waitin' for Darby to dhraw near.

But the knowledgeable man gave a leap backwards, an' as he did from the darkness just behindt him swelled a deep sigh that was almost a groan. From the hedge to his right came another sigh, only deeper than the first, and from the blackness on his left rose another mcan, an' then a groaning, moaning chorus rose all round him, an' lost itself in the wailing of the wind. He was surrounded—the ghosts had captured Darby.

The lad never rayalised before that minute what a precious thing is daylight. If there would only come a flash of lightening to show him the faces of the surrounding spirrits, horrible though they might be, he'd bid it welcome. But though the rain drizzled an' the tunder rumbled, not a flare lit up the sky.

One swift, dusperate hope at the last minute saved the boy from sheer dispair; an' that same hope was that maybe some of the Good People might be flyin' about an' would hear him. Liftin' up his face to the sky an' crying out to the passin' wind, he says:

"Boys," he says, agonised, "lads," says he, "if there be any of yez to listen," he cried, "I'll take it as a great favour an' I'll thank ye kindly to tell King Brian Connors that his friend an' comerade, Darby O'Gill, is in deep throuble and wants to see him imaget," says he.

"Ho! ho! ho!" laughed the turrible thing in the hedge.

In spite of the laugh he was almost sure that off in the distance a cry answered him.

To make sure he called again, but this time, though he sthrained his ears till their drums ached, he caught no rayply.

And now, out of the murkiness in the road ahead of him, something began to grow slowly into a tall, slender, white figure. Motionless it stood, tightly wrapped in a winding sheet. In its presence a new an' awful fear pressed down the heart of Darby. He felt, too, that another shade had taken its place behindt him, an' he didn't want to look, an' sthrove against lookin', but something forced the lad to turn his head. There, sure enough, not foive feet away, stood still an' silent the tall, dark figure of a man in a top-coat.

Thin came from every direction low, hissing whuspers that the lad couldn't undherstand. Somethin' turrible would happen in a minute—he knew that well.

There's just so much fear in every man, just exactly as there is a certain amount of courage, an' whin the fear is all spilt a man aither fights or dies. So Darby had always said.

He raymembered there was a gap in the hedge nearly opposite the clump of willows, so he med up his mind that, come what might, he'd make a gran' charge for it, an' so into the upland meadow beyant. He waited an instant to get some strength back intil his knees, an' then he gave a spring. But that one spring was all he med—in that direction, at laste.

For, as he neared the ditch, a dozen white, ghostly hands raiched out eager for him. With a gasp he whirled in his thracks an' rushed mad to the willows opposite, but there a hundhred gashly fingers were stretched out to meet the poor lad; an' as he staggered back into the middle of the road agin, the hayro couldn't, to save his sowl, keep back a long cry of terror and disthress.

Imaget, from undher the willows and from the ditch near the hedge an' in the air above his head, from countless dead lips aychoed that triumphing, onairthly laugh, Ho! ho! ho!

'Twas then Darby just nearly guve up for lost. He felt his eyes growing dim an' his limbs numb. There was no air comin' into his lungs, for whin he thried to breathe he only gaped, so that he knew the black spell was on him, an' that all that was left for him to do was to sink down in the road an' thin to die.

But at that minute there floated from a great way off the faint cry of a woice the dispairing man knew well.

"Keep up your heart, Darby O'Gill," cried Brian Connors; "we're coming to resky you," an' from over the fields a wild cheer follyed thim worruds.

"Faugh-a-balla—clear the way!" sprang the shrill warcry of a thousand of the Good People.

At the first sound of the King's worruds there rose about Darby the mighty flurrying an' rushing of wings in the darkness, as if thraymendous birds were rising sudden an' flying away, an' the air emptied itself of a smothering heaviness.

So fast came the King's fairy army that the great cheer was still aychoing among the threes when the goold crown of Brian Connors sparkled up from beside the knowledgeable man's knees. At that the parsecuted man, sobbin' with joy, knelt down in the muddy road to shake hands with his friend, the masther of the Good People.

Brian Connors was not alone, for there crowded about Darby, sympathisin' with him, little Phelim Beg, an' Nial the fiddler, an' Shaun Rhue the smith, an' Phadrig Oge. Also every instant, flitthering out of the sky into the road, came be the score greencloaked and red-hooded men, follying the King an' ready for throuble.

"If ever a man needed a dhrop of good whusky, you're the hayro, an' this is the time an' place for it," says the King, handin' up a silver-topped noggin. "Dhrink it all," he says, "an' then we'll escorch ye home. Come on," says he.

The masther of the night-time turned an' shouted to his subjects. "Boys," he cried, "we'll go wisible, the betther for company sake. An' do you make the 'luminaytion so Darby can see yez with him!"

At that the lovely rosy light which, as you may raymember, our hayro first saw in the fairy's home at Sleive-na-mon, lighted up the roadway, an' undher the leafy arches, bobbin' along like a ridgement of sojers, all in their green cloaks an' red caps, marched at laste a thousand of the Little People, with Phadrig Oge at their head actin' as gineral.

As they passed the mill foive dayfiant pipers med the batthered ould windys rattle with "Garry Owen."

# CHAPTER IV

## THE COSTA BOWER

### I

So the green-dhressed little army, all in the sweet, rosy light they made, wint marchin', to the merry music of the pipes, over the tree-bowered roadway, past the ha'nted brakes up the shivering hills, an' down into the waiting dales, making the grim night maylodious.

For a long space not a worrud, good, bad, or indifferent, said Darby.

But a sparrow woke her dhrowsy childher to look at the beautiful purcession, an' a robin called excited to her sleepy neighbours, the linnets an' the rabbits an' the hares, an' hundhreds like them crowded daylighted through the bushes, an' stood peerin' through the glistening leaves as their well-known champyions wint by. A dozen wentursome young owls flew from bough to bough, follying along, crackin' good-natured but friendly jokes at their friends, the fairies. Thin other birds came flying from miles around, twitthering jubilaytion.

But the stern-jawed, frowny-eyed Little People for once answered back never a worrud, but marched stiff an' silent, as sojers should. You'd swear 'twas the Enniskillins or 'twas the Eighteenth Hussars that 'twas in it.

"Isn't that Gineral Julius Sayser at the head?" says one brown owl, flapping an owdacious wing at Phadrig Oge.

"No!" cries his brother, another young villian. " 'Tis only the Jook of Willington. But look at the bothered face on Darby O'Gill! Musha, are the Good People goin' to hang Darby?"

And faix, thin, sure enough, there was mighty little elaytion on the faytures of our hayro. For, as he came marchin' along, silent an' moody, beside the King, what to do with the banshee's comb was botherin' the heart out of him. If he had only trun it to the ghosts whin he was there at the mill! But that turrible laugh had crunched all sense an' rayson out of him, so that he forgot to do that very wise thing. Ochone, now the ghosts knew he had it; so, to trow it away'd do no good, onless they'd find it afther. One thing was sartin—he must some way get it back to the banshee, or else be ha'nted all the rest of his days.

He was sore-hearted, too, at the King, an' a bit crass-timpered bekase the little man had stayed away so long frum wisitin' with him.

But at last the knowledgeable man found his tongue. "Be me faix, King," he complained, " 'tis a cure for sore eyes to see ye. I might have been dead an' buried an' you none the wiser," says he, sulky.

"Sure, I've been out of the counthry a fortnit," says the King. "And I've only rayturned within the hour," he says. "I wint on a suddin call to purvent a turrible war betwixt the Frinch fairies and the German fairies. I've been for two weeks on an island in the River Ryan, betwixt France an'

Germany. The river is called afther an Irishman be the name of Ryan."

"At laste ye might have sint me wurrud," says Darby.

"I didn't think I'd be so long gone," says the fairy; "but the disputaytion was thraymendous," he says.

The little man dhrew himself up dignayfied an' scowled solemn up at Darby. "They left it for me to daycide," he says, "an' this was the contintion:

"Fufty years ago a swan belongin' to the Frinch fairies laid a settin' of eggs on that same island, an' thin comes along a German swan, an' what does the impident craythure do but set herself down on the eggs laid by the Frinch swan an' hatched thim. Afther the hatchin' the German min claimed the young ones, but the Frinchmen pray-imp-thurribly daymanded thim back, d'ye mind. An' the German min dayfied thim, d'ye see. So, of course, the trouble started. For fufty years it has been growin', an' before fightin', as a last raysort, they sint for me.

"Well, I saw at once that at the bottom of all was the ould, ould question, which has been disthurbin' the worruld an' dhrivin' people crazy for three thousand years."

"I know," says Darby, scornful, " 'twas whither the hin that laid the egg or the hin that hatched the egg is the mother of the young chicken."

"An' nothin' else but that!" cried the King, surprised. "Now, what d'ye think I daycided?" he says.

Now, yer honour, I'll always blame Darby for not listening to the King's daycision, bekase 'tis a matther I've studied meself considherable, an' never could rightly con-clude; but Darby at the time was so bothered that he only said, in rayply to the King:

"Sure, it's little I know, an' sorra little I care," he says, sulky. "I've something more important than hin's eggs throubling me mind, an' maybe ye can help me," he says, anxious.

"Arrah, out with it, man," says the King. "We'll find a way, avourneen," he says, cheerful.

With that Darby up an' toult everything that had happened Halloween night an' since, an', indeed, be sayin': "Now, here's that broken piece of comb in me pocket, an' what to do with it I don't know. Will ye take it to the banshee, King?" he says.

The King turned grave as a goat. "I wouldn't touch that thing in yer pocket, good friends as we are, to save yer life—not for a hundhred pounds. It might give them power over me. Yours is the only mortial hand that ever touched the banshee's comb, an' yours is the hand that should raystore it."

"Oh, my, look at that, now," says Darby, in despair, nodding his head very solemn.

"Besides," says the King, without noticin' him, "there's only one ghost in Croaghmah I 'ssociate with—an' that's Shaun. They are mostly oncultavayted, an' I almost said raydundant. Although I'd hate to call anyone raydundant onless I had to," says the just-minded ould man.

"I'll trow it here in the road an' let some of them find it," says Darby, dusperate. "I'll take the chanst," says he.

The King was shocked, an', trowing up a warnin' hand, he says:

"Be no manner of manes," the fairy says, "you forget that thim ghosts were once min an' women like yerself, so whin goold's consarned they're not to be thrusted. If one should find the comb he mightn't give it to the banshee at all—he might turn 'bezzler an' 'buzzle it. No, no, you must give it to herself pursnal, or else you an' Bridget an' the childher'll be ha'nted all yer days. An' there's no time to lose, ayther," says he.

"But Bridget an' the childher's waitin' for me this

minute," wailed Darby. "An' the pony, what's become of her? An' me supper?" he cried.

A little lad who was marchin' just ahead turned an' spoke up.

"The pony's tied in the stable, an' Bothered Bill has gone sneakin' off to McCloskey's," the little man says. "I saw thim as I flew past."

"Phadrig!" shouted the King. "Donnell! Conn! Nial! Phe-lim!" he called.

With that the little min named rose from the ranks, their cloaks spread, an' come flyin' back like big green butther-flies, an' they sthopped huvering in the air above Darby an' the King.

"What's wanted?" axed Phelim.

"Does any of yez know where the banshee's due at this hour?" the King rayplied.

"She's due in County Roscommon at Castle O'Flinn, if I don't misraymimber," spoke up the little fiddler. "But I'm thinking that since Halloween she ain't worrukin' much, an' purhaps she won't lave Croaghmah."

"Well, has any one of yez seen Shaun the night, I dunno?" axed the master.

"Sorra one of *me* knows," says Phadrig. "Nor I," "Nor I," "Nor I," cried one afther the other.

"Well, find where the banshee's stayin'," says King Brian. "An' some of yez, exceptin' Phadrig, go look for Shaun, an' tell him I want to see him purtic'lar," says the King.

The foive huvering little lads wanished like a candle that's blown out.

"As for you, Phadrig," wint on the masther fairy, "tell the ridgiment they're to guard this townland the night, an' keep the ghosts out of it. Begin at once!" he commanded.

The worruds wern't well said till the whole ridgiment had blown itself out, an' agin the night closed in as black as yer hat. But as it did Darby caught a glimpse from afar of the goolden light of his own open door, an' he thought he could see on the thrashol the shadow of Bridget, with one of the childher clinging to her skirt, an' herself watchin' with a hand shading her eyes.

"Do you go home to yer supper, me poor man," says the King, "an' meantime I'll engage Shaun to guide us to the banshee. He's a great comerade of hers, an' he'll paycificate her if anyone can."

The idee of becomin' acquainted pursonal with the ghosts, an' in a friendly, pleasant way have dalings with them, was a new sinsation to Darby. "What'll I do now?" he axed.

"Go home to yer supper," says the King, "an' meet me by the withered three at Conroy's crass-roads on the sthroke of twelve. There'll be little danger to-night, I'm thinkin', but if ye should run against one of thim spalpeens trow the bit of comb at him; maybe he'll take it to the banshee an' maybe he won't. At any rate, 'tis the best yez can do."

"Don't keep me waitin' on the crass-roads, whatever else happens," warned Darby.

"I'll do me best endayvour," says the King. "But be sure to racognise me whin I come; make no mistake, for ye'll have to spake first," he says.

They were walking along all this time, an' now had come to Darby's own stile. The lad could see the heads of the childher bunched up agin the windypane. The King sthopped, an', laying a hand on Darby's arrum, spoke up umpressive:

"If I come to the crass-roads as a cow with a rope about me horns ye'll lade me," he says. "If I come as a horse with a saddle on me back, yez'll ride me," says he. "But if I come as a pig with a rope tied to me lift hind leg, ye'll dhrive me," says the King.

"Oh, my! Oh, my! Oh, tare an' ages!" says Darby.

"But," says the King, wavin' his hand aginst inthurrup- tions, "so that we'll know aich other we'll have a by-worrud bechuxt us. An' it'll be poethry," he says. "So that I'll know that 'tis you that's in it ye'll say 'Cabbage an' bacon'; an' so that ye'll know that 'tis me that's in it I'll answer, 'Will sthop the heart achin. Cabbage an' bacon will sthop the heart achin'," says the King, growin' unwisible. "That's good, sat- isfyin' poethry," he says. But the last worruds were sounded out of the empty air an' a little way above, for the masther of the night-time had wanished. At that Darby wint in to his supper.

I won't expaytiate to yer honour on how our hayro spint the avenin' at home, an' how, afther Bridget an' the childher were in bed, that a growin' daysire to meet an' talk sociable with a ghost fought with tunty black fears an' almost bate them. But whinever his mind hesitayted, as it always did at the thought of the Costa Bower, a finger poked into his weskit pocket where the broken bit of comb lay hid, turned the scale.

Howandever, at length an' at last, just before midnight our hayro, dhressed once more for the road, wint splashin' an' ploddin' up the lane toward Conroy's crass-roads.

## II

A man is never so brave as whin sittin' ferninst his own comfortable fire, a hot supper asleep in his chist, a steamin' noggin of flaygrant punch in his fist, an' a well-thried pipe betwixt his teeth. At such times he rumynates on the ould ancient hayroes, an' he daycides they were no great shakes, afther all. They had the chanst to show themselves, an' that's the only difference betwixet himself an' themselves. But whin he's flung sudden out of thim pleasant surcumstances, as Darby was, to go chargin' around in the darkness, hunting unknown an' unwisible dangers, much of that courage oozes out of him.

An' so the sthrangest of all sthrange things was, that this night, whin 'twas his fortune to be taken up by the Costa Bower, that a dhread of that death-coach was present in his mind from the minute he shut the door on himself, an' it outweighed all other fears.

In spite of the insurance that King Brian had given, in spite of the knowledge that his friends, the Good People, were flyin' hither an' thither over that townland, there crept into his sowl an' fastened itself there the chanst that the headless dhriver might slip past thim all an' gobble him up.

In wain he tould himself that there were a million spots in Ireland where the death-carriage was more likely to be than in his own path. But in spite of all raysons, a dhreading, shiverin' feelin' was in his bones, so that as he splashed along he was flinging anxious looks behind or thremblin' at the black, wavering shadows in front.

Howsumever, there was some comfort to know that the weather was changin' for the betther. Strong winds had swept the worst of the storm out over the ocean, where it lingered slow, growlin' an' sputtherin' lightening.

A few scatthered, frowning clouds, trowing ugly looks at the moon, sulked behind.

"Lord love your shining face," says Darby, looking up to where the full moon, big as the bottom of a tub, shone bright an' clear over his head. "An' it's I that hopes that the blaggard of a cloud I was creeping over at you from Sleive-na-mon won't raich you an' squinch your light before I meet up with Brian Connors."

The moon, in answer, brushed a cloud from her face,

and shed a clearer, fuller light, that made the looded fields an' dhropping threes quiver an' glisten.

On top of the little mound known as Conroy's Hill, an' which is just this side of where the roads crass, the friend of the fairies looked about over the lonesome counthry-side.

Here and there gleamed a distant farm-house, a still white speck in the moonlight. Only at Con Kelley's, which was a good mile down the road, was a friendly spark of light to be seen, an' that spark was so dim and so far that it only pressed down the loneliness heavier on Darby's heart.

"Wisha," says Darby, "how much I'd druther be there merry-makin' with the boys an' girls than standin' here lonesome and cowld, waiting for the divil knows what."

He sthrained his eyes for a sight of a horse, or a cow, or a pig, or anything that might turn out to be Brian Connors. The only thing that moved was the huge dark cloud that stretched up from Sleive-na-mon, and its heavy edge already touched the rim of the moon.

He started down the hill.

The withered three at the cross-roads where he was to meet the King waved its blackened arms and lifted them up in warning as he came toward it, an' it dhripped cowld tears upon his caubeen and down his neck when he stood quaking in its shadows.

"If the headless coachman were to ketch me here," he whumpered, "and fling me into his carriage, not a sowl on earth would ever know what became of me.

"I wish I wasn't so knowledgeable," he says, half cryin'. "I wish I was as ignorant about ghosts an' fairies as little Mrs. Bradigan, who laughs at them. The more you know the more you need know. Musha, there goes the moon."

And at them words the great blaggard cloud closed in on the moon and left the worruld as black as yer hat.

That wasn't the worst of it by no manner of manes, for

at the same instant there came a rush of wind, an' with it a low, hollow rumble that froze the marrow in Darby's bones. He sthrained his eyes toward the sound, but it was so dark he couldn't see his hand before his face.

He thried to run, but his legs turned to blocks of wood and dayfied him.

All the time the rumble of the turrible coach dhrew nearer an' nearer, an' he felt himself helpless as a babe. He closed his eyes to shut out the horror of the headless dhriver an' of the poor, dead men laning back agin the sate.

At that last minute a swift hope that the King might be within hearing lent him a flash of strength, and he called out the by-word.

"Cabbage an' bacon!" he cried out, dispairing. "Cabbage an' bacon'll stop the heart achin'!" he roared, dismally, an' then he gave a great gasp, for there was a splash in the road ferninst the three, an' a thraymendous black coach, with four goint horses an' a coachman on the box, stood still as death before him.

The dhriver wore a brown greatcoat, the lines hung limp in his fingers, an' Darby's heart sthopped palpitaytin' at the sight of the two broad, headless chowlders.

The knowledgeable man sthrove to cry out agin, but he could only croak like a raven.

"Cabbage an' bacon'll stop the heart achin'," he says.

Something moved inside the coach. "Foolish man," a woice cried, "you've not only guv the byword, but at the same time you've shouted out its answer!"

At the woice of the King—for 'twas the King who spoke—a great wakeness came over Darby, an' he laned limp agin the three.

"Suppose," the King went on, "that it was an inemy you'd met up with instead of a friend. Tare an' 'ounds! he'd have our saycret and maybe he'd put the comeither on ye.

Shaun," he says, up to the dhriver, "this is the human bean we're to take with us down to Croaghmah to meet the banshee."

From a place down on the sate on the far side of the dhriver a deep, slow woice, that sounded as though it had fur on it, spoke up:

"I'm glad to substantiate any sarvice that will in any way conjuice to the amaylyro-ra-tion of any friend of the raynounded King Brian Connors, even though that friend be only a human bean. I was a humble human bean meself three or four hundhred years ago."

At that statement Darby out of politeness thried to look surprised.

"You must be a jook or an earl, or some other rich pillosopher, to have the most raynouned fairy in the worruld take such a shine to you," wint on the head.

"Haven't ye seen enough to make yerself like him?" cried the King, raising half his body through the open windy. "Didn't ye mark how ca'm an' bould he stood waitin' for ye, whin any other man in Ireland would be this time have wore his legs to the knees runnin' from ye? Where is the pillosopher except Darby O'Gill who would have guessed that 'twas meself that was in the coach, an' would have flung me the by-worrud so careless and handy?" cried the King, his face blazing with admyration.

The worruds put pride into the heart of our hayro, an' pride the worruld over is the twin sisther of courage. And then, too, whilst the King was talkin' that deep, obsthreperous cloud which had covered the sky slipped off the edge of the moon an' hurried to jine its fellows, who were waiting for it out over the ocean. And the moon, to make a-minds for its late obscuraytion, showered down sudden a flood of such cheerful, silver light that the drooping, separate leaves and the glistening blades of grass lept up clane an' laughin' to the eye. Some of that cheer wint into Darby's breast, an' with it crept back fresh his ould confidence in his champyion, the King.

But the headless dhriver was talking. "O'Gill," says the slow woice agin, "did I hear ye say O'Gill, Brian Connors? Surely not one of the O'Gills of Ballinthubber?"

Darby answered rayluctant an' haughty, for he had a feeling that the monsther was goin' to claim relaytionship, an' the idee put a bad taste in his mouth. "All me father's people came from Ballinthubber," he says.

"Come this or come that," says the deep woice, thremblin' with excitement, "I'll have one look at ye." No sooner said than done; for with that sayin' the coachman thwisted, an' picking up an extra'onary big head from the sate beside him, hilt it up in his two hands an' faced it to the road. 'Twas the face of a goint. The lad marked that its wiry red whuskers grew close undher its eyes, an' the flaming hair of the head curled an' rowled down to where the chowlders should have been. An' he saw, too, that the nose was wide an' that the eyes were little. An uglier face you couldn't wish to observe.

But as he looked, the boy saw the great lips tighten an' grow wide; the eyelids half closed, an' the head gave a hoarse sob; the tears thrickled down its nose. The head was cryin'.

First Darby grew oncomfortable, then he felt insulted to be cried at that way by a total sthranger. An' as the tears rowled faster an' faster, an' the sobs came louder an' louder, an' the ugly eyes kep' leering at him affectionate, he grew hot with indignaytion.

Seeing which, the head spoke up, snivelling:

"Plaze don't get pugnaycious nor yet disputaytious," it begged, betwixt sobs. " 'Tisn't yer face that hurts me an' makes me cry. I've seen worse—a great dale worse—many's the time. But 'tis the amazin' fam'ly raysimblance that's pathrifying me heart."

The dhriver lifted the tail of his coat an' wiped the head's two weepin' eyes. " 'Twas in Ballinthubber I was born an' in Ballinthubber I was rared; an' it's there I came to me misfortune through love of a purty, fair maid named Margit Ellen O'Gill. There was a song about it," he says.

"I've heard it many an' many the time," says the King, noddin', sympathisin', "though not for the last hundhred years or so." Darby glared, scornful, at the King.

"Vo! Vo! Vo!" wailed the head, "but you're like her. If it wasn't for yer bunchy red hair, an' for the big brown wen that was on her forehead, ye'd be as like as two pase."

"Arrah," says Darby, brustlin', "I'm ashamed to see a man of yer sinse an' station," he says, "an' high dictation—"

"Lave off!" broke in the King, pulling Darby be the sleeve. "Come inside! Whatever else you do, rayspect the sintimintalities—there all we have to live for, ghost or mortial," says he.

So, grumbling, Darby took a place within the coach beside his friend. He filled his poipe, an' was borrying a bit of fire from that of the King, whin looking up he saw just back of the dhriver's seat, and opening into the carriage, a square hole of about the hoight an' the width of yer two hands. An' set agin the hole, starin' affectionate down at him, was the head, an' it smiling langwidging.

"Be this an' be that," Darby growled low to the King, "if he don't take his face out of that windy, ghost or no ghost, I'll take a poke at him!"

"By no manner of manes," says the King, anxious. "What'd we do without him? We'll be at Croaghmah in a few minutes, then he needn't bother ye."

"Why don't ye dhrive on?" says Darby, lookin' up surly at the head. "Why don't ye start?"

"We're goin' these last three minutes," smiled Shaun; "we're comin' up to Kilmartin churchyard now."

"Have you passed Tom Grogan's public-house?" axed the King, starting up, anxious.

"I have, but I can turn back agin," says the face, lighting up, intherested.

"They keep the best whusky there in this part of Ire-land," says the King. "Would ye mind steppin' in an' bring-ing us out a sup, Darby agra?"

Misthress Tom Grogan was a tall, irritated woman, with sharp corners all over her, an' a timper that was like an east wind. She was standing at her own door, argyin' with Garge McGibney an' Wullum Broderick, an' daling them out harrud names, whilst her husband, Tom, a mild little man, stood within laning on the bar, smoking saydately. Garge an' Wul-lum were argying back at Misthress Grogan, tellin' her what a foine-looking, rayspectable woman she was, an' couldn't they have one dhrop more before going home, whin they saw coming sliding along through the air toward them, about four feet above the ground, a daycint-dhressed man, sitting com-fortable, his poipe in his mouth an' one leg crossed over the other. The sthranger stopped in the air not foive feet away, and in the moonlight they saw him plain knock the ashes from his poipe an' stick it in the rim of his caubeen.

They ketched hould of aich other, gasping as he stepped down out of the air to the ground, an' wishin' them the top of the avening, he brushed past, walked bould to the bar an' briskly called for three jorums of whusky. Tom, obliverous— for he hadn't seen—handed out the dhrinks, an' the sthranger, natural as you plaze, imptied one, wiped his mouth with the back of his hand an' started for the door, carrying the two other jorums.

Tom, of course, follyed out to see who was in the road,

and then he clutched hould of the three others, an' the four, grippin' aich other like lobsters bilin' in the pot, clung, spacheless, swaging back an' forth.

An' sure 'twas no wonder, for they saw the sthrange man lift the two cups into the naked air, an' they saw plain the two jorums lave his hands, tip themselves slowly over until the bottoms were uppermost—not one dhrop of the liquor spillin' to the ground. They saw no more, for they aich gave a different kind of roar whin Darby turned to bring back the empty vessels. The next second Tom Grogan was flying like a hunted rabbit over the muddy petatie-field behind his own stable, whilst Wullum Broderick an' Garge McGibney were dashin' furious afther him like Skibberberg hounds. But Mrs. Grogan didn't run away, bekase she was on her own thrashol', lying on the flat of her back, and for the first time in her life spacheless.

Howandever, with a rumble an' a roar, the coach with its thravellers wint on its way.

The good liquor supplied all which that last sight lacked that was needful to put our three hayroes in good humour with thimselves an' with aich other, so that it wasn't long before their throubles, bein' forgot, they were convarsing sociable an' fumiliar, one with the other.

Darby, to improve his informaytion, was sthriving to make the best of the sitiwation by axin' knowledgeable questions. "What kind of disposition has the banshee, I dunno?" he says, afther a time.

"A foine creachure, an' very rayfined, only a bit too fond of crying an' wailing," says Shaun.

"Musha, I know several livin' women that cap fits," says the knowledgeable man. "Sure, does she do nothin' but wail death keens? Has she no good love-ballads or songs like that? I'd think she'd grow tired," he says.

"Arrah, don't be talkin'!" says Shaun. " 'Tis she who can sing them. She has one in purticular—the ballad of 'Mary McGinnis'—that I wisht ye could hear her at," he says.

"The song has three splendid chunes to it, an' the chune changes at aich varse. I wisht I had it all, but I'll sing yez what I have," he says. With that the head began to sing, an' a foine, deep singin' woice it had, too, only maybe a little too roarin' for love-ballads:

"Come all ye thrus lovers, where'er yez may be,
Likewise ye decayvers be land or be sea;
I hope that ye'll listen with pity to me
Since the jew'l of me life is a thraitor."

"Here's where the chune changes," says the head, lickin' his lips.

"On goin' to church last Sunday me thrue love
    passed me by,
I knew her mind was changed by the twinklin' of
    her eye;
I knew her mind was changed, which caused me for
    to moan,
'Tis a terrible black misfortin to think she could has
    grown."

"That's what I call rale poethry," says Darby.

"There's no foiner," says the King, standing up on the sate, his face beaming.

"The next varse'll make yez cry salt tears," says Shaun. An' he sang very affectin':

"Oh, dig me a grave both large, wide, an' deep,
An' lay me down gently, to take me long sleep;

Put a stone at me head an' a stone at me feet,
Since I cannot get Mary McGinnis."

"Faith, 'tis a foine, pittiful song," says Darby, "an' I'd give a great dale if I only had it," says he.

"Musha, who knows; maybe ye can get it," says the ould King, with a wink. "Ye may daymand the favours of the three wishes for bringing her what yer bringin'," he whuspered. "Shaun!" he says, out loud, "do ye think the banshee'll give that song for the bringing back of the lost comb, I dunno?"

"I dunno meself," says the head, jubious.

"Bekase if she would, here's the man who has the comb, an' he's bringin' it back to her."

The head gave a start and its eyes bulged with gladness.

"Then it's the lucky man I am entirely," he says. "For she promised to stick me head on and to let me wear it purmanent, if I'd only bring tidings of the comb," says Shaun. "She's been in a bad way since she lost it. You know the crachure can sing only whin she's combing her hair. Since the comb's broke her woice is cracked scand'lous, an' she's bitther ashamed, so she is. But here's Croaghmah right before us. Will yez go in an' take a dhrop of something?" says he.

Sticking out his head, Darby saw towering up in the night's gloom bleak Croaghmah, the mountain of the ghosts; and, as he thought of the thousands of shivering things inside, an' of the onpleasant feelings they'd given him at Chartres' mill a few hours before, a doubt came into his mind as to whether it were best to trust himself inside. He might never come out.

Howandever, the King spoke up sayin', "Thank ye kindly, Shaun, but ye know well that yerself an' one or two others are the only ghosts I 'ssociate with, so we'll just step out, an' do you go in yerself an' tell the banshee we're waitin'. Rayturn with her, Shaun, for ye must take Darby back."

With that the two hayroes dayscinded from the coach, an' glad enough was Darby to put his brogues safe an' sound on the road agin.

All at once the side of the mountain ferninst them opened with a great crash, an' Shaun, with the coach an' horses, disaypeared in a rush, an' were swolleyd up by the mountain, which closed afther thim. Darby was blinkin' an' shiverin' beside the King, when sudden, an' without a sound, the banshee stood before them.

She was all in white, an' her yellow hair sthrealed to the ground. The weight an' sorrow of ages were on her pale face.

"Is that you, Brian Connors?" she says. "An' is that one with you the man who grabbled me?"

"Your most obadient," says the King, bowin' low; "it was a accident," says he.

"Well, accident or no accident," she says, savare, " 'tis the foine lot of throuble he's caused me, an' 'tis the illigant lot of throuble he'd a had this night if you hadn't saved him," she says. The banshee spoke in a hollow woice, which once in a while'd break into a squeak.

"Let bygones be bygones, ma'am, if you plaze," says Darby, "an' I've brought back yer comb, an' by your lave I ax the favour of three wishes," says he.

Some way or other he wasn't so afeared now that the King was near, an' besides one square, cool look at any kind of throuble—even if 'tis a ghost—takes half the dhread from it.

"I have only two favours to grant any mortial man," says she, "an' here they are." With that she handed Darby two small black stones with things carved on thim.

"The first stone'll make you onwisible if you rub the front of it, an' 'twill make you wisible again if you rub the back of it. Put the other stone in yer mouth an' ye can mount an' ride the wind. So Shaun needn't dhrive yez back," she says.

The King's face beamed with joy.

"Oh, by the hokey, Darby me lad," says he, "think of the larks we'll have thravellin' nights together over Ireland ground, an' maybe we'll go across the say," he says.

"But fairies can't cross runnin' water," says Darby, wondherin'.

"That's all shuperstition," says the King. "Didn't I cross the river Ryan? But, ma'am," says he, "you have a third favour, an' one I'm wishin' for mightilly meself, an' that is, that ye'll taiche us the ballad of 'Mary McGinnis.' "

The banshee blushed. "I have a cowld," says she. " 'Tis the way with singers," says the King, winkin' at Darby, "but we'll thank ye to do yer best, ma'am," says he.

Well, the banshee took out her comb, an' fastening to it the broken ind, she passed it through her hair a few times an' began the song.

At first her woice was purty wake an' thrimblin', but the more she combed the sthronger it grew, till at last it rose high and clear, and sweet and wild as Darby'd heerd it that Halloween night up at McCarthy's.

The two hayroes stood in the shadow of a three, Darby listening and the King busy writing down the song. At the last worrud the place where she had been standing flashed empty an' Darby never saw her again.

I wisht I had all the song to let your honour hear it, an' maybe I'll learn it from Darby by the next time ye come this way, an' I wisht I had time to tell your honour how Darby, one day havin' made himself onwisible, lost the stone, and how Bothered Bill Donahue found it, and how Bill, rubbin' it by accident, made *himself* onwisible, an' of the turrible time Darby had a-finding him.

But here's Kilcuny, an' there's the inn, an'—thank ye! God bless yer honour!

# AUTHOR
# BIOGRAPHIES

**Esther Friesner** has written twenty-nine novels and more than one hundred short stories, has edited six popular anthologies, is a published poet, playwright, and has written articles on fiction writing for Writer's Digest Books and *Writer's Market*; her works have been published here and in France, Germany, Italy, Japan, Russia, and the United Kingdom. She has twice won Nebula Awards for Best Short Story, is a Hugo finalist, received the Skylark Award from NESFA, and in 1986 was named Most Promising New Fantasy Writer by *Romantic Times*. A Vassar graduate, she received her M.A. and Ph.D. from Yale, and now lives in Connecticut "with my husband, two children, two rambunctious cats, and a fluctuating population of hamsters." Esther once wrote an advice column, "Ask Auntie Esther," which hopefully did not dispense the kind of wisdom lurking in the curmudgeonly mind of Auntie Elspeth in our opening story!

**Terry Kaye** is a professional actor and singer. She has performed in her home town, New York City, played Europe as the Mistress in the international company of *Evita*, and has also toured Canada, and the United States with numerous musicals and other theatrical productions. A graduate of the O'Neill Theater Center and the Moscow Art Theatre, when she's not living out of a suitcase, Terry usually can be found in New York or Los Angeles auditioning for the next project. "The Witch Who Hated Halloween," written backstage during a national tour of *Fiddler On the Roof* in which Terry played one of Theodore Bikel's daughters, is her first published story.

All Hallows Eve is not a good night to go roaming, especially if you're a chap straight out of Bedlam hospital for the daft. The titular Tom has appeared in several adventures by the prolific **Darrell Schweitzer**, a Philadelphia area fantasist who has written many short stories that regularly appear in honored places in my anthologies. He is the editor of *Weird Tales Magazine*.

**Terry McGarry** is a copy editor and Irish musician from New York City. Her first novel, *Illumination*, was recently released by Tor Books, and other short work currently can be found in *Realms of Fantasy, The Magazine of Speculative Poetry*, and the collections *I Have This Nifty Idea* and *Outside the Box*. She has contributed new Sherlock Holmes tales to the St. Martin's Press anthologies, *The Resurrected Holmes* and *The Confidential Casebook of Sherlock Holmes*. Her Halloween story, "Miasma," is an unusual and shivery *petite guignol*.

If spirits really can walk on Halloween night, who says their only business is to frighten? **Marc Bilgray**, who has another "take" on the notion, has written for television, magazines, and comedians. His short stories have appeared in numerous anthologies, including *Cat Crimes Through Time, Far Frontiers* and *Merlin.*

"Pumpkin Head," a modern classic of Halloween literature, is the work of **Al Sarrantonio**, who, to date, has written twenty-eight novels, including science fiction, fantasy, mystery, horror, and westerns. Author of *The Five Worlds Trilogy, Moonbane, Skeletons, West Texas* and *Cold Night,* he is a winner of the Bram Stoker Award for horror, the British Fantasy Award, and the Shamus Award from the Private Eye Writers of America. He has also edited numerous books, including the acclaimed anthology *999: New Stories of Horror and Suspense.* His short fiction has appeared in magazines such as *Amazing, Analog, Asimov's Science Fiction, Heavy Metal, Realms of Fantasy,* and *Twilight Zone. Toybox* is a recent collection of his best horror stories. Al lives with his family in New York's historic Hudson Valley.

An evangelist once challenged me on a New York subway: "Have you thought about Jesus today?" To which I crabbily responded, "No, but have you thought about Nietzsche?" I never would have dared if he'd been anything like the protagonist(?) of "Trick or Treat with Jesus," a wickedly original Halloween story by **Marilyn Mattie Brahen**, whose fiction has appeared in the anthology *Crafty Cat Crimes,* and in such magazines as *Dreams of Decadence, Fantastic, Marion Zimmer Bradley's Fantasy Magazine,* and, in England, *Scheherazade.* In addition to writing, she spends her "copious spare time" in various art and musical pursuits. Mattie resides in Philadelphia with her husband Darrell Schweitzer, their two cats Amaryllis and Lovecraft, "in a house with more bookcases than regular furniture. The books and cats really own the house. They let me stay as long as I take good care of them—and Darrell, of course."

Magician, entertainer, and author, **R. J. Lewis** leads a colorful life. He has experienced every level of show business from street performing to Broadway, where he appeared in the original production of *Barnum* starring Jim Dale. In addition to his magic career, which includes frequent headliner appearances at New York's popular long-running *Monday Night Magic*, R. J. has been diligently working at his writing and has completed four novels in the past four years. As seen in "Into the Abyss," he is also an expert on special effects makeup.

Crime literature has a tradition of gentleman thieves that include such personable rascals as E. W. Hornung's amateur cracksman Raffles, Maurice Leblanc's Arsene Lupin, and the inimitable Nick Velvet, who positively refuses to steal anything that has any monetary value! Nick's creator is the spectacularly prolific **Edward D. Hoch**, who has written at least nine hundred and probably more short stories for *Ellery Queen's Mystery Magazine* and numerous other publications. He is a former president of the Mystery Writers of America.

**John Gregory Betancourt**, a former editor of *Weird Tales*, is head of the growing fantasy/mystery publishing firm, Wildside Press. He has written many short stories and novels, including *The Blind Archer, Johnny Zed*, and *Rememory*. An affable gentleman, emphasis on the first syllable, it is perhaps paradoxical how dark some of his fiction is, and his Halloween tale is a good example.

An odd meeting at twilight, a minor injury—simple things, and nothing much really happens, does it? And yet... wouldn't a ghost have been less upsetting? "All Souls" is a tale of quiet terror by **Edith Wharton** (1862–1937), usually remembered for her satirical cosmopolitan novels like *The Age of Innocence* or *The House of Mirth*. But she also wrote many chilling supernatural stories, as well as one of America's greatest "conte cruelles," *Ethan Frome.*

"Uncle Evil Eye" is a touching Halloween anecdote by **Carole Buggé**, author of two Sherlock Holmes novels, *The Star of India* and *The Haunting of Torre Abbey*, and three contemporary murder mysteries: *Who Killed Blanche Dubois?, Who Killed Dorian Gray?*, and *Who Killed Mona Lisa?* A popular New York improvisational comedian and "improv" teacher, she also teaches writing. Her excellent comic and fantasy tales have been published in several Doubleday anthologies, and three shorter Sherlock Holmes stories appear in *The Game is Afoot, The Resurrected Holmes*, and *The Confidential Casebook of Sherlock Holmes*. Also a playwright-composer, Carole has written several musicals; her *Sherlock Holmes* is now in development in New York City.

Harry Challenge, specialist in occult and science-fictional cases, appeared in *The Prisoner of Blackwood Castle* and three other adventures in the mid-1980s; this is his first new case since then, so welcome back, Harry! "I even included a pumpkin in the story," says Harry's prolific author **Ron Goulart**, who, in addition to writing the *Vampirella* novels and works based on comic strips/books like *Star Hawks* and *Challengers of the Unknown*, has done many other novels, including *After Things Fell Apart, Clockwork's Pirates, Death Cell, Gadget Man, The Sword Swallower, The Tin Angel*, and (in a twist on an H. G. Wells title) *When the Waker Sleeps*. His nonfiction includes *Cheap Thrills: An Informal History of the Pulp Magazines* and *The Adventurous Decade: Comic Strips in the Thirties.*

# AUTHOR BIOGRAPHIES

**H. P. Lovecraft** (1890–1937), the Providence, Rhode Island, native whose name became synonymous with America's greatest fantasy periodical, *Weird Tales*, was the author of such memorable chillers as "The Rats in the Walls," "The Shadow Over Innsmouth, "The Dunwich Horror," and *The Case of Charles Dexter Ward*. "The Unnameable," set in a New England cemetery as October dusk falls, features an uncommonly autobiographical discussion for a work of Lovecraftian fiction.

"The Halloween Man," an unsettling story from the late, lamented horror magazine, *Night Cry*, is by the prolific screenwriter **William F. Nolan**. His published works include a volume of his short stories, *Impact-20*; two anthologies, *A Sea of Space* and *Man Against Tomorrow*; and the definitive index to the writing of his friend Ray Bradbury. One of the screenplays Bill is justifiably proud of is his BBC adaptation of Henry James's "The Turn of the Screw."

Despite persistent rumors, my friend and erstwhile collaborator **Parke Godwin** was not a changeling elf-child from Faerie. "My parents, both as improbable as their son, were vaudevillians." Parke, who is the author of *A Truce with Time, Beloved Exile, Firelord, Sherwood, Waiting for the Galactic Bus*, and many other genre and historical novels, also wrote *Lord of Sunset, The Lovers*, and his forthcoming novel, *Watch by Moonlight*, under the pseudonym of Kate Hawks. His ghost story, "The Fire When It Comes," won the World Fantasy Award for Best Novella. Short fiction is a pleasurable luxury for him; in "A Matter of Taste," the fine distinction between the mere gourmet and the connoisseur is deliciously(?) explored.

One of the best films produced by Walt Disney is *Darby O'Gill and the Little People*, the mostly comical adventures of an elderly Irish story-teller among the leprechauns. I say "mostly" because there are also some frightening moments with a banshee and the Costa Bower, or Coach of Death. Disney based the film on a series of stories by H. T. Kavanagh (1876–1933) that appeared in two books, *Darby O'Gill and the Good People* (1903) and *The Ashes of Old Wishes* (1926). Born Herminie McGibney in Ireland, the author was twice married—the "T" stands for her first married name, Templeton; her second husband, Marcus Kavanagh, was a Cook County, Illinois, judge. The first Darby O'Gill stories, serialized in *McClure Magazine*, ended with "The Banshee's Comb," which tells what happened to Darby one Halloween when his wife Bridget volunteered him for an errand of mercy that led (more's the pity!) to the worst haunting in the history of the whole blessed county!

# ABOUT
# THE EDITOR

**Marvin Kaye** is the author of fifteen novels, including the terrifying *Fantastique* and *Ghosts of Night and Morning*; the science-fiction classics, *The Incredible Umbrella* and (coauthored with Parke Godwin) *The Masters of Solitude*, and the critically-acclaimed mysteries *Bullets for Macbeth* and *My Son the Druggist*. His short story "Ms. Lipshutz and the Goblin" was included in a DAW Books Year's Best Fantasy anthology, and his horrific "The Possession of Immanuel Wolf" was written with the great macabre comedian, Brother Theodore.

His numerous best-selling anthologies include *13 Plays of Ghosts and the Supernatural* and other theatre collections; *The Game is Afoot* and other Sherlock Holmes anthologies, and many fantasy/science fiction books for the Science Fiction Book Club, such as *Ghosts, Masterpieces of Terror and the Supernatural*, and *The Vampire Sextette*.

He is Adjunct Professor of Creative Writing at New York University, has taught mystery writing in England for the Smithsonian Institute, has served as a judge for the Edgar, Nero and World Fantasy Awards, and is Artistic Director for The Open Book, New York's oldest readers theatre company. He is a reiki master and cranio-sacral therapist, and, as a change of pace, acts and sings in Carole Buggé's New York improvisational comedy troupe, *Please Don't Feed the Actors*.